ONLY A BREATH AWAY

DIANA KNIGHTLEY

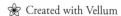

For my husband...
in the time shifting burrito of our timeline,
the drifting ebb and flow of our lives,
the lingering and meandering,
I'm so glad our happy place is the same.

CHAPTER 1 - KAITLYN

I woke from the jump like coming up for air from under water, fighting, terrified, could barely breathe, and — oof. I was face down in grass. I could hear water moving nearby, a river or… I tried to wake enough to count heads. Isla was beside me, then Archie, and Ben. Zoe was on Emma, who was stirring and moaning. Quentin was up. He came into focus, dragging a box toward the trees.

James was lugging a crate. "You up, Katie? We need some help, we're out in the open." To Zach he said, "Get your ass up."

I said, "Are we all here?"

"Yeah, why?" He was panting out of breath.

"I don't know, I just don't trust anything."

I lumbered up, grasped the handles of a rucksack, and dragged it to the underbrush within the tree line.

I stopped and put my hands on my hips. "Wait…? Where's Magnus? Shouldn't he be here to meet us?"

We got everyone in under the trees, hidden from view, surrounded by our things, and took stock. Zach fed the kids from a box of Oreos that he had somehow remembered to bring, saying, "We can go back for more, we have the vessel, we can leave at any time, right?"

For a panicky moment I thought, *Do we have a vessel?*

I said to Quentin, "Show it to me, I need to see it."

He pulled one from his pocket. "Got it, it's here. I just don't understand why Magnus isn't—"

Galloping horses, hooves thundering, an army was coming, though it strangely sounded very far away.

I jumped up. "Mag—!"

Quentin grabbed my wrist and yanked me back. We weren't jumping up to greet Magnus, because there was something odd about the sound. A chill went down my spine. The horses sounded like they were approaching, though it sounded faint as if they continued to be distant.

I held onto Isla and Archie, frozen in fear.

There wasn't a vibration. My eyes settled on the grass in the clearing, wispy wildflowers, straight and still, a small bug flitting from bloom to bloom.

Quentin pressed his fingers to his lips, gestured for us to stay put, and crept from our hiding spot to survey the clearing.

The thundering hooves drew very near.

My eyes were on Quentin's back. He had his hand up — no noise, no movement.

Hooves stamped, a man's voice, very very faint, like a whisper, "Haw!" The sound of horses quieted. A faraway sound of a dog barking.

One horse, barely perceptible, rode in a circle inside the clearing.

I held my finger to my lips to remind the kids to not make a sound. Because it was frightening, I wanted to scream and run.

Suddenly there was the sound of underbrush moving. Right in front of us a horse stamped, something smaller rummaged through the brush beside me. The sound was faint, but present, like the shadow of a sound — I clutched the children — a horse was right there. I heard the muffled puff of its breath, the hardly detectable creak of the leather straps. I could barely hear the man on the back of the horse, but I could sense him, his dim breaths — yet there was no one there.

Archie held tight around me, Isla buried her face in my clothes. The horse was breathing, sniffing, it felt like a horse's muzzle was right there smelling me, the nose of a beast that I couldn't even see...

It was terrifying how it felt — as if there were an invisible horse right in front of me.

To call it invisible though was not exactly right, there was a shimmer there, a shifting, almost like a blurry motion of tiny atoms, vibrating, in the shape of a horse nose, an inch away from my face.

My full attention was held on that shimmering spot. It felt like at any moment a horse would break through from one realm to another up against my skin, horrifyingly close, but I forced my eyes up to where the man would be — a man who was a shimmering vibrating nothingness. The spot could have been the size of a large man, a warrior, was it... could it be Magnus...?

Then the horse drew away. In its place a frenetic rustling through the brush, a smaller something, a growl, then barking imperceptibly, as if down a long long tunnel, more rustling through all the underbrush and then a milling about as if many men were conferring in the center of the clearing — a whispering of voices we couldn't make out.

Quentin motioned for us to stay in place as he crept forward. One hand on his gun, the other feeling his way, he crept into the middle of the clearing, then closed his eyes, as if concentrating.

Faintly I heard, "Haw!" Horses jostled for position and then horse hooves thundered away.

Quentin remained watchful for a moment before returning. "What the fuck was that?"

James said, "I have no idea."

Beaty, whose hands were folded in prayer, said, "Twas as if ghosts walked among us."

I said, "Whatever it was, I did not like it one bit."

Beaty said, "I canna hear anythin', it all sounds verra far away, and m'heart is racin'. Everythin' else is all too loud, m'breathin' is too loud."

I said, "That's part of the time travel—"

Zach said, "Was that *thing* that was right in front of us part of the time travel? I don't think so. I've been traveling for a long time, we are not usually met with ghosts."

Beaty's eyes went wide, "Was it ghosts...? Was it?"

Quentin sat down and put an arm around her. "There aren't any ghosts, I don't know what that was, but it wasn't a ghost." He added, "So where's Magnus?"

I patted Isla's head in a way that I hoped felt soothing, I did not feel soothed at all. "He ought to be here, but... he's been held up. He'll come, it's just...."

James scooped up a few pebbles and nervously shook them in his hand. "We need a plan. We're practically within the shadow of Stirling castle, we should go up and—"

"What're we going to do?" asked Zach. "Walk right up to a thirteenth century castle, one full of ghosts, basically, and ask... what?"

James shook his head. "This is a very good point, I have no idea. Also, most of us are wearing modern clothes. I for one am wearing sweatpants and a t-shirt. 'Um, hi ghosts, we're not from around here, can we make a call?'"

Quentin said, "James and I will scout the area." He passed a gun to Zach, then passed one to me. "You're both armed, protect the—"

Emma said, "But it won't come to that, right? If anyone gets in shooting distance we leave, *right?*"

I held the gun in trembling hands. I didn't even want to think about what any of this meant: if people were shooting at us, we were *not* protected by Magnus. If we weren't protected by

Magnus that meant he was not here. *Not here.* But this was our agreed upon date and time and location for my return.

I asked, "Where will we meet up if we jump?"

Quentin pulled a vessel from his pocket. "If you need to jump, go to the safe house in Maine on July 8th, 2024, we'll all meet there." He worked the numbers into the vessel, holding it up close to his eyes.

James said, "You need reading glasses, old man?"

"No, it's just the darkness of the dark ages. And I'm not that old." He passed the vessel to Emma.

I said, "Have you been to the lake house before, how do you know the coordinates?"

"Magnus and I memorized them years ago."

James said, "I've got them memorized too."

Zach said, "Don't forget, the key to the front door is hidden in the lockbox in the back of the shed."

I said, "I don't know why but I feel better knowing we're using my grandparents' house for a safe space — that we all know how to get there. This is good."

James patted my knee and he and Quentin stood. Using hand signals they crept away through the woods from our hiding spot.

Ben said, "I'm scared."

Archie put on a brave face. "It's no big deal, Ben, we just need to figure—" I clamped my hand over his mouth.

There was a sound behind us.

CHAPTER 2 - KAITLYN

I couldn't turn, I had to sit and wait, every hair on my body bristling. I tensed all my muscles. If I was still enough maybe… whatever it was wouldn't see us or hear us or sense us. I held my children, who were thankfully quiet, sensing the extreme danger.

Peripherally I could see Emma in Zach's arms, holding on around her kids, her eyes tightly shut. Zach was quietly patting around for the gun. He was facing whatever was behind me, and going so slow… whatever it was was *menacing*.

The noise moved closer.

Beaty was curled up around her knees, her eyes pressed to her kneecaps.

Then a giant, hairy, beast of a man grabbed me and yanked me by the arms and hair into the underbrush. The kids were shrieking. I held his wrists, trying to keep my hair from pulling from my scalp, the pain of being dragged by it was agonizing. Where was my gun? Why wasn't I holding my gun? What had I been thinking — whatever that was? It was *not* protecting the kids.

Why hadn't Zach been holding his gun? Why had I let mine slide from my lap? I watched the sky, the tops of trees as I was dragged away, then the beast-man picked me up, his hold around my waist knocking the wind from me. I coughed, gasped for air, and struggled, but I was not getting free.

Far far away in the distance I heard my children crying. That was all.

I beat my fists on his arm, but it just went tighter. I had a wee small comfort that I was alone, no one else had been captured.

But why had I been taken?

The dude carrying me smelled horrible, my nose burned from the rancid stench. I shoved at the fur around his neck and struggled again, pointlessly, as he lumbered through the undergrowth with me in his arms, then we left the woods at a wide field and he picked up his pace on a worn path.

I kicked my legs and craned left and right, we were near the castle. It was much smaller than the last time I had been to Stirling; then the castle had been an imposing stone edifice on the top of rocky cliffs. Now there were timber walls, a thick wood gate, grassy slopes down from it. My captor raced along an uphill path. If I was taken into the castle, even with timber walls, it would be so hard to get out.

I had to get away now.

The man carrying me was growing breathless on the steep climb. I would claw his face, bite his arm — two more beast men emerged from the woods and joined my captor. Great.

I struggled, and the man closest hit me in the face. "Sàmhach!"

Below us Quentin and James raced from the woods, chasing us with their guns drawn.

James's voice yelled, "Hey motherfucker, whatcha doing?"

I tried to go limp to drop through my captor's arms, but the other man pushed me again, "Ow!"

"Sàmhach!"

Quentin and James were running the high-knee run of football players. I tried to get a foot in between my captor's legs, hoping to trip him, wrenching my ankle. I burst into tears.

Quentin stopped running to fire. James continued to chase, yelling instructions at me, "Stop struggling! Curl up!"

I bent around my captor's arm, gripping my legs, shrieking, "Don't shoot me! Don't shoot me!"

Bang!

The man holding me stumbled to the ground. My leg tweaked as I hit the dirt.

Quentin yelled, "Let her go, assholes, or I'll shoot again!"

James got to me, yanked me up, pulled me behind him, and aimed his gun at my captors. "You want to die? I'll shoot you, give me half a chance, I'll shoot you so—"

I couldn't hear James over the sound of my heart clamoring against my chest as I looked up on the walls and saw so many guns pointing down at us. An amplified voice bellowed. "Drop yer weapons."

James dropped his gun to the ground and put his hands on the back of his head. "Fuck."

I heard Quentin race away. Gunfire sounded. I shrieked and hunched down as bullets blasted divots in the dirt around us. The noise was terrifying, everything sounded close, all I could do was hold my head and pray.

James, huddled under his arms, yelled over the shooting, "Quentin got away!"

"Good, thank God." The last shots blasted behind us.

The castle gate rolled up and three big hulking men on horseback rode down the hill.

James whispered, "I think that's Domnall."

I said, "Why the hell is Domnall at Stirling castle?"

We were surrounded. James's arms were bound and he was dragged behind a horse through the castle gates.

I had to walk, my head sore, my ankle tweaked, some big lug shoving my back to propel me forward. They didn't bind my arms, they didn't rough me up, they didn't consider me a threat in any way, and they were right — I couldn't think of a single thing to do, unarmed, weak, surrounded, captive. I was watching James, dragged through the muck and mire of medieval Scotland.

James groaned, "Katie! Once we're in there it's gonna get pretty fucking bleak."

"Yeah. I'd say it's already about as bleak as it can get."

We went through the gate. In the courtyard James struggled and yelled, "Let me walk!"

Domnall chuckled the sound deep and menacing.

James said, "What the fuck you laughing about?"

I chimed in, out of fury, "Right? Why the fuck you laughing? And where are you taking us? I demand to see the lord of this castle. I demand to know who is holding us, and what the hell is going on."

Domnall said, "Ormr is the king, Kaitlyn, and ye will see him when he is ready tae be seen."

"If you know who I am, why in the hell would you grab me? You have to know that my husband will make you pay."

"Och, ye sound frightened, sweet Kaitlyn. I like the sound of it." He chuckled again.

"You are a creep."

James was dragged toward a door in a one-story stone building. He yelled, "Don't tell them anything!"

Domnall muttered something that sounded an awful lot like 'arsehole.'

"What did you say?"

"I said yer accomplice, Master Cook, is a low, blatherskitin' whittret and ye will be better off without him." He shoved me through a door to a stair in another, larger stone building.

"What do you know of Master Cook?"

"He killed my wife, yer granddaughter, Sophie, a great many of my men, and now he has killed m'man Mungo in front of the castle."

"Well, Mungo was kind of a dick, so..." He shoved, causing

me to trip up the stairs, falling on the stone, banging my shin. I rubbed the injury. "That hurt!"

He hoisted me up by the back of my shirt, like a doll.

"Stop lifting me! I'll walk you ass. Get your freaking hands off me!"

He dropped me on the top step. I raised my chin. "I suppose I'm relieved I won't be in the dungeons."

"We hae tae keep ye alive tae lure ye husband here."

He forced me down the hall, and shoved me into a sparsely decorated room.

"Is James Cook in the dungeon?"

He ignored my question. "Do ye ken where Quentin might hae gone? We want tae talk tae him as well."

"I have no idea."

He chuckled again.

"I hate your laugh, what a horrible person, you find all the wrong kinds of things funny."

He said, "I would get comfortable, ye will be here for a while." He closed the heavy door and it was locked from the outside. Great.

I pushed and pulled on the handle, looking for any sort of give, kicking the bottom, and checking the iron hinges for weaknesses. I rushed to the window. It looked out over the courtyard, from very high up, with no ledges, no way to jump, but craning I saw the edge of storm clouds. I figured they were centered over the clearing on the other side of the castle, behind me.

I hoped it was Quentin and the rest of our family headed for Maine — and wasn't it a relief that they were getting to safety? But also, wasn't it horrific that the only people who knew James and I were captive in this castle were leaving?

It had been the plan but it never dawned on me that I would be the one captured and left behind.

But, then again, the storm clouds might be Magnus.

I was here on the day and time agreed upon by us — why wasn't he here to meet me?

. . .

I had been at Stirling castle before in the year 1552, when Magnus and I had gone on a vacation with Mary of Guise. Our room had looked out over the courtyard, much like this, with a small window. From this year, 1290, to the year 1552 would be almost three hundred years. I didn't recognize much in the landscape beyond the basics: a stone castle. A river, its course unfamiliar.

I turned from the window to take stock. It might have been the same room. In the year 1552 there had been a four poster bed along one wall with silk brocade curtains of purple cloth. There had been luxurious rugs, and tapestries on the walls.

It had been warm because of the fire that my husband built in our hearth.

None of that was there now. The fireplace had no fire which explained the chill. The stone floor had no rugs, the bed had a canopy, but instead of the purple silk, there was a thick brown heavy cloth draped around it. Near the fireplace stood an uncomfortable looking table and chairs.

I crossed the room to sit on the bed. There was an audible 'bonk' as my ass hit a plank. "Fucking great."

What could I use as a weapon? There was a ceramic pitcher, I could break it and attempt to use the shards to kill the next man who entered the room, but ceramic was not as sure as glass. I rapped my knuckles on the side of the pitcher hearing a muted clunk, not the clank of strong sharp ceramic. It sounded like it would crumble to clay if pressure was applied.

To kill a man would require pressure.

Also, there was sure to be another man, and another, because it was a castle, there would be more men.

If I was here for a time I could break apart the chair and use a leg to beat the next man who came in. I tried to pick the chair up, it was thick and strong and heavy. I had one pocket in my skirts and all it had in it was some lint, a Burt's Bees lip balm, and a Matchbox car I had picked up off the ground this morning so no one would step on it.

This morning was centuries away.

How come every time I got in one of these situations I didn't have a gun? Or a knife? You would think I would learn. I sighed.

I sat down and carefully lay back on the hard bed and looked up at the stained canopy. Wouldn't it be great if we normalized wearing a sword around Florida? Then I would always have one.

I remembered how Magnus used to want to carry a sword into bars and restaurants and it would have brought me happiness to think of him back then, so innocent and naive about the world, but — *where was he?*

CHAPTER 3 - HAYLEY

*J*t was lunch break, visiting hours at Rehab, and Fraoch was here, waving from the door of the lounge. I joked, "Hey, sweet cheeks."

He said, "Hello, potty mouth," as he swept me up and kissed me.

I laughed. "Where'd you learn that?"

"From Isla. Tis funny."

I laughed and led him to the cafeteria line. We were one of the firsts so there was no wait.

"How is everyone by the way—?" I took a cup for a soda.

He grabbed three cartons of milk. "Not good, m'bhean ghlan, we are a family in crisis as they say on the wall poster over there."

My eyes went wide. "What—? Is everyone okay?"

He glanced around the busy cafeteria and said under his breath. "I daena ken, they hae escaped from the house tae the thirteenth century."

I held my tray out to get a dollop of mashed potatoes. "What the hell, why would anyone escape to the dark ages?"

Fraoch got his dollop of mashed potatoes and said, "More

please." To me he said, "They dinna feel they had a choice. The house is unsafe. They went tae see Magnus."

"When?"

"Yesterday."

"Where have you been?"

He put his tray out for Salisbury steak. "Quentin told me tae stay near yer rehab so I can collect ye when ye are all fixed up."

A slab of meat was tossed onto my tray. "That was very nice of him to think of me and my situation."

"Aye, remember when I said ye ought tae apologize tae him? This is why. Because he is thinkin' of us."

"Yeah, you are right about that." I came to the end of the buffet line and took a small plate with a brownie. "So where are you, really?"

"I am livin' in a tent in the woods right outside."

"That's either the most romantic thing in the world or the freakiest."

"I am Freaky Frookie."

"That you are."

We placed our trays down on a table. "So I will be out of here in a few more days… where are we headed — the house is unsafe?"

"The house is unsafe, we are supposed tae meet everyone in the thirteenth century, unless we hear from them first."

I smiled. "Sounds good, and in the meantime, since you've been living in the woods…" I passed him my piece of bread.

He teased, "Ye ken, I am living in a tent and there might be gators around, I might need an extra brownie as well for fortitude."

CHAPTER 4 - MAGNUS

I had been watching for the storm, but when it arrived twas different, nae like a storm but a shadow. It felt electric, as if the Trailblazer had been in use, and the air shimmered. Twas hard tae describe, but looked as if the atoms of the air were charged and in furious motion, but the usual roar, crash, and booms of thunder were barely perceivable.

I watched Haggis barkin' at the sky, and waited for it tae clear. Then I rode towards the clearing with m'army behind me.

The area was completely still.

I asked m'men tae remain back while I investigated. But there wasna anyone there. I circled the clearing a few times.

I would hae sworn the storm had been one of ours, familiar in strength and its sudden build, its brutal feel, yet this one felt verra different. As if it had occurred down a verra long tunnel, or like a video of a storm with the volume turned down. Now the clearing was empty, quiet, and still. As if there had never been a storm.

My horse intently sniffed the underbrush. Then stepped forward, plunged his muzzle through the branches, and sniffed the empty space. Haggis wanted tae go in, but I ordered him tae stay. I peered into the dimness, but twas evident that there wasna anyone or anythin' there.

Haggis growled, so finally I commanded, "Go!" He lunged intae the brush, barkin' and sniffin'. Haggis came out and growled low and menacin' at the bush.

M'horse snorted.

There was an odd sense about the space, a wavering tae the spot, a quiver. I listened, but I couldna hear anythin' but m'horse stampin' and the loud puffs of his breath.

I pulled m'horse from the woods and drew some of m'men tae the middle of the clearing and I asked if they had noticed anythin'. During the exchange I sensed somethin' behind me. I spun m'horse, sure there would be a man, but I only caught a glimpse, a glimmer of the height and form of a man, the sense of a man, and was not sure about even that.

I turned m'horse twice but found nae one there. Then I led the men back tae the castle, approachin' from the south.

Stirling castle was verra different from the lavish palace Kaitlyn and I had visited in the year 1552. Now, in the thirteenth century it was made up of a few stone buildings, surrounded by timber walls. The castle wasna concerned with royal courts and comfortable rooms, there was a stone chapel, a low stone building for kitchens and storerooms. And there was a three-story stone building that held the royal bedrooms and offices, that we called the King's house. The Great Hall, the barracks for the men, and the stables were all built of timber.

The castle was built upon steep, craggy cliffs, making it strongly defensible. In 1552, the stone walls stood at the edge of the cliffs on three sides, an imposing insurmountable wall. But in the thirteenth century, the timber walls were pulled back, surrounded by sloping fields between the walls and the cliffs. The cliffs were imposingly high, but I wished m'walls were higher and made of stone.

Once I stabled m'horse, I climbed the wooden stair tae the walls tae watch for another storm.

CHAPTER 5 - HAYLEY

*T*he next day and the next Fraoch came to visit. He attended meetings with me, though I told him he didn't have to. "You don't need to do anything but see me for lunch."

"Nae, this is fun!"

"*Fun?* You think it's fun to go to AA meetings? You, sir, are very confused."

"Tis much like gathering 'round the fire in front of the tigh-dubhs—"

"What, my love, is a te-duh?"

"I think ye might call them a blackhouse, ye ken? The low houses at Loch Leven? The men would gather around the fire, sometimes the women as well, and there would be grand stories told."

"What kind?"

"About hunts and battles, stories stuffed full of lies, ye haena ever heard so many lies, m'bhean ghlan, but nae one was listenin' tae hear the truth, twas the telling of them would be the point of it. My uncle, Aymer, after becomin' verra drunk, liked tae tell a story or two. His twists of a tale were astonishin'. He once had me believe that a fish caught him by the foot and swallowed him whole, but he convinced the fish tae spit him out by assurin' him he was rotten. But always there was m'Aunt Margar, and she would talk back tae the storytellers. She would say, 'Nae, tis nae true!' and, 'Ye canna tell it that way, tis nae the way tae tell it!' Uncle Aymer would say, 'Wife! I am tellin' the story, no' ye!' And she would humph and then become so upset at the next part of the story — she was incensed about the fish story. She claimed that she would stuff Uncle Aymer's pocket with bitter herbs, and she felt sure this was why the fish spit him out. Just between us, m'bhean-ghlan, she put the bitter herbs in his pocket tae keep the ladies away, as Uncle Aymer had been known tae wander. But, the point of the story is that tae hear Margar and Aymer bicker meant the world was turning well. And Aunt Margar dinna just criticize Aymer, she kent all the stories, they had been told many times over. Though she had heard them many times, she wanted them told well. She believed a story had a beginning, a middle, and an end and twas how ye got from the one tae the other, in order, without a long blather, much like I am doing here."

I sighed, "This is the longest story ever told, but I can't wait to hear what this has to do with AA meetings."

Fraoch chuckled. "When asked, Aunt Margar would say, 'I just like m'stories, I want tae hear them the way they are meant tae be told.' So, now when I come tae the AA meetings and I see some of the fellas get up tae tell their story, I think, *och, it will be a harrowing tale of crime and punishment and brawling and bawdy behavior,* and *och, I wish m'Aunt Margar were here tae yell at them for nae tellin' it right.*"

I laughed. "Fraoch, have I told you today how much I love you?"

"Ye hae nae told me but three times this day and twas a rainy evenin' and verra lonely in m'tent, so I think I ought tae get at least one more."

We grabbed our coffee cups and entered the meeting room and chose a row near the front.

After introductions, a new person raised his hand and offered to tell his story. The leader of the meeting called him up.

He began with, "My name is Tyrone, but my friends call me the Goatman."

Fraoch muttered under his breath. "Och, this one will be good."

CHAPTER 6 - MAGNUS

*I*n the afternoon I took another turn around the lands around Stirling Castle and returned near time for the evening meal in the Great Hall.

I sent m'horse tae the stables and crossed the courtyard, m'guard pulling in behind me. Cailean rushed over tae walk alongside. "Did ye find what ye went for, Mag Mòr?"

"Nae, but the morrow will come." I meant it tae sound comforting, but twas terrifyin'. I dinna understand why Kaitlyn hadna been at our meetin' place. She could hae come at any time, *from* any time, and arrived at that point.

Cailean said, "The hunting park has a lot of deer at this time of year. I ken ye love tae hunt. It would take yer mind from yer worries."

"Aye, I will consider it later in the week."

In the Great Hall I sat in the chair at the head of the long table with Cailean beside me. "How did ye spend yer day, Cailean, while I was on m'pointless errand?"

We were passed flagons of ale.

He said, "I met with Uilleam Uallas. He has been gatherin' an army tae fight the English king."

I drank from m'ale. "Young Will Wallace wants tae war

with England? Och, he is sharpenin' his sword without ever havin' been faced with the sharp end of one." I shook my head. "On my lands, he is wantin' a war with a king. Next he will need me tae fight. The young men of the world will be the death of us."

"Ye are nae so auld Mag Mòr."

I chuckled. "Aye, but thirty, but I hae aged with every sharp end of a sword I hae faced."

Cailean raised his ale and we drank.

I said, "He is a young man with a drive for mayhem — can we reason with him? He ought tae fight for Mag Mòr! I hae negotiated with Edward. I ken how tae subjugate him."

"Aye, my liege, tae hold Stirling is tae hold Scotland. Ye rule with a strong hand, Edward winna dare cause trouble."

"This is true. I hae nae need for a young Scot with an overblown estimation of his abilities tae begin a war."

"There is much tae deal with, my liege, I will ask Wallace tae come speak with ye, ye can tell him that if an army is gathered it must be under yer command."

I laughed. "That is a diplomatic way of puttin' it."

"What would ye say?"

"I would say, 'Wallace, ye are a radge, a revenge-seeking war-monger,' and then I would say, 'Ye need tae calm yer arse down or I will calm it down for ye.'" I spun my flagon of ale. "Keeping in mind of course, that these words hae been used tae describe me verra often."

Cailean laughed and drank from his ale and banged it on the table. "Mag Mòr, I hae kent ye tae be a thoughtful leader, ye are nae cocksure nor warmongering."

I smiled. "Ye hae tae say it, cousin, as ye are often at m'side during the warring."

He chuckled. "Yer side has often been a just cause."

"I am sure Will Wallace thinks his cause is just as well. Hae ye heard anythin' of Ormr or Domnall?"

"Nae, and Wallace hadna heard mention of them, he

believes they died in battle — ye did soundly defeat them for the crown. Perchance they hae retired tae a wee pigsty tae the north?"

I said, "A pigsty would be too civilized for them."

He chuckled.

A wind blew through the walls, adding a chill to the hall. I called for one of the men tae raise the flame in the hearth.

We ate a plentiful supper as there had been food delivered from Cambuskenneth Abbey and I had asked for a feast tae be prepared tae celebrate the return of Kaitlyn.

I had hoped after dinner tae take her tae m'room, wooin' her with banter and some modest fondlin', perhaps tae bed her along the way — maybe in the stairwell of the stone building we called the King's House.

When we had been stuck in the sixteenth century, we had visited Stirling while on a tour with Mary of Guise, and one night we had been verra drunk and I had taken liberties with her in a spot behind the stairs. Returned tae Stirling as king, I thought I might like tae do that once more. I kent she would like the doing of it, she did like tae be taken on stairwells, and she would have enjoyed the historical reference of it

I exhaled. *Where had she gone?*

I left the Great Hall and slowly walked up the stone steps tae the top floor, Haggis paddin' along beside me. I wondered about Fraoch and Quentin. They ought tae come inform me if there was somethin' wrong with the timeline. Why hadna they come? M'thoughts on it were verra dark — that whatever had happened, had happened tae all of them at once.

For now I would hae tae watch the skies.

I entered m'room with m'guard stationed outside.

M'room was nae the best. The best room was farther down the hall, twas warmer as it had a longer time with direct sunlight on its walls, but I had heard Cailean grumble enough about how the chill pained his joints. He felt it dearly in his knees — I had given the room tae him.

And I had chosen this one because twas the same room I had stayed in when Kaitlyn and I had visited Stirling in 1552. At that time, it had been a guest room in the oldest part of the castle, in this time twas one of the newest rooms. I convinced everyone that I believed it just right for my needs as it was defensible, bein' in the middle of the building. Its drawback was that it had a view of the courtyard instead of the lands.

It was sparsely decorated: a bed, canopied with heavy fabric, thick wool and fur bedding over a thin wool-stuffed mattress. The floor was covered with woven rugs. I had a desk and a chair, and a carved seat for two, its backrest covered with pillows. And a large fireplace, with a smolderin' fire. I used the poker on the coals and added a log tae bring up the flame. It reminded me of the summer of 1552, when I was buildin' a fire tae warm the room and turnin' around had found Kaitlyn undressed, beckonin' for me from the bed.

I slumped ontae the couch and leaned on the carved arm, my chin resting on the heel of m'hand. "Where are ye Kaitlyn?"

Haggis perked his head up and cocked his ears, tryin' tae understand what I said. I scratched his head as I watched the flames dance in the hearth, the heat of them shimmerin' much like the air that morn in the clearing. What had caused it? Why had my horse been so interested in it?

I leaned forward with m'elbows on m'knees and my hands clasped against m'mouth. This had always been our biggest fear, that somehow we would lose track. Nae, twas nae right, our biggest fear was that we would lose track and nae remember the having lost it. So this was the second biggest fear.

I turned tae look at the seat beside me and caught a glimpse of a shimmer there. My brow drew down as I tried tae focus, my heart raced. I reached out tae touch it, but there was naethin' there, nae movement or heat or...

But I felt a presence, as if someone were there.

I concentrated on that spot.

And then I whispered, "Kaitlyn?"

There was nae answer, but then... twas difficult tae understand, the sound dinna come from m'ears, but from inside m'head. It felt like I heard, *Magnus? Magnus, where are you?*

CHAPTER 7 - KAITLYN

I climbed from the uncomfortable bed, dragged the gross blanket across the room, and sank down on the bench in front of the cold hearth. It was full of ash, no fire, no heat. I wrapped myself in the blanket and huddled, staring at the space as if there was a fire anyway. I pretended like I was warm.

Even I didn't have that good an imagination, it was as cold as day-old soup in Alaska.

I turned my head to look at the seat beside me, there was…

It seemed like someone was there.

I listened and beyond my own heart beat, louder than usual, my breathing, there was another breathing — a deeper, heavier breath. I couldn't hear it so much as feel it inside. Was it a weird echo? I paced it with my own, drawing in and drawing out. It had a different rhythm.

Was it a memory of Magnus?

The room was so cold, devoid of life, lonely and quiet. I concentrated on the spot, matching its beat. "Magnus?" It felt like he might be here, sitting beside me, and I could swear there was an indent in the seat where his form would be, as if the molecules of the space were moved aside for him. And there seemed to be a warmth emanating from this spot beside me, yet he wasn't there. "Magnus, where are you?"

CHAPTER 8 - MAGNUS

*M*y room was warm but this spot beside me held a chill. Was it an apparition? A ghost on the seat beside me? Haggis leaned against m'leg looking up at m'face then lookin' at the seat. "Dost ye feel it, cù math?"

He whimpered.

"What is there, do ye think?"

I scratched him behind his ear, both of us focused on the space. "It feels as if Kaitlyn is beside me."

Haggis's tail went back and forth happily.

I leaned back and took a deep breath. Haggis rested his head on my thigh. I put my hand ontae the pillow beside me and I could hae sworn there was a hand enclosed in mine.

CHAPTER 9 - KAITLYN

I reached out toward the seat beside me, and then pulled away, it felt as if it was touched by... I tentatively placed my hand on the pillow beside me. There came the faintest feeling of warmth and a slight pressure as if it was enclosed in... what? I pulled my hand back and rested it in my lap.

I had an overactive imagination, always had, it was one of the worst things about me. I looked down at my hand and felt, with certainty, as if there was a hand clasping mine. A feeling of calm settled over me. I just didn't understand what was happening, what if...

What if Magnus was here as a ghost? What if he had died?

Despair threatened to drag me under. I was alone, captive, was I lost forever? Tears welled up in my eyes...

But wait! If Magnus was dead, the king of this land, it would have happened in the past week. Wouldn't there be signs of a battle, a war, the death of a king?

I thought back to crossing the courtyard, the people milling about... they had looked like normal castle dwellers, going about their day's work. There was no despair, beyond the despair of living in the dark ages.

Most significantly, Domnall hadn't mentioned… oh! I remembered… he was using me as bait. He assumed Magnus was alive.

They weren't planning to rape and torture me, I was a part of their trap… I did not like that one bit. I returned to the bed, shivering, and pulled the blanket up to my chin.

I was a lure for Magnus.

I stared at the underside of the canopy, considering every scenario I could think of — none of this situation was good. And the worst part was, I couldn't think of any reason for them to keep James alive.

It was so freaking cold. I wrapped the coarse, stiff, smelly blanket tighter around me. But then I felt it, or heard it, though it wasn't actually there — a warm breath beside my ear.

CHAPTER 10 - HAYLEY

*F*inally, I was done with my rehab and released to the wider world. I walked out the doors to the parking lot, lugging my bag, and there, leaning on a signpost outside, was my husband. "Hey babe."

"Hello, m'bhean ghlan, how are ye on this fine day?"

"I am awesome, glad to be going home. I have to continue to 'work the program' though, I promised."

"Aye, ye will hae naethin' but water and soda and juice from now on, ye ken? If ye think on it they are all the best drinks anyway."

"That's kind of you to say."

We bumped fists, shook, thumbwar, bumped our elbows, ran a hand through our hair, did a chicken flap, wiggled our hips, hooked our fingers around each other's, waved them up and down, bird-fly-away, and said, "Och aye," with jazz hands. I had taught him the handshake during visiting hours one day when we were bored. He thought it was hilarious.

"Where are we headed to…?"

"The thirteenth century unless Emma answers her phone."

I made a call.

Emma picked up.

"Hey! Are you here in Florida—?"

Emma said, "No, listen, we're at the northern safe house, come, we'll talk about it."

Fraoch and I found a clearing in the woods by the rehab center and jumped to a small field in the woods by Katie's grandparents' lake house in Maine.

CHAPTER 11 - MAGNUS

*T*he feeling of the apparition left, the space beside me had gone quiet and uncharged, so I climbed intae bed, pulled the covers up, and adjusted the thin pillow. But then I felt the presence once more; twas on the side of the bed where Kaitlyn would normally lie.

I concentrated on that spot, listenin', tryin' tae understand what was happenin'. There was a slight shimmer, a barely perceptible coolness. I wondered at it — what was happening here? Was Kaitlyn beside me in the room? Had I lost my mind?

Was she dead and her ghost in bed beside me tae torment me?

But it dinna feel frightenin'. It felt as if the presence needed tae be comforted. It seemed alone and lost and cold, much like myself. I was overwhelmed by the need tae protect it.

I was reminded of Barb sayin' that Kaitlyn and I were entangled and that our strands had become woven taegether. I worried that I had unwoven our strands.

Because I would never ken how tae re-weave them again.

I had a vessel, but I dinna want tae leave without Kaitlyn. I was expectin' her here. What if... Och, I dinna want tae be stuck here in the thirteenth century, a king in a land that I dinna want tae rule. I had gained the throne tae send a message tae m'family: bring me home.

They had come, Quentin, m'bairns, Kaitlyn, but I had sent them home again, promisin' tae join them later, and now I wondered at this... how had I become left behind?

Nae one had returned. We dinna hae a contingency for this.

Och, I was a tragedy.

I rolled ontae m'side and placed my hands intae the space beside me. I held ontae nothingness, and tae keep myself calm and strong, I concentrated on m'breaths.

Just as I was falling asleep, I startled tae hear a whisper, one that seemed tae come from inside my head — *I love you.*

I said, "I love ye, mo reul-iuil."

CHAPTER 12 - KAITLYN

I heard it warm beside my ear. *I love ye, mo reul-iuil.*

I turned onto my back, looked up at the underside of the canopy, and began to speak. "Are you there?"

I paused.

"I don't know what has happened, my love, but I am here and you are there. I think we are beside each other... Do you feel it too?"

I sighed. "Domnall has captured me. Apparently Ormr is king. James is in the dungeon. You aren't here, you... I need you to come."

I pulled the rough blanket over my nose to keep it warm.

"I don't know what I mean by that, how you can be here and *not* here, but maybe you're on a different timeline? We need Zach to explain this to us. I don't know what you should do, how we should solve it, but... will you please go check on the kids?"

CHAPTER 13 - MAGNUS

*I*t came tae me, a certainty — I needed tae check on the bairns. But I wasna sure where everyone was and I dinna want tae risk loopin' upon m'self. Everythin' had been shiftin' for so long that I was uncertain about m'best step. I decided tae jump tae the future and check with grown Archie. I said, in case whoever I was havin' this moment with was listenin', or could even hear me, "Aye."

CHAPTER 14 - MAGNUS

I landed on the western lands about thirty miles away from my castle, the year 2405.

I roused myself, mounted m'horse, and began the ride tae the city. I kept tae the edges of the forest, and traveled through a mountain pass, doin' my best tae be unnoticed. I dinna come across anyone, so I grew more courageous as I approached the Lots, a place with a great many industrial parks and warehouses. Everywhere was bereft of people. I stood on the edge of a wide empty parking lot and surveyed the area. It was like a town of ghosts.

I urged my horse into a brisk pace, passin' through, headed toward the edge of the city.

A mile on I came across a lone store with a hangin' sign: Lots Hardware and Goods. I tied my horse tae the post and crept tae a window tae peer inside. Twas dim and dusty and looked unused. I entered and found shelves of dusty food cans and drink bottles. In an office I found books and papers dated 2389, the year I had left, a poster on the wall for my battle, Magnus vs Domnall. I blew upon it, sendin' dust flinging.

I searched for any sign of life, but twas as if there hadna been a soul here since that long ago year when the time had become fragmented.

I mounted my horse and continued on for miles, deep intae the city, checkin' shops and restaurants and offices. All had that layer of dust, and were abandoned as if all at once. The final place I investigated had been a home, and inside, on a table, there was a lump of decomposed and disgustin' glop inside a bowl with a spoon beside it. A spider had spun a web across the rim of the bowl. It looked verra much as if the occupant's meal had been interrupted, tae never return.

I couldna understand what this meant — how was an entire city abandoned? How was my kingdom, *Archie's* kingdom, gone?

I sat in a shady spot under an awning tae rest my horse, pulling a hunk of bread from a leather saddlebag. I had meant tae interview someone about the kingdom, tae find out who was in charge, afore I entered the castle grounds. I wanted foreknowledge of who I would be meeting. I had assumed it would be Archie, but now I thought it might be Ormr, perhaps it was someone even more malevolent.

Once there, I had intended tae look through records for Kaitlyn and the rest of our family, but now I couldna access it.

M'only option was tae time-travel blindly intae Florida.

I chewed my bread and considered. *Where was Lady Mairead?*

I shook my head, wiped my hands of crumbs, led m'horse tae a wide part of the road, and began the jump that would take me home.

CHAPTER 15 - HAYLEY

We landed in a field with wildflowers growing high all around. I groaned from the pain of the jump and lay there for a bit, looking up at Fraoch who was already sitting up.

I pulled myself up and saw Zach running toward us.

"Hey! Phew, am I glad to see you!"

I asked, "Is everyone here? And why are we here?"

He said, "It's me and Em and Beaty, with all the kids."

I said, "Damn. Here we go again."

On our walk down the old stretch of road that led from the field to the lake house, he explained, "We got to Stirling, and some weird shit went down, first there was this fucking... I don't know how to explain it, like a ghost, we could hear it and—"

"Zach, was Magnus there? Where's Katie?—"

"Nah man, no Magnus, just this apparition. Then James and Quentin were scouting and Katie was snatched by this big dude and carried away—"

My eyes went wide. "Oh my god, the kids saw it? Are they freaking out?"

"Totally freaking out. *Then* James and Quentin got into a shootout with the guys. I don't know what happened because I was in the woods, but it sounded like guns, modern guns. A couple minutes later, Quentin ran into the woods, yelling, 'They got James, too! I'm going to stay and figure out what's going on!' He ran on by. Em and I jumped here with Beaty and the kids. This is the spot for meeting up, so yeah, that happened." He opened the door and let us into Katie's grandparents' cabin.

I had been here, years ago, invited by Katie to come for the summer. Every day she and I had played for hours on the dock, jumping into the water, canoeing.

The kids were all on the couch looking dismayed, so I sat in the middle of them. "Man, I missed all of you so much, Aunt Hayley's been in a hospital for wayward, problematic humans, but now I'm all better." I hugged them to me. "I am *not* going to do that again, I am someone you can count on. And, hate to say it, but this is our life, am I right? We have big scary things, plus adventures. I'm so sorry that the big scary thing is so darn scary. But I know one thing, and that is that your mom and dad are coming back."

Archie put his head back on the couch, the expression on his face looking very much like his father. "How do you know, Aunt Hayley?"

Fraoch said, "I ken because I met ye, when ye were about twenty-two, and ye had known yer father and mother yer whole life. Ye canna argue with it, tis yer fate, it canna change."

Archie narrowed his eyes. "Is that true, Uncle Fraoch?"

Fraoch shrugged. "Tis, and I'm willin' tae stake m'reputation on it as the smartest person in the room."

Zach said, "Hey!"

Fraoch didn't look over at Zach as he stage-whispered to the kids, "Chef Zach will argue that he is smarter, but daena listen tae him. He canna feed himself without a grocery store."

Zach laughed. "For that, no dinner."

"Och, please, I take it back, Chef Zach, I hae been living in the woods, eating in a cafeteria once a day. Ye canna keep food from me, tis nae fair. Also, I was just sayin' it so Archie would ken I was in earnest, ye are definitely smarter, ye ken how tae cook lasagna."

Zach said, "And don't you forget it."

I asked, "How long will we be here, do you think? As long as we're stuck we ought to make the best of it. I remember that Katie's grandparents had canoes. We ought to pull them out. We can have fun paddling until they get back. Magnus just has to rescue Katie and James and find Quentin and yeah, *again*, we just need Magnus to figure it out."

I followed Zach into the kitchen and he opened the fridge to get a snack for Fraoch and me. He said, "Hayley, there was this apparition — it was so real. We *all* saw it, or didn't see it. There was a horse sniffing around us. A ghost dog was barking."

I said, "I have no idea, Zach, but in all this time we haven't had ghosts, it's not... it just doesn't make sense. We can't get bogged down, we just need Magnus to figure this out."

CHAPTER 16 - KAITLYN

*D*ay was fading and I was freaking out, plus I was very bored. Also hungry.

I lay on the bed, tossing and turning for lack of anything else to do.

A filthy brute of a man entered, and dropped a wooden plate onto the table with a bit of porridge on it, and a hunk of hard bread. Beside it he slammed down a mug with a bit of ale. I was impossibly thirsty and the dry food wasn't making it any better.

The only thing that kept me from panicking was knowing Magnus was out there, somewhere.

And Quentin knew where we were.

Those two things would mean escape, definitely, probably.

But Magnus was supposed to be here. It was as if I were in the right place at the wrong time. We had set the right numbers into the vessel, I was sure of it, but I ended up in a place that wasn't the *right* place.

Or Magnus was gone.

That thought kept pushing into my brain, I kept tamping it down, no. He was fine.

He just got held up somehow.

CHAPTER 17 - MAGNUS

I jumped alone to the beach at the end of the island. It was a warm day, the sun baking me as I awoke. *Ah Florida, how I had missed ye.*

I lumbered tae m'feet and began the long walk tae m'house, aware that m'garb was verra wrong for the time: I was wearin' a tunic, a fur wrapped around m'shoulders, leather boots with nae proper soles upon m'feet, belts slung at m'waist, and a sword at m'hip.

I adjusted my face intae a friendly, jovial expression, *look at me, wearing a costume at midday, walkin' down the street, there is a funny story here, ye might guess.*

Though truly there was nothing funny about this story. Kaitlyn hadna come tae the thirteenth century as she had promised. The future kingdom of Riaghalbane was a desolate wasteland. Now I had traveled home and m'family hadna met me when I arrived. Twas worrisome was what it was. But I smiled anyway.

A small lizard scurried across m'path.

I grew apprehensive as I drew near the house. Twas dark and lifeless. The gate locked, I skirted the dunes tae the north and snuck up from behind the sheds. From my guard station on the walls, I knew there was a blind spot here and I was the only person who kent about this weakness.

I watched the empty house for about an hour, because I saw a glimpse of something on the upper walls, a shimmer as if there were someone there. I craned tae see, and wished I had binoculars. Twas difficult to make out what it was — then I saw it in another place, on the walkway, a glimmer in the air, near where we would stand.

I walked down the main road to the small food store. I was dripping wet from sweat and worry, but tried for a pleasant expression again, askin' the lady behind the counter, "What say ye—" I stopped myself. "M'apologies, I was in character."

She laughed. "Where are you going in that costume?"

"This? Och, I hae a play tae put on."

"Oh," she said and narrowed her eyes. "It's very authentic."

"Can ye tell me the date?"

She laughed, then said, "Oh, you serious?"

"Aye."

She told me the date and it matched what I had thought.

I returned tae the house and watched it for a bit longer, wishing I had remembered tae bring money.

I decided tae jump tae our safe house, the one in Maine, the most recent one, tae see if I could find them.

I kent there was a safe there with cash in it.

I landed in a faraway field and trudged a few miles up the road. We had three dates planned for convening here. I had picked the nearest date, and was worried nae one would be there.

But as I neared the house I saw a canoe in the water. I approached cautiously, until I saw Isla run across the dock with orange floats upon her upper arms.

Relief washed over me. "Isla!" I jogged toward her.

She ran intae my arms, "Da!"

I scooped her up.

She said, "Da, you weren't here. Emma said I could not call you."

"I ken, wee'un, I dinna hae a phone."

"You ought to get a phone da, so I can call you to tell you Archie is being a pain in the arse."

I laughed as Zach rushed out of the house sopping wet. "Shit! I was in the shower and didn't notice your storm, but I just saw the vessel on the tracker."

"Nae worries, I was nervous, I jumped tae a place farther away." I could see Fraoch and Ben, I assumed more were in the house. "Where is Kaitlyn?"

"She's not here, she and James were captured when we were in the thirteenth century."

Och. "Where?"

He said, "Just outside of Stirling castle. Where were you?"

"At Stirling castle."

I looked around at the gorgeous blue sky, the floating dock, and the lapping lake. "Madame Beaty, will ye watch the bairns while we go in tae discuss?"

Beaty said, "Aye, but I heard ye were bringin' a dog with ye?"

I laughed. "Ye already heard about m'surprise?"

Archie and Ben ran up. I hugged them both and crouched down when Archie held on around m'neck and seemed tae weep that I was finally home. "Och I hae missed ye."

"I missed you too."

"I am a king now, *another* king."

Archie wiped his eyes and said, "Och it sounds like a lot of trouble."

I laughed.

He said, "We heard your dog was really great, didn't we, Isla?"

She nodded her wee head against my shoulder.

"Haggis is verra braw. He is back at Stirling castle, guardin' for me. I will introduce ye soon enough—"

Archie said, "Where is mom? We were going to see you and…"

"That is more complicated, Archibald. I need tae discuss this for a moment with Uncle Fraoch and Chef Zach. She is in the thirteenth century, I just hae tae go get her."

He blinked, his face screwin' up a bit as if he would cry again, but he swallowed it down and nodded instead.

I said, "Ye hae tae be strong on it, Archibald, ye ken there are risks when we are time-traveling. Good outcomes can be difficult and complicated tae find. We hae tae 'work the problem' as Colonel Quentin would say. It will help me if ye are strong for Isla, Zoe, and Ben."

Zoe toddled up, holding Emma's hand, and said, "N'wee!"

Emma explained, "That's how she says her name."

I said, "Ye are speakin', wee'un, verra well. That is a perfect way tae say yer name, because ye are a verra wee, little one."

We left the kids and went into the house.

Everyone sat down and Zach said, "First, before we get serious, I have to ask the question on everyone's mind: what's up with the clothes, Magnus?"

"What, *this*? Tis the ordinary garb of the time, inna it funny?" I pulled the tunic out and curtsied.

Emma laughed, "No kilts back then?"

"Nae, they haena been used yet."

Zach said, "You know what would be crazy? If *we* are the ones who invented kilts in some weird kind of time loop. Maybe Scotland was never going to have kilts, until one of us went back in time to the thirteenth century in a kilt, and then the men back then liked the kilt and—"

Fraoch grinned. "Och, it could be, Zach. Archie came tae visit wearin' a kilt and Cailean greatly admired it. What if he started wearin' one? What if the history of the kilt in Scotland was started by Magnus's son when he visited from the twenty-fifth century."

Emma said, "However they got to Scotland, I do like a man's knees."

Zach said, "My lady is hot for knee porn."

She said, "This is true."

Zach said, "But Fraoch just gave all the credit to one of the kids. Magnus, I want the credit."

I said, "All right, ye can have the credit for the invention of the kilt."

Emma said, "But you haven't been to the thirteenth century yet, Zachary."

"I haven't? I felt sure I had, what about when..." He stared off into space.

Fraoch said, "I daena like any of this, tis too confused. We are loopin' around and messing with history. I daena want any of us tae be the start of anything, history needs tae be unaltered."

Hayley said, "So how did the kilt get invented then?"

Emma sighed. "Probably when a proper Scottish wife said, 'Honey, I made you this cloth to warm you up, but can you raise it just a wee bit so I can see your knees, I do really like your knees.'"

Zach laughed. "And the husband said, 'I *guess* so, if that's what does it for you, babe.'"

I asked, "Tae get serious, where is Quentin?"

Zach said, "He is behind in the thirteenth century with Katie and James."

I shook my head. "Ye never came, none of ye came."

"We were there, we arrived at the specified time. We were running from Ormr, some weird shit went down in Florida, we got scared and left under duress. But we were there on the agreed upon time."

I said, "I was there, waitin' for ye."

Zach said, "Nah man, you weren't there."

"I had ten men accompanyin' me—"

Zach said, "On horses?"

"Aye."

Emma and Zach looked at each other wide-eyed.

I continued, "I arrived later than I liked, because the storm was different, twas barely perceptible, tis difficult tae explain, but I rode around the clearin' lookin' for ye, I searched the bushes lookin' for a sign of yer havin' been there."

Zach looked at Emma and said, "Oh shit."

Hayley said, "Explain all of this, we weren't there, *what* happened?"

Emma said, "We got up from the clearing, Quentin and James were dragging stuff to the side, under the trees, because no one showed. We sat behind some bushes, waiting for Magnus, when the strangest thing happened…"

Zach said, "It was insane, weird, mind-blowing: we heard horses. We heard a horse, right fucking there." He held a hand in front of his nose. "It was practically breathing on Katie."

Emma said, "And a dog barking! But very very faintly."

I said, "Och, I was there, but nae there."

Fraoch frowned. "I daena like the sound of this, tis as if there are demons afoot."

I said, "I returned tae the castle, and when night fell I had a strange feelin' as if she were in the castle with me, as if she was sittin' beside me."

Zach said, "Have we ever, in the history of these vessels, ever ever, in the—"

Emma rolled her hand, "Get to the point, Zachary."

"Have we ever glimpsed multiple realities or I don't know, an alternate timeline?"

I said, "Ye mean side by side?"

"Yeah — I mean, we haven't, right? It's always been up and down the timeline. Past, future, present, up and down, jumping forward and back, but it's never done this before."

I shook my head. "So ye think Kaitlyn might be in the thirteenth century and I might be in the thirteenth century but one is written over the top of—"

"Or untangled, unwoven, lying side by side. I don't know…"

I exhaled. "I hoped ye would tell me that I was not sensible and none of this could be true. I was relyin' on ye tae come up with a better explanation than, 'something that has never afore happened is happenin' and we need to figure it out.' It sounds like a great deal tae figure out."

Fraoch said, "One thing I hae learned is whenever we need Zach tae explain what is happenin' we are in a verra complicated situation."

I chuckled. "This is true."

Zach said, "So we have Katie in a castle with James, Quentin is there somewhere. We need to write all this down."

I asked, "Colonel Quentin has a vessel?"

"Yeah, and he knows we're here."

"Then I expect he will return any moment, or we will go get him."

CHAPTER 18 - QUENTIN

I crouched in the trees eyeing an encampment up the river from Stirling. I supposed it was military, but being the thirteenth century it was really just a bunch of men in rudimentary tents. They each carried a sword, which was something, I supposed. Overall there were fewer weapons than at a NASCAR race.

I was exhausted. Since James and Katie had been taken a few short hours ago, and Zach, Emma, Beaty, and the kids had escaped, I had lugged the crates full of weapons and food into a ravine and hidden them with leaves and branches.

I needed to figure out how to rescue James and Katie, but the castle was occupied by assholes and I was alone.

I hoped more men were on their way, but beyond watching for a storm, which was boring and made me feel useless, I needed to do something. What I really wanted to do was kick some ass. Those guys on the castle walls had used real honest to god guns, it wouldn't be an easy fight without knowing what I was up against.

I thought about jumping away and jumping back but—

I was hit on the back of the head with something big and painful, and...

. . .

I came to a while later on the ground inside the camp.

A man on a nearby piece of log eyed me while holding my semiautomatic rifle in his hand. Because of the safety though, he couldn't do anything with it, thank god.

I groaned. "Where am I?"

"Ye are in m'camp, and who are ye?"

"My name is Quentin Peters. I need to see Mag Mòr."

The man shook his head.

"The king? Mag Mòr?"

The man said, "The only king around here is Ormr, but we are tryin' tae solve that trouble." Then he stated the obvious, "Ye are black as night."

I said, sitting up, "I don't know about that, I mean there are shades. Compared to your pasty white ass I might be dark, true, but 'black as night'? I've been in black-as-night, you need to get a…"

His eyes narrowed.

Why was I arguing with a man in the thirteenth century about skin color? My head ached and I was losing patience. I changed tack, "You're looking to overthrow Ormr? He's holding two members of my family prisoner inside Stirling. I'm willing to help with any plans you might have."

His eyes narrowed more. "Why would I allow a stranger tae help?"

"I have weapons. Good weapons. Firearms like that one." I held out my hand for it.

He shook his head. "Show me how tae use it."

"We need to be pretty far away. The castle will hear a gunshot."

He nodded looking down at the weapon. "What did ye call it? What will it do?"

"A gun, you've seen one before — the men in the castle have them, right? It's a little like an arrow, it will pierce an enemy right through."

"Aye, we canna mount an attack. Ormr's men have many of

them."

"Have you confiscated any?"

He picked up a cloth bundle, dropped it in front of me, and pulled the cloth away, uncovering three firearms.

I checked them: all were loaded, the safety made them useless to these guys.

"I'll help you wage war against Ormr, using these weapons and more, if you will help me get inside the castle for my family."

"I will take ye tae a field so ye can show me how they work." He held my weapon over his shoulder and rose. The whole time I was grateful the damned thing had the safety on.

He commanded one of his men to pick up the other confiscated weapons, then said, "Follow me."

I was weaving a bit, holding my head as I followed them into the woods. We walked a good while, away from Stirling, until we came to a distant field. The main guy passed me the firearm.

"Cover your ears." I pointed the semiautomatic rifle, and fired.

It was loud and terrifying. Birds rose from the woods. "Want me to show you how to use them and help you mount an attack? I help you — you help me get my family members out. Do we have a deal?"

"Aye." We shook hands.

I asked, "What's your name?"

"Will Wallace."

I grinned. "Okay, Will Wallace — is that really your name?"

"Aye."

"Okay, then, that's cool, so um… let me show you how to use guns."

I spent the next couple of days instructing him and his men how to use the firearms, and planning an attack on the castle.

CHAPTER 19 - MAGNUS

"*W*hat do we know?" asked Zach.

I said, "I hae been able tae use m'vessel tae leave the thirteenth century. I jumped tae the twenty-fifth century and dinna see any sign of m'descendants—"

Fraoch said, "Ye dinna see Ben or Archie?"

"Nae, I dinna go tae the castle, but I searched the outskirts of the city, twas desolate, it led me tae believe that something had gone wrong on our timeline."

Zach said, "Or your vessel might be on the wrong timeline."

Hayley said, "But he's here!"

"Maybe we're the axis of two different timelines."

Emma said, "Jesus Christ, Zachary, you always say crazy stuff that is just a little but funny and also terrifying."

He shrugged.

She checked her laptop, open on the coffee table. It took a moment, then she announced, "Ormr is king in three different time periods."

I said, "What are ye talkin' on, Madame Emma?"

"I thought you knew, Ormr is still king in three different time periods, Domnall in two."

I leaned back on the couch with a groan.

Then I leaned forward and said, "But... ye ken I..." Then I leaned back again. "All that time and trouble tae become a king and what has it gotten me?"

Fraoch said, "A great deal more trouble."

Zach said, "And likely an empty stomach. You haven't been home in a long time, you hungry?"

"Verra." I rubbed m'face, tryin' tae get m'energy tae deal with this. "I daena understand what has gone wrong — we were alone on the timeline, the only actors. Now Ormr is a king?"

"He is a king many times over." Fraoch added, "If ye think on it, ye are in a battle through history for kingdoms. Ye might need tae call for a ceasefire, possibly a treaty."

"I winna sign a treaty with Ormr or Domnall, they are evil."

Zach called from the kitchen. "Want me to reheat lasagna?"

"Och, would ye? But remind me tae eat slowly, m'stomach is half the size it once was."

"I was going to mention you've lost weight, but so had Fraoch when he returned."

I heard the microwave buzzin' from the kitchen, a sound that had become familiar through the years. It meant I was about tae be fed, a verra fine thing.

Zach leaned on the door between the livin' room and the kitchen, waitin' for the food tae cook. "So what *else* do we know?"

I said, "I ken with certainty that I hae tae return tae the thirteenth century. Perhaps I'll arrive on the right timeline."

Zach said, "But if you do, it doesn't sound like it will be your kingdom."

I slowly shook my head considering it — *If I found Kaitlyn I would be on another timeline.*

Emma said, "What I want to know is if the vessels are causing it — maybe Magnus's vessel is taking him to a different time. We ought to trade your vessel with one of the extras."

I nodded. "I will return tae the thirteenth century and test yer theory. Could I take the tracker with me? I will look for other vessels, it means ye will be without the protection of it."

Zach said, "I'll feel naked." The microwave beeped and Zach ducked into the kitchen again.

I raised my voice so he could hear me from the other room. "I ken, I daena like the idea of leavin' ye without it, but I need tae find out which vessels are in the thirteenth century."

Zach called from the kitchen, "Who are you taking with you?"

"Nae one, I need ye and Fraoch tae remain here."

Emma got out a notebook and a pen. "Let's go through all the possibilities, everything that could go wrong, and come up with as many scenarios as we can." She ripped out two pages. "What date in the thirteenth century?" She began to transcribe our thoughts.

I ate a meal, then dinner was ready and I ate a second meal. We had lists of ideas, scribbled plans, and worried solutions, and I had traded out my vessel. I sat on the dock that night with Archie and Isla and Ben beside me. "I plan tae be gone for two days. I ken tis a long time, but I hae much tae figure out. I believe I will be jumping quite a bit, twill be difficult, we need tae be strong."

Archie said, "You keep saying that."

I exhaled. "I ken, and tis a dumb thing for me tae say. I daena need tae tell ye tae be strong, Archie, ye are plenty strong enough a'ready. Tis as if I am sayin' it tae m'self. I am remindin' myself tae be strong and ye are just close enough tae hear it."

"I think grown ups do that a lot. Say things without anyone supposed to hear it."

I chuckled. "This is true."

Isla said, "I think so too."

I kissed her forehead. "That is a verra grown up thing for ye tae think, little one. Allow me tae tell ye something, I want ye tae nae be so grown up. I want ye tae be the wee bonny bairn I push on the swing for a time longer, while I figure this out. Daena grow up too fast."

She laughed. "I have to grow up, Da, it's my job."

"Just not too verra fast, please."

"I won't grow up too fast but Da don't stay away too long."

"Absolutely, only two days — do we hae a deal?"

Archie and Isla said, "Deal."

Emma and Zach had gone tae the store while I was showerin' and had packed me a box for m'trip tae the past. I had gifts for Cailean: a Hydro Flask and a fancy pen, as well as some food and weapons for m'self.

CHAPTER 20 - MAGNUS

I jumped tae a far away clearin' because I hoped I was jumping intae the time where Kaitlyn and James were held, a time when Ormr was a king. I also hoped Colonel Quentin would be looking for a storm and would meet me. I was verra concerned he hadna returned home even though he had a vessel.

I began to come to, and realized I'd arrived at night, feelin' the darkness of the time, both clock time and history time. I lumbered tae my feet and usin' a headlamp, found a footpath and hiked through the woods toward the castle. When I approached I found not a castle with a different occupant, but my own, as I had left it — I was a king returned.

Kaitlyn wasna there.

CHAPTER 21- LADY MAIREAD

There were terrible things afoot. Firstly, I had nae seen Magnus in a verra long time.

Secondly, there were issues with the historical record.

I was seeing Ormr's name far more often than I liked, and that of his brother, Domnall. Both were born of Agnie MacLeod with different fathers: Ormr, a son of Donnan I; Domnall, a son of Donnan II; both of them unclaimed bastards. The fact that they had any historical importance at all was outrageous.

They were uncivilized brutes, gaining dominance in time, and I did not like it.

In the meantime Magnus was lounging around in the thirteenth century, an inattentive king, leaving me tae run his future, civilized kingdom.

I did not like it at all.

At dinner General Hammond asked, "What do you want to do, Mairead, what would set your mind at ease?" He was sitting across the table refilling our glasses from our bottle of Lafite-Rothschild 1996.

"I suspect I ought tae go see him, Hammond. I prefer he

come tae me, but," I sighed. "I suppose I must make an exception."

General Hammond said, "I will place Jones in charge and attend you. Where are we going?"

"We will go tae the thirteenth century to visit Magnus. Then we will stop by Balloch castle tae see Lizbeth and Sean, then we will return home. Twill take but a day tae anyone who cares tae pay attention."

"Good, a little vacation will do you good."

The following day we jumped intae the thirteenth century, landing in a sheltered spot well away from Stirling castle. General Hammond was fully armed. Once I was able tae rise, he sat me upon an ATV, and drove me tae the castle, parking the ATV a distance away, and covering it with leaves and detritus. We wore cloaks tae cover our clothes, as they were near the style but nae perfect for the age — I felt though that Hammond looked verra fine in his tunic and belt, I admired his form greatly.

I did like him, he was kind and held me in the highest esteem, his only drawback was he was excessively boring. If only he would paint, or perhaps take pleasure in the stage.

We approached the castle on foot and fell in with a snaking queue of market tradespeople entering the castle tae sell their wares. At the guard gate, General Hammond approached and spoke tae the men.

General Hammond returned and whispered, "Mairead, we are allowed an audience with the king, but it is not *our* king. His name is John Balliol."

I said, "Well, that is absolutely absurd." I looked up at the walls. "The walls are timber, if he is king, this John, he is nae trying verra hard."

We were led before this pretend-king, who was sitting upon a chair in the middle of the room, as if twas a throne.

He narrowed his eyes. "What say ye?"

I raised my chin. "How long hae ye been a king?"

The crowd murmured.

"I daena answer tae ye."

I kept my sight leveled upon him. "Who was the king afore ye?"

He said, "I am the king of Scotland, how dare ye interrogate us in our court!"

"I hae traveled from verra far away, and I was told there would be another king upon the throne. His name is Mag Mòr."

He said, "I hae never heard this name."

"Och, nae even an ancestor, nothing? Och, this is worse than I expected."

"I come from a long line of kings, none of them are named Mag Mòr. I hae been wearing the crown for almost a year."

"Well daena that just crumble the stone tower, and yer father was…?."

Hammond behind me whispered, "Careful, Mairead."

The king asked, "How are ye Scottish, yet ye daena ken the history of Scotland?"

"I am Scottish, I hae just forgotten, my liege. I was wondering about yer lineage, how ye became a king, was it yer father who wore the crown before ye?"

"My rule has been determined by fiat, after the deaths of our king Alexander III and then his heir, Queen Margaret, God rest her—"

"Neither of them were a Balliol?"

His gaze was hard. "Are ye going tae continue tae be insolent, or ought we finish this conversation afore I become angered?"

I huffed and curtsied low. "May your rule be long, sire."

I kept my head down as I backed out of the room.

. . .

At the door, Hammond took me by the elbow and escorted me quickly to the courtyard. "You were too blunt with him, Mairead!"

I said, "I daena have time tae be polite tae a pretend king, he is in my son's hall, wearing my son's crown. The true king is Magnus! It is in all the history books. Tis maddening tae hear him deny it."

We crossed the courtyard as he looked left and right. "We must leave in haste."

"We are armed, we hae eight weapons hidden upon us."

"Yes, but we do not want to use them against a hundred men."

"Well, we can leave but we should find the nearest inn tae make more inquiries."

He wove us through the crowded courtyard. "It will definitely be safer to inquire about the kingdom from a lowly pub-goer than to demand answers from the king."

"Tis my way, Hammond! How am I tae be cowed intae silence by that usurper of the crown? I think not."

We left the gates of the castle at a brisk pace and went down the path, headed in the direction of the village beyond the walls.

In the Red Lion pub, Hammond ordered two ales and paid with gold. Thereafter though, he had tae look menacing by keeping his hand upon his sword hilt, as we sat at our table near the hearth.

He shook his head. "I swear you will be the death of me, Mairead."

I said, "And ye will be on yer deathbed, complaining about how I hae nae one ounce of care and attention for ye, but who would ye be complaining tae?"

"You."

"Aye, I would be at yer deathbed, listening tae ye list my faults."

He chuckled. "I appreciate that."

I joked, after a sip of ale, "Ye should put that on yer list of my positive attributes, I was an excessive irritation and with certainty brought yer untimely death upon ye, but I was with ye tae the end. There is at least that."

"You joke, Mairead, but it is your most admirable quality, you are loyal to a fault."

"Except with ye tis nae a fault. Being loyal tae ye has been a verra wise thing, ye hae been a good friend."

"I have done my best, Mairead. I have always wanted to be of service to you."

I pulled my book from my pocket and a pen tae write. "When we are done with these dramas, we should return tae our previous task: listing all of Donnan's sons and nephews. We ought tae hae a record of them, so we arna caught unawares."

"I have found four so far, yes... I will begin the search as soon as we are done with this. What are you writing there?"

"I am listing that I hae come tae the year 1290 and dinna find Mag Mòr a king. So I can keep the memories straight." I put the book back in my pocket.

We sat quietly and then my eyes settled on a couple of farmers. "Ask them about the king."

General Hammond called one of them tae the table and slid a coin across. "Has there been a Mag Mòr around Stirling? Mag, Magnus, a Campbell, from the Campbell Clan, a friend of Cailean?"

The farmer's brow knit. "Cailean Mòr?"

"Perhaps?"

"I ken of a Cailean Mòr from Loch Awe."

I had promised myself tae allow Hammond tae be the one tae speak, but broke the promise immediately. "Yet ye haena heard of a Mag Mòr?"

The farmer shook his head.

General Hammond said, "Are there any men contesting King John for the throne?"

The farmer leaned forward and quietly said, "Just William Wallace, he is raising troops near Falkirk."

"On what grounds?"

"He wants tae overthrow the King of England's power here in Scotland. I am nae part of it though, no' at all, I am satisfied with the present king, God keep him."

I met Hammond's eyes.

He said, "Thank you for your time," and sent the man away.

I said, "Tis as if Magnus has never been here, yet when I was in the future in our kingdom, the history books listed Mag Mòr as king." I fished the book from my pocket again and wrote: the common farmer has nae recognition of the name Mag Mòr.

General Hammond said, "When did you first notice these things that seemed to be shifting?"

"What do ye mean?"

"I have noticed that things once seemed orderly, and now they are shifted and disorderly, I am sure you noticed the same."

"I have." I pursed my lips.

"Mairead, is this one of those instances where you think if you say it out loud it will make you seem weak?"

"Nae, but… perhaps a little of it is true. I have been noticing the disorder for a while."

"It seems to have been a *long* time that things have been disordered."

I nodded. "I daena ken why, but…" I brought the book out for the third time, thumbed through it, found a note, and tapped the page. "Twas on the night of the ball, in Riaghalbane, that I told Master Cook that he could find his wife, my great-great-granddaughter Sophie, at Dunscaith castle in the year 1589. I believe that was when our trouble started."

"It can not have been that you told him, that is not…"

"It was that he acted on it, he looped there, tae 1589 and now we have…"

Hammond leaned forward. "A what?"

"An unraveling."

CHAPTER 22 - MAGNUS

I was sore from the jump and without comfort in the castle and wasna sure what my next plan would be. I had been certain that I would be in the different timeline. I was usin' the vessel that had transported Zach there and back.

I supposed our test proved that twas nae the fault of the vessel, but if nae, what *was* delivering some of us tae a different timeline?

I met Cailean for dinner in the Great Hall. Over a horrid meal of overcooked, unspiced salmon, he asked, "How come ye are quiet Mag Mòr?"

I shook my head. "I hae a great deal on m'mind, m'wife has nae returned."

He nodded solemnly. "It weighs on ye, I understand."

"Beyond all the troubles of the kingdom: the English king at the border who wants power, William Wallace gatherin' an army, beggin' for turmoil, the terrible fish for dinner; I am worried upon m'Kaitlyn."

He remained quiet and sipped from his ale.

I asked, "Do ye ever think about the long line of time?"

"What dost ye mean, Mag Mòr, a long line?"

"That we start on a path, headed in one direction. Our

grandfather also traveled this path, we are all on the path — but dost ye think there might be other paths?"

His brow drew down. "Are ye speaking of heaven and hell? Ye ought tae choose the righteous path and follow it dutifully. Ye canna stray from a divine—"

"Nae, Cailean, I mean… tis hard tae describe. Ye ken how ye are in one path, and yer children are walking along behind ye, following ye? Could ye step ontae another path…?"

I stood up a bit drunk at this point. "I will act it out, ye will be amazed at m'talents." I chugged some ale and called two men over. I instructed them tae follow me in a single line as I walked around the room.

They were laughin'. "Why are we doin' this?"

I said, "Daena question, follow me, I am tryin' tae model somethin'."

More men joined and the group of men, laughin' and drunk, followed me down the Great Hall. I said, "Now ye keep walking while I…" I stepped away and continued walking beside them. "Keep walkin' in yer line."

They kept walking in their line, until they grew confused and forgot the instructions. Young Clyde turned from their line and joined behind mine.

I laughed. "Nae, tis nae how it works!"

As we passed the table I dropped down in m'chair. "They are useless for modelin', but I'm tryin' tae show ye how tis tae have a life that follows a line and what if someone stepped from their line, could their life continue on? Separate from the original path?"

His brow drew down. "If ye hae stepped from the path of yer life, ye hae died, Mag Mòr."

"Nae, that is nae what I mean." I exhaled. "I meant…" I thought for a moment, studyin' my hands. "If ye were livin', nae dead, could ye live on beside yer own life?"

Young Clyde asked, "Like a ghost, sire?"

Jim the Braw, who was kent for saying things twice as loud as he ought, yelled, "Och, I ken! Ye would be a shadow!"

I banged my hand down on the table, almost knockin' over m'ale. "Exactly! Like a shadow. Ye ken how yer shadow is there beside ye? What if ye could live a life as a shadow of yerself?"

Cailean stared intae the rafters for a moment. I could tell he was drunk by the way he held his mouth. "I daena really understand."

I exhaled. "That is all right, I daena understand either, nae really." I lifted m'ale tae m'lips and sipped.

He continued tae stare intae the rafters, then said, "What I daena understand is how ye can think that life goes in one straight path — this is nae how it goes. Ye are mighty confused on it."

"I am nae confused, from birth tae death, ye take one step after another along a path." I walked my fingers on the planks of the table.

"Nae, Mag Mòr, nae, tis nae a long path, yer life is a wheel and time is rollin' by."

I laughed. "How does that work?"

"A life goes from the beginnin', a bairn born of God and turns around becomin' reunited with God in the end. Ye are alone at the beginnin' and again at the end, ye ken, ye canna think of it as a path — tis a wheel. Ye might collect people along the way but they are their own wheel, they are going tae live and die as well." Then he laughed. "I canna believe ye think it is a path. Where are ye goin' on the path?"

"I am going tae the future of m'life." I waved m'hands. "I suppose tis a pig-stupid idea." Then I added, "Daena tell m'friend, Madame Beaty, that I said 'pig-stupid', she believes a pig tae be the wisest of animals."

Cailean said, "Mag Mòr, if ye think of yer life as a wheel, ye daena hae tae worry about goin' anywhere, except back home intae the arms of God."

I said, "So if yer life is a wheel, what if ye were on a different wheel — or a cart rolling tae a different place?"

He said, "Mag Mòr, why dost ye want tae be on a different path or a wheel? Ye ought tae be content tae remain where ye are, tae shift from yer life is tae die."

"Och, Cailean, dost ye think if I am livin' a life alongside another life that holds m'family, that I may be dead?"

"Tis exactly what I believe, ye would be a spirit unleashed from the world, a lifeless soul, a wandering, untethered entity. Tis nae somethin' ye should wonder about — ye ought tae ask God for forgiveness. He has given ye yer life, ye must live it in gratitude."

I exhaled, "Aye, I will stop wonderin' on it." Yet I continued on, "Or ye might think of it like this, hae ye seen the spindle that Mary uses?"

He groaned, but was laughin' as well. "Ye canna drop the idea, Mag Mòr? All right, aye, I hae seen a spindle."

"Hae ye seen the yarn, when it has been wrapped tightly?"

He chuckled. "Aye, I hae seen yarn. What is yer point?"

"What if a life is like that wound yarn... tis a bit unraveled at the beginning, wound tightly through the middle, then unwound again at the end, frayed out." I raised my glass. "Aye, this is more what I mean, Cailean, ye might hae yer past and yer future wound taegether, and what if they become unraveled at the end?"

He raised his brow. "How long is the strand, is it long like a path? Are ye tryin' tae convince me that life is a long path and now a long strip of yarn?"

"Nae, not like a path." I stared off intae space.

"Ye are goin' tae upset yerself, Mag Mòr, thinking on this — if ye believe it like a wheel, ye will be pleased. Life goes in a circle: the seasons, the years, the day, the life. It all begins with sunrise and ends with a sunset, up and down, and around."

"That is all it is?"

"That is all it is. If ye want off it, ye daena get tae decide. Tis up tae God when ye will leave the wheel."

I allowed the conversation tae wane, wishin' that Chef Zach were here tae discuss the matters of metaphor and time.

We finished our ales and our dinner and I climbed the stair tae my room. There I knelt beside my bed tae pray. "God, in yer infinite wisdom, please help me tae understand what I am experiencing, I used tae be afraid of being dead in the past, or livin' out of time, but I hadna considered how terrifyin' it would be tae live *beside* time — nothing more than a ghost in one realm, with people I love as ghosts in another. Please, I beg of ye, help me tae find my..." I thought tae say 'my correct path' but decided tae follow Cailean's beliefs. "Please Father, give me guidance within the wheel of time. Bring me round, through this dark time without m'wife, separated from our bairns, returned tae their arms..." I continued on for a while, and then, done with the prayer, lay with my cheek on my bed.

After a moment I felt a barely perceptible, warm hand, brush through my hair as if I were being comforted.

I did feel comforted.

I said tae Kaitlyn, "I will do everything I can tae get ye returned tae yer bairns, I promise."

CHAPTER 23 - KAITLYN

*T*wo men entered, the first was Domnall, who I had already met. The second seemed likely to be Ormr, though I had never met him. He was not as ugly as Domnall was, not quite as big, but a gross brute all the same.

I was pissed. I sat on the bed and glared.

His brow raised. "Ye are angry, little bitch."

"And you are a dipshit, you're evil and vile, and yes, I am a bitch, sure. These two things are both true."

Ormr sat down in the chair, adjusting his furs around his shoulders.

Domnall leaned against the wall, his expression stupid and leering, dangerous.

Ormr said, "Are ye enjoyin' yer new home?"

"Fuck you."

He laughed.

I said, "Why am I here? Why haven't you killed me yet?"

"I wouldna give us any ideas."

I huffed.

He said, "Where is yer husband?"

"I have no idea, don't *you* know?"

"Nae, I think he is hiding from us, like the big coward he is. Tis loathsome."

"Says the man who kidnapped someone else's wife. He's not a coward, he's going to learn where I am and he's going to come and kick your ass so hard you'll be crying to your mother that the bad man hurt you—"

"We are countin' on him learning where ye are and waitin' for him tae arrive."

"And until that happens you'll just keep me indefinitely?"

"He winna leave ye here that long, though he's been known tae be irrational." He shrugged. "Perhaps yer pull is nae so strong with him?"

I huffed. "Where is James Cook?"

"The dungeon."

"He's still alive? He hasn't been harmed?"

"He's alive, but nae for long."

CHAPTER 24 - MAGNUS

I woke up the next morn, and sat for a long time on the edge of the bed, considerin' what tae do. I was sure I was in the presence of Kaitlyn, that somehow I was separated by a shroud of time between us. I was worried about leavin' this time, twas a risk, what if I couldna return?

I kent she was in one place, I was in another. What if we never once more came taegether again?

If this was it, I couldna bear leaving her.

But I had tae find a solution tae our separation.

I had found naethin' in the future. The past was splayed intae segments.

I held m'vessel and turned it over and over. I kent every marking, every part— when I had lived in Maine with Kaitlyn's grandparents I had learned tae work it. Through the following years my understandin' had grown. I kent a great deal about the vessel, more than anyone else in the history of the world — except m'mother. She always knew more. I would need tae remedy this imbalance.

In the meantime, in all these years, neither of us had ever landed on a different timeline.

I needed tae think this through methodically, tae begin jumpin' tae try tae get on the correct timeline. I just needed a plan.

CHAPTER 25 - QUENTIN

I was leading a charge, wondering what the hell I was doing. Men were on the castle walls shooting down at us, and as I ran I thought, *where the hell did they get these fucking modern weapons?*

I was pissed, enraged, waging-war, and I was irritated — if this was Ormr and Domnall shooting at my ass from those old-as-shit timber walls. I was sure that the cause was James looping to save Sophie. Somehow we had effed up the world and given these assholes an easier way to kill us.

I had designed a battle plan based on a football end-around play. We were charging, but as bullets flew I raced from behind the lines, around the army, alongside the castle walls, to the back where the timber walls were up on the top of cliffs. There I would try to find a back entry and force my way in, kill the guard, or scale the wall and kill the guards, and fight my way to the roof in a surprise attack. I had my semiautomatic rifle, a grenade, and a rope from my supplies.

There wasn't a door. There was no guard to kill, but no one noticed I had run around back. *The guards had one job.* I looked up at the walls, *could I climb them?* I ran farther, checking the wall for holes or doors, finding a spot that seemed — I was surprised by how quiet it was in the castle beyond.

I waited in the shadows, listening.

The shooting, the yelling and mayhem, had gone quiet.

Was everyone dead?

I crept back around the castle walls to the front. No one was there.

I looked up at the walls and all around to find no one. I snuck in through the front gate and clung to the walls in the shadows, staring out at the courtyard.

The castle was completely still, there was no sound at all but the wind, and it was echoing, a sound that didn't happen in an occupied castle.

Humans in a castle dampened the echoes and a castle needed at the very least ten people to make it operable. There needed to be guards, a kitchen crew — and what about the guns that had been shooting?

There had been a battle not more than ten minutes ago and now... I stood in the shadows, clutching the gun to my chest, trying to understand the silence.

With my gun aimed, I stepped from the courtyard into a store room, empty, except for some barrels and bottles on a shelf. There were cobwebs. It had been a while since someone had been in here.

I swept the gun left and right and crept into the next room which was the same, cold and bare. Stirling castle was a huge important castle in the history of Scotland, it had just been full of people, defensively protecting the walls. Now it was empty? I stepped from the kitchen to a wooden stair and climbed, aiming my gun up as I mounted, breathless, to the top of the walls. Not a soul.

I crouched low and crept along to the east side, where Will Wallace and I had staged our attack and peered down.

There was no one there. *What kind of mindfuck was this?*

The valley stretched in all directions, not a road to be seen. A river glistened in the sun, a village lay beyond, a field looked disused and abandoned, an endless, uncivilized landscape, an unpopulated land, a castle that was unnecessary.

I searched for the stairwell that led down to the dungeons and found it inside a low stone building. I turned on my head-lamp in the long corridor, finding no prisoners, only a few furi-ous-to-be-interrupted rats. In the far cell I found a carving in the stone: JC and marks counting one plus five and then eight and then nine, a sum of 24 days.

It had been four days since he and Katie had been captured. A chill ran down my spine. I felt my sporran for the vessel, it was still there.

I left the dungeons, emerged from the stairwell at the court-yard, and crossed to a three-story high building. I went up to the upper rooms and opened door after door, finding one broken door that looked as if someone had hacked away at the wood from the inside, and looking through bedrooms and sitting rooms. I found an office that held nothing but a piece of furni-ture. All the rooms were unlocked.

I called, "Katie! James!"

I returned downstairs to the front gate, and used a side door to exit. I walked out onto an overgrown path, down the hill, and returned to the encampment, where I found nothing but my crates, the weapons still inside.

I stared down at them for a long time.

With certainty, I had been in the middle of a battle. The planning of it had taken days — how had I...?

I knew Zach would call this a time-discrepancy, a time burrito, but there was a little bit of me that wondered if I might be losing my mind.

CHAPTER 26 - KAITLYN

I pressed my ear to the door. I was so freaking famished. I listened and called, "Hello? Hello? Who's there?!"

The castle echoed. A wind howled. An echoing, howling castle was a frightening castle. "Hello?!"

While I slept, had the world ceased being a world? The room was so cold. I tried to budge the door. "Hello! Hello! Are you there?"

The echo circled the room and ricocheted down the halls and returned to me, *are you there?*

I backed up to the bed. "Can you hear me? Hello!!!"

I pulled my knees up and wrapped around them. "Magnus! Magnus, can you hear me? Help me!"

CHAPTER 27 - MAGNUS

A plea hit me with a cold dread — *Help me.*

I jumped up. I had tae act, I had tae get tae her.

I began m'first jump.

I went tae Balloch castle in the eighteenth century then returned tae Stirling, I went tae the seventeenth century, the eighteenth century, tae Edinburgh, tae Stirling over and over in different years. I left marks upon a stone, tae note where I was, and when, and I felt as if I lost layers of m'soul in the work of it, an agony from inside m'self that ached me through.

I dinna go back tae the bedroom, tae ken she was alone and scared was maddening enough.

In the eighteenth century the marks on the stone were aged and hard tae read, I rubbed them with cloth tae make them out. In the thirteenth century they were fresh, marked the day afore. It wasna lost on me that I had become a part of the past.

It was the wrong past.

I thought, with every jump, perhaps this time will be the one time.

Perhaps she will be there.

Finally, I rose at Stirling and stared down at the marks upon the stone. M'sight was blurred, my soul weary. I prayed tae God tae help me from this turmoil.

The marks upon the stone would turn intae fifteen afore I finally gave up.

~

I woke in the field and found Fraoch, Zach, and Quentin, looking down on me. I blinked at the sky.

"Is she home?"

My voice was barely audible, weary from the exertion, agonizing.

Fraoch said, "Nae, Og Maggy, she inna—"

I wept for a long time, layin' in the field starin' up at the sky. Fraoch crouched beside me and put a hand on m'shoulder until I finished cryin' and made m'self calm.

He stood and outstretched his hand tae help me sit.

I exhaled, looking up at the men, nae feeling well enough tae stand. "I am sorry about my grief, I hae jumped many times."

Zach said, "It's okay, Magnus, we got you."

"When did ye arrive, Colonel Quentin?"

Quentin looked solemn. "Just a few moments ago—"

Fraoch said, "Twas two storms, one right after another."

I nodded and scrubbed my hands up and down on m'face. "I am frightfully hungry, I haena eaten since Balloch castle, the fourth time I jumped there. Lizbeth and Sean send their regards." The field we were in was blooming with wildflowers, I picked a stalk of grass. "Is she lost, how will we recover her?"

Colonel Quentin said, "I don't know, Boss, I had a full blown rescue operation with William Wallace—"

"William Wallace? Och, I daena believe it, he is an unhelpful bawbag."

Colonel Quentin said, "You met him too? Holy shit."

Chef Zach said, "William Wallace, *the* William Wallace?"

I said, "Ye hae heard of him?"

Chef Zach said, "Of course I've heard of him! He's the most famous Scotsman in the world, have we shown you Braveheart?"

I peeled away leaves from a long wildflower stem while they spoke, it was calmin' tae m'mind.

Colonel Quentin said, "We're off topic I think, Zach, crazy shit just went down—"

"Right of course, carry on."

Quentin said, "I was attempting to rescue Katie and James and we had guns blaring and I had taught Wallace an end-around play..." His eyes went vague and far off, then he said, "I was proud of that, but it's only something that James would understand — wish he were here to hear it."

"From the west?" I asked.

"Yeah, and while I circled the castle it was like the world had vanished, all the people were gone, it was a creepy-ass ghost town."

I peeled another long leaf. "Did ye see or hear any ghosts?"

"No, but I did see a sign from James. His initials carved in a cell wall. He had been keeping track, it looked like twenty-four days or something."

"Nae sign of Kaitlyn? I believe she might be kept in a room on the second floor."

"I checked all the rooms, but..." His eyes went wide. "Should I go back? Maybe I didn't look hard enough...?"

"If James was gone, she was likely gone as well, but..." I stood. "I need ye tae write all this down, we ought tae map out what ye saw. We hae tae make sure we daena miss any clues."

As we headed tae the house, lugging some of Quentin's crates, the winds picked up again. Chef Zach looked up at the sky. "Fuck, another storm is coming, three in a row."

We ducked behind a stand of trees, the wind was brutal and dangerous.

I called out. "How many weapons do we hae, any extra?"

Colonel Quentin lifted the lid on a crate and passed out weapons.

Chef Zach said, "Look on the bright side, though, it's probably not going to be a shootout, it's probably Katie and James."

I said, "Aye Zach, but can ye run tae the house tae protect the kids?"

"Absolutely." He raced down the road.

But it wasn't Kaitlyn and James. The time travelers this time were Lady Mairead and General Hammond.

CHAPTER 28 - MAGNUS

*W*e waited for them tae waken, finally Lady Mairead groaned, sat, and then nudged General Hammond. "Get up, if I must, ye must."

He sat up without a word.

She looked around. "What are ye men doing there with yer mouths open, agog? Ye ought tae help me up, and tell me what the hell is going on — we hae gone tae three different times. They are all empty, nary a person exists, nor a memory of us on the timeline."

I greeted the bairns and had a sandwich in front of me. Lady Mairead sat primly on the sofa. "I daena suppose we could meet anywhere else? I hae a fine house called Elmwood in the Upper East Side, tis nae nearly so..." She brushed something off the cushion and looked around at the paneling in the room. "I daena ken why there is so much wood everywhere."

Emma pulled a long sheet from a roll of butcher paper and taped it tae the wall. She pulled the cap off her marker and drew a long horizontal line. "Where are Archie and Ben supposed to be in the future? We ought to make contact to see if they can help."

I said, "They ought tae be in the year 2405, I went there and dinna find them, twas an empty desolate land."

Emma wrote 2405 on the right side of the paper. "Great."

Beaty, sitting on the couch, said, "Why dinna ye bring Haggis with ye this time, Magnus?"

"I think he needs tae remain at Stirling until I hae figured out how tae get tae Kaitlyn. He senses she is there, perhaps she senses he is there as well. Perhaps he is familiar while I am away."

Hayley said, "You really heard her ask for help?"

"Aye."

She had her arm around Fraoch and was rubbing his shoulders, comfortingly.

I said, "Are ye well, Fraoch?"

Hayley said, "He hasn't slept, he's been up guarding every night."

"I canna sleep with all this goin' on, I might as well watch on the high walls."

In unison we all looked around the interior of the room. We were inside a one-story cabin, tucked in the trees. He chuckled. "The walls may nae be high, but the dangers are."

The kids ran through with Mookie trotting along behind them. Emma called after them. "We're working and we're all necessary for it. Archie and Ben, watch your little sisters, don't let them near the lake."

Isla announced, "We going to bunkhouse."

Emma said, "Perfect."

Beaty called after them, "Daena feed Mookie anythin'! He gets a tummy ache from too many treats."

Isla said, as they left through the back door, "That's silly Aunt Beaty, there no such thing as too many treats."

"For Mookie there is!"

Then Emma asked, "What about the year of Magnus's arena

battle with Domnall?" She wrote the year on the paper and circled it. "Empty?"

Lady Mairead said, "Aye. Then I went forward a few years, and twas empty, and before it was also empty."

Quentin said, "The year that Magnus was in the arena with Domnall was empty too, like a ghost town?"

General Hammond said, "Completely desolate. We couldn't find a year in the kingdom of Riaghalbane that wasn't affected."

I moaned.

Emma circled another date. "What about 1707, has anyone checked in on Lizbeth and Sean?"

I said, "I visited them."

Emma said, "Was it empty?"

I said, "Lizbeth and Sean and the rest of the family were unaffected."

Lady Mairead said, "I visited them as well, everyone was there, but tae be safe I dinna make contact... but *honestly*, what hae the rest of ye been doing? This is a disaster! Hae ye all been here playing in the lake while every subject in Magnus's kingdom has vanished?"

I said, "Ye canna hold any of this against us, I hae been jumping tryin' tae reach Kaitlyn. Quentin has just returned from a rescue attempt. Someone had tae remain with the bairns. This is not a time for recriminations."

Lady Mairead pursed her lips.

Emma put an exclamation point beside the year 1707. "What did you mean, Lady Mairead, by 'safe you didn't make contact...'?"

She raised her chin. "I believe that the moment this all went awry was when Master Cook began looping at Dunscaith castle tae rescue his wife, m'great-great-granddaughter Sophie. I think the times which hae been altered are ones we hae visited after that fact. I want tae make sure we arna altering more of them. I saw enough tae ken the year 1707 is nae empty."

Quentin said, "I was in the year 1290, it is also empty."

I said, "But I have been tae 1290, when I go tis a kingdom under my rule."

Emma wrote the year on the paper twice and circled one and drew an exclamation point by the other.

Zach was scrutinizing her code. "Em, you think this is helping?"

She put her hands on her hips, looking at the chart. "I think so, yes." She drew a dotted line down the middle of the timeline. "On the left side you have dates doubling, emptying, shifting, like alternate universes. On the right you have empty years, like an unraveling."

She wrote the current year in the middle. "The present is not empty, we are all here, we are able to jump in and out of this place."

Lady Mairead pointed, "Put the year 1589 there as well, that is, I believe, the central point of this entire situation. It was the year I told James that Sophie would be at Dunscaith."

Chef Zach said, "Figures it would come down to James."

Emma wrote a one then a five and—

Quentin groaned, "*That's* what James carved into the wall in the dungeon at Stirling!" He jumped up and grabbed a red marker from the box on the table. He uncapped it and wrote, JC one plus five plus eight plus nine. "I added them together. I thought it meant that was how many days he was in the cell, but that's a year. Was he telling us to go to that year?"

Lady Mairead said, "I will go, someone needs tae tell Master Cook—"

Quentin said, "What makes you think he is there?"

"Of course he is there, he is looping! I will go and tell him tae calm his arse down, or I will be forced tae stop him with my dagger. He is ruining everything."

I chuckled. "I think we can send someone with a better bedside manner tae intervene with Master Cook."

I said, "Tis clear we believe 1589 is the moment when we unleashed Ormr and Domnall and certain doom?"

Colonel Quentin asked, "But what exactly happened to the timeline? And what tools do we have to fix it?"

Zach said, "We have the vessels and we have the tracker."

Fraoch said, "We hae the atrocious Trailblazer."

Emma said, "We have the gold strands."

I watched Lady Mairead as she sat immobile, staring straight ahead.

I said, "Lady Mairead, where is the rest of it?"

"I daena ken what ye mean?"

"There are other tools, I ken there are, and ye hae had access tae them or ye ken of them. What else is there? Tis the time tae be forthcoming."

Her lips pursed, she shifted in her seat.

I said, "Once ye almost killed me with a small ring, an addition that grounded my vessel. Where is that ring?"

"I am nae sure where it ended up."

I watched her face, a barely perceptible lie in her expression, holding back information. "All right, ye daena ken where that is, how about this? Donnan could retrieve vessels remotely, where is *that* tech?"

"The last I saw of the ring and the remote retrieval, they were held in our vault, but there was also a locked metal chest."

My eyes narrowed and I held my hands about a foot and a half apart. "Twas a metal chest, locked, about this big?"

"Aye, ye stole it from the origination moment."

I exhaled. "So I was guarding it in the cave at Kilchurn?"

"Aye."

Quentin said, "This was the chest we couldn't open, right? I tried everything."

Lady Mairead asked, "Did Magnus try?"

Quentin and I looked at each other.

He said, "I don't remember, we tried everything, I thought, but... Did you try, Magnus?"

"Nae, why? I thought twas enough tae hae my colonel attempt it."

Lady Mairead said, "Twas nae enough, Donnan had the chest coded so that his male descendants could open it. Ye ought tae hae tried, Magnus."

I exhaled, long. "These are the things ye ought tae tell me. Where is it now? Last I kent of it the chest was in m'vault in Riaghalbane."

She glanced at General Hammond. "I hae passed all of it tae m'great-granddaughter, Rebecca. I asked her tae guard the chest. Tae keep it away from the males of the family, so twould be safer."

"Safer with a great-granddaughter?"

"Aye," she added, "I dinna think we *needed* it — tis verra dangerous, Magnus. Donnan was serious about keeping it hidden. We dinna want it laying around for any descendant tae find and use, so I hid it away from the males of the family. Tis safe with her. Donnan called it the Bridge, I daena how it works but it changes the—"

She clamped her mouth closed, her eyes widened.

I said, "What does it do?"

Her eyes shifted as if she was calculating. "I daena ken, exactly, but Donnan said it would control the timeline." Her hand shook.

I said, "We *need* tae control the timeline! Let me get this straight, we need the chest containin' the Bridge *now*, but ye hae hidden it away? I am a descendant of Donnan, I took the chest from the origination moment, tis mine, tis my son Archie's, and ye hae hidden it from us?"

She said, "Donnan had too many sons, tis ridiculous. I had tae hide it, or they would all come around, accessing *your* birthright, simply because they are born of his sexual antics."

Chef Zach laughed.

Fraoch leaned forward. "Sophie was yer great-great-grand-daughter, could she hae been kidnapped in order tae gain access tae the items her mother was guardin'?"

Lady Mairead smoothed back her hair. "I suppose that might be—"

I looked around at the room. "Aye, ye daena just '*suppose*'... Ormr and Domnall could hae applied pressure tae Sophie tae find all of it."

Fraoch said, "And they could hae opened the chest."

Zach said, "How...?"

Fraoch said, "Ormr is a son of Donnan I, Domnall is a son of Donnan II, they are brothers of ours." He waved his finger between us. "If they found the items, they could open them."

Zach said, "Fuck, I forgot they were brothers, but one is also an uncle...? This is Game of Thrones level crazy."

Fraoch said, "I daena think of them as brothers, Magnus and I agreed tae either nae talk about it, or tae call them distant cousins, at best."

Zach said, "Yeah, I get you, distant cousins, I'm more comfortable with that, and we're fucking grateful they didn't get their hands on the chest."

I turned tae Lady Mairead. "Ye used Isla in a deal for the Trailblazer, now ye use Rebecca tae hide the Bridge." My voice turned steely. "Ye ought nae tae use your granddaughters tae protect the tech. Tis too dangerous. This is a weakness."

Lady Mairead huffed. "There is *nothing* weak about my granddaughters."

Quentin said, "We need to arm to the teeth and go fight Ormr and Domnall before they come for anything, or *anyone* else."

I said, "It would be a suicide mission, we are losin' our place in history and losin' our minds in the meantime. I daena think we can find both Ormr and Domnall *and* the chest and surprise them *and* kill them... nae while time is unraveling."

Zach said, "Maybe it's a moot point anyway, we don't know if we need to battle for the Bridge in the box because it might not be the bridge or box we need, it's baffling."

Emma said, "Nice alliteration, babe."

"Yeah, I get weird when I'm stressed."

Quentin said, "I suspect it is what we need. I think if there is a possibility of the timeline being corrupted, the people who invented time travel tech probably also had tech to fix it."

General Hammond said, "I agree with Colonel Quentin: the vessels have a ring, like a leash, that keeps them close. We have a Trailblazer to build new time roads. There is a way to set the vessel to call it home. We can assume that the inventors planned for complications. I believe they would worry about the unintended consequences of unmitigated time travel power. We can assume they had an antidote to time-unraveling."

Beaty said, "Wouldn't they have more than one Bridge then?"

We all looked at Beaty for a moment.

She said, "If ye think on it, they had verra many vessels. They had more than one Trailblazer, and we hae multiple golden strands. Do we hae more than one of the rings?"

Lady Mairead said, "Aye, there are at least six."

Madame Beaty said, "Then I think there ought tae be more of the Bridges, where would they be?"

Hayley waved a hand excitedly. "Emma! Start a new list! Where are all our hiding places?"

Lady Mairead said, "We arna sure where our chest is hidden *or* where m'great-granddaughter is."

Hammond said, "The question would be, did Donnan give any tech tae his other sons or nephews?"

I exhaled. "We ken he did. He often gave them vessels for when they were of age, then he would send for them. I hae already fought—"

Chef Zach said, "I mean, holy crap, Mags, haven't you killed them all yet?"

Lady Mairead said, "There were many sons, but nae all of Donnan's sons or nephews *want* the throne. General Hammond is a cousin, he has a claim tae the throne, but he inna interested in it. It takes having the mindset of a king tae want tae fight for a kingdom. Hammond is too soft for it." She patted the back of his hand. "I daena mean any offense by it, ye are a wonderful protector. Ye are courageous in guarding us, but ye daena want tae *start* a fight. There is a difference."

Hammie chuckled. "I am glad you finished that thought more in my favor, Mairead."

CHAPTER 29 - MAGNUS

*L*ady Mairead pulled her book from her pocket. "I daena ken *all* of Donnan's sons and grandsons and nephews, but there are a few I keep tabs on. There is one who has connections here, in Maine, in this time period." Her finger scrolled down a page, she read then flipped a few pages. "Here he is, Finch Mac, he's a singer—"

Beaty said, "Finch Mac, the rock star, *Finch Mac?*"

Lady Mairead said, "Aye, ye hae heard of him?"

Hayley said, "He's crazy famous, you're kidding right? Mags! You're related to Finch Mac!"

I said, "Last I heard I was a king in two centuries, but I am supposed tae be impressed that he sings some songs? Maybe he ought tae be impressed tae be related tae a king."

I asked Lady Mairead, "And speaking of relations, how many are on yer list of sons and cousins, as of now?"

She said, "There are a great many. Ye daena need tae worry on them much. Only the ones who want tae challenge ye are necessary. Fraoch dinna want tae challenge ye, so we dinna need tae worry about him, he is inconsequential."

I glanced at Fraoch, he looked bemused. Hayley looked furious.

Lady Mairead continued, "Donnan never even *met* with Fraoch when he was of age, did he?"

Fraoch shook his head. "I consider m'self lucky."

She said, "Well, he dinna intend for ye tae hae the throne, so aye, ye were lucky that ye dinna hae tae fight Magnus." She looked down at the pages of her book. "I have a notation beside each name, marking who I believe are the more consequential sons. Finch Mac's mother was visited by Donnan more than once. Promises were made tae her. Donnan met him on more than one occasion when he was verra young. Donnan dinna ask for him tae train with a sword though, but he might hae given him gifts or asked him tae hold things for him in safekeeping."

Hayley said, "It's worth a shot. Emma and I will research Finch Mac and try to make contact."

Emma sat on the floor and opened her laptop on the coffee table. "Finch Mac will be hard to get in touch with, but…" She went quiet, while her fingers worked on the keyboard. "He's recently married into a local family…"

Lady Mairead said, "Aye, Finch Mac is listed in m'book as living in Maine."

Emma did some searching and then said tae Hayley, "Look up his tour, he's on tour, while I look up this family — his in-laws."

Hayley and Emma were quiet while they investigated.

I said, "Chef Zach, dost ye hae anything more tae eat? I am famished."

He jumped up for some more food.

Emma said, "He's on a big tour, we might be able to get in touch with his manager." Then she said, "Wait! Check this out, his father-in-law wrote a book about the Earl of Breadalbane!"

Lady Mairead said, "About m'brother? Who on *earth* would want tae ken about m'brother? He is naething but a sniveling fool." She took a deep breath. "Dost ye hear it Magnus? Someone thought tae write a book about yer uncle."

"I canna believe it, he never did anything that was worth tellin' the story."

Lady Mairead said, "If *anything* he was a hindrance tae a good story. Nae nae, it is ridiculous, ye must hae read it wrong, Madame Emma, ye canna believe everything written down on the internet."

Emma said solemnly, "I completely agree. They should tell your story, Lady Mairead— Picasso, that guy in London..."

I saw Hammond fluster.

Lady Mairead said, "Aye, tae tell my story would be verra interesting, but who would read a story of the sister of an earl, the mother of a king? Though I do think, at a small press, it might have a few readers. Thank ye, Madame Emma, for the suggestion."

Emma said, "Whoa, look at this, this is Finch Mac's father-in-law." She turned the laptop tae show us a photo of the historian, holdin' a broadsword, beside a desk. We all peered at the photo.

I said, "Ye ken, it looks as if there is a crest there on the sword, do ye see?"

Lady Mairead said, "It is difficult tae decipher, but it does look a bit like Donnan's." Then she excitedly tapped the screen, "There! Behind him! See it? That's the chest! The Bridge is right there."

I scrutinized the photo. "It does look much like the one we had at the cave in Kilchurn."

"It is it, I ken it, we hae tae go retrieve it from him."

Emma grinned. "Okay, I'm going to call this guy, try to set up an appointment, who wants to go?"

Hayley said, "Fraoch and I will go."

Lady Mairead said, "I will go with them... I speak tae historians and art collectors all the time."

My eyes went wide. "Are you *sure* you want to go with us, all of us in the Jeep?"

"Aye, we will go taegether, all of us, in the Jeep. Hammond, what is a Jeep?"

Hammond said, "It is one of those vehicles that ye swore in 1947 ye would never ride in again."

"Och, twas horrid in the backroads of Italy, but in Maine it should be fine. Ye will attend me."

Emma said, "When I call I will tell him I'm the assistant of a descendant of the Earl of Breadalbane and that she wants to speak to him about some of the artifacts he's collected."

Lady Mairead said, "May I see a photo of Finch Mac?"

Emma turned around the laptop showin' a picture of the rock star. "This is from a Vanity Fair photo shoot."

Lady Mairead scrutinized the photo. "This is a brother tae Magnus?"

Emma nodded.

Lady Mairead raised her chin. "He looks weak. He canna fight in an arena. We are reminded why Donnan picked Magnus tae be his heir."

I said, "Ye will go and get the Bridge, we will meet back here in two days and then we will use the Bridge tae fix the timeline. Somehow. In the meantime I want tae go back tae the thirteenth century tae check it again. Perhaps this time the timeline will be straightened and we winna hae a problem."

Zach said, "The old, 'Hope the issue fixes itself'?"

"Aye. Twould be great if it would." I stood. "I need tae say goodbye tae the bairns again, I will make sure they are nae feeding treats tae Mookie for ye, Madame Beaty."

CHAPTER 30 - MAGNUS

I returned to the past. It was very difficult tae leave this time, as Archie begged me nae tae go. He was adamant and that worried me. I was concerned that I might be on a death errand and without their mother I might be leavin' them orphaned. But I was torn. I had tae go, Kaitlyn needed me as well.

I felt as if I was forsakin' her, if I wasna listenin' tae her breathin' in the timeline next tae mine. That I might be desertin' her tae fate. A terrible fate. It haunted me that she was lost in time. More so than when she had jumped tae the past. I had found her in that instance, it had been verra practical and ordinary when I did, she had been captured, I rescued her there.

But now she was in an otherworldly place, a time between times, nae dead nor alive. I couldna accept she was nae within reach. I had tae find the solution.

I ate dinner beside Cailean, and then retired tae my room, I prayed, then sat with my head on the bed and spoke tae Kaitlyn. "We are trying to figure this out, mo reul-iuil. We have some ideas, everyone is working on it.... We are staying in the lake house... I miss ye there, and the kids are... the kids are swimmin' in the lake. Ye would be so happy tae see it. We put the floats upon Isla's arms and she shivers and says, 'Cold! Cold!' but she goes in all the same because Archie and Ben are in the water. They winna do much else but swim." I took a deep breath. "I hope ye will be comin' home soon, I am verra worn out from tryin' tae find ye and livin' here in the thirteenth century. Twas verra many months without the comfort of home, and then I saw ye for a matter of days — how long was it, do ye remember? I thought ye were on the pilgrimage between Scone and Stirling. I thought ye were just behind me, and then I turned around and ye were gone, vanished in air. I was…"

I exhaled. "I was verra alone while I waited for ye tae return and then ye dinna, and now I hae had the chance tae go home twice, and in between I jumped so many times, I hae a sore heart and soul… I hae seen the bairns though, but I am nae able tae enjoy it, tae relax… Zach made me a meal. He made pasta with red sauce, och tis m'favorite. He says tis too simple, that I ought tae hae better taste, but when he makes it so that tis a bit spicy on the tongue? I am growin' hungry again. There is never enough food here… I imagine ye are hungry as well. We are tryin' tae get tae ye. I truly hope time is goin' at the same rate as tis here… Ye hae been captured now for three days — hold on, mo reul-iuil, please hold on."

I grew quiet then, and listened, and felt sure I heard breathing beside my ear, a voice urging — *help*.

CHAPTER 31 - KAITLYN

I hadn't heard from anyone and the outer corridor was eerily quiet, *what the hell was going on?*

I called through the door and then pressed my ear to it: nothing, not a pin drop, a... anything. I went and lay down on the bed. What was happening? I listened to the shrouded breathing near my ear and then swung my feet off the bed to sit and really listen. I tried to hear.

But beyond a sense that there was something, *someone* there, I couldn't hear anything. I did feel calmer though, as if it were going to be okay.

But I was so very thirsty.

I looked around the room, there were tapestries upon the walls. I began peeling them aside and feeling along the walls, for cracks, possible doors, hopeful passageways. The window was too narrow, too high. And it was cold all day. I called out, "Hello! Hello!" On a sidewall I found a stone with a bit of cool air coming around it. I shoved and shoved against it, but it was not budging.

The other bad news was that I was getting thirstier and thirstier by the minute.

CHAPTER 32 - HAYLEY

I was driving to Orono in the old Jeep that Kaitlyn kept in the garage. It was rusty and only started because the caretaker of the lake house was paid to drive it occasionally. Zach had already driven it to the grocery store three times, but this time I was driving it for about an hour. I had Lady Mairead and Hammond in the back seat and she was carrying a bag of what she called priceless artifacts to sweeten the deal.

Fraoch was in the passenger seat, watching the map, and talking back to Siri as she read the directions. "Och, it says we are tae turn ahead, are ye ready?"

I rolled my eyes, "Yes, I'm listening, I know to turn, Siri just said it."

"Ye ought tae note that yer turn is in two stop signs there…"

"I know. Man, you are a backseat driver."

Fraoch looked over his shoulder. "I am nae in the backseat."

"It's just an expression."

"I am just excited, ye daena hae it readin' ye directions usually, how does it ken where ye are goin'?"

"I forgot this would be exciting, we don't need it in Florida, because I know how to get basically everywhere. I think it's satellites up in the sky."

He craned to look up out of the front window. "Dost ye think tis right above us? Is it followin' us?"

I turned at the intersection. "It's not right above us, it's so high that it can see a lot of cars, or something like that. I don't really know."

Lady Mairead said, "Daena be ridiculous, of course the satellites arna followin' us. If ye canna see it, tis nae there."

I pulled up in front of a suburban house with a mailbox out front, solidly middle class. It reminded me of the neighborhood I grew up in before my parents split, before I had to move to an apartment with my mom.

"This is the address I was given."

Lady Mairead looked up at the house. "This is it? The man who told the story of my brother, the Earl of Breadalbane, lives here in this wee house?"

I said, "It's not *that* small."

To Fraoch I said, "You have to pretend like we are normal people from Florida, just doing some historical research about the Earl. Don't mention the family connection, that Finch is your half-brother, that gets weird, we're just with Lady Mairead, the Earl is her ancestor, other than that, he knows nothing about us, right? To reiterate, you can *not* let him know we are time travelers."

"Twill be easy. I haena ever told anyone that I am a time traveler — what do ye think, twill simply come up in conversation?"

"No, but it might."

"Daena worry on it, m'bhean ghlan, I can handle the secret."

Lady Mairead said, "What did ye call her?"

"M'clean wife."

She exhaled. "Well, now, *finally*, I hae heard everything."

We left Hammond in the Jeep, and went up to the front door. I rang the bell.

An older man with bushy gray hair and a thick gray mustache, came to the door. He was wearing Doc Martens, tight jeans, and a summer-weight sweater that had 'The Replacements' embroidered across the front. He said, "Ah, you must be Lady Mairead!"

She raised her chin. "Aye, I am a descendant of the Earl of Breadalbane." She was stiff and didn't introduce us as if we were unimportant.

From behind her, I put forward my hand. "I'm Hayley, this is Fraoch MacLeod."

"Hayley and Fraoch MacLeod... good, good. MacLeod, like Duncan MacLeod, 'There can be only one!' Loved that movie, time traveling, immortal highlanders, just loved it." He added, "MacLeod. I mostly research Campbell history, that's where my interest lies, but I have been know to meet someone with a Scottish surname then spend the next two weeks in a rabbit-hole learning their clan's history."

I said, "Fraoch is a bit of an enigma, he was raised by a step-father as a MacDonald, but his mother was a MacLeod, his real father was a Campbell. I use MacLeod as my married name."

Fraoch said, "I daena care what ye call me as long as someone is calling me, preferably tae supper."

I glanced at Lady Mairead, as she rolled her eyes.

"I'm Joe Munro, interesting that you're a Campbell, are you Lady Mairead's son?"

Lady Mairead said, "Nae, dear God, nae."

Joe said, "Oh, my apologies, but anyway, so glad to have Campbells visiting, my new son-in-law is a Campbell, that was a happy turn of events. I've been researching the clan for years and now my daughter married into the family." He stepped aside, held his dog by its collar, "Down, Howard!" and led us down the hall.

"I'm *thrilled* to have a descendant of the Earl in my house. After all that research I feel like I know him. It's a little like having a celebrity in the house, I'm fan-girling." He called to someone down the hall, "Lydia, we have guests! I'm taking them down to my office."

To us he said, "Follow me," and led us down a carpeted stair and through a big basement, into an office in the back corner. The office had a window on one side that was lawn level, and the yard sloped gently up and away to some woods.

His wife, Lydia, stuck her head through the door. She had spiky black hair, wore lots of earrings, and had dramatic, dark makeup like Joan Jett. "Hey, everyone, want something to drink?"

I asked for a soda for both of us. Lady Mairead, her eyes sweeping the room, said, "I would like tea, a bit of sugar."

Fraoch gazed at a weapon on the wall. "Tis a fine sword."

Joe said, "Yes, my son-in-law left it in my care, he said it once belonged to his father." Joe pulled it off the wall and held it out for Fraoch to appraise. Fraoch held it in two hands, one on the hilt, one under the blade. Joe pointed at an engraving, "I haven't been able to find any record of this crest though—"

Fraoch interrupted, "It's Donnan's crest."

I nudged him, a reminder not to say anything else. "My husband thinks that's a seal for the king of… um, we've been studying a… Donnan and… did I mention we're historians? We don't know where the crest is from, any who… yes, that's a D might be for Donnan."

Joe looked at me, then the sword, completely confused. "You know Donnan? That's his name… but I didn't mention it…"

Lady Mairead said, "This is all very confused, what on earth are ye talking on Madame Hayley?"

I muttered, "I literally have no idea."

Lady Mairead said, "My apologies, Master Munro, we found ourselves overly interested in the crest, perhaps there is nae history of it. Tis likely Donnan had the crest made for himself."

Joe said, "Like a novelty? I never thought about that before. It is a very nice broadsword — wait, do you know Donnan, personally?"

Lady Mairead said, "I hae known him."

Joe said, "This is so interesting, a direct descendant of the Earl of Breadalbane also knows Donnan, Finch's father? It's a small world."

"Scotland is a small country."

"It's part of the UK now and wanting—"

Lady Mairead gave him a withering look.

"Ah yes, my apologies, you're a descendant of the Earl, you're titled, you probably want an independent Scotland, correct?"

"I rarely speak of the politics of the present day." Lady Mairead inspected the sword, I could have sworn she kept the point of the blade pointed at his chest while she did. "Ye are *certain* Donnan gave it directly tae Finch Mac?"

"Oh yes, that's what I was told, he passed it to him when Finch was about eight years old, I think—"

She asked, "Is Finch Mac here?"

He said, "No, he's on tour. I spoke with him last night and told him that you were coming to see the artifacts. He wished he could be here to show you."

I nudged Fraoch to take the sword from Lady Mairead. He eyed it down the blade. "Tis a verra good sword."

Joe said, "You've worked with a sword before?"

"Aye, I've been known tae swing one."

Joe leaned against his desk.

Lady Mairead said, "What other artifacts do ye hae?"

"I have some wonderful letters, one addressed to the Earl of Breadalbane—"

Fraoch said, "I met him once—"

I smacked his arm.

"From the seventeenth century?"

Fraoch winced. "Och, I thought ye meant the most recent one."

He passed the sword to Joe who hung it back on the wall. "So, Lady Mairead, you're obviously named after Lady Mairead from back in the Earl's day. His sister, a bit of a tragedy."

Lady Mairead's eyes widened in horror. "I am named for her. Her life was nae tragic, beyond the trouble her brother caused — where ye see a tragedy, I see the fount of her power."

"You found her to be powerful?"

"If ye dinna learn of her power then ye ought tae do more studying—"

I interrupted, "But then again, you've *already* studied that time period and you weren't actually studying Lady Mairead, you were concentrating on the Earl. I think what Lady Mairead means is she prefers her namesake's story."

Joe said, "I would love to interview you sometime, Lady Mairead, to learn about her. Maybe that could be my next book." Lydia delivered our drinks.

Lady Mairead sipped daintily from her tea, sort of sneered at the taste, and placed the cup down on the edge of the desk.

I asked, "Joe, what are you writing now?"

"I'm working on the history of a little known king of Scotland, Mag Mòr."

Fraoch sprayed soda from his nose on the corner of the desk.

I said, "Oh my god, we're so sorry."

Joe said, "Quite all right." He passed Fraoch a tissue. "I surprised you with that?"

"I've heard of Mag Mòr, I was... aye, surprised."

"You've heard of him? Now that's unexpected, very little is known about him. I've been working on some of the dates leading up to his coronation."

Fraoch narrowed his eyes and nodded.

I could see he wanted to say a lot of things but instead said, "Aye, tis good tae…" and went over to a table to peer down into a display case.

Lady Mairead said, "The reason we asked tae visit is because I am curious about my history and the history of the..." She cleared her throat as if it was painful to say. "The Earl of Breadalbane and the Campbells in Scotland. But I am also a collector and I am very interested in some of these... artifacts passed down from Donnan, they would fit in my collection." Her eyes settled on the chest that we had come for. "I am especially interested in... something that might be a... box, about this big, similar tae that one, there, something that might not have a reason or a purpose or..."

"I do have that one, yes." He pulled it from under a stack of books. He brought the metal chest closer. "Finch gave me this as well. It has the Campbell crest upon it, I can't open it though, it's locked tight."

Fraoch took it and turned it, looking it over from all directions.

Joe said, "He asked me to keep it until he had a safe place for it." Then he added, "I also have this." He opened a display case with a small key and pulled out a velvet bag, opened the drawstring top, and rolled a vessel out onto his palm.

I said, "Oh," and tried to be cool. "Did Finch give you that too?"

"No, I got this from an estate sale, one of the math professors passed away and I bought it. The velvet bag has a Campbell crest, and it's old, very old, but this odd thing was inside and..." He shrugged. "I just kept it together."

Lady Mairead sitting on a chair beside the desk was attempting to look disinterested. She stared straight ahead, with sideways glances, flitting eyes, I could see in her expression though, her eyes were recording everything in the office.

I wanted to grab the vessel, but I didn't want to freak Joe Munro out. Embroidered above the Campbell crest on the velvet bag was an 'M'. It could've been for Magnus or Mairead — and weren't Kaitlyn's grandparents professors—?

Joe said, "I wondered if the crest might be for a Malcolm Campbell or—"

Lady Mairead sneered and raised her chin. "Nae, this is the crest of Lady Mairead."

"Oh, well how about that? Right under my nose all along."
He asked, "Have you ever seen one of these?" He placed the
vessel on his desk and poked it. "I can not figure out what it—"

The chest sprung open on Fraoch's lap.

I said, "How the hell did that happen?"

"I daena ken."

Joe looked shocked, "I've seen Finch open it before, he said
he was the only person who could. I've never been able to get it
open. How did you do that?"

"I just touched it."

Inside the chest was a... machine or tech or an apparatus, it
was hard to know what to call it, the whole thing actually looked
like it was something... unexplainable. There was a place,
smooth and oval, black obsidian, as if it was a river rock. There
were grooves and markings around it. The markings reminded
me of the markings on the vessel. It was difficult to not see that
the vessel on the desk and the Bridge on Fraoch's lap had the
same origin.

Fraoch put the Bridge down on a table and poked at the
interior.

Joe said, "Do you have any idea what it might be?"

I glanced around at all of our faces, you could see that we
did know what it was, but we all said 'no' anyway.

Joe continued to peer down into the chest, "I suppose this is
not what you're looking for, it's an apparatus of some kind. I
might need to take it down to the school to have it looked—"

Fraoch closed the lid and it audibly locked.

Lady Mairead, keeping her voice steady, said, "I would be
verra interested in studying this chest. I do believe it might have
some interest as a collector, as it came from Donnan's collection
and..."

I said, "Yes, how can we... can we...? How can we talk to
Finch about borrowing it to figure out what it is?"

Joe looked from one of us to the other.

I added, "We just want to look at it, to study it, then we could bring it back, or… we could pay you for it."

He checked his watch. "What about you all wait here, let me call Finch and talk to him about it first."

He stepped from the room.

CHAPTER 33 - HAYLEY

I said, "Oh my god, we found it, we found the Bridge, right?"

Lady Mairead said, "Aye, tis the Bridge."

"I hope it does what we need it to do."

Fraoch stared down on the chest. "I hope we can figure it out, it daena look like it has instructions."

Lady Mairead said, "There is nae way Joe Munro will allow us tae walk away with it."

I said, "Well, that would suck."

"Aye, ye ought tae be memorizing the layout of the room."

I said, "Oh shit, seriously?"

Fraoch said, "I am already on it."

Joe was gone for about fifteen minutes. Then he returned and said, "Finch sends his regards, and his apologies, but thinks you would be better off waiting until he gets back, *then* he could meet you. He's very mistrustful, comes with being famous."

He extracted the chest from Fraoch's hand.

Fraoch ran a hand through his hair. "Ye are writing a story

about Mag Mòr? I hae some missin' details, I could tell ye, I ken a great deal about him..."

"What sources are you using?"

"Primary writing, passed down, directly through the family."

Joe Munro placed the chest beside him on the desk and tapped his fingers on it.

I was trying to think if I could somehow grab it and run.

The dog was sitting beside Fraoch looking up at him adorably, wanting to be petted. "Hae ye heard about the battles he fought? I could fill in the gaps in yer knowledge..."

"Look, how about we set up an appointment? Finch will be back in..." He called from the room. "Lydia!"

She stuck her head in the room.

"When will Finch be back? I forgot to ask."

"He's back in three weeks, officially." She tapped on his calendar where it said, 'Finch and Karrie get back.'

"Good, we won't have to wait long, we'll plan a meeting next month."

Lady Mairead stood. "Of course, you must honor your son-in-law's wishes." She smoothed down her skirt.

"I really appreciate that you understand the situation, it's not mine—"

Fraoch and I stood. Lady Mairead said, "Thank ye for your time."

We left the room, climbed the stairs to the front yard where General Hammond was waiting by the Jeep.

He asked, "Mairead, what did you find out?" as we climbed in.

Lady Mairead said, "He has the Bridge we are looking for, Fraoch is capable of opening it, but Joe Munro, the historian who believes the Earl is a worthy subject, winna give it tae us. Madame Hayley and Master Fraoch will be returning tonight tae abscond with it."

I looked at her in the rearview, my jaw dropped. "You're kidding?"

"Nae, I never kid. Magnus and Kaitlyn's lives depend on the Bridge. Are ye willing tae wait for three weeks for an appointment tae beg for it, or will ye take it? The silly man daena even ken what tis!"

I said, "I guess I'm willing to get the chest."

Lady Mairead said, "Fraoch, ye ken how tae get in?"

"Aye, I will pry the window, twill be easy."

"Good, we are decided."

We began the drive back tae the lake house barely speaking, until Lady Mairead said, "Hammond, we need a peerage title for myself and Magnus, he ought tae be a duke or something. Twill need tae be back-dated, as I assure ye, Joe Munro is researching our lineage."

Hammond replied, "It is already done." He added, "That's a time travel joke."

Lady Mairead said, "Nae one thought twas funny."

Fraoch said, "I thought twas hilarious."

Finally Fraoch asked, "Lady Mairead, why do ye think Donnan dinna pass down anythin' tae me?"

Lady Mairead was quiet for a moment, then she said, "Donnan had an evil nature, Fraoch, he enjoyed pitting one son against another. How he decided who tae support and who tae put down I canna understand. Instead he played games with his son's lives. I believe twas all about power. Why dinna he give all his support tae Magnus and end it there?"

Fraoch nodded. "Aye, tis too bad he dinna see what a braw son he had in Magnus, what a good king he would become. Magnus is lucky he had ye in his corner."

Lady Mairead said, "Thank ye Fraoch, that is verra kind."

CHAPTER 34 - KAITLYN

*T*he room was empty. I needed something to use as a tool and the only thing I had was the Matchbox car. I spent a second prying the plastic undercarriage from the metal casing of the car and ended up with a small scoop.

The door was thick wood, but I was able to jam the nose of the car between the planks. It pried one of the pieces of wood farther away from the other. I had to be careful though — if the toy car broke, it was literally all I had. I got it jammed in the space, and peeled away a splinter, making the gap wider between the planks, and pried again and again, each time pulling off a long thin splinter, making the gap ever wider. In all this time no one came.

Finally, I had a two-inch gap. I peered out trying to see. There was no one in the hallway. *What the fuck was going on?*

I had a blister on one hand, a cut on my other, a scrape on my knuckle. I shoved the car in again and pried. I managed to get a wide strip split away, got my hand around the top and levered it down. The wood cracked at the bottom and now the strip was wide enough to get a big bit of my hand through. I was excited so I took some deep breaths and paced around the room. Then I rushed the door, and chiseled down the middle of a plank with the nose of the car. The fender chipped, but it made it sharper, now it was an even better chisel. At the bottom of the plank I had a wide strip, I pulled and plied, and finally, a third of the plank was gone. My full arm was out. I struggled trying to get the handle and then... It was a simple wooden plank in a groove. I lifted it with a groan, then it dropped away.

I pushed the door open and crept down the hall, my footsteps echoing in the day. Where was everyone?

I was all alone.

I made it down to the courtyard and located the back stairs and went down into the dungeons. I prayed while I felt along the wall in the dark.

It was too quiet for there to be anyone living in there, and god I did not want to find James dead. I checked the first cell. "James?"

"Katie? Oh my god, Katie?"

I rushed to the end of the tunnel and peeked through a crack, seeing James's eye looking back at me. There he was, sitting. "What the fuck, Katie?"

"James! Oh my god, I can't believe..." I pulled the crossbar from its brace and dragged the heavy door while James pushed from his side.

We hugged. He asked, "What are you doing? Where is everyone? Are we escaping?"

"No, not, everyone has just vanished and we are, yeah, we're getting out of here."

"I don't think I've ever been this happy to see you in my life."

I held him at arm's length. "Same to you, buddy, this was really scary when I was alone." I held up my fingers. "Look at this shit, I cut myself all up."

"How?"

"Digging through a door."

He said, "And no one is here?"

"Not a soul, hopefully just in the castle, maybe the village?"

"I was yelling for help, and my voice echoed back at me, it was pretty fucked up."

"Yeah, me too. Follow me. " I led him into the kitchen, finding absolutely nothing, "Should we go up on the walls, or—"

He blew on the dust on the kitchen hearth. "I need water faster than that."

We went outside the castle walls and down the banks to the river's edge and drank, scooping handfuls of water into our mouths. I watched James, drinking and groaning with happiness.

"In all this time I haven't seen a soul besides you." I gulped and gulped.

Then, a man's voice behind us, "Dost ye ken where anyone is?"

CHAPTER 35 - KAITLYN

*J*ames jumped to his feet. I clambered behind him.

There was a man, young and very tall, angry, and armed with a dirk.

James tried to look ready to fight, but he was wearing sweatpants with the 'Relax the Contractor is here' t-shirt. We had no weapon unless a broken Matchbox car counted.

The man looked menacing, but also confused. "I was… I was preparin' tae battle, I was… I had men around me, then I turned tae call back and they were gone. Ye are the first souls I hae seen since it happened." His eyes narrowed angrily.

James planted his stance protectively. "You haven't seen anyone?"

"Nae and I am goin' tae kill ye for it."

I said, "So we're the first people you've seen and you plan to kill us? That seems unhelpful."

James said, "Katie."

"No, seriously, dude," I said, "we didn't make everyone disappear, we're just innocent. No reason to kill us, think this through, maybe we can help each other." I looked around, at a loss for what I could offer.

He said, "Do ye hae any of the firearms?"

James said, "What the... the guns? You know about guns?" Under his breath he said, "Do they have guns this far back?"

"The guards in the castle had guns."

James said, "Oh, right, they did, but out of time, right?"

The guy said, "Aye, I hae seen them, I want a gun."

James said, "I have crates of weapons here somewhere, a *lot* of guns, so many guns. As soon as I find them, I'll give them all to you. Just don't kill us."

I added, "And I am very hungry. Do you have any food, good sir? I've been in the castle, there wasn't any..."

He reached into a leather bag at his waist, pulled out some dried meat, and tossed a piece to James, who broke it in half and passed me a bit.

"Thank you." I shoved it in my mouth and chewed happily. Then, with that solved, I sized him up. *What could I say to explain this?*

I asked, "Are you a time traveler?"

James said, "Shush, Katie, what the hell?"

I shrugged. "As far as I can tell we're in some kind of a time slippage. Homeboy here is with us, ergo: he must be a time traveler."

The man asked, "Och, a time traveler? What dost ye mean?" He kept his dirk dangerously pointed at us.

I narrowed my eyes. "You really don't know?"

James said, "He doesn't really know, look at him."

The man asked, "What did ye mean by time slippin'?" He remained on edge, ready to strike.

"Like, we went to bed in one time, and then when we woke up it was a different time. Have you ever been in a river, when there is an eddy?"

"Aye, the current will pull ye under if ye arna careful."

"*Exactly!* And yes, we all ought to be *very* careful. No one needs to kill *anyone*. What's your name?"

"I am William Wallace."

I said, "Like, *the* William Wallace?"

"Tis what I said."

"Oh, hell, anyway, I'm sure someone is going to fix this, we just need to wait. Do you have more food? James and I don't have any, but we will have so many guns when our shipment is found."

"Aye, I will find somethin' tae eat." We followed him from the riverbank, speaking in facial expressions to each other — *what the hell are we going to do?*

James asked me, under his breath, "Where's a vessel?"

I whispered, "Nearest one is under a tree near Balloch, I think."

"How many days walk?"

"A couple of days at least."

James said, "And honestly, without a gun, I am not going to be able to hunt for us, probably."

"Where's Quentin? Why isn't he here?" I was calculating — without food we would die. I felt sure that Magnus was trying to figure out how to rescue us, but until then I had to stay alive. This dude, could it be *the* William Wallace? Would he be willing to keep us alive? He seemed like a hothead willing to fight anything that moved.

But he was our only choice, and actually, as far as I could tell, he was the only person living within a distance.

He had a horse. He untied it and led us past the clearing — the bare clearing, then farther along in the woods, where there was trampled down grass, footprints, some disarray. There was a recently used fire-pit.

James asked, "Was there a camp here?"

Wallace said, "Aye, now there is nothing." He narrowed his eyes and pointed at me with his dirk blade. "Because she is a witch."

"What would make you think I'm a witch? And no, to be *very* clear, I'm not a witch. But why?"

"Because ye are all that is left and there is a magic afoot."

"You're left too, James is left. It's not just me. Maybe you're the witch."

He scoffed. "I'm no'the witch, daena lie."

"Well, I'm not a witch, either. James and I are stuck here, same as you, not sure what's going on." I appraised the area, noticing a square place of heavy indention in the grass. I pointed it out to James, because it could have been made by one of Quentin's crates. "This looks the size and shape of our boxes."

James nodded. "William Wallace, did you see a black man here? About this tall?" He gestured Quentin's height about the same as his own.

William Wallace looked shocked. "Aye, was he the witch?"

I shook my head. "No, he was a friend."

James said, "He has the crates of weapons I was telling you about, did you happen to see which way he went?"

"Nae, I daena ken. He trained me tae fight. He had a battle plan for takin' the castle, yet when he stormed the castle he passed intae oblivion with everythin' else."

There was a leather sack hanging from a tree branch. He opened it, fished out a hunk of bread, and passed us bits, tearing off some for himself too.

I said, "So Quentin was trying to rescue me and James, right?"

"Aye he trained me tae use his weapons."

"Why did you need weapons, why were you helping him?"

"I was attackin' the castle, because I am goin' tae rid the lands of Alba from the barbaric warring pig-men, Ormr and Domnall."

"Oh." I sat down in the middle of the clearing and chewed the bread.

James asked, "But what about your revenge on England? You have um… a vendetta against the king of England, unless that's later on…"

"I am nae fightin' the English crown, I am fightin' the scab-encrusted, vile bawbags, Ormr and Domnall."

James said, "Uh oh."

I said, "Yep, it's all messed up." Then I asked, "Was there another king, a Mag Mòr?"

"Tis what yer friend asked as well, nae, there inna a Mag Mòr."

I shook my head slowly. "This is very, very confusing. You're really supposed to be fighting the English. I'm sure of it. That's the story I heard."

His brow drew down. "Ye heard tales?"

"Yes, you're a warrior, you fight for Scotland. I suspect someday there will be monuments erected in your honor."

James nudged me, but I didn't care, history was already trashed — buttering up this guy, perhaps the only person around who might be willing to help us, was my only chance.

He chuckled. "I daena think ye ken what ye are talkin' on, I hae won a couple of battles, aye, but King Ormr has evaded the sharp end of m'blade every time."

"Well, once my husband finds me, he's going to kill them. He will help you, I promise you that." I licked crumbs off my fingers.

"What is yer husband's name?"

"That's Magnus, or Mag Mòr, the one I was telling you about."

"Your husband is named Mag Mòr? He is a king? He is the one with the weapons?"

James said, "So many weapons, all for you."

"Then I will hae tae keep ye alive."

"Yes, definitely, I expect him *any* moment."

We all turned to look down the path.

CHAPTER 36 - MAGNUS

I had a meetin' with William Wallace, but I was in sour spirits. I couldna hear the voice, or sense the presence of Kaitlyn since the night I heard her beggin' for help. I was verra concerned that she had died, but I dinna want tae think on it.

I sat in my chair while William Wallace was ushered in. He bowed out his chest, bellowed, "What are ye lookin' at?" and lunged at one of my guards as he passed.

Then he stood in front of me, unbowed, his hand remaining on the hilt of his sword.

I watched that hand.

My guards watched his hand.

I asked, "What ye up tae, Bill?"

He scoffed. "What dost ye mean?"

"Ye walk intae the king's hall, with yer chest bowed out like an insolent child, yer hand on yer hilt, tis an agitatin' state of affairs. Ye hae my guards on alert, they want tae kill ye. Ye are causin' trouble throughout m'kingdom."

"I am fightin' the king of England, I hae too much on my mind tae worry on yer guards."

The guard on my right shifted.

I remained seated, but placed m'hand on my hilt.

I chose an expression tae show him I was amused. I *was* amused. I possessed four weapons that would kill him where he stood. He would not see it coming.

He said, "Ye ought tae be behind me, Mag Mòr, ye are king of Scots, we ought tae raise arms taegether."

I smiled. "Ye ought tae raise arms for *me*, nae taegether — ye forget yerself, ye are m'subject."

He snarled.

I said, "I will back ye though. As long as ye are fightin' my enemy, for *me*. What dost ye need?"

"Guns and men."

I narrowed my eyes. "*Guns*? What dost ye mean, guns?"

He looked confused and shook his head. "Guns? I... meant... I want weapons, that's what I meant."

I watched him for a moment, looking for something behind his confusion, but findin' naething asked, "I will arm ye once Colonel Quentin returns." I watched him as a flash of recognition passed over his face. "Hae ye met Quentin? He is a black-skinned man. I am lookin' for him."

He shook his head but his brow was drawn down.

I added, "When ye are fightin' king Edward, will ye be fightin' him in the borders?"

"Aye, we will call him tae the field near Falkirk."

"And what strategy would ye use? I canna imagine what yer plan would be, ye are but a man with a small army, Edward has a large army—"

"I would use the end-around reverse..." His voice trailed off and he looked confused.

I leaned forward. "Describe it tae me."

"The men charge while a runnin' back man goes around from behind, and—"

"Who taught ye this battle plan?"

"I daena ken, I thought of it on m'own."

"I am awaitin' my wife, Kaitlyn, she is travelin' here, as well as my man, James Cook. Dost ye ken them?"

His brow drew down. His eyes shifted as if he were calculating.

"Does any of what I mentioned seem familiar tae ye, William Wallace?"

"Nae, I daena ken these names."

I calculated.

I felt like he had come in contact with my wife, yet I couldna read his mind. He seemed verra confused and I could only think he was a man with a confused timeline such as mine — such as all of us.

"I will send ye a shipment of weapons verra soon." I sent him from the room.

Tae Cailean, I asked, "What do ye think of him?"

"I think he sounds much like yerself, as if he has come from far away with ideas and words that are different from our own."

"I was thinkin' the same thing. I haena decided if he is a friend and I ought tae arm him, or if he is an enemy and I ought tae kill him."

"He will be more useful alive."

CHAPTER 37 - HAYLEY

"*H*ow the hell did we get talked into doing this?"

Fraoch said, "Quentin ought not tae, as he is a black man, if he gets in trouble he will hae tae go tae jail. Twould be dangerous for him as he has a prior record. Hammond canna, he daena ken his way around this time, and he wasna in the house. Zach is too necessary for all of us, we canna let him get in trouble. Lady Mairead offered but that is unseemly and she had a party in New York anyway, remember, she said she is 'verra busy.' So tis up tae me tae do it, plus m'wife, because she does everythin' with me because she is a verra braw wife."

"Okay, the sweet talk made me feel better. I wonder where James is?"

"I daena ken, he has disappeared, it is worrisome."

We drove in silence down a two lane highway. Then we pulled off on an exit for the small college town of Orono.

I said, "Joe Munro has a dog, what are we going to do about—"

"The dog is a sweetheart, I will tell him tae wheesht. I brought him a treat."

"Okay, but no one dies, right? Especially not me or you or the dog."

"Nae one dies, we will just purloin the chest off his desk. He probably haena even moved it since we were there. Twill be easy."

"Sure, but also, what are we doing?"

"We are parking the Jeep in a hidden spot and then hiking intae their yard, this will be easy as well. Then we will shimmy open the window and crawl through. I will go in and pass the chest out tae ye."

"What happens if we get caught?"

"If I get caught ye run. Ye hide it in the woods. We need it, nae matter what comes."

I parked the Jeep, we pulled on our gloves and hats though it was a little too warm. I strapped a headlamp to my forehead to light our way from the Jeep through the woods. The map on my phone led us right to the back of their property.

There was a wire deer fence. Fraoch clipped the wires, peeled them away, and we climbed through. We watched the house for a moment.

Fraoch said, "The light is still on."

I said, "We have to sit here and wait — whatcha want to talk about?"

He said, "Remember when we went tae find the vessel that was triggering the storms and we had tae sit and wait under the tree?"

"I do, how fun was that? I miss those simple issues, a vessel here and there, missing — the occasional bad guy."

"We hae had tae fight a great many murderous, maniacal evil men, and sometimes we hae had tae do it at great personal risk. What are ye talking on?"

"I don't know, maybe I miss the clothes."

He chuckled. "Ye miss the Frayley adventure."

"Did you just call us Frayley?"

"Aye, Beaty said it the other day, tis tae smash our names taegether."

"Oh my god, you are adorable."

"I am glad ye think so."

I sighed. "What if we can't get the Bridge? What if it's not the right thing? What if none of this helps? What if Katie never comes home? Last time this happened I *saw* her disappear, I was able to go into rescue mode. I took care of the kids, focused on her — but now it's too vague. She isn't gone but just slipped away somewhere. It's terrifying to think of getting lost in time, but maybe worse yet, to slip from time into somewhere else when we can't get to her."

He kissed the top of my head. "We will get tae her. This box with the Bridge inside is the key, I can feel it. Lady Mairead said there was another one of those, she has seen it. She is sure it is capable of doing what we need. Else why did Donnan give it intae safe keeping?"

The main light in the house turned out.

"This is safe keeping?"

"Nae, twas only safe before we kent it was here, now tis verra unsafe, we are about tae steal it."

We waited longer until every last light in the house went out, then we waited longer still.

"Let the Frayley adventure begin!" We crouched as we ran across the back yard headed tae the ground-level basement window. He put his finger to his lips and mouthed, wheesht.

He tried to slide open the window. It was locked, of course. He cut a hole in the screen, peeling it away from the frame. I jammed my knife into the wood between the windowpane frames and jimmied it, sliding the knife back and forth while he pulled on the bottom. Finally I got the latch flipped and he slid open the window.

We stilled and listened with our backs against the house.

Fraoch said, "All right, I am goin' in." He climbed through the window, carefully dropped down to the table, dislodging some things, and perched balancing on the edge, trying to keep stuff from sliding off in every direction. When it was quiet and clear, he dropped from the table to the floor. He took one step, immediately tripped over something, and stumbled against the desk with an "oof."

From somewhere in the house a dog barked.

I couldn't bear to look, muttering, "Please please please…" It was very quiet in the house. A pile of papers slid to the floor. I stuck my head in the window to see in the moonlight, Fraoch up against the desk, totally still, with the dog in front of him, wagging its tail.

When the dog saw me it cocked its head.

Fraoch whispered, "Good boy," fished a treat from his pocket, fed it to the dog, and patted it on the head. Without taking his eyes off the dog, he felt behind him for the chest, pulling it slowly into his arms.

The dog whimpered. Fraoch tossed it another treat.

Sideways walking, he slowly brought the chest over and passed it through the window. He fed another treat to the dog.

He whispered, "Should I take the vessel too?"

A light went on upstairs.

I said, "Shhh."

I dug in the messenger bag for the stack of things Lady Mairead gave us to leave for Joe Munro. I passed it through the window with shaking hands. In it were a small bundle of very old letters, wrapped in an ancient faded-crimson ribbon, an old journal that once belonged to the Earl of Breadalbane, and a newer letter, sealed with Lady Mairead's wax seal. She wouldn't tell me what the bundle of old letters were, just that they were the most important, formerly missing, priceless letters in the history of the world.

I had asked her what her letter said, and she said she had

explained that Finch and Magnus and Fraoch were brothers, because she had been thinkin' on it and there was more tae gain from the connection than tae lose. The rest of it she said was none of my business, except that she said her letter explained everything.

I would have broken the seal and read it on the drive over, but without a way to steam a seal open, or reseal it, there would have been a broken seal. And I was already breaking about ten laws. I felt pretty sure that if tampering with the mail was an offense, breaking a wax seal on Lady Mairead's private correspondence was probably deserving of the death penalty.

Fraoch tiptoed over and placed the pile on the desk.

The light in the outer-room's stairwell went on. A young woman's voice from up the steps called down in a whisper, "Howard! Stop barking!"

Howard whimpered, looking from Fraoch, who was up against the wall just inside the door, and then at the stairs. I hid, praying, peeking, as Fraoch tossed the dog another treat. Then the dog trotted out of the office to go meet the voice.

The light clicked off.

Fraoch waited a minute longer, crept to the window, climbed up on the table, and dislodged a pile of books. They slid across the table and down to the floor.

He jumped-leapt onto the windowsill, so his front-half was in the yard, his back-half, dangling in Joe Munro's office. I grabbed the back of his shirt and pulled, he whispered, "'Tis nae helpin'."

He grasped the side of the window, heaved himself through, sat up, pulled his shirt down, and slid the window closed.

I glanced in and saw that damn dog sitting in the doorway, his head cocked to the side, his tail wagging slowly.

Fraoch leaned the screen up against the window, picked up the chest, whispered, "Go!" and we raced across the lawn to the woods. We barreled through the trees, crashing through the underbrush, until we got to the spot where our Jeep was parked.

I said, as I dropped into the seat, "Och!"

"Och aye, twas a frightenin' thing, but we hae what we went for, except... we dinna get the sword, I had my eye on the sword."

I laughed. "You're jealous that Finch Mac got a sword from Donnan and you didn't?"

"Aye. I am so jealous, so so so verra jealous."

I drove us back to the lake house through the middle of the night and kept checking the rearview mirror.

"Do you think they'll send the police?"

"Why would they? Joe dinna ken what the box was, he winna miss it."

"Not entirely sure that's how laws work. We do not want our Frayley Adventure turned into the Frayley Felony."

He laughed. "If the police come I will explain it tae them, nae worries." He dug through the bag of snacks I brought for the ride.

"Pass me the Pirate Booty."

He chuckled, he always chuckled when he heard the name of it.

I shoved some cheesy corn puffs in my mouth and chewed. "You know if you think about it, we're pirates, we just totally pirated that treasure."

"Och aye, ye canna send the police after pirates, I hae watched all the movies with the bairns, tis nae how it works."

CHAPTER 38 - KAITLYN

*J*ames and I followed Wallace to the closest village and found it, like everywhere else, empty. Wallace said, "I daena understand where the world has gone. I will kill the man who has done this."

James nodded, "I'm pretty pissed at the men who have done this too, I blame Ormr and Domnall."

William Wallace said, "Then ye ought tae help raise arms against them. We must fight them afore they take our lives. Once ye hae given me the guns, we will overthrow the crown."

James nodded. "As soon as I find my friend, Quentin, as soon as I get to the crates of weapons..."

I shaded my eyes and looked around the empty lands, with overgrown unused gardens.

They had stopped speaking so I asked, "Where do you think everyone has gone?"

I sighed and said, "I can't go too far away, definitely not in search of weapons, I um... I need to wait for Magnus. He's going to come for me. I need to be here."

I turned around to speak to them about it, but there was no one there. I spun, a bit of dust coming up from my heels.

Terror filled my heart — *where was I?* In the thirteenth century and literally all alone? I yelled, "James! James!!!"

Someone had just been here, I had been talking to someone, I was sure of it.

I sniffed my fingers, they didn't smell like food, but... I had just been eating, hadn't I? I had been talking to someone, I had been talking to James, right? And someone named William and...

I looked all around at the completely empty world. *What the hell was I going to do?*

Had I lost my mind? Was I all alone?

I slowly turned, taking it all in.

Nothing-no-one-empty-quiet-stillness filled my head.

Frightened, I turned and fast-walked, then, closer to the castle, I ran. It felt like the omnipresence of quiet was behind me, chasing me. I raced to the castle, through the open gate, up the stairs — panting and breathless, I made it to the bedroom where I collapsed on the bed.

And burst into tears.

CHAPTER 39 - HAYLEY

*I*t was the middle of the night at the lake house and we all looked down into the chest.

The interior looked a lot like the vessels, but with divots and grooves and markings and nothing really made sense.

Quentin pointed. "What if we touch that?"

Fraoch said, "Daena do it, I daena trust it."

Zach said, "Me either. We shouldn't touch *anything* until we know, right?"

Quentin said, "Yes, absolutely. The vessels hurt, the Trailblazer wants to kill us. If we activate this horrific piece of machinery it will likely raze the neighborhood. Imagine!"

Fraoch shivered.

"When will Lady Mairead be back with instructions?"

"Tomorrow," said Emma, then she looked at the clock, "I mean today. It's almost morning."

I yawned, "I gotta go to sleep. You coming to bed, honey?"

"Nae, I must do guard duty, ye ken, Og Maggy would want me tae."

Everyone shuffled off to the paneled bedrooms to sleep under the vintage quilts in the wooden beds that had been there since Kaitlyn's grandparents had owned the place. Fraoch and I had the pullout bed in the living room. I made it ready, and collapsed onto it, and was asleep before I could even worry about anything.

CHAPTER 40 - HAYLEY

During breakfast there was another storm. Fraoch tossed down his napkin. "Lady Mairead is right on time, the earlier the better."

But Lady Mairead wasn't in the grass: it was Magnus.

Fraoch and Quentin and I sat around the field waiting for him to wake. I had a bottle of fresh vitamin juice for him, but it took him a long time to rouse. Finally his eyes opened and he looked up at the sky. "Och."

He turned his head to look at us, "I daena ken if Kaitlyn is goin' tae make it if we daena hurry."

Quentin said, "That's the problem, boss, we don't know where we're hurrying to or how."

I said, "But Fraoch and I got the Bridge, it's… hopefully it's the answer to all of this."

"Did Finch Mac's father-in-law give it tae ye?"

Fraoch said, "We stole it."

Magnus sat up, not disturbed at all by our confession. "So we hae tech, do we ken how tae use it?"

Fraoch said, "I was hopin' ye might be able tae figure it out, once ye saw it. Ye ken the most of all of us."

Magnus ran his hand through his hair. "If I ken the most,

Lady Mairead will ken more." He put out a hand and Quentin hefted him up to his feet.

We strolled back to the lake house.

Fraoch said, "On an up-note, we will soon get tae meet our new brother. I figure once he kens we stole from his father-in-law he will be comin' round tae meet us." We all laughed.

Magnus said, "He can come around as long as we can get tickets tae his concert. I hae never seen one, I would love tae someday."

I said, "I'll have Kaitlyn add it to her list."

He exhaled, kicking some gravel from his path. "Did this brother hae a great deal of tech?"

Fraoch said, "I am nae sure, his father-in-law showed us a few things."

"How was Lady Mairead? He has written a history of my uncle, I assume she was infuriated. If I ken her well, she tried tae explain her side of the story?"

Fraoch said, "She had us deliver a stack of letters and a book tae him, a journal, along with a letter that she said explained everythin'. But I think she means tae meet with him again."

"Och aye, she is vyin' tae hae her story told. She is verra predictable. Someday someone *ought* tae tell her story for the whole world tae ken, but daena tell her I said so, it would be one more thing tae go tae her head."

CHAPTER 41 - MAGNUS

*L*ady Mairead came later in the evening, as I was pacin' back and forth in front of the house. Colonel Quentin and Beaty came tae check on me near dinner time. I said, "Another full day wasted, every day becomes more dangerous for Kaitlyn."

Beaty said, "King Magnus, please daena say it, it is giving me the chills tae think it."

I understood. I nodded and stalked up tae pace by the road.

Lady Mairead was alone.

She wore clothes that looked as if she had come from the early twentieth century. She rose soon after jumpin' and when I asked where Hammie was she said, "Ye ken, we daena always hae tae be taegether."

"Where were ye?"

"I was visitin' Pablo. And if ye must ken, Hammond went tae the future tae try tae learn what has happened tae the kingdom."

"He is a good man, he is always concerned about the right things. Ye ought tae take that intae consideration when ye are decidin' who tae spend yer days with, the man-child Picasso inna worth—"

"Magnus, I dinna come here tae listen tae ye carry on about m'lovers. Tis my business who I bed."

"Och aye, leave me out of it. I was simply mentionin' that ye ought tae settle down and think of Hammond as yer—"

She stopped dead in her tracks.

"Ye want me tae settle for Hammond? I will hae ye ken, Magnus, son of mine, Hammond is nae at *all* in m'station. I am one of the most sought after women in the history of the world and I am the mother of a king. Ye want me tae settle for Hammond! Och, he is able tae keep me warm in bed, tis enough. He is lucky tae be invited. Now wheesht and tell me about the Bridge. Did Hayley and Fraoch steal it?"

"Aye, they hae stolen it." I opened the door for her and followed her intae the living room. Fraoch brought the Bridge down from the top shelf of the bookcase where it had been out of the reach of the bairns.

Fraoch placed it in front of me. "Ye should try, Og Maggy."

I put m'hand on the lid. It clicked open.

Quentin said, "All that time trying to figure out how to open it and that's what did it?"

Chef Zach said, "It's Donnan's fucking paternity test."

We all stared down intae it.

It was verra like the vessels, fascinating, but twas impossible tae understand how it was tae be used. Lady Mairead said, "This is exactly what I hae seen before. Donnan was verra protective of it."

Quentin said, "So it's called the Bridge, will it bridge between two times or is it just a bridge like a command central?"

Hayley said, "Whoa, what if it's both?"

Lady Mairead said, "I daena ken about the two times, because never before in the history of time has there been a split. I daena ken what is happening but someone is responsible."

I said, "Aye, we need tae stop whoever is doin' this."

Lady Mairead pulled three small books from her messenger bag, and set them in a stack on the table and flipped through the top one. I glimpsed her familiar handwritin'; twas orderly and small and filled the pages from side tae side, unlike Kaitlyn's which was large and full of flourishes, with a great deal of space around it.

She came tae a page and pulled from it a piece of oft-folded paper that looked verra old. She uncreased it, spreadin' it upon the coffee-table. She said, "I haena seen the Bridge since Donnan was alive, and I was only able tae see it over his shoulder when he needed tae set a vessel remotely tae turn it on, so he could find it."

While she talked, my eyes were drawn tae the bottom book of her stack. "This is the book from Johnne Cambell that Kaitlyn gave ye…?"

She pulled the book away from me. "Aye, as she ought, twas nae her's tae keep."

She turned it tae a page with diagrams and lay it beside the other and opened the third book and laid it flat as well. One page had her notes, one had very ancient diagrams, one had writin' and diagrams.

She read over all of them and then looked inside the chest, as if she were comparin' the instructions tae the machine.

We all looked from her face down at the Bridge, tryin' tae see what she was figurin' out.

She pointed at the top left area. "This is where he would trigger the return of a vessel. See this spot here? Ye can set it in motion, with a finger-press."

I leaned in. "Och, I hae always wondered how Donnan accomplished it. Can ye turn it on?"

She said, "We can experiment, what vessel do ye want tae return?"

Colonel Quentin said, "Wait, don't do anything, we'll use my vessel." He held one up. "Let me get it out of the house."

He rushed away, a few moments later he called Zach on his phone.

Chef Zach signaled tae Lady Mairead. I watched her carefully as she pushed and revolved parts, checked a page in her book, then twisted somethin' more. Then she said, "It ought tae begin. Tell him nae tae grab it, I am nae sure where it would go. I am new tae the process."

Chef Zach explained it tae Colonel Quentin over the phone, and then we waited and waited. He asked, "Anything?" And then, "What about now?"

He shook his head.

Lady Mairead read down a page of her notes, and looked inside the chest, pushed somethin' and asked, "What about now?"

He shook his head again.

She said, "Well, I daena ken—"

A clap of thunder sounded outside the house. A deluge of rain poured down.

The dripping wet kids and the pig came squealing from the bunkhouse.

Chef Zach said, "Yep, that worked, whatever you just did."

"I did nothing new, ye just needed more patience. Tis nae baking biscuits, tis turnin' the time of the world on end."

Zach said, "Yes ma'am." And added, "Anyone need a beer while we think?" He went tae the kitchen and returned with drinks for everyone.

With an opener he popped tops off beer and soda bottles and passed them around. For Lady Mairead he poured the beer intae a chilled mug.

I acted incredulous. "What of my frosty mug, Chef Zach?"

"I only had one, Mags, please forgive."

I sighed. "Tis fine, I hae only been livin' with the privations of the thirteenth century while m'mum was in Paris, partyin' with artists, daena worry, I hae grown used tae it by now."

Zach groaned and joked, "Och, the boss and his mother will be the death of me."

Lady Mairead joked, "Stop yer bellyaching, Chef Zach, ye might think tae hae two beer mugs next time. Or a frosted mug for my son, the king, and chocolates for me, tis the way tae my heart."

He said, again, "Yes ma'am."

She said, "Explain tae Colonel Quentin that I hae turned it off, tae give it a moment, then it should be fine tae retrieve and return it."

She wrote notes in her book.

I asked, "And what are ye writing?"

"*Exactly* how tae accomplish it. I winna always have young men around tae help me experiment. I must note it down so I can use it again."

I said, "Ye are remindin' me that ye are ever growin' wiser in yer dealings. This tech might be too powerful for yer inclinations."

She jokingly smacked m'shoulder. "Wheesht Magnus, there is nae such thing as too powerful."

She wrote some more, and I noted that she turned a wee bit, tae keep me from seein' the page.

Colonel Quentin entered through the backdoor, dripping wet from the rain. "That was not fun. "

Isla said, "Uncle Quentin, you're wet!"

He shook, sprayin' the bairns with water then came intae the living room, dryin' his hair with a towel. "We're pretty sure we know how that part works now."

Lady Mairead said, "Aye, thank ye, I do. This is verra good." She wrote more, and looked verra secretive about it.

Zach passed Quentin a soda.

Quentin asked, "Do I get a frosty mug?"

Zach groaned.

Lady Mairead closed the book and clutched it tae her lap.

I asked, "Tell me what ye hae written."

She said, "Nothing."

"Will this Bridge solve our timeline unraveling?"

"I daena ken — twill take time."

"Take time? We daena hae time! Ye ken ye hae the instructions there in yer book. Let me see it."

She raised her chin and moved the book away. "Nae, I will take the Bridge and—"

"Nae, ye winna, ye canna hae it."

She closed the other books, stacked them and, and placed the stack in her messenger bag. She pulled it tae the side away from me. I said, "Madame Beaty, would ye please take the bairns tae the bunkhouse?"

"Aye, King Magnus."

CHAPTER 42 - MAGNUS

I watched them depart and then said, "Lady Mairead, if ye think ye are leavin' here with yer instructions and this chest, ye are sadly mistaken. We daena hae time. I want tae ken how tae use the Bridge."

"These are my books, I hae taken a great deal of care and I winna share them. We hae plenty of time, we are *rich* with time.
"

"Lady Mairead, I am askin' ye, as yer son, tae share yer knowledge with me, so that I can—"

"Nae, they are mine and I will use the Bridge and—"

"Ye canna open it! Ye need a son of Donnan tae open it!"

"There are other sons, Magnus, I hae a list."

I stood, strode across the room, grabbed m'sword from the corner, spun around, and pointed it at her heart. "I will repeat m'self, but twill be the last time I ask—"

"Ye are going tae use brute force against me?"

"Ye are hiding notations and diagrams, keepin' books in secrecy, and planning tae conspire with m'enemies. Ye tell me, as yer king, or aye, I will take the books from ye by force."

"Ye wouldna dare!"

"Try me. Ye arna takin' the Bridge anywhere. Tis mine."

Colonel Quentin stood by the door. Fraoch had risen tae his feet.

I said, "The Bridge opens tae my hand and tae Fraoch's. Fraoch do ye give Lady Mairead permission tae take the Bridge?"

"Nae. She canna take it." He leaned forward and closed the lid, the lock clicked intae place.

I asked, "Fraoch, do ye demand, as I do, that Lady Mairead reveals tae us what she kens about the Bridge?"

Lady Mairead narrowed her eyes, looking unafraid. "Ye wouldna dare. I ken *everything*. What ye ken, is one page. The book is mine, but even if ye steal it, ye will never know all I understand."

I said, keepin' the sword point still and true. "I hae been losin' my grip on reality for a long time. There are memories comin' that arna real. There is a history that I daena remember, and though we hae tried, we are unraveling our pasts. There are madmen loose in time and ye are primly sittin' in our safe house as if ye daena hae a care in the world. Ye hae come from a party in Paris. Ye are in possession of instructions that ye are keepin' from me and — ye are so sure of yerself. I am pushed tae the edge, I am pushed past m'edge. Kaitlyn is stuck in a long ago century. What are ye going tae do, test me? Ye are going tae see if I would prefer tae trust ye or live my life free of ye?"

She said, "This is all verra unnecessary, Magnus, ye daena need tae hold me at knife point."

"I am nae holding ye at knifepoint, I am frozen in the verra second afore I run ye through with a sword. One moment. In that moment of action, will ye decide tae be helpful? Tae save yerself?"

My sword was still, unwavering. I was intense. I said, "I am keepin' the Bridge, ye must instruct us tae use it tae rescue Kaitlyn."

"Twould be much easier if I just did it m'self."

"I am not going tae let ye take this machine away. Either ye tell us what it does, or ye will hae tae move aside, easiest for me will be for ye tae help us. I tell ye, I am in nae mood. Ye took the last frosty mug, I would hate for our descendants tae believe ye died for such a ridiculous reason."

"Wouldna our descendants find fault with ye for killing yer own mother over a frosted mug? I daena think yer reputation would come out verra well from matricide."

"I would be alive tae tell the story. How dost ye want it tae go?"

She raised her chin and looked down her nose. "I would prefer a story in which ye told all that yer mother was helpful tae ye in yer hold on power."

"Exactly. My hold on power requires that I bring the timeline back in order. Right now. I canna take one more moment of uncertainty and Kaitlyn will nae survive much longer. She is m'focus right now. Ye are either a help tae me or ye are dead."

"I daena see ye demanding all the other people in the room tae help or die."

"I daena need tae threaten them tae be helpful. Ye are the only one who has proven that ye will only cooperate under threat of death. Ye want the machine so badly that ye are willin' tae lie and cheat tae gain it. This is somethin' ye might want tae work on with a... Madame Emma, what is the word?"

Emma had her eyes covered, she pulled them away from her face tae say, "A therapist?"

"Och aye, a therapist."

Lady Mairead scoffed. "I daena need a therapist, I need a son who for *once* would stand down his brute force and show his mother some respect."

With m'arm absolutely still I slowly shook m'head.

Lady Mairead huffed. "Fine, I will tell you all I know."

I said, "Good, this is how twill go, I will lower m'weapon. In return ye will tell me all ye ken, and ye will conspire with us tae rescue Kaitlyn and fix this timeline. After, I will allow ye tae return tae yer parties and we winna speak of this again. Twill be nothing we remember. And when ye die a decrepit auld woman with a long line of descendants, I will tell them that ye were a wonderful mother and always a help tae her son and daughter-in-law."

"I accept, though I find it verra rich that ye believe I will die first, ye canna truly believe it!"

I shrugged. "I am the one with m'blade pointed at yer chest, at this moment I think tis likely."

She said, "Put it down, I agree tae the terms, I will share what I ken and ye will be less of an uncivilized brute who is driven tae threatening me over a frosted mug."

I lowered m'sword. "Twas a verra braw looking mug."

Chef Zach groaned. "I will fix this, more mugs are going into the freezer right now." He strode intae the kitchen and we soon heard the sound of glassware, and the door to the freezer opening.

CHAPTER 43 - MAGNUS

I sat down on the couch and slid the sword under it, within reach. Then I put my hand on the lid so that it clicked open again.

Lady Mairead exhaled, then leaned forward. I watched her carefully as she investigated the interior of the chest.

She pulled her books from her bag and opened the auld book that originally belonged tae Johnne Cambell. "Do ye see, this smooth black piece in the center? It looks like an obsidian river rock, embedded in the metal. It is labeled in this book: the drochaid—"

Quentin said, "What does that mean?"

I said, "It means a bridge. This is where the chest gets its name."

She tentatively touched it and everyone said, "No!"

"Why?"

Chef Zach said, "Lady Mairead, respectfully, you can't just touch it in the middle of the living room in the middle of the lake house in the middle of Maine. Think about the damage the Trailblazer does, there are kids here!"

She huffed. "Fine, if ye are feeling fearful I winna touch it. Besides, it says here in this book that 'in ùine air fhuasgladh.'"

Hayley whispered tae Fraoch, "What does that mean?"

"Time and unraveled."

"Oh."

Lady Mairead continued, turning the page to the next and pointing, "Ye hae tae activate the bridge at the 'steach far a bheil bruachan na h-aibhne air leth.'" She looked triumphant.

Quentin asked, "Boss, a translation, please."

I said, "Och, right, m'apologies, Master Quentin. The words mean, 'the place where the banks of the river are discrete,' m'guess is it means as opposed tae where the banks of the river are connected, ye ken? I suspect we are supposed tae use this at the place where the timelines become unraveled."

Lady Mairead said, "Aye, see here, this word?"

I read aloud, "Fhuasgladh."

Fraoch explained tae Hayley, "Unraveled, like when ye are weavin'."

I pulled the book around and read, "'An abhainn dhubh,' the words are out of order and misspelled, but it means the black river."

Hayley asked, "So we need to stand on the bank of the black river?"

Quentin pointed at the chest, "No, I think it means this, the stone here, that's like a black river stone."

"Could be. If this is the bridge and the stone is the black river, where are the banks? And where are the banks 'discrete' and where are they separate?"

We all shook our heads.

Zach said, "Fuckin-A, this is confusing."

He sipped from his beer. "The thing about this situation is it all fucking started with Sophie, she was the beginning of all the messy timeline stuff."

We all turned tae him.

He said, "Am I right? I mean, she was out of time, right? Then she was grabbed by Ormr, married off to Domnall, was pregnant, died, long before she was born, married to a friend of her great-grandpa. She was basically a big gigantic time loop."

Lady Mairead said, "Nae, she was nae a time loop. I am out of time, Magnus is out of time. It daena change the timeline of the world. Tis nae a *person* who is a loop."

He shrugged. "Sure, fine, she wasn't the loop, but we do have timelines unraveling all over the place, people stuck in time, kings rewriting history, a loop of everything and everybody... Is it because James tried to rescue her by looping? I mean... he was looping and looping and looping did he set this nightmare in—"

Lady Mairead narrowed her eyes. "Where *is* James Cook?"

We all looked at each other.

Quentin said, "Last I saw of him he was being dragged into the castle by Domnall."

She said, "Magnus, when ye sensed Kaitlyn was near ye at Stirling, did ye sense James Cook?"

"Nae, but I dinna go tae the dungeons."

Zach said, "Quentin, what was it James chiseled into the rock of his cell?"

Quentin said, "His initials and the year 1589."

Lady Mairead said, "And that was the year James Cook traveled tae try and rescue Sophie. He is looping. Who would like tae attend me tae go keep James Cook from his madness?"

Hayley said, "What do you mean? He's not there, he's been in the thirteenth century, he's somewhere else—"

"Nae, he is stuck, looping in the year 1589. This is what he is trying tae say."

Fraoch said, " I daena ken if I am followin' this exactly. We ken we hae a bridge, we need tae use it at the banks where the time unraveled? We ought tae go tae the year 1589 and use it then?"

We nodded.

He said, "I see two issues. One, we daena ken what happens when we 'use' it, and is it painful?"

Quentin groaned. "The vessels are awful. The Trailblazer

takes us to the brink of death. I figure using the Bridge to knit time must be really really excruciating."

I nodded. "We daena ken what happens after we 'use' it. How does it bridge time? Does one time override the other? Or does it stitch taegether? I am a king in the year 1290, Kaitlyn is in Stirling Castle in the year 1290, held captive by Ormr and Domnall, yet we are not in the same time."

Lady Mairead said, "I went tae the year 1290 and ye were nae king, twas a man named John Balliol."

Quentin said, "And Ormr and Domnall are like fucking whack-a-moles, they keep disappearing and coming back in different places."

"I daena ken what a whack-a-mole is but I agree with the sentiment."

Zach said, "We totally need to take Boss to a fair. Put that on a list."

Hayley said, "Katie is the one to keep the lists."

Emma typed on the laptop. "I'm listing it for her."

I nodded. "So if we bridge time, who is the king? Where does Kaitlyn turn up? Does she turn up? This might be the last time we..."

Colonel Quentin put his hand on m'shoulder. "Sorry boss, we have to hope that's not the outcome."

Chef Zach said, "We don't know which timeline will be superior, which will overwrite the others— will people from one timeline be able to cross to the other? It's like a conch shell of time, we could be all spiraling around, who's on the spiral, who isn't?"

Quentin said, "And also, I hate to say... maybe once the Bridge sets the timeline straight, the people who are out of time are... um, no longer with us... so it won't, um... you know... matter."

I said, "Before we use the Bridge we ought tae say goodbye tae those we love."

Quentin let out a long breath. "Yeah, Boss, I agree."

I stood and pulled m'sword from under the couch.

Lady Mairead said, "Not *this* again."

"Nae, 'not this again.'" I said, "We believe loopin' caused the timeline tae unravel. We hae tae stop the looping afore we can use the Bridge, or else the timeline might unravel again. We are going tae the year 1589. Colonel Quentin we need guns, many guns and swords. Ye hae been there, what was the weather?"

Quentin said, "Coats. But…"

I said, "We need coats, guns, a great deal of food."

"How long will we be there for?"

"Nae, I am just hungry. And ye canna go, Colonel Quentin, ye and Fraoch and Madame Hayley hae been there before."

Chef Zach said, "So you think James is still…?"

Quentin passed me a holster from our locked cabinet

"Aye, he is looping. We must stop him afore we can solve anything else. Only Lady Mairead and I can go, the rest of ye ought tae stay here and do yer best tae say goodbye."

I exhaled. "Everyone ought tae consider carefully what they will do from now on. We need a vessel for each person, in case we are separated. We are goin' tae go tae the year 1589 where we will try tae stop James from looping, but we may verra well meet up with Ormr and Domnall and they may be verra fresh and ready tae battle. They might hae a full army."

I buckled the holster and adjusted it tae m'shoulder. "Also, ye ought tae say goodbye tae yer family. If ye are married tae one of us who are out of time, there is a chance they winna be able tae bridge across once the time is affected."

Lady Mairead said, "I daena ken if it is as dire as all that."

"Are ye sure that we are supposed tae be in this time?"

"Nae."

"From that first moment when I put my foot on the shore of Amelia Island I hae known I was out of time. Tis a folly tae imagine that time exists for all else in the world but us, what makes us so special?"

Lady Mairead said, "Maybe we ought nae do it if it is so dire?"

"Kaitlyn is in the past."

Lady Mairead nodded.

I said, "Chef Zach and Madame Emma, I am leavin' ye in charge of the bairns, as their guardians, please…" I was nae sure how tae continue.

Quentin said, "I'll arm you up."

I said, "I need guns for James as well."

Then I asked Lady Mairead, "Do ye need tae say goodbye tae Hammie afore we do this?"

"Nae, whenever I leave him we say goodbye. He kens that when I time travel away it means I will likely never return, he is relieved when I do."

We packed tae go to the past once more.

CHAPTER 44 - MAGNUS

I went tae the bunkhouse and asked Archie and Isla tae come with me tae the end of the dock.

They were quiet as they walked alongside me and then we sat down and both tucked under my arms and I held them while we looked out on the water. I said, "I am goin' tae do something difficult, m'bairns, it will be—"

Archie interrupted tae ask, "Where is Mom?"

Isla watched my face, intently. I would not lie tae them, they would see it.

"She is in the year 1290. I hae been there also and somehow we canna find each other. I am verra sorry tae tell ye that I haena been able tae find her for a time now. I dinna want tae frighten ye, but ye must ken. Now, yer aunts and uncles and yer grandmother and I hae a plan. We hope it will succeed."

Archie said, "There is a chance it won't?"

"In life there are a great many risks, in time travel there are even more. There is a great deal of reward, but many risks. This might be the riskiest thing I hae ever had tae do."

Archie tucked his head back to my side.

Isla asked, "What's risk?"

I opened and closed my mouth a couple of times. "Tis verra hard tae explain."

Archie said, "Isla, it's like this, if you want a cookie and you want to go get it, maybe Uncle Zach will be mad if he catches you up on the ladder."

She said, "Like yesterday."

He said, "Aye. So when you climb up on the ladder you have a reward that is a cookie. You have a risk that Uncle Zach will catch you."

I said, "That is a verra good explanation, Archie, thank ye," to Isla I said, "Ye hae been stealing cookies?"

She hooked a pudgy hand under her arm, and humphed lookin' verra much like her mother. Then she sounded like me by sayin', "I was hungwy."

I said, "I have risked a lot in my days because I was hungry, I understand. Just ask first, Chef Zach will probably give ye a cookie if ye ask."

We sat quietly for a moment and then I said, "So that is what I mean, I am takin' a risk, I am going tae go find yer mom."

Archie asked, "Do I want to know what the risk is?"

"Nae, it would be better if we just hugged and if ye would listen when I tell ye that I love ye. I am verra proud of ye, and that ye will hold my words inside ye."

He threw his arms around my neck. "I love you, too."

We hugged verra tightly and then I put out an arm for Isla and she hugged us, too. Then she said, "I love you too, Dada."

Archie let go so I could center the hug around Isla. I said, "I ken ye do, bairn." I took her face in my hands. "Did ye ken that I was the first person on earth tae hold ye? I was. We hae a special bond ye and I. Tis how ye ken what I am thinking."

She nodded. "Now you are thinking you will miss me when you are away."

"Ye always ken my mind." She hugged me again. I stood and then we walked up the dock tae the shore.

She pointed down in the muck of the shoreline. "Do ye see the wee fishes, Da?"

I crouched down tae look. She said, "They don't know they are wee fish in a lake, they think they are in the whole world. If I splash a rock into the water they will swim away and their life goes on. They come right back and they don't remember what happened. They have tiny brains."

We laughed. Though my laughter covered a heavy heart. I knew I was about to dislodge our world with a rock thrown right into the middle and prayed that somehow I would find a way tae come back.

CHAPTER 45 - MAGNUS

*L*ady Mairead and I jumped tae the year 1589. We made sure tae land well away from Dunscaith castle, but also away from the village, and then we walked along a path with a view of the coast. Colonel Quentin had mapped our route and warned us about the frigid weather. It was a verra cold day, a high contrast tae the warmth of the summer day when we had left Maine.

The sky was gray and dreary, the wind brutally cold. As we climbed the hill we were cautious, Quentin having warned us that the men from the castle might come tae fight us if James was here causin' trouble.

Lady Mairead said, "Ye hae yer rifle? We need tae be able tae take men out afore they get tae the crest of the hill."

"I hae what I need."

"Good."

Lady Mairead kept her head down, walking alongside me. She wore a gun, but she wouldna draw it, tellin' me it wasna her style.

We were coming tae the crest and found in the distance, against a gloomy sky, under a hilltop tree, a lone person.

It was James Cook staring out over the landscape, Dunscaith castle beyond, dark and foreboding.

Lady Mairead and I strode up. "What ye doin', Master Cook?"

He startled as if he dinna ken we were approachin'. "Oh, what are you doing here?" He looked around. "Where's Quentin?"

I sat down beside him. Lady Mairead stood a few feet away.

"Colonel Quentin has gone home, Master Cook, he couldna watch ye do this anymore."

"Do what?"

Lady Mairead said, "Master Cook, ye are looping."

He looked at her as if he had just noticed she was here. Then went back to staring at the castle. His eyes were vague, almost unfocused.

I asked, "Ye hungry?"

"Nah, just got here, ate before I left."

I opened my pack and brought out a sub sandwich and held it toward him. He grabbed it and ate ravenously. I placed a Hydro Flask of vitamin juice between us and after he had eaten the sandwich he chugged from the flask. I said, "Ye are hungry because ye hae been gone longer than ye think."

His brow drew down. "That doesn't make sense." He shook his head. "Doesn't make sense at all, what makes sense is that as soon as the telescope goes up I'm going to get her. You here to help?"

I said, "Aye, I'm here to help. Tis time for ye tae come home, this inna working."

"What do you mean? What's not working?"

"Ye are trying tae get tae Sophie afore she dies but she's—"

Lady Mairead interrupted. "Ye are using yer weapons instead of yer brain, what hae ye tried?"

He shook his head, vaguely. "I don't know... I'm just... I need to be here when she gets to the castle, so I can..."

I said, "Ye hae tried over and over, Quentin told me. Ye hae tried everythin', it inna—"

Lady Mairead asked, "Hae ye tried speaking tae my contact, Auld Arthuretta in the kitchen?"

I groaned. "Lady Mairead, that is nae why we are here, we are here tae stop him from loop—"

She waved her arms around. "Look at it, look at the landscape, the dire circumstances, look at his demeanor. Dear God, he has lost his mind at this. Hae ye ever seen such a thing—?"

Master Cook screwed up his face up. "I haven't lost my mind, these assholes are going to pay for—"

I said, "Ye are both wrong. Master Cook has nae lost his mind, he is just spiraling in grief. He needs help, and Master Cook, this is nae acceptable. Ye hae been looping for so long that ye are breaking the timeline. Ye hae ruined a great deal of history, we are losin' track, Kaitlyn is stuck in the past, ye need tae stand down."

"Katie?"

"Aye."

Lady Mairead got out her weapon. "But that is nae what we need tae do. Look at him, he canna stand down. Are we going tae allow Ormr and Domnall tae do this tae Master Cook? This is nae acceptable!" She looked at the castle. "Is Sophie there?"

Master Cook said, "I think so, but I... There was a huge storm yesterday, then I watched a column of men dragging their goods and horses into the castle through the gates. I didn't see Sophie, but it was raining at the time, visibility sucked."

I said, "Lady Mairead daena fill his head with dangerous ideas."

"Ye be quiet Magnus, ye ken if ye were in this position ye wouldna stop, ye ken it. Besides tis nae a dangerous idea if it works." She added, "I ken we canna save the life of someone who has gone, that it is a terrible precedent tae believe ourselves God-like, but as I look upon the castle, I am thinking we could save m'great-granddaughter and that would be an important—"

"Sophie is your — wait, what?"

This James Cook remembered nothin' of the past months. I said, "Aye, Master Cook, she is Mairead's descendant and ye hae already been told this in a loop."

"How did I take it?"

"Ye took it much better than we expected."

Master Cook asked, "Lady Mairead, do you see a solution?"

"Aye, I will go tae the castle, where I will speak with Auld Arthuretta in the kitchen. I will demand Sophie. You will wait here on the hill with this gun." She passed him a sniper rifle. "Dost ye think ye can shoot it?"

"Hell yeah."

I asked, "How do ye ken this will work?"

"Because, as I told ye, the woman in the kitchen works for me, she has the most power in the castle and I am going tae demand she help us. What ye men ought tae hae done months ago, but ye are too busy wavin' yer weapons around tae be reasonable."

"'Tis a fair insult. What are we goin' tae do while ye handle it?"

"Ye will wait here on the hill, aimin' yer cocked guns at the walls, until I return."

She began down the hill.

I called, "What are ye plannin' tae do?"

"I am planning tae get Sophie, I hae had enough of this." She pulled her cloak down, covering her face as she went.

We watched her stalk across the grounds, approach the bridge, and cross intae the castle. She remained unhindered. A man accompanied her inside. I watched through binoculars. "She has entered."

Master Cook said, "I don't see how she survives."

"She keeps survivin' somehow."

CHAPTER 46 - LADY MAIREAD

*A*s the guard accompanied me across the courtyard, I could see the men, just returned from battle, lookin' verra weary. I nodded as I passed a man who looked gravely injured.

I asked the guard. "Has Laird Ormr returned from the battle yet?"

He said, "He got in a few hours ago."

I said, "I could see that ye hae traveled verra far. I am sure it is good tae be returned tae the castle."

He gestured toward the door of the kitchen.

I entered and met my acquaintance. "Auld Arthuretta! Tis wonderful tae see ye!"

She started when she saw me, her whiskers waving in the flurry of her excitement. "What! Mairead! What ye doin' here? Ye shocked me!"

There were a dozen people at work on the meal, and my co-conspirator was in the middle running everything. I lowered my voice, "I told ye once that I would need yer help, tis today."

She looked around, tae make sure we were nae overheard. "The laird has just returned, the men are hungry, I daena ken. I am nae sure I can—"

"What would ye want me tae do for ye in return?"

Auld Arthuretta put her hands on her wide hips. "Ye could do what I asked years ago, tae take the orphan intae yer care."

"Och nae, I daena hae time tae deal with the orphaned bairn."

"He has been kept here for long years and ye ken where he is from. Tis verra dangerous for him here. Ye ought tae take him and give him a castle and some land, make a proper laird of him."

"Och, ye are driving a tough negotiation..." I shook my head. "I think he will cause a great deal of trouble, can I do anything else for ye, dear Auld Arthuretta?"

"Nae, this is all I want, for ye tae take the—"

"Fine, I will take the orphaned bastard bairn intae my care."

"Will ye promise he will hae land and a title?"

A woman rushed by with a pot of porridge causing me tae step from the path.

I resumed, "He will hae land and a title, *fine*, he can come with me, in trade — is there a young woman traveling with the laird? She is named Sophie, I believe she is here."

"I daena ken, I heard tell of someone... I will find out her name."

She rushed away.

While she investigated, I took stock of the kitchen. There were bread loaves baking, a deep brown color, a thick stew bubbling on the hearth.

I opened my messenger bag and took out a large vial of powder that I carried with me, just in case. It had been invented in Riaghalbane, and was enough for an army because of that time in Boston when I swore I would never be without a proper sleep potion again. I strolled across the room, hiding it in the folds of my skirt, tae the cauldron. I wafted in the scent and spoke tae the woman stirring it. "Is this the stew for the laird of the castle?"

She nodded.

I smelled again. I said, "It needs salt. Do ye hae some salt?'"

She went for salt while I popped the cork from my vial and dumped the entire contents in, and as she returned I grasped the spoon and stirred the pile of white powder down intae the stew before she could see. "I found the salt already."

She left me tae the stirring.

Auld Arthuretta returned. "A young woman accompanied the men from the battle, she has been placed in the dungeons."

"Och nae, I will not leave until she is returned tae me."

Her eyes wide, "How will... how do we...?"

"Daena worry on it, after ye feed Ormr and Domnall and the guard, weariness will overtake them, once they are asleep, I will free Sophie and I winna bother ye again."

"And ye'll take Lochinvar with ye—?"

"Who is Lochinvar — the bairn?"

"Aye, daena forget, he has lived here since he was wee, and he will die at Ormr's hands."

I said, "How auld is he? I thought he was still a wee bairn!"

"Nae, he is a fine lad, he works hard and has a strong sword arm."

"Och, he sounds even more trouble. But aye, I will be a woman of m'word. Just feed the stew tae the laird and his guard and I will take Lochinvar and Sophie verra far from here."

Her eyes glanced nervously at the soup.

"Should I eat the soup?"

"Nae, stick tae bread today."

She nodded, turned, and began directing everyone that it was time tae serve the meal.

CHAPTER 47 - MAGNUS

*M*aster Cook and I sat on the hill overlooking the castle, our guns beside us, binoculars up tae our eyes. He said, "This is taking a long time, how long are we supposed to wait?"

"I daena ken." I swept the binoculars back and forth. "I suspect it will take her a moment tae subdue a castle and rescue a maiden, alone."

"This is nuts."

"Aye."

We sat and watched. He asked, "Have I really been looping? I mean, I haven't, I know I have not. I remember leaving Florida just yesterday and I didn't do anything else. I know I haven't looped, logically, but… when you said it I felt like… like there's something going on and I feel kind of dazed. Like I wasn't fully aware of… I feel kinda out of my mind."

"I hae looped before, I remember the feeling."

"I wonder why you remember looping, but I don't?"

"Perhaps because I pulled m'self out — we are interruptin' ye mid-loop. Ye are startled that we came upon ye. I daena ken if it is fair tae stop ye in mid loop, I think ye are nae going tae under-stand where ye are and in what time. Ye will hae missed a lot —

we are in hidin' at the lake house in Maine, and I truly am sorry that ye might hae tae grieve for Sophie all over again, but I hae tae interrupt ye. Ye are ruining the whole wide history of the world."

"I am? How?" He shook his head. "We are in hiding, why?"

"Ormr and Domnall, the two arseholes in that castle, are after us."

"How much time has passed?"

"Months, centuries, time travel, ye ken? Enough time for me tae become a king."

"I'm confused, weren't you already a king?"

I tapped the side of my head, "Aye, but now I am a king in the thirteenth century as well."

"No shit, how'd you get back there? Did someone have to drive the Trailblazer? Who was it?"

"The bairns: Archie, Ben, and Isla — all grown up."

"Shit, that is so cool. The kids still like each other?"

"Aye, they do, they were careful tae only speak on themselves, we dinna glean any information about other bairns, about other relationships, I would hae liked tae ken how it all works out."

"The kids were probably keeping it from you. No one really likes a spoiler."

I chuckled. "I suppose that is true."

We sat for a very long time.

We both stood and stretched and we talked a bit here and there about how tired we were of waiting, and then finally, tugging a stalk of grass and tearin' it tae pieces, he said, "So shit, my ex's husband is a king twice-over?"

"Aye."

"And I'm freaking ruining everything by looping?" He grimaced. "And my ex is missing?"

"She is on a different timeline. Tis verra frightening, I can feel her in the room, but I canna speak tae her."

"And, this is all my doing?"

"Aye, the looping is causin' it, but we daena blame ye. Ye dinna ken, none of us did. I hae looped afore, there is a grave power in these vessels, tae control time, tae want tae hae power over life and death. I daena think there is a man alive who wouldna want tae try it."

He picked up the binocular strap and looped it around and around his fingers. "I'm sorry for causing it, I just..."

"I ken, ye daena need tae apologize, ye daena need tae apologize at all. We ken ye are in grief — I want ye tae ken, that what Lady Mairead is doin' right now... tis unlikely tae work, she is—"

CHAPTER 48 - LADY MAIREAD

*A*s the workers finished the meal, rushing around, following orders, I stood near the cauldron, nae allowin' anyone tae taste from it. The line formed and the men went by and the stew was ladled onto their hunks of bread. I whispered tae Auld Arthuretta, "Hae the boy meet me by the gate," then I busied myself in a back storeroom, and tried tae blend intae the stonework of the castle. Twas easy tae do, I had a great deal of practice with it.

I witnessed when a large pot of stew meant for the laird was carried tae the Great Hall. I was watchful in every direction. I needed the laird tae eat from his stew afore any of the other men fell unconscious. I couldna allow a… through the door I saw a man slump tae the ground in the courtyard. My scheme had begun.

I rushed from the kitchens tae the doors of the Great Hall. Clinging tae the shadows I watched Ormr and Domnall at the front table shoveling food intae their mouths, one, two, three spoonfuls, then Ormr glanced up and his eyes met mine. I ducked away tae hide behind a group of men, but heard a commotion at the front of the room.

I skirted through the shadows tae the door, escaping the

Great Hall tae the closest stair as men began tae follow. I raced down the steps intae a storeroom and ducked behind a large cask and waited, but nae men came looking. The commotion remained on the grounds above. Men's voices yelling, but then slowly, a silence spread across the castle.

I crept through the storerooms, until I came upon the weapons room. I crept along until I found a dungeon with a wooden bar bolted across its heavy door. I whispered, "Sophie Campbell, Sophie Cook?"

She said, her voice a whimper, "Aye, who is there?"

"Tis me, yer great-grandmother, Lady Mairead, ye must be ready tae run as soon as I hae the door open." I dislodged the bar tae the side. Then I pulled the heavy door scraping along the floor until it was ajar, turned, and rushed up the stairs with Sophie just behind, clutching my skirts. We emerged in the courtyard where most everyone had fallen tae the ground or was too dazed tae stop us as we fled.

I glanced over my shoulder. She was wide-eyed at the horror of it all. "Did ye…?"

I dinna answer, keeping a straight path tae the front gate, the guards there, leaned sleeping against the wall, their half-eaten meals dumped tae the ground. At the gates ahead of me stood a young man, tall and strong, waiting with a sword slung on his hip. "M'Lady Mairead, Auld Arthuretta sent me tae—"

I said, "We hae nae time for this, ye are the boy? Ye are much too big for a boy!"

"I am Lochinvar."

"Och, ye look a great deal of trouble, but if your sword inna decorative ye ought tae draw it tae protect me as we escape." He faltered. "Draw yer sword!"

"Och aye, Lady Mairead." He drew his sword.

"Follow, if ye are coming!"

I led Lochinvar and Sophie through the castle gates, where we left the path tae race up the hill.

·　·　·

Magnus and Master Cook rushed down, Master Cook yelling, "Sophie!" They fell intae each other's arms.

I said, "We daena hae time for your affections, ye must run!"

Magnus called, "Lady Mairead, who is this man?"

I called over m'shoulder, "He is part of the deal tae get Sophie."

Master Cook and Sophie fell in behind me, Lochinvar behind us, with Magnus at the rear, though twas unnecessary. There was nae following army, only a silent castle, everyone asleep.

We made it tae the woods and fled along the river's edge.

CHAPTER 49 - MAGNUS

*F*inally, we came tae a place where I felt we could rest. Lady Mairead leaned against a tree, breathin' heavy. James and Sophie embraced.

I said tae the young man, "Ye are verra ginger, what is yer name?"

"Lochinvar the… um… Fearsome."

I narrowed my eyes. "As pink as ye are, that is what they call ye?"

"Aye, um…" He scowled. "Nae… but they ought tae."

"And who are ye, why are ye in m'presence?"

He said, "Auld Arthuretta bargained for m'safe passage from Dunscaith."

Lady Mairead, still breathless, said, "Och, he is nae in your presence, he is in *my* care. Tis a long story." She tugged at her bodice. "Auld Arthuretta asked me tae look after him, in return she allowed me tae poison the castle with sleeping potion."

"Poison or putting them tae sleep?"

"Could be both, I daena ken." She dabbed at her face with a cloth. "I *meant* tae put them tae sleep, but if there was too much, then it is likely a poison. Tis nae easy tae get the proper dosage, but I canna be blamed if it goes wrong, my intentions were for them tae sleep and awake later."

"I daena think that is how a crime is looked upon, yer intentions are nae matter."

"*You* would think that! Ye daena understand the subtleties of poison, ye are a brute."

Lochinvar looked between our faces as we bickered.

I looked back in the direction of the castle. "So ye might hae poisoned a whole castle worth of people?"

She waved her hands, "A whole castle full of *evil* people. Ye canna expect me tae consider their lives worth anything."

Lochinvar said, "They were vile, except for Auld Arthuretta, the rest can ride deamhain straight tae hell."

I asked, "Auld Arthuretta was yer mother, who was yer father?"

Lochinvar scowled. "Nae, Auld Arthuretta only cared for me when I was a bairn. I daena ken who m'father is, I was born a bastard, and then I was kidnapped. I hae lived at Dunscaith since."

"Who kidnapped ye?"

"Domnall."

Lady Mairead exhaled. "Ye are speaking, Magnus, tae one of yer brothers. He is yet another unclaimed son, I hae had my eye on him for years tae make sure he dinna cause us trouble."

I groaned. "Och nae, ye are *another* son of Donnan? The man was an unbridled libertine. So what are we goin' tae do with ye?"

Lochinvar said, "I was promised land and a title."

Lady Mairead said, "We hae some difficult work tae do first, but aye, at some point in the future, I will make sure ye hae land. If there is any land left once we destroy all the timelines in the world."

I looked over at James and Sophie, in an embrace and whisperin' tae each other. "Speakin' of, James inna time-looping anymore, tis time tae use the Bridge tae fix the timeline."

James, his arms around Sophie, asked, "Wait… what… destroy all the timelines? What exactly are we doing?"

I said, "We are goin' tae use an apparatus called the Bridge tae do something unknown and unprecedented — tae fix what has been broken."

"And that is…?"

"Everythin'." I pulled the chest from my bag.

Lochinvar took a step back. "Are ye talkin' about witchcraft?"

Lady Mairead said, "Nae, daena be ludicrous, everything ye see that is new is nae witchcraft, and ye will need tae be quiet and let us speak, Lochinvar, we are saving the world."

I said, "Savin' the world? I daena ken if that is necessarily true, but we are saving our small part in it."

"Says a king in two different times." She added, "But what you said is true enough, we might break everything. Lochinvar ought tae be quiet and let us set about our work."

James said, "So we are… what exactly are we doing?"

I said, "Saying goodbye tae the people we love." I strapped on a holster and checked m'gun was loaded. "I am going tae the thirteenth century, I will be in the room near Kaitlyn—"

James said, "We really don't know what's going to happen?"

Sophie clung tae him.

"Nae, but we think twill be verra painful. There is a chance we winna see each other again. This could be the end."

"Sounds fucking terrible." He said, "Lady Mairead, do you want to leave? I will stay and push the button…"

Lady Mairead said, "Nae, because then ye would be able tae take all the credit. Magnus will go tae the thirteenth century tae be near Kaitlyn, ye will take Sophie tae Maine, and twill be down tae me and Lochinvar, a man I just met, tae push this world-altering button." She held out the chest tae Lochinvar. "Place yer hand on there."

He placed his hand on the chest and the top clicked open.

"Just as I suspected." She added, "Once ye all jump away, I will give ye an hour, then I will operate the Bridge."

I passed James a vessel.

Sophie said, "The bairns will be there?"

"Aye, Madame Sophie, and I am verra pleased that ye are with us once more, the bairns will rejoice tae see ye."

James said, "We'll make sure someone is holding their hands while this shit is going down."

"I would appreciate that."

Sophie said, "Do ye have a message for them?"

I looked off intae the horizon. The sun was goin' down, the world was cycling through. The river rushed by, making the comforting sound that meant there was fresh water and good fishing, life would go on. It seemed a terrible thing for life tae carry on without us, but it was the truest part of a life. It would always come tae an end.

"Nae, I already spoke with them on it. They ken." I added, "Kaitlyn dinna get tae tell them how much she loves them, make sure they understand, she never did anything without considerin' them."

James said, "Sounds good. I will make sure they know." He glanced over at the new guy who was tapping his fingers on his arm, waiting. "And we shouldn't take this dude with us?"

Lady Mairead said, "Nae, he's my responsibility. Also, he's verra braw and if I am tae be without a hero at the end of the world, I suspect he will raise his sword for me if I request it." Her eyes glinted merrily.

I said, "Och nae, is this a double entendre? What of Hammie?"

She said, "Hammond understands that when one needs a strong swordsman sometimes a young man is a better use."

I said, "Dear God, mother, ye are disgraceful."

The side of her mouth turned up in a smile. "Lochinvar, are ye good with a sword? I might need yer handiwork."

Lochinvar smiled broadly. "I am verra braw with m'sword,

the best in the castle, and tis verra large, I must use two hands tae raise it."

I groaned. "Just what we need, a braggart and a rogue, he will be lookin' for fights and bringin' danger tae us all."

Lochinvar said, "I am nae a braggart, tis all true, I am a good swordsman. All the lasses sought me out for it." He giggled.

I said, "What was that noise? Och, ye laugh like a bairn."

Lochinvar clamped his mouth shut.

Lady Mairead said, "This is all in good fun, Magnus, I am nae looking for a swordsman, nae at the end of time."

"Is this the end of time?"

"Tis likely."

James said, "On that note..." He hugged me, clapping me on the back, then said, "Hey, you're so thin!"

"I hae been living in the thirteenth century, I am wastin' away. But ye are thin as well, Master Cook."

He looked down at himself. "Aw man, I've been doing this for a long time, haven't I? How long did you have to live in the thirteenth century?"

"Too long, but tis all fair in time travel. I and m'mother started it, after all. My life has been enriched by time travel: my marriage, my family, my bairns. If I am called upon tae fight, twill be my fight. If I am called upon tae live in some long ago land, I will go there. I will do it."

Lochinvar listened with his brow drawn.

Tae cut the gloom I smiled. "I winna be happy about it, but I will do it."

Lady Mairead joked, "Ye will complain and complain but ye will do the right thing, tis how I raised ye."

James said, "On the bright side, we got Sophie back."

I said, "Aye, we got Sophie back, tis a verra good thing."

Lady Mairead said tae Sophie, "I am verra glad ye are with us once more, Sophie, ye must, when ye see yer mother, tell her what we hae done in case we arna seen again."

"Aye, Lady Mairead."

Sophie and James walked a ways away and set their vessel intae motion. I said, "We must go fast, the castle might awaken, they might see the storm."

Storm clouds build overhead. I asked, "What are our odds that we will live past the usin' of the Bridge?"

She looked down upon it. "There are three scenarios I hae thought of… one, we will be stranded wherever we are, tae live as we must, never tae be heard from again. We might even lose our memories, twould be blessing though if ye think on it."

"Twould be a blessing if we were forgotten, but if this is the way it goes I wish I had brought more food."

She said, "Two, we will die. Never tae be seen again."

"Och nae, and what is the third?"

"A fiery pit of hell with unimaginable pain, perhaps unending."

"There is a fourth? I think we might need a fourth."

"Nae, I canna imagine a fourth. I canna imagine there is a chance for us tae come away from this pleasantly. We ken the vessels are painful. We ken the Trailblazer is torturous. Tae stitch time taegether, must be horrible." She pulled a gold watch from her pocket. "Use this." She pointed at the face. "See the time? In an hour I will use the Bridge. Where will the sun be here?"

I looked up at the sky. "Ye can see it is here? Twill move tae there." I pointed. "When it is time tae use the Bridge, twill look as if it is nestled in that branch of the tree."

She and I looked at each other long.

She said, "Ye hae always been a good man, I ken I haena said it tae ye, but I am proud ye are m'son. I love ye. I am glad ye are the kind of man who will go tae wait upon his wife in a moment of uncertainty. This is a good trait in ye."

"I love ye as well. Thank ye, Lady Mairead."

"Ye're welcome, now go, get ye tae the past. I will stay here with…" She and I looked over at the fellow, standing, staring up at the branch that we had looked at a moment earlier.

She sighed. "I will stay here and be comforted and protected by Lochinvar."

I said, "Aye."

I walked a few feet away and turned and said, "Twas a good life, Lady Mairead, I daena regret it."

"I daena regret it either."

I left her on the shore of the river.

CHAPTER 50 - HAYLEY

*T*here was a storm, and then Quentin called, telling me there was a surprise and then, "Sophie!" I was so excited I was screaming her name before she even got through the door. She was timid, hiding her face, and very frightened. "Sophie! You're alive, oh my god!"

The kids ran in, looked as if they had seen a ghost, and ran out again.

Emma said, "Sophie, I'm so glad to see you, so so glad, but let me go explain this all to the kids."

She hugged Sophie and rushed out after the kids to explain that Sophie had been rescued.

Everyone hugged Sophie and made a huge loud fuss.

I said, "Sophie, what do you remember?"

We all sat down on the back porch, around the table, with a view of the lake.

"We were at Kilchurn, there was a battle, terrible machines from the sky — a war on the walls, and then I was taken, a terrible pain, much like this, and..." Zach slid a pair of sunglasses across the table toward her.

She fumbled with them and then with James's help got them on over her eyes. "'Tis a relief."

Emma entered the screened porch with the four kids in tow. Archie and Ben sat beside Sophie, Isla climbed up in her lap, and Zoe tugged on her skirts.

Sophie said, "Zoe! Ye are so big! How did this…? Och ye are…" She kissed and hugged them all. "Ye all look so forlorn, yet I was only gone for a verra short time."

I said, "Finish your story."

She said, "I was dragged tae a dungeon and was there for a few hours when Lady Mairead appeared and…"

Fraoch said, "Lady Mairead…? She was the one?"

James said, "She poisoned the whole damn castle, nabbed Sophie, and picked up a boy-toy in the process."

Zach said, "What the fuck? Where was Magnus through all of this?"

"He was waiting with me. Lady Mairead is a force of destruction. Thank *God* she's on our side." He put his arm around Sophie and kissed her on the temple.

Emma sighed. "I suppose since you're back… they're going to do it, right? How long do we have? When are they going to use the Bridge?"

"Magnus went to the thirteenth century, to be near Kaitlyn, while it happens, in case. And… I left. She was going to activate the Bridge soon after."

Emma frowned.

Zach said, "Hey kids, who wants a treat?"

Fraoch and the kids yelled, "Me!"

Zach disappeared into the kitchen and returned a moment later with ten bags and four bowls. He began pouring: pretzels, Chex mix, nuts, and M&Ms into the bowls. Then he added sour gummy worms, some Oreos. He poured Doritos on top. "Isn't anyone going to stop me?"

Emma laughed, "It seemed like you had a plan."

He used a big spoon to stir the bowls and placed them around the table. He carried the empty bags back to the kitchen and returned with a box of sodas. Everyone popped a soda can. He sat back down.

Emma patted her lap for Zoe to climb up and she wrapped her hand around Zach's. She said, "Ben, will you come sit in your dad's lap?"

"Why?"

"Just for a moment, just… please."

Ben sat in Zach's lap. Isla climbed up in Beaty's lap. Archie moved to a seat beside Fraoch and Fraoch and I held hands while he put an arm around Archie. Quentin had an arm around Beaty and James and Sophie were embracing. And we sat like this for a long time. Quietly eating, drinking, and holding onto each other. A tear streamed down from Emma's eyes.

Isla asked, "Why you crying, Aunt Emma?"

"I just love you all so much and this is one of those moments where I want it to be known, I love you all, and if I had my way we would be together forever, and we would have everyone with us."

We all raised our cans. "Here here." I tucked my head to Fraoch's shoulder and he kissed my hair. And then we were quiet, except for the tick tick tock of the clock on the wall.

CHAPTER 51 - KAITLYN

I sat on the straw mattress of the hard bed, really truly freaking out. I was completely alone, but also, the room was cold, the comforting presence absent. What if slowly over the next few days the whole world was slowly chipped away? Bit by bit — how long would I be here doing nothing while it happened? And what else could I do?

I couldn't leave the castle for Balloch, I would get lost in medieval Scotland — I mean, I was already lost, but that would make me doubly lost, unable to ever be found again.

This harkened back to the lesson I learned a million years ago, or a thousand years in the future: *who was lost?*

It had to be me.

I was lost in the thirteenth century and slowly, Quentin, James, that Braveheart dude, and everyone else in the world, had all disappeared. Now I was oh so hungry, so very hungry, and cold and I goddamned had nothing to build a fire.

I dug through my pockets. Nothing but a broken Matchbox car. I really needed to make sure I had a fanny pack on, with survival supplies like fire-starter and a multitool with me, whenever I jumped.

As if I ever had a plan when I jumped, *that* was wishful bull-shit thinking.

And if I ever had a chance to jump again.

Was I just supposed to wait like a damsel in distress in a castle tower?

As I ran over and over every idea, there was no solution. I had no string for fishing. I didn't have enough knowledge of the flora and fauna of the area. I had not studied enough to survive. Instead we had been packing and carrying matches and fishing poles with us. Coolers of food and coffee. I knew this was a mistake, but I also knew I would not survive without coffee in the morning. At the very least I wouldn't have been happy without coffee.

So I had brought coffee to the past instead of learning to forage and hunt for food.

Mistakes were made.

It was so cold. It would take some time to build a fire, it would take effort, and I was really too hungry to expend the effort and that made me sure that this was the end.

I lay down on my side, pulling the scratchy wool blanket over me. My hands lay in the empty space beside me on the small short bed.

I thought about how I should be a better rescuer of myself than this. But also, that the world was supposed to be not quite so dire, so freaking perilous.

CHAPTER 52 - MAGNUS

I strode up tae the castle gate and waved up at m'guard. A few of m'men came tae follow me, but I told them tae go on tae the Great Hall. "Find Cailean, send him tae see me."

I looked hard at the castle walls, I had lived here a long time, but it dinna feel like m'home. Twas cavernous and lonely and full of strangers, though... I surveyed in every direction. There were nae enough men on the walls, the courtyard was empty, a verra rare occurrence—

William Wallace strode through from the Great Hall, he was also lookin' in all directions for anyone.

I called out, "What say ye?"

"Och, I was here tae see ye, Yer Highness." He bowed low.

I said, "Ye may rise."

"I wanted tae tell ye that I remember, I was — I saw yer wife. She was at the riverbank this morn, hae ye found her?"

I said, "Nae, I haena, was she returnin' tae the castle?"

"She was with a man by the name of James, he seemed a scoundrel, ye haena seen them?" His brow drew down, he seemed verra confused.

"I haena, but I am sure they will appear soon enough. Was that all ye needed?"

He lowered his voice. "I hae had something I needed tae—

Cailean rushed toward me across the courtyard, almost breathless from his pace. "Mag Mòr! My apologies, I was goin' tae warn ye that Wallace was demandin' a…" He looked around at the empty courtyard. "This is odd, where is yer guard…?" His brow drew down, but he continued, "I hoped tae announce Wallace afore he found ye. I told him ye were nae in the castle, and I ordered him tae nae accost ye once ye returned."

I clapped m'hand on his shoulder overwhelmed by a need tae say some kind of farewell. "Tis all right, Cailean, ye hae been a good friend and a wise advisor, I appreciate all ye did as I rose tae power. It has been an honor tae hae ye by m'side, though we hae had some difficult times."

"Aye, the loss of m'dear wife."

"Twas a desperate loss."

"It has been an honor tae be at yer side as well, Mag Mòr."

"Would ye see tae a cup of ale, Cailean? I will speak with Wallace for a moment."

I fished the watch from my bag, I dinna hae much time left.

I said tae Wallace, "I hae a few moments. It must be brief."

William Wallace said, "I was trained by a man, he went by the name Quentin. He was black-skinned, as ye mentioned. I daena ken why I dinna remember it afore. It came tae me a few hours ago, as ye asked, ye said, perhaps I had been trained by a black man, and I *had*. This is why I hae come, tae get some of the weapons from ye."

I eyed him while he spoke, his cloak opened so he was showing his sword, his hand rested on the hilt, his fingers poised tae draw it.

I shook my head. "Nae, I winna give ye any weapons. Was this what ye needed tae speak tae me on?" I made tae walk away, but noted that he stepped in front of m'path.

I noted his stance — he was always on edge, lookin' for a fight, but today he seemed unusually edgy.

"Where are yer men?"

I smiled. "They are just behind ye, in the Great Hall, ye shouldna start trouble."

He sneered, "I demand the weapons, liege." He spit in the dirt.

"Ye are goin' tae demand them of me? As if I am nae yer king?" I pulled my cloak closer around me tae hide m'holstered gun from his view.

He drew his sword. "Give me the weapons, or I will kill ye and take them for m'self."

I drew my own sword. "Ye daena want tae fight yer king, this winna end well for ye."

"I daena think ye are a king, I think ye are a usurper. That ye hae taken the throne."

"Tis treason that ye are speakin'." I prowled around him.

"Ye're no' my king."

"Ye are rash, William Wallace, just a young man, beggin' tae fight. Ye are going tae need tae be wiser than this if ye are tae wage war against the English king."

He stepped back and looked at the walls. "Says the man who daena hae a guard. Yer men are nae here tae fight alongside ye." His voice echoed against the stone: *ye daena hae a guard, where is yer guard...*

I glanced at the walls. Twas true, all m'men were gone. There was a breeze blowing through, sending a bit of dust spiraling intae the sky. The space seemed ominously empty — William Wallace lunged, slicing my left shoulder, a deep cut that brought with it intense, knee-buckling pain.

Blood soaked through the arm of my tunic.

I swum up through the pain tae focus — *focus!* I roared, swung my sword, hard, down, furiously knocking his blade away, and charged him, slamming against him, wrestling him tae the ground. Holding my sword aimed down upon him, I growled, "Ye are weak, ye are lost, ye are too stupid tae ken ye arna ready tae aim yer sword at a king."

He said, "Yer blood is pouring from ye."

"Aye, tis, but I will survive it. Will ye survive my blade aimed at yer skull...?"

"Nae."

"What say ye — if I allow ye tae walk from this courtyard, will ye go?"

He nodded.

I stepped off him.

He slowly stood, then lunged again. But I caught him with a step and stabbed him clear through, shoved him tae the ground and yanked my sword from his stomach. He groaned desperately as he died.

I swept my eyes around the courtyard, the wind picked up, a howl through an empty courtyard. Blood dripped down my fingertips.

I strode tae the Great Hall, tae ask Cailean for help with m'wound, but he wasna there. There was nae cask of ale, nae ash in the fireplace. The benches were grey and splintered. All signs of life were gone.

I felt like I could hear Haggis nearby. I yelled, "Haggis! Haggis!" My voice rasping. "Haggis!"

I felt for sure twas a sign of what was tae come. I was tae end here, dissipating intae dust within this timeline, inside this desolate world — without Kaitlyn.

I peeled m'shirt aside tae see the wound. It was deep, pouring blood. I dropped m'cloak tae the ground, pulled my shirt off, and pressed it tae the wound. I felt woozy from the loss of blood and — I looked back at the courtyard. William Wallace's body was nae there. Twas as if all I knew was bein' taken from me. Twas maddening tae lose the world, one person by one person, each piece one at a time. I picked up the cloak, draped it over my arm, and dragged the sword while holdin' the shirt against my wound.

I couldna carry it all. I dropped the sword and dragged m'self up the stairs, resting against the wall, and crawlin' the last few steps. Once I gained the floor, I clamored tae my feet, and lumbered down the hall tae m'room. It was bare and cold and dusty.

I fell intae the bed, pressin' the cloth tae m'shoulder. "Och, Kaitlyn, I am injured, how can it be? Tae hae drawn the sword so many times, and then tae hae a lad, barely trained—"

I peeled the cloth up tae look, blood poured from the wound. "I need tae…I daena ken if we make it from this…"

Yet warmth filled me.

I sensed her nearby. It was good because it had been a long time without her. I turned my head tae look at the space beside me. "I pray ye are well, mo reul-iuil. This is… this is naething, I am going tae be fine. We are going…"

I dug through my bag for the watch. It took a moment tae focus, I was disoriented and weak, but twas five minutes until…

I whispered tae the empty space, "We are usin' the Bridge, we are tryin' tae fix the timeline. I want ye tae hold ontae me, stay here, we are… it may be awful, I imagine twill be very painful, but… "

"Magnus? Magnus?"

M'eyes opened and there was Kaitlyn's face just within a few inches of mine.

CHAPTER 53 - HAYLEY

*A*fter about twenty minutes of sitting like that we kinda grew bored.

Zach said, "Well, hmmmm… what does this mean?"

Quentin said, "It must not have worked."

Beaty said, "Unless it worked so well that we daena ken how much it worked."

Fraoch nodded. "Aye, this is exactly how it might be."

James shook his head. "Nah, something didn't… that was supposed to be a huge thing, this was nothing, this wasn't an option. That was our one big shot. Damnit." He kissed Sophie on the head. "Well, we got you back, that was important. We'll figure the rest out."

I asked, "How do we *know* it didn't work?"

James said, "Because Katie isn't here."

We all looked at the tracker hanging on the wall. He said, "Just us, that means we didn't do shit."

Emma said, "It's too early to know, I mean, what if they're traveling right now? We don't honestly know how long it might—"

Fraoch said, "We know it doesn't take long, time wise, it just takes a hunk of life from your flesh."

I asked, "But how would we know if it worked? We're waiting for Katie and Mags to get back, right? And they're in… where exactly?"

Everyone looked blank.

James said, "Shit, that sucks."

Emma said, "We could look things up on…"

She jumped from her chair, ran for her laptop, returned, and plugged it in. Then with her hands poised over the keyboard she asked, "What would we look up though…?"

We all remained quiet.

I said, finally, "We don't know what to look up, there's nothing, no way to prove if it worked or not."

Zach scratched his head. "How long have we been sitting here? Do you know?" He tipped one of the bowls to look inside, they were all empty except for some crumbs.

He narrowed his eyes. "I'm hungry though, are you?"

We kind of vaguely nodded.

Sophie said, "I am famished, I haena eaten since lunch at Kilchurn, right afore the battle."

"Whoa, Sophie, that was months ago, time-travel speaking. Let me organize dinner. That there's an emergency." Zach left the porch for the kitchen.

Emma typed some things into the keyboard and read. "Nothing. No mention of Magnus, that's what it was, right, we were looking for Magnus?"

We all nodded and finally she closed the laptop. "Why are we in Maine?"

Quentin said, "I feel like we're missing part of the story here, and that worries me." He stood. "I'm going to arm up, and take a guard shift."

James said, "You've got a gun in a shoulder holster."

Quentin looked down. "Oh right, good."

James said, "What are we worried about?"

"I have no idea. But I better be ready."

CHAPTER 54 - KAITLYN

*M*agnus's eyes fluttered open.

"Magnus, oh my god, is that really you?"

I touched his face. "You're right here, oh thank god!!" I leaned forward and kissed him, I kissed him hard and he kissed me back. "You are right here, I can't believe it, wait…"

It was wet under us. I pulled away to see blood, *everywhere.*

I shoved him on his side, he moaned and I found the blood coming from a cut on his shoulder. He had his shirt wadded up beside him. I pushed him over on his other side, jumped on him, side-straddled his waist, and used the shirt to put down-pressure on his shoulder. There was a lot of freaking blood, but I tried to swallow down my panic.

"What happened?"

He croaked out, "William Wallace."

"William *Wallace,* that asshole cut you? I knew I didn't like him."

He chuckled.

I said, "Thank god, please laugh, please make it through this, please *please.*" I kept the pressure going, but blood had soaked through the cloth. I pulled up my skirts, wadded up the hem with one hand and pressed the wad down on top of the soaked-red cloth.

I kept pressing like I had learned in all my first-aid training way back when. I knew it was going to be a while, like ten minutes or fifteen — "Do you have a clock?"

He turned his hand over, he was clutching one of Lady Mairead's pocket-watches. His eyes closed, wincing with pain, he asked, "What time is it?"

I squinted at the timepiece. "It's three minutes after the hour."

"Och, she activated the Bridge on the hour. It only took a moment, did ye feel anythin'?"

"Nothing, what's the Bridge?"

"Tis another new thing we hae tae worry about."

"Well, if it brought us together, and took only a minute and didn't hurt, maybe we don't have to worry at all."

He was facing away but the edge of his mouth turned up in a smile. I said, "I am going to kiss you so hard when this is over — you're going to survive it, right?"

"How long must ye press?"

"About five more minutes."

"I will probably survive it, mo reul-iuil, as long as nae one comes, as this inna my bedroom."

I looked around. The room was nice, there were tapestries along the walls, there was a fire burnin' in the hearth.

"Are you sure? Because this is much better than my room and I broke the door to get free and I lay down right here, on this bed and…"

"Tis nae m'room. There was nae fire when I went tae sleep, there was naething left, everythin' had been removed from the room and here we…" He raised his head a bit and looked around. "Nae, see the table, that is nae my pitcher. This is a different man's room, hae we been moved?"

He patted around his waist. "Do ye see m'bag… Och,

m'sword is down in the courtyard." He was looking up out of the corner of this eye.

I gestured with my head. "I think that's your bag. It's beside you." He patted around, found it, then opened it and felt inside.

"Is it there?"

"Aye, we hae a vessel. We just need tae escape this room."

"Okay," I looked at the clock again. "We ought to wait at least four more minutes. Note, we have good news, the blood isn't pouring out anymore. I didn't need another cloth. Don't get me wrong, my love, that is a lot of blood. It looks like a fucking massacre in here. But it's slowing down. I am not letting you move though, not yet."

He said, "I wish I had some vitamin juice."

"Why?"

"Because we might hae tae fight our way out of here."

"Crap, and your sword is downstairs?"

He said, "Aye, but there are two hangin' there on the wall, do ye see? As soon as ye let me up, we are goin' tae grab them both. Then we will walk straight down, ye ken the castle?"

"Yes, we'll go by the south stair?"

"Aye, we will go directly tae the south stair, down, and intae the kitchen."

"With a bloody arm?" I retched, half jokingly.

He said, "Twill nae be the worst thing tae happen in a thirteenth century kitchen."

"Is it the thirteenth century? Maybe we're in a different time? How do you know this isn't your room in your castle — sometime in the future...?"

"I ken it is the thirteenth century, because of the furniture. But see there over the door? That is the crest of John Balliol. I fought him once, when I was seeking the crown. He was easy tae beat, but here he is with his crest upon the door. Tis plain that I am the usurper and dost ye ken what I would do tae a man I found bleedin' in m'bed?"

"Probably kill him?"

"Aye, especially if I had fought him afore."

"Great, do you have a blade on your belt?"

"The other side."

I felt around and unsheathed a small dagger. I dropped it beside his hand. "I need you to cut off my skirt here, see?" He got both his hands twisted around and sawed at the cloth.

He asked, "Where is yer blade?"

"I don't even want to tell you that I somehow dropped a gun and the only thing I had to dig through the door was one of Archie's Matchbox cars. Don't ask, mistakes were made."

He cut the fabric free from my skirt. He said, "Now ye can move."

I said, "Hold this here, as firm as you can."

He held the cloth to his shoulder while I found a cord holding back the drapes on the bed. I cut it, hoping it would be long enough. "Sit up."

He sat up and groaned as he swung his legs off the bed.

"Feel woozy?"

"Aye, ye are a bit blurry."

"Smile."

He grimaced.

"Your gums are still pink, pale, but you haven't lost too much blood. Please be okay, because I do not want any more twists. I truly hope this is all real and happening, truly I do. That was weird how you were here but not here. I did not like that." I wrapped the cord around his shoulder, across his chest, and tightened it under his other arm. "We need a vacation. We need to go on a cruise or something as soon as we're out of here." I tied it as tight as I could.

I asked, "You can't move that arm, right? Don't do it, this is... shit this is a lot of blood, it looks like a pig was murdered in here."

"Nae one will be murdered as long as I am on my..." I helped him stand and held him up. He swayed for a moment. "As long as I'm on my—

The door flung open. By flung I meant, *scraped,* but still, it opened and there stood a young maid, carrying a pitcher. She took a look and then screamed.

I said, as she backed away from the door, "Here we are, my love," I did my best to hold his weight up. "It's go time."

~

We rushed to the wall. Magnus grabbed a sword with one hand, making it look effortless. I lugged one down with both hands making it look like 'maybe I should not be carrying a sword.'

He said, "I want ye tae stay on my left side, just behind, as we go. Ye be aware of m'left flank and my rear. Ye remember our lessons?"

I said, "Yes, I totally remember."

We left the room, his feet slow but steady. I stayed right beside him, a step behind. His path weaved a little but aimed down the middle of the hall, keeping his right hand clear for fighting. I kept close tight against him, between his left flank and the wall.

He gasped out, "Up ahead." It scared me that he was so winded.

We came to a circular stair. His downward descent was practically a fall as he raced down, his feet correcting him upright and his injured shoulder banging against the wall for balance keeping his fighting arm free. His face wore a grimace as he dropped three stairs, his knees buckling, his wounded shoulder struck against the spiral as he stumbled. I muttered prayers, *please let him be okay.*

I was in my head, freaking out — *this was too much, too much for him to do.* But then we made it tae the bottom step, and he led us down a tunnel headed toward the kitchens. We passed a few of the kitchen girls, but not a single guard. Not one young man with a knife. It was a miracle.

Or maybe they were so shocked by the couple who were both covered in blood and were racing past that they couldn't imagine how to mount a defense or a proper chase.

In the kitchen he said, "Daena pay us any mind, we are going tae go past ye tae the door."

"We are friendly, see us? See how nice we are?" I held my sword up like a baseball bat. "We are really truly the nicest people, we are just fleeing. We'll be out of here in no time." Side-stepping, with caution, we moved through the kitchen, making sure Magnus faced the kitchen workers, while I watched the door behind us.

We made it to the outer door, then the kitchen garden, three steps later we were running down the slope. We paused so I could dig in his bag for the vessel. I pulled it out, and we ran while I twisted it

"Where to?"

He said, "I need a hospital," as he stumbled and fell forward, crashing intae the grass. "Our family is at the lake house."

I set us headed to Maine.

CHAPTER 55 - LADY MAIREAD

I stood looking down at the Bridge.

At the appointed time I had placed my thumb atop the obsidian river stone.

Nothing happened. *Och nae.* I pressed and prodded, panic rising.

"Lochinvar!" He looked verra confused, much like a lost boy, though he was as big and tall as a man. "Lochinvar, come here, right now, hold this." He shuffled over. "Hurry! Put your thumb there." He placed his thumb on the black rock, and it briefly turned tae liquid, as if twas quicksilver.

He said, "Och nae!" His thumb was pulled in, then pushed away. He withdrew his thumb and rubbed it.

"Did it hurt ye?"

"Nae, but twas surprisin'. What was it?"

"I daena ken." The obsidian stone was solid once more. The whole event had taken only a moment.

I looked down at the Bridge. "Was that all it was tae do?"

Lochinvar shrugged. "What was it supposed tae do?"

I asked, "Ye dinna feel anything?"

He said, "Nae, Lady Mairead, what would it be?"

I looked back down intae the box. "I daena ken, *something*, like a pain or a headache or... naething?"

"I felt naething, except I am verra hungry."

I pulled one of my favorite treats from my bag, a Reese's Peanut Butter Cup, and passed it tae him.

"I can eat it all?"

"Of course, eat up, ye need some weight on ye."

He pulled the wrapper open and ate it in two bites, moaning in pleasure. "Bha e blasta!"

"I ken it was delicious, that is why I keep many of them in my bag when I travel." I poked inside the box hoping it would do something, *anything*.

His eyes widened and he put out a hand.

I huffed and dug out a second peanut butter cup for him. "Ye daena get fed much?"

"Nae, there is never enough."

"What am I going tae do with ye, ought I leave ye here?"

He shook his head, a smear of chocolate on his beard. "Nae! Ye must take me, I will do anythin', daena make me stay."

I sized him up. "Do ye ken how tae fight?"

"Aye, I fight all the time."

"Were ye with Ormr and Domnall when they went on their raids?"

"Aye, I trained with the lairds, I fought, I am one of their best warriors."

"How do I ken ye will be on the side of Magnus?"

"Who, Magnus? The man who was here?"

"Aye, Magnus, he is my son and he is a king, nae a barbarian laird, but a real king. He will be fair, but he will demand loyalty of ye. Will ye be willing tae declare yer fealty tae the king? Keeping in mind, ye must be especially loyal tae me as I am the king's mother, his regent, and I run absolutely everything. Can ye?"

"Aye." He stood straight and adjusted his sword.

I looked him over. "Good, I can always use more brawn in my work."

"Will there be food?"

"Aye, there is a great deal of food, Lochinvar. Ye can close the lid on the Bridge."

He closed it and it locked with a click. Now I wouldna be able tae open it again, as I hadna the bloodline of Donnan and it seemed verra irritating that Lochinvar had been the one tae actually do it.

And that it had been unchallenging. It was always this way with men. I had hoped tae use my selflessness in the face of great challenge for praise and respect, but men would get the glory in *everything*.

Lochinvar put out his hand again. "May I hae one more?"

And now there was this strapping young man in my care.

I passed him a third peanut butter cup and appraised him as he ripped the package open.

I was torn, I kent the Bridge was powerful, but tae keep it I would need tae also keep Lochinvar around tae use it for me. And he was a verra dim and useless young man. He would need tae be trained.

Also, if I kept Lochinvar around I would hae trouble with Hammond and though I was irritated by Hammond's unwavering attention, I needed Hammond tae protect the kingdom.

He was important, I just dinna want him tae ken how much.

Lochinvar tossed down another peanut butter cup wrapper, his wide shoulders stretching his shirt.

Perhaps I could take him tae New York for a time? Show him the world?

I said, "We must go. Hae ye time-jumped before?"

"I daena... Is it witchcraft?"

"Och, if ye are going tae be modern, ye need tae stop being so superstitious. Ye canna believe in witchcraft, Lochinvar, ye must open yer eyes and watch the world around ye. Daena live in fear, ye must live by what is real: your family and your sword."

"Aye, Lady Mairead."

"Now hold my arm, this will hurt, but ye will survive it and all will be well."

"Ye promise there will be more of the food?"

I sighed. "Aye, ye sound like Magnus. There will be more. Now hold on."

CHAPTER 56- KAITLYN

*T*hat thing happened again — we were jumping to one place and then we were grabbed, like from my middle, and dragged in a different direction. It hurt like hell and my internal brain-screaming echoed in a different way. Instead of streaming out behind me it spread from the side — it was unexplainable but it was like screeching around a corner and then…

I was lying face down in the dirt. Stadium dirt, the sound of a galloping horse circling, Magnus's voice from above me. "Kaitlyn, get up, get up Kaitlyn, I daena ken how we are here, I am fightin' Domnall, ye must get up."

I came to enough to see he was standing over me, protecting me. His shoulder bound with my haphazard wrap, blood all over him, a sword in his right hand, the tip down in the sand.

I looked up. The open sky was above us. I looked around, holy shit, we were in the stadium. Shifting faces all around us, a roar of cheering crowds.

He said, "Kaitlyn, run tae the door!"

I scrambled to my feet.

He was prowling around Domnall in the middle of the stadium.

To Domnall he said, "I demand ye give her passage tae the door!"

Domnall grunted, kept his face still, his expression unchanging, meaning literally nothing — was he going to chase me? I ran anyway, as fast as I could because I had had enough training, if my husband was facing off against an asshole and said, "Run!" I shouldn't ask questions. Second guessing could get us both killed.

I did not want either of us dead.

But where the hell, *when* the hell, were we?

We were in the stadium, and it seemed like we hadn't left from his battle before — it was still going on.

I heard the audience go wild. *Keep running.* I made it to the door, threw my shoulder against it, looked back to see Magnus swing his sword, one-handed, Domnall stumbled to the ground.

I fled through the weapons room and raced up the stairs — *he should not be fighting, he was not ready to fight, he was injured, he had lost so much blood.*

I heard the audience groan.

I made it to the second level, hearing a cheer erupt from the audience, and rushed into the royal box, taking a seat beside Lady Mairead.

"What is happening? I can't believe we are in this again."

Lady Mairead said, "We hae had yet another shift and we are back, watching Magnus battle Domnall as if twas never interrupted."

"How did this happen?" Magnus was struggling to hold up his sword.

"Stop asking questions, Kaitlyn, I am trying tae keep Magnus alive through sheer will."

There was a young man in the chair beside her, licking a wrapper from a peanut butter cup. He wore a kilt with a sword slung on his back, looking a little like Magnus when I first met him, though this guy was ginger, almost pink he was so ginger. His beard was sparse because he was young, unkempt because he was disgusting, and he had a robust smell.

"Who is this?"

Lady Mairead huffed and glanced at him. "Nae one important, just a boy — answer me, why is Magnus injured? Did ye hae difficulties when we used the Bridge?"

"No, he was injured in a scrap with William Wallace."

She scowled. "He ought nae be scrapping. He ought tae save his strength for the important fights, now he is injured and—"

Magnus swung toward Domnall but looked weak and exhausted. The audience groaned.

"We didn't *know* we were going to be in the stadium, we had no idea. Did you?"

"Nae, we were jumping elsewhere and we were grabbed and dragged here."

Magnus was thrown off balance and stumbled back. I clapped my hands over my mouth to stopper my scream.

Lady Mairead held onto the railing in front of us, her grip whitening her knuckles. "General Hammond just signaled tae me from the command booth, he believes the fight is lost, we must prepare."

The young man with Lady Mairead asked, "What is happenin' down there? Why is Magnus fightin' Domnall?" He wadded up the wrapper, tossed it to the ground, and licked his fingers.

Lady Mairead said, "He is trying tae protect his kingdom, Domnall is trying tae take it from him."

"Do ye hae any more of the sweet food?"

"Nae, I will get more, right now we are in the middle of—"

"What are these things all around?"

"Those are videos, can ye wheesht?"

He clamped his mouth shut, then said, "Magnus is too injured tae fight, what happens if Domnall wins?"

Lady Mairead said, "His brother Ormr will become king, and all of us will likely die."

He said, "Och, I daena like the sound of that, Ormr is a maniacal arse."

"On that we are agreed."

He stood. "Tis tae the death?"

Lady Mairead said, "Why — what? Aye, this is a battle tae the death."

He pointed, "See Ormr waitin' on the side? If Domnall loses, Ormr will fight, he means tae kill Magnus if Domnall daena. Tis nae fair." He drew his sword.

"What are ye doing?"

He jumped on the rail and balanced there crouched, watching. "I'm joining the fight on Magnus's behalf!" He jumped, landing deftly on the ramped floor below. He raced down into the arena.

Magnus and Domnall looked shocked.

CHAPTER 57 - MAGNUS

"*W*hat are ye doin'?" Lochinvar stood beside me, spinning his sword.

"Comin' tae help ye, auld man, ye are injured, tis nae fair. Ye will die and then I winna get the box of sweet cups yer mum has promised me."

My shoulder was desperately sore, damp from bleeding again. "I am hardly older than ye, maybe a few years..." My sight was doubled, I dinna ken if I was strong enough tae lift m'blade. "But aye, I am verra injured."

Lochinvar tossed his heavy sword from one hand tae another. "Ye are at least a decade older, enough tae hae fathered me."

I laughed.

Domnall said, "I ken ye, ye are Lochinvar! What are ye doin' here?"

Lochinvar set his stance. "I am Lochinvar the Fearsome, and I hae decided tae live and fight alongside King Magnus." He whipped the sword around, showin' off. "Ye ready tae fight, auld man? Why nae bring yer brother over, I can fight ye both at once."

Ormr stepped from the shadowy side of the arena and called,

"Mag Mòr, ye goin' tae allow this lad tae fight for ye? He is a nobody, a bastard. Ye canna allow him tae fight in a stadium battle for the kingdom of Riaghalbane, tis—"

I looked from the young man tae Ormr and then tae Domnall. "I can, he carries Donnan's bloodline. As a descendant of Donnan, and as my brother, he can be called upon tae protect my kingdom, tis all fair in thrones and family."

Domnall said, "He is a bastard, Donnan never claimed—"

I chuckled "He never claimed ye either, his father never claimed Ormr, none of it matters. Donnan had many bastard sons, I daena care at—"

Lochinvar charged past me, straight for Domnall with all the fearlessness of youth. Takin' him by surprise, he whipped his blade back and forth, then with a quick jab he nicked Domnall at the waist.

Lochinvar yelled, "I marked his weakness with m'blade, King Magnus!" He skirted Domnall, and raced toward Ormr, swinging.

The crowd cheered.

Ormr rushed tae meet Lochinvar, their blades meeting with a loud clang, but Lochinvar was faster, quick on his feet, driving Ormr tae fury. Twas a good strategy, tae enrage an opponent, one I often used when I was in better condition.

I had taken the moment tae catch m'breath, but I was verra weakened and I was givin' Domnall a chance tae recover as well. His injury was — I glanced from the corner of m'eye. There was a great deal of blood seeping through his shirt.

I watched his movements in my periphery as I looked down at my sword tip, pretending tae be too exhausted tae fight. In my far vision I could see the movement of Lochinvar against Ormr.

I couldna worry on them, if the young man was killed, at least Ormr would be worn down by their fight. I was sure that if I killed Domnall, Ormr planned tae immediately challenge me for the throne. One after another they would fight me and in my weakened state it was likely to cause m'death in the end.

Domnall moved his weight to his right leg. There was a bit of hesitation, a barely noticeable swerve as he tried tae protect his injury. He was preparing tae raise his sword — time stood still. The sky above was overcast, the temperature cool, the crowd roared but I pushed the sound aside. I focused. The twitch of a muscle on his right hand, the small wince at the edge of his eye. The slight crunch of the dirt as his weight switched, from his front foot tae his back, he was swinging... left.

I lunged right. I went from standin' still tae an explosion and afore he could raise his sword I had stabbed him through.

His eyes locked tae mine and there was deep hatred there, we had been locked in battle for many long centuries.

I shoved him tae the ground and tugged m'sword from him.

I was breathless, pantin'. I eyed the young man fightin' across the field. He was winnin', but Ormr had witnessed the downin' of his brother, now writhing in the dirt.

Ormr bellowed, rounded Lochinvar, and charged toward me with his sword held high, Lochinvar chased him, but I calculated — he wouldna stop Ormr in time.

I thought tae myself, *Och, twill be more of it,* and shakily raised m'sword.

His pace: one, two, three, *he would be on me*—

I waited for Ormr, closing fast, then as he shifted tae swing, I lunged with all the strength left in me, a deadly stab tae his chest, a death blow — as Lochinvar's sword stabbed through his stomach, thrust from behind. Our two swords struck through him, he convulsed. I let go.

Lochinvar lifted Ormr with his sword and dropped him down in the dirt.

Lochinvar panted hard, still holding the hilt of his sword. The cheering was thunderous.

I clutched m'shoulder, dripping red with blood again. Twas hard tae get on top of my breath. But Lochinvar's eyes were wild, his excitement dangerous. There was a moment I thought, *He could turn on me now, and finish me,* but his sword had entered Ormr in my defense. He had sided with me.

He was now in front of me, a young warrior gasping for breath, battling with himself.

"Ye can let go of yer sword now, boy, ye daena want tae look too murderous. We hae won the battle, smile at yer fans."

He let go of his sword.

I clapped my hand on his shoulder. "Ye good?"

I could see the rage in his eyes, he was tryin' tae dampen it down, twas a dangerous moment when a man had gone full-rampage, when he had just killed an enemy, two enemies, twas a verra dangerous moment. I had long practice recovering from it.

I said, "Ye ken, ye just need tae breathe, in and out, dost ye hear the applause? Aye?"

He nodded, breathing heavy, and gasped out. "Aye, I hear it."

"Good, yer comin' back tae the civilized world. Pull yer sword from Ormr." We pulled our swords free. He dropped his sword at my feet, declaring his allegiance.

I dropped mine on top of it.

I said, "I need tae walk from the stadium on m'own two feet, but I am feelin' verra weak. Would ye let me lean on ye?"

"Aye." He straightened up.

I announced for the crowd, "M'name is Magnus Archibald Caelhin Campbell, King of Riaghalbane, and I hae defeated the usurpers trying tae take the throne." A cheer went up. "This is Lochinvar the Fearsome, m'brother." Another loud cheer, the mayhem was deafening.

I said tae Lochinvar, "Are ye good tae walk now? We are goin' tae the door, but I am nae sure I can make it."

"Aye, hold on."

I clapped my arm around his shoulder and leaned on him as we walked tae the door, my gait unsteady. He walked slowly beside me and waved at the audience's video faces as they yelled and cheered celebrating the kingdom's win.

Hammond met us at the door. "Magnus! Well done, ye remain a king!" He led me tae the room where Kaitlyn fell intae m'arms.

"I can't believe it, you're still standing. I can't believe all that you had to do and you—"

Twas the last thing I heard as I slipped down collapsing at her feet.

CHAPTER 58 - KAITLYN

I was wearing a simple pair of slacks and shirt having taken the quickest shower in the world and now I was once again waiting for Magnus to survive in the royal infirmary, but I had heard from the physician that Magnus was going to be okay. He had his wound cleaned, his skin sutured, and his blood replenished. Now he was sleeping while I watched, because I hadn't watched him sleep in so long it felt like forever.

I held his hand, calloused and worn, strong and noble. There were cuts and bruises on it. I wrapped around that hand, pressed my lips to it, and nestled my cheek against it, waiting for him to awake.

His fingers shifted. I said, "Hey."

"Hello, mo reul-iuil." His voice was weak.

I said, "Your voice sounded stronger when you were in the stadium, are you feeling better?"

He said, "I was pretendin', I daena ken if ye realize this but I am an amazin' actor."

"Are you now? Really? I knew you had a good singing voice,

and your dance moves are epic." I chef-kissed my fingers. "But I didn't know you were an actor too."

"Aye, I was dyin' out there. Totally beaten and ye dinna ken I had lost."

"Here's a secret about me, my warrior, watching you fight makes me feel really scared, I have to look through my fingers like this, so I'm not surprised that I didn't realize you were losing." I sighed. "I'm teasing though, playing along, I knew you were injured, I knew you were dying, I knew it was lost. Thank god for Lochinvar jumping in the ring."

"Aye, he is goin' tae crow about it. I barely ken him, but I can see it in his eyes and I ken the type, because he is just like me. He is goin' tae be braggin' about how he saved m'life and calling me an old man through it."

"Dear god, an old man? But you're young!"

"Thank ye for saying it, but I was feeling m'age out there."

"You had lost buckets of blood, you were too thin from living in the thirteenth century, *and* you had been worrying about me."

He grinned. "Speaking of, do ye think they will bring us food? I am hungry."

I rang the bell for him. "Can you please bring Magnus a meal?"

Then I said to him, "We have to get home, we need to see the children. How long was I gone?"

"A few days, enough for them tae be verra worried, but they ken this is the nature of it. They daena understand but they ken. They were verra brave when I spoke tae them."

I spread out his fingers and stroked his hand finding comfort in caressing him, then I rested my cheek against his palm. "They're okay, right? I'm so surprised by how the Bridge worked — what if they aren't there? What if something has happened?"

"Do ye remember our bairns, mo reul-iuil?"

"Yes."

"Then they are there. Ye remember the lake house?"

"Yes."

He grinned. "Now put those memories taegether."

I chuckled. "Okay, got it." Then I said, "Which kid is the one that's afraid to jump in the water? Wait, let me guess — it's Ben. Ben is nervous about jumping in, but when he sees Isla do it he jumps in out of pressure. Archie goes in and out easily but he spends time fussing and worrying about the little sisters and Zoe... Zoe is...?"

"She is fearless, so she is wearin' those floaties on her arms, ye ken? They hae her in them from morning 'til night, because if she decides tae she will just go swimmin'."

"I bet that is cute as hell and also terrifying."

"Aye, Emma is feelin' it."

"Can I climb up on the bed? That was a long time without you and it was scary, echoey, and so alone, now the kids aren't here and..."

"Aye." He patted the bed. "Just nae yer usual side, m'left shoulder has stitches in it and I think twill need therapy, but nae the talking kind, twill be a physical kind."

I climbed up slowly and curled against his right side with my head on his right shoulder. "Stupid William Wallace."

He said, "Aye, he was stupid. All the rage and ill-judgment of a young man who needs tae grow up. Which makes me wonder, where is Lochinvar?"

"Ha ha. He's following your mother around, and General Hammond is giving her the silent treatment about it."

"Och, I hope they can get through it. Can ye imagine m'mother without the calm influence of Hammie?"

"He is an excellent Lady Mairead wrangler."

Magnus chuckled.

I said, "So Lochinvar just saved your life."

"Aye, he did. Twas my blade that killed Domnall and Ormr, but I wouldna hae been able tae do it without him. Twas respectful that he allowed me tae take the final blows."

"And he is a brother?"

"Aye, yet another bastard son of Donnan, an orphan with nae allegiances. Apparently Donnan had many sons and I am meant tae guard against them or for them. This is m'lot in life."

"You're so young to be the patriarch-guardian of this many sons."

"Young? I am the age of ten men stacked upon each other. I was young when ye met me, but think on it, that time we spent in Edinburgh? That added forty-five years tae my life."

"True, the time I was abducted in Scotland added fifty years to mine."

"Ye daena look a day over fifty."

I laughed. "I will pretend like you were joking."

"I was, ye are more beautiful than when I met ye."

"Really?"

"Aye, ye hae rounded verra nicely, ye hae gained stature, and ye are verra much the wiser."

"Jesus Christ, this is either the greatest compliment I've ever received or I'm horribly insulted."

He chuckled. "Ye would be insulted because I said ye were rounded from havin' a bairn? Ye hae added pillows upon yer chest, handles tae hold ontae, but inside ye are stronger, ye hae gained stability, strength, and wisdom. I ken I can count on ye. They are all exalted compliments."

"I suppose so... But you say you can count on me? You couldn't before?"

"When a man first marries, he daena count on his wife, he only wants tae take care of her, tae protect her, and keep her. It takes some time for a man tae hae her grow tae be his equal, tae be someone he counts on tae keep him safe as well, ye ken — tis normal."

I chuckled again. "I never thought of it that way, I think when I first met you there was a very protective thing about you and an anger when you couldn't keep me safe, a desperation, but now I think you know that I am capable, yeah, I can see how that change happened. I think I've done the same thing, I grew to trust you." I nuzzled my face against his skin and kissed there. "We ought to spring you from this place so we can sex it up."

He said, "My captors mean tae keep me til the morn. We will hae tae wait, but also I am on pain medication and canna feel this whole middle area." He waved his hand around his crotch. "Ye winna like tae sex me up, I will be boring."

"Stupid William Wallace."

"Aye."

We sat quietly for a moment. Then he said, "Where will we live, mo reul-iuil?"

"No more bad guys?"

"I daena ken if there are more bad guys, but I ken that Ormr and Domnall were made tae die at m'feet in a pool of their own pig blood and I think we ought tae count that as a win against all bad guys everywhere."

"After all that drama, all we needed to do was bring in one of Donnan's other bastard sons and have him be your second?"

He chuckled. "Aye, tis all we had tae do — fight them at Kilchurn, battle them in the stadium, fight them in front of the king of England, war against them a few times in long ago Scotland, live in the past, gain a kingdom, and then at the verra end, really after a *verra* long time, in the verra last second, Lochinvar got tae run ontae the field and help me kill them dead. He was a great help, couldna hae done it without him."

I laughed.

He said, "I am teasing, Lochinvar saved my life, he was more than necessary. Only daena tell him I said that, I need tae feign that he was unnecessary or he will be insufferable."

"How do you know?"

"Because I would be insufferable, if our positions were reversed."

"Who dragged us here? How did we get from the thirteenth century to here? Who did it?"

"My first suspect is m'mother."

"She was dragged here too. She's incensed about it."

His eyes narrowed as he searched his mind for who it could have been. "I daena ken. Our bairns hae access tae the tech, perhaps they dragged us there tae handle Domnall and Ormr."

"Well, I don't like that one bit, if there is any dragging to happen, it needs to be *us* dragging *them*. We are the parents. Remind me to tell them, they are not allowed to mess with us. Besides, you were injured. You easily could have died in the arena. It was a terrible risk to take. That's why I don't think it was them."

"Ye think someone else has the tech and can move us around if they want?"

"Yes."

Magnus said, "I wonder how far back we can time travel. We ought tae test if the times that we opened with the Trailblazer are still passable. We can go back tae a day beyond the dates, and see if we can return."

"I agree, just not you. You are wounded, but we can send other men, like James, Fraoch, and Quentin. We need to keep the vessels under our control, And that bridge thing, that is... We ought to test. If it's powerful enough to close off time, we need to know how many Bridges exist."

"Aye, twill take some investigation."

"So many unknowns."

"And so many brothers tae challenge the throne. I hae a new one, his name is Finch Mac."

"The rock star? Finch Mac the freaking rock star?"

"He is a son of Donnan."

"What the hell? How do you know?"

"Because his father, named Donnan, gave him a sword with Donnan's crest on it, and the Bridge is in a box that only sons of Donnan can open. He was able tae open it. Fraoch and I can both open it. Tis indisputable."

I raised my head and looked down at him. "Let me get this straight, a rock star is a son of Donnan? A rock star could challenge you for your throne? A guitar solo challenge?" I laughed.

"Aye, but he winna challenge me, look at me, who would want tae fight me? I am lethal."

I put my head back down on his shoulder. "How many sons of Donnan are there?"

"I daena ken, how many sons can one man make?"

I groaned.

He said, "Finch Mac though is proof that just because Donnan sired a son, daena mean he meant for them tae take over the kingdom. He gave that power tae me. Fraoch wasna offered the chance tae be a king. Finch Mac daena even ken about time travel. So how many sons of Donnan—"

"Or Samuel or Roderick or all your ass-backward uncles and cousins, are there?"

"Aye, how many are there that actually want tae take m'throne? I think, ten tops."

I groaned again. "That's ten too many."

"Aye, I hae tae kill them all afore Archibald becomes old enough tae fight. Or he will hae tae train tae be lethal like his da."

I clamped my eyes shut. "I can't think about that, he's too young. It's impossible to imagine him fighting."

"Aye, I hae become so modern I canna even imagine what Baldie must hae thought when he placed a sword in m'hand and began trainin' me tae fight. I was verra wee. He frightened me terribly with his instructions: kill or be killed."

"That's a terrible thing to teach a kid."

"Tis terrible, but tis also necessary. There will always be someone who wants what ye hae, ye must be willing tae defend it. But, that being said, I am going tae stop acceptin' challenges. I am the king, I will change the rules. My throne is assured, my bloodline is strong. I hae a brother, possibly two, who would fight at my side against any encroachers, I hae a clan full of men who would fight for me, and I hae a son. It daena mean we winna hae tae defend the kingdom, but I winna allow would-be usurpers tae demand I fight."

"Good, yes, I agree." I sat for a moment thinking. "So who are we defending ourselves against?"

"I daena ken, but m'mother has a list." He yawned.

I said, "Your mother, huh?"

"My whole life has just been one verra long struggle tae keep her busy so she winna be so meddlesome."

"She is so freaking meddlesome."

"Aye."

"So is this a respite?"

"Aye, mo reul-iuil, tis more than that, we need a vacation."

"Truly? A vacation? That would be amazing, we can eat and drink, play in the lake, hang out with the kids?"

"Aye, especially the eat and drink." He smiled. "Once we get me out of the hospital and—" His head shot up. "Where is Haggis?"

My eyes went wide.

He dropped his head back and groaned. "Och, I left a man behind."

"Oh no, poor Haggis!" I gave him a sad frown. "I'm so sorry, Magnus, where do you think he is?"

"I daena ken, he was never far away from me, but when I returned he was gone. He wasna nearby. Och nae!"

"He's in the thirteenth century, poor poor Haggis. Do we even know if we have access to the thirteenth century? And if he wasn't there when we left, is he still there...? He never left your side before — I don't know, my love, I think he might be gone."

"Och nae, I promised him a run on the beach with the bairns."

I clutched around his shoulders and held him tight. "I'm so sorry."

He moaned. "Och I ken, me too, I made the poor dog a promise."

CHAPTER 59 - KAITLYN

I went out to the waiting room and Lady Mairead buzzed in with Lochinvar following, he was still wearing the same clothes, holding a bag of cookies in one hand, a box under his arm, shoving handfuls of cookies in his mouth. I pulled Lady Mairead to the side and whispered, "Why haven't you sent him to get washed up, there's dried blood on him still!"

Lady Mairead huffed. "I ken, but I daena ken what tae do with him, General Hammond is verra unhappy with me that I hae brought him along."

"But, he's a hero, he can't even get a shower? Don't we have people for that?"

"Just between us, Kaitlyn, he is frightened of everything, and daena want tae be without me. He is also verra hungry. All I do is give him cookies and try tae…"

Lochinvar sat in a chair with the metal box in his lap. He had a small bag that had once held cookies but was now empty. He turned it upside down over his face, pouring crumbs all over his beard. Then he tore open the bag and licked the inside.

Her eyes widened. "General Hammond thinks I hae taken him tae be my lover." She smoothed back her hair. "I would nae dream of it, look at him, there are crumbs in his beard." She gave a slight shiver, but her eyes glinted. "Daena get me wrong, he has a fine jaw, a verra braw arse—"

I said, "Holy shit, did you just say that?"

"Aye, ye ken, ye can see it."

"I only have eyes for my husband, your *son's,* arse."

She rolled her eyes. "Well, ye daena ken what ye are missing, Kaitlyn, in taking a young man tae bed. But this one is more trouble than he is worth. I prefer my lovers tae be kept at a distance so I daena hae tae hide them. Also, I want tae tell them tae go home after, I daena like them tae stink up my sheets."

"There is so much there to unpack, but firstly, Lady Mairead, Lochinvar saved your son's life! You ought to show some gratitude."

"I am grateful, I just am nae taking him as a lover because of the aforementioned stench."

"Hammond doesn't stink up your bedding?"

"Hammond is a fine man, he is a willing, capable lover, and we hae a relationship. He kens I am allowing him tae share my bed as a *favor* for as long as he stays within my good graces. Now he is upset, I hae never kent him tae put his foot down, but Lochinvar is a man too close. Hammond has warned me that he will leave the castle if he finds Lochinvar in my quarters, so I brought him here tae put him in Magnus's care." She said, "He just needs some land, tell Magnus he will need tae clean him up, educate him, and take him tae a time period where he will sensibly fit, and drop him off."

"Fine, Magnus and I will take care of him."

"Good, I wash my hands of it."

"What is that box he's got in his lap?"

"Tis the Bridge."

"The Bridge! Is it dangerous? He's just carrying it around?"

"Aye, likely, but I canna open it, I canna work it, I wash my hands of it as well. Tell Magnus tae keep it safe."

"You have another one, right? I've never known you to give something up like that."

She chuckled. "Tis likely, ye are right, it daena sound like me tae give away m'power."

"I've wanted to ask, who do you think dragged us here?"

She said, "I hae nae idea, but tis at the top of my list of things I need tae understand, as well as finding *all* of the sons of Donnan."

She looked at her bag. "Tell yer husband that I want my pocket watch returned and if he daena ken where it is, I want a new one, or an old one, rather. That one was built by Thomas Wagstaffe and belonged tae Benjamin Franklin, given tae me personally. There is a long history behind it. I expect it replaced with a timepiece of a similar pedigree."

"What about the one you keep in your apartment, I never see you carry that?"

"The Supercomplication? Because tis verra precious, twas given tae me by Donnan, when he was promising me the whole world. I canna use it, I must keep it special."

I said, "Do you think it might have been Fraoch's mother, Agnie MacLeod, who is messing with us?"

"If twas I am sure she is enraged that I hae seen tae the death of two of her sons, Domnall and Ormr, I imagine she will be driven tae avenge them."

"The two of you have been locked in this avenge battle for a long time, huh?"

"Nae, not a battle, Kaitlyn, it has been *me*, the rightful consort of Donnan, and her, a verra deceitful bitch who beguiled him intae siring her son. I am nae locked in a vengeful thing with her, she is trying tae steal what is rightfully mine. I winna allow it."

"My apologies, I misspoke."

"The thing is, Kaitlyn, imagine if ye had Bella still, trying tae ingratiate herself in the kingdom and intae yer husband's good graces. Would ye be 'locked in a vengeful thing'? Nae, ye would be the wife and she would be the bitch and she would deserve the death ye brought tae her."

"Yes, you're right, I won't say that kind of thing again, you're right about it."

"Good, tis the first time ye hae properly taken my side; I hae taken yer side for a verra long time."

I bit my lips because I wanted to mention all the *millions* of times she had *not* taken my side, but decided that as Magnus had said about Lochinvar, after a long time of fighting he swooped in at the end, for Lady Mairead after a long life of being adversaries, she was only going to count the last few adventures when she had somehow been on my side.

She said, "Now, I am going tae go see tae Hammond, and then I will leave him in charge of the kingdom while I go tae New York. My dear friend Abby is having an opening of her new museum, November 7, 1929, all will be there."

I said, "Do you think we are still able to go before the year November 1, 1557? Do you think the Bridge removed the Trailblazer's effects?"

"We winna ken until we test. Master Cook may be willing tae do it, he will want tae make sure the timeline is safe and stable from his looping. He has Sophie tae protect and she is—"

I said, "Wait... Sophie is back?"

"Aye, I resolved it. James was looping all around. I daena ken what the other men were doing. I strode intae Dunscaith, met with m'contact in the kitchens, Auld Arthuretta, and put some sleeping powder in the food. Once the potion took effect, I was able tae procure Sophie from the dungeons and deliver her tae James. Ye ought tae pay attention, Kaitlyn, there is a great deal goin' on—"

I threw my arms around her shoulders. "Thank you. Thank you. That means... thank you."

She pulled away, "Aye, well, tis done."

I blinked back my tears of gratitude.

Then I looked over at Lochinvar. "Hey, I'm Queen Kaitlyn."

He bowed awkwardly. "Yer Highness."

"Would you like me to show you to your room?"

CHAPTER 60 - KAITLYN

*T*here was dried blood on his shirt, chocolate smeared in quite a few places, and he smelled to high heaven. He also wore a pair of sunglasses. I said, "I remember how bright it was the first time I came, and you're from more centuries before that." I led him down the hallway. On route I passed our household manager, apprising her of the situation, then she led us down the hall, and opened a door on an opulent guest room.

"You've never time traveled before, this is your first room in a future house?"

He nodded.

"Well, then, this is going to be fun." I walked into the bathroom. "You've been introduced to the toilets?"

"Aye, General Hammond told me how tae use them."

"Great." I led him tae the shower, turned it on, and brought it to a good temperature. I pointed, "There is the soap for lathering your whole body and I mean *whole* body, then you will use this in your hair, and this. Then when all the soap is rinsed off your body, you will turn off the water, here, step out, and dry yourself with this towel."

He nodded and began taking off his shirt, showing his stomach with some jagged pink scars.

"I will be outside, don't undress in front of me—"

He stopped me as I left. "Where will ye be, Queen Kaitlyn? Ye winna go far?"

"I will be right outside, yell if you need anything."

He nodded.

I asked, "Why are you so nervous?"

"Daena ken, tis verra bright and loud, my heart is racin' in m'chest."

"Well, the murderous rampage and the time jumping were bound to be upsetting."

He chuckled, "The rampage wasna upsettin', that was usual. M'name is Lochinvar the Fearsome, with m'broadsword I will kill anyone who crosses me."

I gulped. "Great, just what we needed, another big sword swinging, another man covered in the blood of his enemies."

His brow drew down. "Ye dinna like it when I was a hero?"

I sighed. "No, I am very grateful you saved Magnus's life, it's just... if you're going to be around us we need you to sound less bloodthirsty."

He looked down at his bloody clothes. "Yet, I am a brave warrior, and a skilled swordsman. I fight tae win."

"That's good, these are good qualities, and as the king's brother you need to say things like *that* — less rampaging, more considered and thoughtful."

He squinted. "Ye daena want me tae say, 'I will make m'enemies writhe at m'feet, beggin' fer mercy, as I bash their lives from them...?' Even if tis true?"

I exhaled. "Even if it's true. Instead you ought to say, 'I am a skilled swordsman, I will win when called upon to battle.' No bashing."

"Aye, Yer Majesty, I daena ken why I tried tae sound so brutal. I daena rampage unless it is in a battle, and usually tis when the laird has commanded me tae fight or die. Today was the first battle I fought for m'self, because Magnus is a fair laird, and m'brother, and I promised I would protect Lady Mairead's family."

I said, "That's a much better way to talk about it, Lochinvar, here in the future we do not want fearsome, uncivilized, rampaging men."

His brow drew down. "'Tis confusin' as there was an arena battle tae the death just hours ago—"

A knock on the door interrupted. The house manager passed in some basic clothes and a pair of shoes for Lochinvar.

I passed him the stack. "There are contradictions in the future, you have to be civilized and never fight, but you might want to always be ready to fight. *Especially* as a son of Donnan."

"Donnan must hae been a strong king tae hae such a glorious kingdom, tae hae raised such a brave son in King Magnus."

"Obviously you never met him. Donnan was a horrible person. King Magnus turned out brave and wonderful *despite* his horrible father. Give credit for his wonderfulness to Lady Mairead and his Uncle Baldie."

"I will give credit tae his Uncle Baldie. Ye canna give credit tae his mother, mothers make warriors weak, everyone kens it."

"Another thing to never say, especially not where Lady Mairead can hear you."

I pointed at the clothes in his arms. "After your shower you'll put this on. Then we'll take you for a beard trim and haircut, you're hairy as a ginger bear."

He made his voice sound like a growl, "Aye, Yer Majesty, I will get cleaned up so I am nae a bear, but I will go fast because m'stomach is a'growlin' a'ready."

I laughed, "I can absolutely tell you're related to Magnus."

I sat on a chair in the outer room while he showered. After a long time I knocked. "It's all right in there?" He emerged a long time after that. He had some greasy conditioner and some bubbles in his hair still, his shimmery pale blue shirt was stuck to his body with dampness, but he smelled like a flower garden.

He smiled, the blue of his shirt contrasting against his ruddy pink skin. "I feel a great deal better, thank ye."

"Now here's the thing, I want to go back to Magnus. Do you want me to take you to the kitchens first for some food?"

He nodded.

I led him down the hall, passing the elevator, and instead taking the stairs. Everyone backed to the wall and bowed as we passed.

He looked all around dumbfounded.

"You probably want to know what everything is, right?"

"Aye," he cast his eyes down, "But tis too much tae look at."

I led him into the kitchens where the house manager rushed up to help as this was *not* somewhere I was supposed to be without a lot of fanfare. I said, "This young man needs to be fed a hero's feast, but," I glanced at his face, he licked his lips looking around at all that food. "while that's being whipped up he needs a sandwich to tide him over."

"Of course." She rushed around ordering the staff to prepare a sandwich. She seemed shocked that I stood there. "Will you be waiting, Your Highness?"

"Yes, and how about a small one for me and one for Magnus as well."

"The king wants a sandwich? We just fed him!"

I joked, "Well, I haven't asked him, but it's safe to assume."

A few moments later I was followed through to the royal infirmary with three people: the manager to manage our progress, a steward to carry the tray, and one of Magnus's nurses, alerted to the fact that the king was hungry. They all followed me as I led Lochinvar to the infirmary waiting room. I said, "Sit."

He sat and the food was placed in front of him.

Then I went with the entourage into Magnus's room. He

exclaimed, "M'wife and a sandwich! She has read m'mind, I was just thinking how hungry I was!"

The nurse said, "My apologies, Your Majesty, I thought you had just eaten."

They all bowed out of the room.

I huffed, jokingly, with my hands on my hips. "I told them I wanted to bring you a sandwich and about set off a five-alarm emergency. I forgot about all the bending and scraping they do about you here, Mr King. Now that I think about it, you were a king in the thirteenth century too, all the 'aye your majesty' and fussing about you — we need to get you back to the present day so you can stop thinking *everyone* is going to make *everything* all right for you *all* the time."

"Tis how it has been for me? Everyone is always makin' it all right for me?" He took a big bite of his sandwich, chewed, swallowed, and moaned happily. "Ye forget I was *months* in the past. It dinna seem like everyone was always makin' it all right, there was a great deal of blood sausage and fish served tae me though I wanted something, *anything* else."

I chuckled. "Yeah, I'm so sorry, you're right, you're the one making sure it's all right for everyone else. The very *least* you can get is a sandwich. Lochinvar got one too, and there is a feast planned for later."

Magnus asked, "Where is m'mother?"

"She's packing, she's planning to head to New York tomorrow night. She has a party."

He grinned. "We are in charge of Lochinvar now?"

"Yes."

"I figured m'mother would get bored with him. Guess what? Speaking of bored, I am allowed tae leave in the morn. I will meet with General Hammond and m'mother, then we will take Lochinvar tae Maine. He can try tae drive Chef Zach crazy."

"We will have our hands full, all those kids and two people, Sophie and Lochinvar, fresh from the past, plus Beaty and Fraoch, ai ai ai." I grinned.

He said, "Ye forgot me, I am from the past."

I smiled. "I forget sometimes, you're such an important part of my present."

I led Lochinvar to the barber to get his hair and beard trimmed and later we visited Magnus who asked, "Lochinvar, how old are ye? Ye look a verra young man. Far too young tae hae saved m'life in the arena."

I said, "He doesn't look that much younger than you did when I first met you."

Magnus's eyes went wide. "I never looked that young! There is nae way, he looks fresh as a mewlin' kitten!"

Lochinvar laughed. "I daena think a fresh mewling kitten would be able tae save yer arse in an arena."

Magnus chuckled. "Aye, I thank ye Lochinvar, I am verra grateful tae ye for joinin' the battle."

"Ye were goin' tae lose, ye ought nae fight arena battles if ye are goin' tae lose!"

"Ye ken, Lochinvar, I wasna tryin' tae lose. Every stadium I enter I plan tae win, ye just caught me on a bad day."

"How many of those arena battles hae ye had?"

"I daena ken, seven or eight? Donnan would make me fight tae the death tae prove m'worth."

I said, "So many, too many."

Lochinvar winced. "He sounds a shite da."

"Aye, he was."

"Ye had tae fight for the kingdom, it winna just given tae ye?"

Magnus said, "I had tae fight, the kingdom is passed by bloodline, but anyone with a drop of blood can challenge for the throne. I call m'self a descendant of Normond I but tis tenuous, some in the line of kings were distant cousins. Not all were

Campbells, but they all took the name Campbell as they took the throne."

"Och, I think tis a barbarous way tae decide a succession."

Magnus nodded. "Tis. Now I hae a young son, I plan for him tae take the throne and for the succession tae be less barbaric. I want tae do away with the challenges. I am telling ye this because I want ye tae ken, I winna allow ye tae challenge me for the throne. Dost ye understand?"

"Aye."

"Ye will hae land and a title and all I will ask is that ye offer yer blade in my defense, when necessary. But ye must take an oath that ye winna raise arms against me or my son."

He knelt down on one knee. "I swear, Yer Majesty, I winna challenge yer rule."

Magnus watched his bowed head for a moment, then said, "Thank ye, ye can rise."

He stood.

"Ye pledged yerself without considering it first?"

"Tis an easy decision, Yer Majesty, ye hae fought many battles and ye are still standing. I take that tae mean ye can be fierce. I hae heard ye speak and ye seem tae be a fair man. Tis a simple calculation that I would rather be on yer fair side than yer fierce side."

"Good, Lochinvar, thank ye. And ye still look verra young, how auld are ye?"

He shrugged. "I think I am young enough tae nae be married, too auld tae be alone at night, dost ye ken where I can find a woman for m'bed?"

I had been listening quietly, but that was too much, I jumped in, "No, that… holy moley, no. I do not know where you can find a woman, you will have to wait until you meet someone who is willing to date you…"

"Tae date?"

Magnus said, "What m'dear wife is saying is ye will have tae take a woman tae dinner, to get her tae fall for yer charms, and *then* ye can marry her and then ye can take her tae bed, tis the order of it." His eyes twinkled. "Unless she is a widow."

Lochinvar said, "Aye like Lady Mairead — where is she anyway?"

Magnus groaned. "Ye leave m'mother alone. Ye will need tae hold yer appetites in if ye are tae live in civilized company. We are goin' tae take ye home with us, there winna be any unmarried women there, but we will find someone tae introduce ye tae."

I joked, "There's always Tinder."

They both blinked at me. This was not the right crowd for dumb jokes. I said, "We will do our best to find someone."

He grinned, "In the meantime I get tae live with yer family — there will be plenty tae eat? Will there be horses?"

"Aye, ye will hae plenty tae eat, and there will be horses... at our home in Florida, once we are back there."

"Good, thank ye, Yer Majesty, when do we go?"

CHAPTER 61 - KAITLYN

The following day, after being shadowed constantly by Lochinvar, who, on the whole, was trying to be good. He would be quiet and respectful, then out of the blue something would intrigue him and he would hound me with a relentless number of questions.

"What's that?" He pointed at a video playing on the wall.

"The video? That's the same as the audience in the stadium, and the wall of the waiting room in the infirmary. I told you then, 'A video.' And the wall of the kitchen, I said when you asked, 'A video.' And the wall on the hallway, 'Still a video.' It's been everywhere, you've seen it now lots, it's a video."

His eyes narrowed. "*What* is it, though? Really what is it?"

"Like um... a light, making an image, telling you a story... right? Does that make sense? It's not real, it's... it's a recording of something that happened... you know what, it's a recording that is telling you a story, that's the best explanation."

"But how is it?"

"How is it telling you a story, or how is it recorded?"

"I daena ken."

"Tomorrow at the lake house we'll put you on a stool in the kitchen with Zach and let him explain everything."

He ignored me and asked, "What's the story?"

I watched it for a moment. "This one is about the battle happening in the outer provinces."

His eyes swept around the image and I wondered if he could actually see it or if it was too abstract. "What is that dark thing up there?"

"That's a drone, they fly around filming the video, or they can shoot—"

"I have seen one before but I daena remember where."

There was a loud explosion on the video, he winced. "The whole thing hurts m'head and m'eyes."

"Yeah, I remember what it was like, but maybe we can just sit quietly for a moment?"

He was quiet for a moment, then he asked, "But how does it fly?"

"What, the drone?" And we were off again.

We left for the rooftop to jump to Maine.

Lochinvar had the Bridge in a messenger bag; we had decided tae put it in a safe house in the twenty-first century.

We arrived at night, and Zach, Quentin, Fraoch, and James, met us. "Welcome back Katie."

I pushed my hair out of my eyes. Magnus was already sitting up.

Quentin asked, "Why is your arm in a sling, boss?"

Magnus winced and explained, "There was this terrible man, he cut me."

Fraoch said, "In an arena?"

"Nae, in the courtyard of Stirling, he was mouthin' off and wouldna calm his arse down. He was askin' tae be run through, but I was tryin' tae be nice, and then he cut m'shoulder. I had tae fight in the arena with a wounded shoulder."

Fraoch said, "Twill teach ye tae be nice."

I mumbled from my jump hangover, "Tell them his name."

Fraoch said, "Who was it? Ormr, Domnall? Some other arsehole?"

Magnus said, "Nae, twas William Wallace."

Quentin said, "I met him! He helped me, I trained him in modern warfare."

"Aye, that is why he wanted more guns, he cut me because he demanded them."

Quentin grimaced. "Shit, that sucks."

"Aye, but I killed him. Ran him through with a sword. He dinna remain dead?"

"Nae, he is still a major player in history."

Magnus exhaled irritatedly. "Well, I got Kaitlyn back."

"Then you came right here?"

"Nae, then I fought in the arena against Domnall and Ormr, they winna be bothering us anymore."

Quentin said, "Sounds great, also sounds like there are a lot of war stories to tell. Let's get you to the house and then you can fill us all in. You brought some ginger dude with you?"

"Aye, this is Lochinvar the Fearsome."

Lochinvar struggled to get up.

Fraoch said, "He is pink as a newborn pig."

Magnus said, "He daena look like much, but he joined me in the arena. He helped me kill Domnall and Ormr."

Fraoch sized him up. "Really? He looks a scrawny as a spring peahen."

Lochinvar moaned. "I am nae so wee, auld man."

Fraoch's eyes went wide and he laughed.

Magnus said, "He is also yet *another* brother."

Fraoch said, "Och, we canna throw a rock without hittin' one."

. . .

We walked to the house through the dark. Archie and Ben came running in their pajamas and Archie threw himself in my arms. I squeezed him tight. "I missed you so freaking much!"

Behind him was Isla, sleepy from waking up to see me. She pushed past her brother, knocked me backwards to my ass on the gravel driveway, climbed into my lap, and burst into tears. Magnus sat down beside us and held Archie. Everyone else walked on toward the house leaving us there in the dark of a summer Maine night, cool but beautiful, on the gravel drive, finally reunited with my bairns. They had missed me desperately.

I had been lost, had felt completely lost, and desperate as well. I was so grateful to be found by my husband, to have the world set right, and have a short rest in the kingdom before coming back home, because it was still so very emotional. I had been lost. I still felt raw. I cried, too.

Then I fished the Matchbox car from my pocket. "Look at this Archie, your car saved my life."

"Really?"

"Yes, I dug through a door with it, I'm sorry it's broken."

"I don't mind, that's cool."

"I was thinking whenever we jump we ought to keep a Matchbox car in our pocket in case of emergencies."

Magnus chuckled. "Archie, tell yer Mum, we ought tae carry a proper weapon in our pocket, then we might hae far less emergencies."

I laughed and hugged Archie and Isla and said, "This is true, but I'm going to make sure I have both."

Finally Magnus stood up, lifted Isla from my lap, and carried her into the house, I held hands with Archie and we walked in together.

Magnus called to Lochinvar, who was standing on the dock alone, looking out over the lake, "Ye ought tae come inside and meet everyone."

Lochinvar strode up the dock toward us. "Ye were right, King Magnus, Florida is verra braw!"

"This inna Florida, ye will see, this is Maine."

"Is this yer kingdom as well?"

"Nae, this is the New World, Lochinvar, here we are not the sons of a king," he held open the screen door for us, "here we are just men."

CHAPTER 62 - KAITLYN

*W*e all hugged and greeted each other and then sat around the dining room table, the one in front of the plate glass window. I said, "Wow, look how many of you there are."

Zach joked, "Don't I know it, so many mouths to feed."

Emma said, "We're almost to the point where we need to hire someone to do the cooking while Zach plans the meals…"

He grabbed his chest. "Are you trying to kill me, Em? You take that back."

She laughed.

I said, "And Magnus and Lochinvar have just arrived and they are very, very hungry."

"Are you?" asked Zach, "Need a midnight snack?"

Magnus said, "Och aye, if it can be ice cream. And we need tae put the Bridge away somewhere."

Zach said, "I know just the place, there's a board loose in the back of a cabinet above the fridge."

Lochinvar pulled the Bridge from his messenger bag and passed it to Zach who said, "So this is the little fella that fixed the world? Wow. You're amazing, little box. Good job. Now I'm hiding you in a dark dusty place."

He walked into the kitchen and we could hear him dragging the step-stool across the floor. Then he called out. "I have vanilla with cookie chunks."

Lochinvar's eyes went wide. "There are cookies here as well?"

Archie said, "There are cookies *everywhere*."

Isla sat on Magnus's lap, but her eyes were glazed over with sleepiness. I whispered, "Do you want to go to bed?"

She shook her head no, her face buried in the folds of his shirt.

Quentin said, "First question, did you feel anything when Lady Mairead used the Bridge? Because none of us felt anything."

Magnus said, "I felt nothing, just instantly Kaitlyn was beside me."

I said, "He was covered in blood, and we were in another king's bed."

Quentin said, "That is insane."

Emma said, "What king?"

"John Balliol."

She said, "Phew, yes, that's what Wikipedia says. There is no mention of you at all, it was freaking me out, but I didn't tell anyone, been keeping that secret since yesterday."

She looked around at all our shocked faces. "Don't be pissed, I just didn't know what it meant. I sort of remembered Magnus was a king in the past, but now I couldn't find a record of it. I wondered if it meant I misremembered, or worse, that something terrible had happened, but either way I waited until I had proof. Here's proof." She gestured to Magnus and me. "Magnus is no longer king in the past."

Magnus exhaled, then looked at Fraoch and shook his head. "All that time and effort in vain, I gained the kingdom of Scotland and lost it in an instant."

Fraoch shrugged, "We could win it again, we just hae tae go—"

Everyone said, "No!"

I said, "No regaining kingdoms and changing history, no leaping, or looping, or... *nothing*, we are going to be calm and chill."

Lochinvar asked, "Queen Kaitlyn, what is chill?"

"That's when we sit around and relax."

His face screwed up in a grimace. "Sounds awful, will there be any cattle reiving? Might we go on a warrin' party along the Viking coast?"

Magnus shook his head, "Nae tae cattle theft, nae tae Viking fights, nae arena battles or fights tae the death — we are on vacation." Zach placed a bowl of ice cream and a bottle of chocolate syrup in front of him. He moaned happily, turned the bottle upside down, dripped chocolate all over the top, then started eating.

Lochinvar watched him, took the bottle, turned it upside down accidentally pouring chocolate everywhere, dripping down the side of the bowl, scowled because his looked different from Magnus's, but took a spoonful up, ate it, and smiled. "I think I did it better King Magnus, ye ought tae try it with more of the sweetness."

Fraoch's brow was drawn down. "And *who* are ye again?"

He had a drip of chocolate on his ginger beard. "I am Lochinvar the Fearsome, second tae King Magnus in the arena during the slaying of Domnall and Ormr, I am a son of Donnan, and brother of Magnus. And ye are?" He took another big bite of ice cream and grinned.

Fraoch flustered. "I am a brother tae Magnus as well, and... ye ken, I rescued him once from a swamp in Florida."

James said, "Lady Mairead took Lochinvar from the castle in exchange for help in releasing Sophie, who, as you see, is home with us, so Lochinvar is welcome, right Fraoch?"

"Aye," Fraoch raised a glass of ice water to Lochinvar. "Tae Og Lochie, for yer help in vanquishing my enemies and deliverin' Sophie home tae our family."

"Ye're welcome, twas naethin', really, I had trained tae fight with Domnall and Ormr. I kent their weaknesses. I saw Magnus was wounded and asked if I could join the fight, and if I did, could I kill them — Lady Mairead said, 'Aye, ye can join,' and I did." He acted out this part, waving his spoon with wild movements. "I sliced Domnall, like this...! Then I fought Ormr, like this!" His spoon plug a bit of chocolate across the table. "And Magnus dealt the death blow through Ormr's stomach as I stabbed m'sword through from the other side, like this! And Ormr died writhin' in the dirt like the mucag he was—"

Beaty said, "Och nae!" She looked at her pig. "Daena listen tae him, Mookie, ye are a noble animal."

Fraoch's brow drew down even more, he muttered, "I dinna get a chance tae kill Ormr or I would hae, I dinna ken twas an option."

We all laughed. Hayley hugged him.

I said to Sophie, "I am very glad you made it home."

She tucked into James's shoulder. "I am verra thrilled tae be home, we hae had a worrisome day with what I learned is too much candy and sweets, I hae a stomach ache, but I am verra much looking forward tae the morrow and exploring this land." She yawned, hiding it behind her hand. "James has said we will get a telescope on the morrow. Did ye ken, we can get a telescope here, if we want one, we only hae tae ask?"

"I did know that, it's a magical shopping world. Where is your other telescope?"

"I daena remember, James and I wondered on it, tis likely... twas left in Dunscaith, but I..." She shrugged. "I am truly nae worried about it, I daena want anyone tae risk their lives for it. Twas nae important compared tae all of ye."

I said, "In the looping it turned up a few times, maybe it will turn up again. Is this the first time you remember being in the modern day?"

She nodded. "Aye, tis verra loud, is it always this loud and bright?"

"Yes, yes it is, but you'll grow used to it." I patted the back of her hand.

Beaty yawned. "I am up verra much later than usual and the bairns will hae me up early, but King Magnus, ye dinna bring what I hae been promised. Ye said you would bring a dog, where is the dog?"

Magnus sighed. "I ken, Madame Beaty, when the time travel shifted Haggis was lost and—"

Beaty's eyes went wide. "But we must go get him, King Magnus! We ought tae put it on yer list as the *verra* first thing."

"I daena ken if it is possible."

James said, "I'm not sure that going to the thirteenth century to find a dog is the first thing we need to do. That's got to be farther down on the list."

She said, "Maybe nae *first* thing, but verra close after."

"Och, we canna go back for the dog, that would be foolish, I ken, I canna even think on it..." Magnus shook his head. "And we daena even ken if tis safe tae time travel on this newly stitched timeline. We need a discovery mission tae figure out how far back we can go."

James said, "I volunteer. I've been thinking about it: I looped and Sophie is out of time. I need to go back and make sure it's all stable. It was my doing, it ought to be me."

Hayley joked, "To be fair you basically broke the world, so yeah, seems like it ought to be you."

"But... is it me all by myself?"

Magnus joked, "Ye canna guilt me, James, I hae an injury and I was many long months in the thirteenth century."

Quentin kissed Beaty's cheek. "I can't go with you, James, I promised Beaty that I would take a vacation, just relax and do nothing."

James sighed. "Without Quennie? I have to go all by myself to test the timeline, without Quennie?"

James looked at Fraoch and batted his eyes.

Fraoch said, "James, it sounds like a wonderful adventure for ye, but Hayley and I hae planned tae go fishin' on the morrow—"

Lochinvar said, "I will go with ye."

Magnus said, "Dost ye ken what ye are volunteering for, Lochinvar?"

He said, "Nae, but ye canna send a man alone tae do it. Ye daena want tae test the fae. They will lie in wait and seduce him, ne'er tae be seen again. I will go along if needed."

Fraoch sighed. "If Og Lochie is goin', then I will do it as well."

Beaty said, "Tis okay Quennie, ye can go with James, but *after*, ye must promise tae relax."

Quentin said, "Beaty, are you saying it's okay, because you think if the timeline is safe, Magnus will go get the dog?"

Beaty said, "I hope he will go get the dog, but also I think we need tae be certain the timeline is safe. If someone comes upon us and we are forced tae jump, we need tae ken that we can trust where we are going. We hae tae ken. Tis verra important."

James nodded. "I'm glad you agree, Beaty. We need this to happen and I'll take Quennie with me. Everyone else can stay and enjoy a little down time. We'll arm up and we'll make sure that we keep it safe, day by day. And no fairy seduction, promise."

Magnus said, "We will make a plan on the morrow."

Emma said, "But for now we all need sleep. Zach and I will give up our room and we can—"

Magnus said, "Ye daena hae tae give up yer room for us. Kaitlyn and I will bunk in the bunkhouse. I think Kaitlyn wants tae be near the bairns since we are newly returned."

She said, "And we can put Lochinvar on the…"

"Lochinvar dost ye want tae sleep on the daybed out on the porch?"

"Aye, looks verra comfortable."

Fraoch said, "We need tae assign him a guard duty, he needs

tae take the middle of the night shift so I can sleep. And has someone taught him tae use the toilets—?"

"He has been with us in the future-future, he's up to speed on some of that."

Lochinvar said, "I am verra hungry."

Zach laughed and went to the kitchen, returning with a box of Oreos and placing them in front of Lochinvar. He said, "Before anyone else asks, there's only a few Oreos left in the box and they're Lochinvar's. Everyone else goes to bed, don't make me regret getting them out, no fighting."

Magnus joked, "Fine, I winna remind ye how long it has been since I hae seen an Oreo cookie." He winked at Archie, who giggled and then yawned.

CHAPTER 63 - KAITLYN

*W*e all went to our rooms. It was a three bedroom house, and one bunkhouse with two bunk beds. Quentin and Beaty had a room, Zach and Emma had one, James and Sophie had one, and Hayley and Fraoch had taken the pull-out sofa in the living room.

Magnus led us into the bunkhouse, Zach carrying Ben, and as we walked through the night I glanced back to see in the dim light of the moon, the lights going off in the house, and Lochinvar as he dropped down onto the daybed on the porch, placing the box of cookies on his stomach.

I said, "He is going to put on fifty pounds in cookie fat if we don't teach him moderation."

Magnus chuckled, "It haena hurt me."

"But you just spent how long in the past?"

"Months, there is a hungry pit in my stomach that is nae satisfied."

Zach groaned. "Now I feel guilty that I didn't give you the Oreos. I will make it up in the morning, I will cook you a breakfast feast of eggs and—"

"Bulgin' waffles?"

"I forgot you called Belgian waffles that." He laughed. "Yes, I might have to go to the store, but hell yeah, Bulging waffles it is."

"There were many a night that I dreamed of them."

We opened the bunk house door and Zach dropped Ben into the top bunk, Archie climbed up into his top bunk, Magnus took a bottom bunk, and I lay down beside Isla. Zach said, "Light on or off?"

I said, "Off, and Zach, we need toothbrushes and stuff, can you add it to the list?"

"Absolutely."

He turned off the light, throwing the room into darkness except for a nightlight-glow coming from the bathroom.

I curled on my side and looked at Magnus across the floor. I put my hand out, but it was four feet away, close, but not quite close enough. He reached out his hand and we entwined our fingers for a moment and then withdrew. "Feels familiar, like that horrible time in the past."

"I ken."

"I'm surprised you didn't opt for one of the bedrooms."

He said, "I dinna want tae pull m'king card. But I do regret leaving the kingdom afore I had a chance tae wander in yer gardens."

I grinned. "There will be plenty of time for that. And I'm glad you did. I did *not* want to stress anyone out with changing rooms, making beds, I just want to sleep."

He whispered, "Aye, we are home, we are on vacation in Maine, and the bairn hae needed us, our long lingerin' meander through yer gardens will hae tae wait."

I whispered, "A long lingering meander? How long, like really long, like longer than I can handle? And by lingering do you mean… like *really* lingering, like excruciatingly long lingering, and… meander, oh how I love meanders. You're being so sensible and humble and it's actually kind of hot and…"

He laughed, "Och, ye hae turned the words long and lingering and meander intae foreplay."

I whispered, "*Maybe,* if you're lucky, we can find a place with a locking door in the morning for a bit of Good-Morn Master Magnus."

Through the dark room, the comforting sound of his voice whispering, "A night in a bunk, under m'son as he snores, a Good-Morn Master Magnus awaiting me from m'wife, who I hae missed terribly, and then a bulgin' waffles breakfast? I am the luckiest king in the world." There was a bonking noise from the foot of his bed.

He chuckled. "The bed is verra short."

I giggled, and then yawned and curled up around Isla and fell asleep.

The following morning Isla woke up, climbed on me, looked down, and said, "Mommy I am glad you here."

"I'm glad I'm here too."

She climbed off the bed and climbed up Archie's ladder, "Archie!" She called to the other top bunk, "Ben! We have to wake up now, it's morning."

Archie groaned. "It's early Isla."

"If we don't get up we will miss the loons and we have to see the loons. Beaty said it's magical, the loons only laugh in this one place in the whole wide world."

Archie and Ben climbed down their ladders. Archie said, "Morning Da, Mammy."

"Good morning," we said.

Ben and Archie went into the bathroom.

Isla said, "I go get Zoe and Beaty." I glanced over at Magnus, his eyes twinkling.

I whispered, "They are almost all out…"

Finally the door clicked behind them, Magnus said, "I hae missed them terribly and I thought they would never leave."

I jumped up from the bunk and accidentally bonked my

head, "Ow! Holy moley, that hurt!" I rubbed the spot as I locked the bunkhouse door. I climbed over onto Magnus's bed and sat astride him, hunched because of the low bunk above me.

I said, "It's going to *have* to be a Good-Morn Master Magnus because we cannot get acrobatic in these bunks." I kissed his nose and trailed my lips down his chest.

He said, "I think we can do anythin' we like tae do, and if m'wife wants tae do flips and spins I think I will figure it out."

I giggled, "Flips and spins? Ha!" I drew my lips to his waist and pulled his pajama pants down his legs. "The good thing about Good-Morn Master Magnus is that it doesn't require acrobatics at all and *how* long were you in the past without me?"

"Months and months, so many long months."

"*That's* why…" I settled down between his legs. "For our lack of space, I'm taking one for the team and giving you a Good-Morn Master Magnus all for yourself."

His eyes twinkled. "I will get ye back the next time."

"Oh definitely," I said, as I took him in my mouth, my tongue up and down the length of him, his fingers entwined in my hair, his low moans. I brought him to a climax, with some long lingering of my own… Then I lay my cheek on him and rested there. I was content, so happy, but also, for some reason, overwhelmed. "I missed you so much, I was so scared."

"I ken, I was as well." He pulled me up to lay on his chest. An arm around me, his lips pressed to my forehead. "We hae tae make sure nae one loops, tis a terrifyin' thing tae hae our memories turned inside out like that."

I nodded.

He said, "The good news is, though, I thought twas Domnall or Ormr that were causing it, but twas James. I find comfort in that we are the center of the timeline, *we* are the ones that create the chaos and also the calm."

"That's a good point, the vessels are ours, and you are the king of all time."

"I used tae be king of all time, now I am back tae just a man, king in the future, but just a man in the present. I just had a braw Good-Morn from m'wife and now I'm going tae hae a feast. We canna be sad."

"We canna be sad!" I wiped my eyes on my arm and jumped from the bed. "I love you." I kissed him. "Let's get you something to eat."

CHAPTER 64- KAITLYN

*W*hen I got outside there was a strange car in the driveway with its trunk open and grocery bags overfilling it. There were more bags in the back seat, there was a lovely young woman making trips in and out of the house along with Emma.

I said, "Hi!" as I went into the kitchen where Zach was shoving food into any cupboard that would fit it. The young woman laughed. "How many people is this now? I've been delivering groceries here twice a day all week."

Emma counted on her fingers. "Fourteen, I think."

I said, "Lochinvar makes fifteen."

"Fifteen and some of them are very hungry." Emma introduced me, "Kaitlyn, matriarch of the house, just arrived—"

"I'm the motherfucking matriarch." I clamped my mouth shut. "Sorry about that."

The young woman smiled. "No worries."

Emma said, "This is Tracy, she delivered our groceries the first day, and now I have her on speed dial. Because Zachary will not plan two meals ahead."

Zach grumbled, "I want to make everyone special food, what

they want, when they want it, to do that I have to keep my options open."

"Nice to meet you, Tracy." She went out to the car for the last load with Emma following.

Zach was struggling to close a cabinet door, a box fell out onto the counter. He joked, "Guess we gotta eat what's in that box first. This is a tiny kitchen."

I said, "Somehow Grandma Barb managed to cook whole meals here."

"For fifteen?"

"Rarely."

Soon coffee was brewed. Zach said, "Once you have your coffee you have to move to the other side of the room, stop hounding me, I'm trying to get these waffles made."

Emma made a coffee for Lochinvar, black.

Fraoch seeing that said, "I want mine black as well."

Hayley said, "You usually love cream in yours?"

He scowled, "Nae, I want mine black this morn."

We stood around the kitchen table drinking coffee. Emma casually said, "It's going to be even more crowded in here tomorrow, I just hired Tracy to come help you cook, Zachary."

He dropped a pan. "What? You hired someone to come help... what?"

"Don't look shocked, or offended, you need the help. Do you want one of us to help you?"

"No, that is... no, I—"

"Beaty helps with the kids, you don't like me to help, Quentin and James aren't good at cooking or taking orders from you, Hayley hates it. Want Kaitlyn or Magnus to help?"

"No, don't be ridiculous."

"So you need help, at least while we're on vacation, so you can relax too."

Zach scoffed dramatically. "I don't need to fucking relax, does she even know how to cook?"

"She said she cooks at home, but that's unimportant, she

needs the work. She's delivering groceries, and I think she's great. I asked if she would come and help you make meals."

Zach sputtered. "I feel insulted."

Emma looked around. "Does anyone in this house think that I asked Tracy to come help Zach because I think he's incompetent?"

We all shook our heads.

Beaty said, "She asked her tae help ye, Chef Zach. I daena think ye ought tae take it as an insult. In the castle kitchen there were ten people makin' the meals."

"But here there are… now I've got Madame Beaty ganging up on me." He huffed as he pulled a tray of warming waffles from the oven and started scraping scrambled eggs off a pan into a bowl. "Does she have *any* restaurant cooking experience?"

Emma said, "Zachary, would you like me to go to town and get you a trained chef to come in here and you can have all kinds of issues, arguments, and power struggles over whose kitchen it is? Or do you want me to hire someone who wants the work and is willing to let you run things and tell them what to do."

He pouted. "The second one, I guess."

"Exactly, Tracy will be here tomorrow morning to help you make breakfast. Don't worry, it will be like the castle kitchen at Kilchurn, you've been missing Eamag, this is to give you someone to talk to."

Zach said, "Fine, I suppose this is acceptable, as long as everyone knows that I *can* do the cooking by myself, I'm just choosing not to because we're on a relaxing vacation. And by the way, your five-course breakfast is ready."

We piled waffles, eggs, sausages, fruit, toast, and bacon on our plates and all went out to the porch to eat.

At the table Quentin said, "Now that you have kitchen staff, what are you going to do with all your free time, Zach?"

He groaned. "I don't *want* free time, but probably swimming with Ben and Zoe. Why?"

Quentin said, "Because once I get back from my trip with James, Beaty asked me to take some time to relax and do things that are not security related, and I am having a hard time figuring out what that is."

Beaty said, "Swimming, or ye could paddle around on the boats, or ye could go for a walk in the meadows. Ye could play board games with the bairns."

Fraoch said, "Ye could go fishin', Hayley and I are goin' tae fish."

He narrowed his eyes, "Yeah, no, none of that…"

James said, "We're going to leave in a couple of hours, we'll be back tomorrow."

Quentin took a big bite of sausage. "Yeah, I'll figure it out then, for now there's a lot to do."

Magnus said, "Ye can take the gold threads so ye are rested when ye jump. Zach will send some vitamins with ye."

I grabbed a notebook and a pen. "Emma and I will come up with a list of dates. The origination date of the vessels is November 1, 1557. So first we want you to jump to October 31, 1557. If your vessel disappears, you'll wait for a day, you'll miss your return date and someone here with a vessel and the Trailblazer will mount a rescue. But if your vessel is still there, awesome, you'll jump to the next date. If your vessel is gone, wait there. If you don't return someone will go back with the Trailblazer to the first date, then the second date, then the third and fourth until they find you." I circled a date, and wrote a check mark beside another.

James said, "Just not 1589, not Dunscaith castle, no looping for me."

I said, "Exactly. We'll pick safe dates, and uncomplicated destinations. If you go to each of those dates and you have a vessel you won't need a rescue, that's great, if not, stay there, don't move, we'll come get you — using the Trailblazer, and so on, until you get to 1290."

Quentin said, "Who's using the Trailblazer in this scenario?"

I said, "It sounds like Lochinvar, Magnus, and Fraoch."

Fraoch groaned.

Lochinvar shoveled in a forkful of waffles and moaned happily, "Does all the food taste as if God placed heaven upon it?"

Magnus said, "Just Chef Zach's food — his is the best."

Lochinvar said, "Ye want me tae use the Trailblazer? If I can come back and hae these fancy cakes with honey sauce and whipped clouds, I will do anythin' ye ask of me."

Fraoch said, "Ye are only sayin' it because ye haena done it before."

We stayed long at the table, eating breakfast and drinking coffee, but then we began loading up food and supplies for James and Quentin. Zach packed a cooler and Quentin went to town, returning with a small, non-military ATV. We were able to pack some supplies on it.

He said, "It's noisy though, we can't drive it around, but it will work for escapes."

Sophie said, "Escapes!"

James said, "It's for worst case scenarios. We're only going in and out of time periods, checking the path. Quentin's packed a couple of beacons, we'll put them out wherever we land, and if I have any trouble, I'll just stay tight. Fraoch and Magnus and Lochinvar will come for us. Right, that's the plan?" He looked around. "Sophie is nervous so we need to make sure she knows, that's the plan. Someone promises to come, right?"

Magnus nodded. "Of course, we will come for ye."

Fraoch said, "That's the plan, we will be ready tae go if ye daena return on the morrow."

CHAPTER 65 - KAITLYN

*I*t took all day to pack the stuff, many meetings to plan the strategy, there was a printed calendar with dates, times, and a ton of research to come up with the coordinates of out-of-the-way time-jump zones.

I spoke to Sophie after dinner, "Are you very nervous about James leaving?"

She said, "Aye, but he will return verra soon, on the morrow, and I will make m'self busy with the bairns until then."

I said, "This is a very weird situation because I have memories of you that you don't have. They're fading though, it's like they're weak."

"I ken, I was speaking with Master James about it. He has memories of mourning me, and yet I am here. Tis verra complicated." She looked down at her feet. "I dinna want tae say anything, but because of losing me, James is verra frightened. He was pretending earlier when he was persuading *me* tae be brave. He daena want anyone tae ken, but he is desperately afraid of losin' me again. This is why he is so determined tae go on this test of the timeline. He is worried that if the timeline inna stable I will simply disappear."

She looked out over the lake. "I daena ken how tae help him, he is afraid something will happen tae me, but he canna say what it is, he needs tae relax, tae 'chill', is that what ye call it? Tae chill?"

"Exactly, you want him to chill." I added, "I don't know how to help him either, except that with time he will relax, once he knows the timeline is stable he'll feel more secure. We hope. And those memories will fade for him too. Then he will totally chill."

James came down to the dock to check on her and she smiled, and they wandered toward the clearing to kiss goodbye.

And then James and Quentin were gone.

The following morning Tracy came to help. Emma helped her get acquainted with Zach's needs, then said, "I'll be out on the porch, if you need help with anything, tell Zach. If Zach is who you need help with, just come outside and yell, 'Emma!' and I'll come running. He curses all the time, my apologies in advance."

Tracy said, "That's okay, he dropped five f-bombs when I delivered groceries yesterday, I won't be surprised."

Emma said, "See Zachary, you're going to get along great."

Zach said, "Hope you like music." He cranked up the volume. "It's the Idles, you gotta have it on loud."

Tracy squinted her eyes and pursed her lips. "I've never heard of them."

"Greatest band in the world. So fun, you gotta listen to the lyrics."

She said, "I don't know about *that*... I like hip hop, have you heard..." Emma and I hightailed it out of the kitchen before the coming music debate really heated up.

Fraoch and Hayley went fishing at dawn. Emma, Sophie, Beaty and I took the kids for a brisk morning swim. Zach was calm and there had even been laughing coming from the kitchen. Breakfast was called.

We put a plate out for Tracy and she asked, "I can eat with you?"

I said, "Yes, we all eat, we all help, I mean, I know that's a weird thing to say because none of us want to help Zach in the kitchen because he's just so... *territorial.*"

Magnus sat down at the table with a big plate of food.

Lochinvar sat beside him. He watched Magnus's every move: how he filled his plate, what he chose, and the order he ate it in.

Fraoch served himself then turned around and said, "Och nae!"

Hayley asked, "What do you need, love of my life?"

He pointed with his utensils. "He has taken my seat."

"Who has?"

"Og Lochie has taken m'seat, I sit tae the left of Og Maggy, near the whipped cream. Tis better for me so I daena hae tae reach and I can see out the window at the loch."

Lochinvar looked around confused.

Hayley said, "You can sit on this side, just this once, right?"

He dropped his plate in front of the nearest seat. "But I canna see the loch, I winna ken if the fish are tuggin' on my pole."

Magnus clapped him on the shoulder. "Twill be good, Fraoch, we will sort it out later."

Lochinvar scooped some whipped cream onto a pancake, poured cereal onto it, and ate it with a spoon. "These are delicious!" He asked, "Why are we fishing, if the food tastes like this? How can ye like tae eat fish when ye can eat sweet circles and cookies with whipped cream whenever ye want?"

Fraoch looked outraged. "Of course ye want fish, fish is the greatest food tae eat! They are just in the water, wanting tae be brought tae shore tae feed ye. Ye hae tae like fish better than any other foods!" He made a great effort to turn around and point at the lake. "There is so much food, right there, the best food."

Hayley asked, timidly, "Is this truly true, my love?"

"Och, ye are goin' tae question me in front of…?" He jerked his head toward Lochinvar.

"No, I mean, I know fish is good but aren't you a wee little bit overstating it?"

"Nae, not at all, Og Maggy, back me up, ye like fish, daena ye?"

"Well, Fraoch, ye ken, I ate a lot of fish in m'time away. I think I do verra much like hamburgers and ice cream. This breakfast is verra good, too, pancakes and syrup with sausage and whipped cream."

"Och, ye are takin' a side against me."

Magnus said, "Tis nae purposeful, I just canna believe ye would take the side of 'fish is better than all other food'. Hae ye tasted blueberries with whipped cream and a bit of sugar?"

Fraoch scowled. "Ye are a sweet boy with yer love of sweet foods."

Magnus said, "I like what I like."

Tracy asked, "Lochinvar, where have you been that you haven't eaten cereal before?"

We all looked at him with apprehension. *What would he say?*

He answered, "I lived on Isle of Skye, we dinna hae these — what are they called?"

Zach quickly said, "Honey Nut Cheerios and homemade whipped cream?"

"Aye, Cheery-nut-os with cream, we dinna hae them."

"Oh, for a second there I thought you meant you never had cereal at all! That would have been so weird, I think everyone in the world has had a bowl of cereal, maybe not with whipped cream." She asked, "Well, what's next?"

Zach said, "We do some dishes and then you're off for an hour until lunch and then you come back in the afternoon, when we make dinner. Tonight's dinner will be light, because—"

The men all groaned.

Zach raised his fist and pretended to threaten them all to be quiet.

Emma smiled. "If you don't want to drive too much you can swim, whatever, read a book, do what kids do these days."

She said, "*Seriously?* I can come, do a bit of work at breakfast, and then at lunch, and then dinner and you're paying me a full giant salary?"

Zach jokingly put his finger to his lips. "Shhhhh, I *know*, pretend like we're busier than we are, it's the only way I keep the guise up."

CHAPTER 66 - KAITLYN

*L*ater I found Magnus in the room we had given to James and Sophie. He said, "I was verra tired, Sophie said I could take a nap in here. Tae think I need a nap between breakfast and lunch like a bairn."

"You're still healing. Can I come join?"

"Aye." He patted the bed beside him.

I kicked off my shoes and curled up there, in my sweats. "This is a nice vacation. I wasn't expecting one, I didn't plan — I have a million lists of 'things to do on vacation' but here we are on a surprise one and it's nice. I like the birds singing and the kids laughing, and the water rocking the dock. It's lovely."

"I ken, I hope Master Cook and Colonel Quentin return with no incident and that all is well so I daena hae tae leave tae rescue them. There hae been too many rescues a'ready."

"So true."

He was quiet, then he said, "For many long months, whenever I slept, Haggis would sleep right beside my feet."

"You miss him, huh?"

"Aye, we were in many a battle taegether, he was a fellow soldier."

I chuckled, nestling my head into his shoulder. "And you didn't want a dog."

"Aye, I hae learned a lesson, I dinna ken what a good friend he would be. He was an excellent listener."

"What did you talk about?"

"We talked a great deal about steaks, because I was hungry. He had never tasted one afore. I told him about soft beds and warm houses."

"Those are all things you love."

He chuckled. "Aye, Haggis would love them too, he and I hae a great deal in common. We spoke of it on those long nights in the rain, looking out over a battlefield — he dinna want much, I wish I could give him a steak and a warm house, he risked a great deal for me."

"He sounds like he was great."

"Aye, he was a cù math, a good dog."

He kissed the top of my head, his lips pressed there as he fell asleep.

When we woke from our nap I came out to the kitchen and Zach was organizing cupboards and making a list. "Whatcha doing?"

He said, "Waiting for Tracy to get here so we can make lunch."

"How is she, was Emma right?"

"Of course Emma was fucking right, Emma is *always* right, but don't tell her I said so. Tracy is great, her only drawback is that she has terrible taste in music. She calls it *eclectic*, I told her it sounded like fucking jazz and I wasn't going to stand for it in my kitchen. She alluded to me being old. I'm a millennial, I'm not old."

"You're also a dad in his thirties with two kids. She's what, twenty? I think you're old in comparison."

He joked, "For *that* you get out of my kitchen, this is a

Zach-bashing free zone. Only Zach adulation allowed, no complaints, no criticisms."

Lochinvar was sitting on the end of the dock and the kids were all around him, Zoe with her floaty arm bands, the boys, and Isla, they all looked like they were listening to him tell a long interesting story.

I leaned against Magnus's shoulder up at the outdoor sitting area. "What do you think Lochinvar is telling them?"

We watched for a few moments and then Lochinvar started making a stabbing motion in the air excitedly. It looked like Zoe burst into tears.

Magnus said, "Och, I better intervene."

We rushed down the lawn tae the dock. Beaty had scooped up Zoe. Magnus picked up Isla whose eyes were huge. Magnus asked Zoe, "Och, wee bairn, what are ye crying about?" She shook her head and clung to Beaty.

I asked, "Archie, what's going on?"

"Lochinvar was telling us a story about when dad killed Domnall and Ormr in the stadium."

Magnus said, "Och nae, Lochinvar, ye canna tell the bairns these stories. Tis too frightening!"

Lochinvar pointed at Archie. "This one is almost a man, he's going to have a sword soon enough."

I said, "Dear god, I hope not!"

Beaty said, "Come on bairns, we all will go up and get some treats from the house."

I looked at Magnus, and he said, "I will handle it with Lochinvar."

I saw Fraoch pulling his canoe up tae the side of the lawn.

CHAPTER 67 - MAGNUS

J said, "Lochinvar, these kids are bairns and ye canna
tell them scary things about death and murder, ye
canna."

"Magnus, ye are raisin' yer son tae be weak, he is tae be a
prince, he will hae tae fight in the arena."

"I am nae, he has seen more death and destruction than
most wee'uns his age. Ye canna think him weak, he is protected.
He is gaining strength, he is nae ready tae—"

"At his age I had a sword in m'hand and was training every
day."

"But here ye are tae be a modern man, do ye like the food?
Ye ken ye like it. Twas modern men that made it. Tae live among
them and enjoy their food and homes and the warmth and the
soft bed and hot water, ye must follow their modern rules. One
is ye canna kill anyone, ye canna even fight. Once Quentin fired
a gun at an enemy and he was held in jail as a criminal for a
time. The rules are verra strict on this. When ye are in the
modern world ye hae tae put yer weapons aside, but ye also hae
tae think on…"

Fraoch walked up. "What're ye talkin' on?"

"I am explainin' tae Lochinvar about how tae behave in the modern world."

Fraoch said, "Tis easy, Og Lochie, ye do the opposite of what ye might think tae do. If ye are goin' tae take a piss, and ye think, here is a good place — it probably inna a good place. And importantly, ye hae tae be much cleaner than ye think ye ought."

I laughed because his feet were covered in mud from the shoreline.

Fraoch looked down. "Tis a lesson that is hard tae remember. But ye hae tae remember it tae get along with the Moderns."

I laughed again, "I had forgotten that is what we called them when we were in the past together all those long months."

"We are the Historics, they are the Moderns. The Moderns have a way about them that is hard tae understand but ye must, tae live here."

Lochinvar narrowed his eyes. "Are ye sayin' ye daena hae tae fight here?"

Magnus said, "I am sayin' we hae tae guard, we hae tae protect, sometimes we are in a great deal of danger, but if we live in modern times we must pretend we arna doin' any of it."

Lochinvar screwed up his face.

Fraoch said, "We are only advisin' ye. Ye daena hae tae listen, but we will drop ye off in the eighteenth century and then ye will regret ye dinna listen when ye are back tae eatin' blood sausage and—"

Lochinvar said, "I like blood sausage."

Fraoch retched. "Figures, Og Lochie, tis yer problem because ye daena like fish."

Lochinvar's eyes traveled up the driveway where Tracy was parkin' and stepping from her car tae help with the meal. I said, "And ye canna be interested in modern women, if ye canna behave. They are verra tricky, ye must ken and follow many rules."

The screened door banged behind Tracy as she walked inside.

Fraoch shook his head. "I daena think Og Lochie can handle a modern woman, I think we ought tae return him tae the past."

Lochinvar said, "What are the rules?"

Fraoch said, "Ye daena get tae decide if they like ye, if they want ye. Ye hae tae ask nicely."

I chuckled. "Tis true. Ye hae tae ken tae be gentle with them."

Lochinvar said, "I can do that."

I said, "Perhaps, but tis far more likely ye daena even ken what I mean by 'gentle'. I think that ye ought tae wait until we take ye tae the Earl's castle, Balloch. We will go soon, I will introduce ye tae my sister and brother and the Earl and ye can live there with them. Twill nae be as confusing as this time, ye will get along verra well I think. And Lizbeth will set about finding ye a woman." I clapped him on the back. "In the meantime, ye must leave our kitchen assistant alone, and ye canna tell dark murderous tales tae the bairns. Ye must listen more than ye speak."

"Aye, King Magnus, but ye ought tae make sure ye change the rules about the challenges tae yer kingdom, I took an oath tae protect ye and yer son, but he is already almost a man and he canna lift a sword yet—"

Fraoch said, "He is barely seven years auld! He is too wee — Och, this is what Og Maggy was just saying, listen more, Og Lochie, daena speak if ye are going tae be an—"

I interrupted, "I will change the rules in the kingdom, we will all agree that Archie is too young tae fight, and Lochinvar, ye will listen more. Now how about we go tell Chef Zach that we are hungry and we can share some treats with the bairns so they will forgive yer story earlier."

CHAPTER 68 - KAITLYN

*H*ayley was standing near the house phone when it rang, we all looked shocked, because frankly I didn't know it worked. She said, jokingly, "What do I do?"

"Answer it… I think."

She said hello and yes and yes and um… and um…

She put her hand over the receiver. "It's Joe Munro, what am I going to do?" She waved Fraoch over for support.

Then she said, "Yes sir, yes, I know sir. Yes, I know, Lady Mairead is a special lady, yes sir." She put her hand over the receiver again and said to Fraoch, "He wants to talk to Lady Mairead about the letters and book we left."

Fraoch's eyes went wide. He said to Magnus, "Tis the man we robbed for the Bridge."

Hayley continued, "Yes, of course. I… yes he's here. Yes. Okay, yes. Okay at seven."

She hung up and called into the kitchen. "Um, Zach, we have company for dinner."

He stuck his head around the corner. "Who?"

"Um, Finch Mac and his wife and son and her mother and father and her sister, are all coming. Apparently Lady Mairead explained that Fraoch and Magnus are Finch Mac's brother and now he wants to meet us and… yeah."

Magnus said, "This is the man ye broke intae his house and stole his things?"

Fraoch said, "Aye."

Magnus said, "Then it needs tae be a verra fine meal."

Hayley said, "He seemed to think the letter from Lady Mairead explained it well enough, he was blown away by what she gave him, like *really* excited, but still… he said Finch Mac left his tour to come home and yeah, we robbed them, broke the window and…"

Beaty said, "Finch Mac? He will be here? Finch Mac, dost ye think… Finch Mac! I hae tae dye m'hair, the blue is too faded!"

I looked down. We were all wearing sweats and t-shirts. It was all we had, basic clothes, the bare essentials all bought from Walmart.

Magnus said, "We ought tae clean up."

Zach said, "Tracy and I will grill, sound good?"

Tracy had been looking back and forth from all our faces. "You guys stole from Finch Mac and now he's coming here?"

Zach said, "Yep, it's a pretty ordinary day-in-the-life for us, the point is, it's going to be great." He counted in the air. "Twenty! I think this is dinner for twenty people. Wait… twenty-one? Or no, nineteen…? How many?" He counted on his fingers.

I said, "But… but… we're waiting for James and Quentin, they could arrive at any time, we can't do this… we can't have company while we're doing this! Call him back and tell him—"

Hayley's eyes went wide. "I can't tell Joe Munro no! He wants to talk to us about the items Lady Mairead left for them, and Finch Mac is upset and wants to meet his brothers. I didn't know what to say! What could I have said?"

"I don't know? Like we were going out of town."

"He knew our home number!"

I sighed. "I suppose there's nothing we can do. And how bad can it be? They must not be too angry, they're bringing the whole family." I looked around at all the kids. "What are you waiting for, everyone get pretty for Finch Mac!"

We all raced around straightening up the house and getting it ready for company. I said to Hayley, when we passed. "Do you have any idea what Lady Mairead said in her letter to Joe Munro? How much did she tell him?"

"I have no idea. There was a stack of priceless letters, a book, I think it was a journal from the Earl of Breadalbane, and her letter had a wax seal."

I said, "We have to say *nothing* until they let us know what they know."

To say we were excited was an understatement. We were also nervous.

We were worried though too, about James and Quentin. I asked Magnus when he was staring at the far edge of the lake. "Wouldn't you think James and Quentin should already be here?"

He said, "Aye, but there are still hours remaining in the day."

I passed Hayley and Fraoch in the living room. "They should be here, right?"

She said, "Soon, I think, I'm not worried yet, late afternoon, then I get worried."

Fraoch mumbled. "I should hae gone with them."

Hayley said, "Then you would be lost too! Plus you're part of the rescue if they're not back."

"Aye," he scrubbed his hands down his face. "Me and Magnus, using the Trailblazer, twill be good."

"And Lochinvar."

He scowled.

. . .

I looked at the clock on the wall. "They need to come, we don't want to mount a rescue. We want all of it to be good, a normal life for once, for the timeline to be ordered and stable."

Beaty walked through the room. "I hae been praying on it, Queen Kaitlyn, I haena asked for m'self, but for the bairns, for there tae be peace and a timeline that is nae in disarray, tae calm our minds."

"Yes, we need to calm our minds."

Beaty dyed her hair a vivid blue. Sophie helped and had blue hair-dye staining her hands. Beaty was frantically tying a bow around Mookie's neck. "Ye must be handsome, Finch Mac is comin'!"

We met to talk about our story. Sophie asked, "Why haena James and Quentin returned yet?"

Magnus said, "They will be back soon, I am sure of it, daena worry."

I said, "Again, how the hell did any of this happen?"

We all looked over at Hayley.

She said, "I panicked!"

I said, "We just need to concentrate, get our stories straight. We are all just normal people here on vacation, right?"

Hayley said, "Someone needs to coach the kids, no time travel."

Fraoch said, "Make sure Og Lochie daena run his mouth, he is goin' tae start trouble."

Hayley said, "When did everyone move here from Scotland? Make sure you have a date set in your mind."

Magnus said, "I moved here in 2017, Kaitlyn and I are the Duke and Duchess of Awe."

Fraoch said, "When did that happen, Og Maggy?"

"Lady Mairead arranged for us tae receive the title, she told me about it when I was in the hospital." He looked around at our disbelief. "Tis a real current title, ye can see it listed in Burke's Peerage."

He joked, "But be quiet on it, I am going tae tell Colonel Quentin I hae *always* been the Duke of Awe, he will think tis maddening and twill be funny."

Fraoch said, "I moved here three years later."

Magnus said, "And Lochinvar is fresh, movin' here just the other day." We looked over at Lochinvar, flicking the light switch up and down confusedly.

Magnus added, "Lochinvar, be verra verra quiet."

Lochinvar switched the lights off. "Aye, I will listen more and speak less, like ye said — how does this light work?"

I ignored him. "What if James and Quentin return while we are at dinner?"

Magnus said, "Fraoch and I will discreetly go up tae the field tae meet them."

We all checked our watches or the clock on the wall.

I said, "Where are they? Shouldn't they be back by now?"

Emma said, "Some of us need to change. We are wearing so many sweats, in too many colors, we look ridiculous."

CHAPTER 69 - KAITLYN

*A*n Escalade pulled up in front of the house with six people inside. They all stepped out and congregated at the top of the sloping lawn.

Magnus and I shook hands and introductions were made. Joe said, "The Duke and Duchess of Awe, I've read about it in the peerage, what a long glorious history your title and lands have. It's really great to meet you."

Magnus said, "Aye, tis a pleasure to meet you as well."

Finch Mac was big and handsome, tall, and had a glow of celebrity around him. That had been what we called it when I lived in LA: the celebrity glow. He wore rock star clothes, all very expensive, designer. His wife, Karrie, was beautiful. Their son, Arlo, was cute and about the same age as Ben and Archie. Finch Mac had a Scottish accent and when he shook Magnus's hand he said, "Joe tells me we're brothers?"

Magnus said, "Aye, tis a surprise tae me as well. This is our half-brother Fraoch, and also, our half-brother, Lochinvar."

Finch said, "I went from an only child tae havin' three brothers."

"Och aye, our father, Donnan was a real…"

Finch said, "A player, an arse, a piece of shit?"

Magnus smiled. "Aye, all of that, I am verra glad ye agree."

Finch shook Fraoch's hand. "I heard ye stole somethin' from me?"

Fraoch ran a hand over his beard. "Och, m'apologies, I..."

Finch said, "M'father-in-law, Joe, inna much bothered by the robbery, he has a pile of new historical artifacts tae be excited about. But I hae been receiving threats... I dinna ken what they meant, but now... this is why we rushed home from m'tour." He looked around.

Magnus said, "We ought tae sit down so we can talk."

We led them to the picnic tables and I introduced Arlo to Archie, Ben, Zoe, and Isla, and they went down to the dock together.

Finch continued, "Being famous, I have had tae be on guard, there are always threats, but recently there hae been threats related tae m'father, Donnan. M'mum warned me, never talk about m'father, we were supposed tae be secretive about him. But the threats kent about Donnan and sent a chill down my spine. The threats mentioned ye, Magnus, and I dinna ken ye — it dinna make sense, until I heard from Joe that yer mother, Lady Mairead, had visited the house. It all clicked intae place."

His wife, Karrie, held his hand and lay her head on his shoulder.

Magnus said, "Dost ye ken who they were?"

"There was a man going by Ormr, he showed up at the Vegas show. A woman named Jeanne Smith—"

Magnus said, "Fraoch, this was yer mother's alias?"

Fraoch said, "Aye, and when she is using her alias she is up tae nae good."

Magnus said, "Finch, some of the things ye hae stored at Joe's house are wanted by dangerous people. I hae been trying tae locate all of them. My apologies about the theft but once we kent ye had the artifact in yer possession we needed tae get it tae safety. We felt as if it couldna wait." He said to Emma, "Can you get the Bridge from the house for us, Madame Emma?"

She went inside, then returned with the Bridge, and placed it in the middle of the table. Magnus put his hand on top and it clicked open. He locked it again. "Fraoch, put yer hand there." Fraoch triggered the box to open. Then Magnus had Lochinvar open the box. Then Finch. Magnus said, "No one else can open the box, only sons of Donnan."

Finch nodded, chewing his lip. "So havin' this in m'father-in-law's house could hae been dangerous?"

Magnus said, "Aye."

Finch said, "Ye arna goin' tae tell me what it does?"

"Which are ye more likely tae believe, that it is an intricate paternity test, devised by our father, Donnan? Perhaps it is a time travel device? Or Maybe it is just a box and ye ought nae know what else it does?"

Finch said, "I don't believe any of those, one is ridiculous, one is impossible. The last is boring."

"Aye, true." Magnus nodded. "Let me put it in m'safe, I will keep it from falling intae the wrong hands."

Finch pushed the box away. "Aye, I agree, I daena want it, it's too much tae worry about. But if I give it tae ye, that's the end of it, right? Nae one is going to come after us?"

"Aye, this is what they wanted. Unless... unless ye hae anything else?" Magnus pulled a vessel from his pocket. "Ye hae one of these? We ought tae put that in my safe as well."

Joe said, "I have one of those. I could give it to Lady Mairead when we meet. Will she still meet me?"

Magnus said, "Aye, she is lookin' forward tae it, she would love tae hae an audience for her stories. And m'apologies for the trouble with yer window. I will pay tae replace it."

Finch said, "Good, thank ye." Finch said to Joe, "Does that make up for the robbery?"

Joe waved his hand "Yes, sure, it's already forgotten."

Emma asked, with her phone in her hand, "Do you take Venmo? I'll go ahead and pay you now."

Magnus said, "Ye ought tae build better cases and hae a

stronger security system, I hear much of what ye hae stored there is priceless. The sword for instance, Fraoch tells me it is worth a great deal."

Finch Mac chuckled, "Nae need, we hae removed the rest of the artifacts, they are stored somewhere more secure. Daena come lookin' for them."

Magnus laughed. "We winna. But if ye need anything stored with me, let me know. Lady Mairead for one has an extensive art collection, she kens how tae keep it safe."

Joe said, "She is a lovely woman, so knowledgeable about the history of Scotland. I look forward to meeting with her, did you hear what she gave me?"

"Nae, what was it?"

"The lost casket letters! It's amazing, I have the lost casket letters in my possession!"

Lydia said, "You'll need to explain what those are, dear."

"Mary Queen of Scots wrote letters to the Earl of Bothwell that were used to incriminate her, they ultimately led to her beheading. Many assumed they were faked, but the letters were lost so if they were real or fake, it couldn't be proven. There were copies that have been passed down through history, but no way to know if the originals were real and—"

Lydia rolled her hand for her husband to hurry.

He finished with, "Lady Mairead gave me the originals! I, Joe Munro, will get to the bottom of it: were they faked, were they real? It'll be me!" He rubbed his hands together. "It could take *years* of research!"

Zach called over, "Dinner will be ready really soon!"

Magnus said, "Thank ye Chef Zach."

Joe said, "She also gave me a book that was..." He shook his head. "Breathtaking, it's the journal of the Earl of Breadalbane, absolutely fascinating."

Lydia Munro said, "Ha! You said it was infuriating."

"It's both fascinating and infuriating. It opened my eyes to a part of the Earl of Breadalbane's life I never knew before. It also basically makes my life's work useless. I'm going to have to go back and revise the whole thing."

Karrie's little sister, Tessa said, "Dad, we talked about this, just write a volume two!"

Lydia said, "Better yet, tell the story of his sister, it can dispute the facts of his life, but that's part of history, right? To tell *all* sides of the story."

Magnus chuckled. "Lady Mairead would love tae hae ye tell her side of the — I mean, her ancestor's side of the story. I am sure she looks forward tae meetin' with ye on it."

I said, "She thinks the Earl gets too much credit. She believes Lady Mairead has the better story of the two."

"Well, I have my gears turning, I was going to write about the king of Scotland, Mag Mòr but—"

Magnus sprayed beer, coughing. "My apologies, I was…"

Fraoch joked, "I had the same reaction."

Hayley nudged him.

I handed Magnus a wad of paper towels and he dabbed at his shirt.

I asked, "What were ye saying about that king of…?"

Joe Munro said, "I was writing about this man, Mag Mòr. Some sources had him as a king of Scotland, but it's gone very murky. Some of my research I'm having trouble duplicating. He was a king from the late thirteenth century, but most records have John Balliol as the king at about that same time. It's very confusing—"

Karrie's little sister, Tessa, said, "Dad, you promised you weren't going to talk about your books while Finch was meeting his brothers."

Joe, put up his hands, "I know, I know, I'm hushing up."

Finch Mac asked, "So yer mother's real name, Fraoch, was…?"

"M'mum is named Agnie MacLeod, she—"

Joe said, "That's funny, when I was researching the Earl,

there was an Agnie MacLeod who lived in the village there, very small world." He sipped from his drink.

Finch said, "And Lochinvar, what is yer mother's name?"

Lochinvar had been cutting open a box of chocolate chip cookies with a stab to the side with a gold and silver dagger. He said, "I dinna ken m'mother, she died when I was young. I only met Donnan once, I was kidnapped by Ormr and—"

Joe said, "Ormr? Now that's a name you don't hear every day, and now I keep hearing it."

Finch blinked and looked around at the faces. "Ormr kidnapped ye?"

Magnus nodded.

Finch said, "Now I want the Bridge off the table, I daena want it anywhere near my son."

Emma hopped up to move the Bridge and the vessel back to their hiding places.

Magnus dug in the cooler for more beers and passed them around. "Ye said ye met Donnan, Finch Mac?"

"The last time I saw him I was about twelve years old. He sent m'mum and me tae live here in Maine."

"Ye are lucky he was nae in yer life, he was an arse. I saw him enough times tae ken he made most people miserable."

"I agree, I tell m'mum tae beware of him, but she winna listen."

Magnus met my eyes then said, "I daena ken if ye hae heard, but he has passed away. We lost him a few years ago. I ken it is always difficult tae lose a father even when he was an arse, so I winna begrudge ye having some trouble with it, but he was a verra bad person and the world is infinitely better now that he is nae in it."

Finch's brow raised. He nodded. "I was tellin' m'mum recently that I thought we'd be better off without him."

Joe said, "So how long have you lived here, are you...?"

I said, "This was my grandparents' house, I grew up

spending summers here, we're just visiting on a little family vacation."

Finch joked, "Just Magnus and all his brothers, all their wives, all the kids, and his personal chef?"

Magnus said, "And the personal chef's wife and kids, tis a verra large family growin' larger by the day."

Joe asked me, "So who were your grandparents?"

"Jack and Barb Sheffield."

"I knew Jack and Barb!" He looked at his wife, "Remember Jack and Barb, we would see them every year at the faculty dinner? What a lovely couple, such intellects."

Lydia said, "I adored them, so sorry for your loss."

Joe said, "We got a few of their things from the estate sale, and..." His eyes went wide. "That's where I got the..." He pointed at the house. "The thingie that looked like that thing, what do you call it?"

Magnus said, "Tis called a vessel."

"I always wondered what their connection was to the Campbells but now I know it was their connection to Magnus, the brother of Finch, and whoa, this is a really small world."

Chef Zach and Tracy rushed from the house carrying a fruit platter, a bowl of potato salad, a green salad, and some rolls, placing them down on a serving table.

Magnus called, "What are we havin' for dinner, Chef Zach, and how long until the meal is ready?"

"We're having lobster rolls, shrimp skewers, and a bunch of other treats, twenty more minutes."

"Och, m'mouth is waterin'. Did I hear the ice cream churn goin'?"

"Ayuh, as they say here in Maine."

CHAPTER 70 - KAITLYN

A few minutes later everyone had gone in different directions. Karrie and I were sitting beside each other staring out over the dock where Magnus, Finch, and Fraoch were standing. "Thank you for coming, Karrie, it means a lot to Magnus to meet your husband, family is really important to him."

She smiled. "It was a bonkers scenario: first Dad gets a visit, then he gets robbed, but he gets a rare historical artifact during the robbery so he's not that upset about it. But Finch was, he's been really worried for a while. Then Dad says the family that robbed us has invited us to dinner. We weren't sure what to expect, but this is lovely. Sort of surprised how many knives and swords there are, hope his brothers won't be a bad influence on him."

"We live in Florida most of the time, so we won't be around enough to get him in too much trouble." The kids ran past. "You said you're newlyweds...?"

"Arlo is my stepson, his mother passed away about ten months ago, after a battle with cancer."

"Oh, Archie is my stepson too. It's complicated isn't it?"

"Yeah, it's also really simple, I love him so much, but yes, it's complicated."

"I one hundred percent agree." We grinned.

She said, "I remember you, your YouTube channel, I wondered what happened to you."

"Yeah, here I am. Traded in the dickhead for Magnus Campbell."

"So you won in the end, married a duke, and you don't need my PR help?"

"I don't need PR help, but thank you."

She said, "The thing is, we're really relieved to have Magnus take that box away, Finch was really worried about the recent threats. It's rough on him, he's very private."

"Magnus is too, he's very guarded."

"I know, I Googled him and came up with nothing! In this day and age it was astonishing."

I nodded. "We all keep a very low profile."

"Good, it's such a relief to meet new family members and have it be low pressure, and no one wanting anything from Finch."

I chuckled. "Have we mentioned we would like concert tickets?"

She said, "Well that's a given!" She looked out over the dock. "What do you think they're talking about, all those brothers?"

"I have no idea," I lied. I was pretty certain he was telling Finch Mac about time travel. I could see it in his body language. "I think he's just really happy to have another brother. Donnan was so awful, finding brothers is the one good thing from it all."

The kids rushed up, Isla said, "We go swimming?"

"No, dinner is about to happen, just wait… maybe after dinner."

Chef Zach called out, "Dinner is ready!"

We all stood to go down a buffet line then settled in different places all over the yard. Joe and Lydia spoke with Beaty about Mookie, some sat, some stood around the table, it was convivial and fun. I leaned my head on Magnus's shoulder. "This is so cool, right?"

"Aye, I like him, did ye ken we get tae go tae a concert?"

"Awesome. Did you hear that, Beaty, we get to go to a concert!"

Beaty squealed and clapped her hands.

Archie said, "Really? Can we all go?"

Magnus said, "I daena ken, can we all go, Finch? I hae never been tae a concert afore."

Finch laughed. "My brother hasna gone tae a concert? Well, that is goin' tae be remedied. Aye, everyone can go."

I whispered to Magnus. "This is going great, we seem totally normal."

"Aye."

Lochinvar right then took a big bite of lobster roll and moaned happily. "Tis m'favorite." Then his eyes went wide. He grabbed a cookie, placed it on top of the lobster, and took a bite. He considered and then shook his head. "Och I might hae ruined it."

Magnus laughed. "I will save ye trouble, Lochinvar, ye canna think because something tastes good twill taste good with yer other favorite thing. Ye hae tae listen to Chef Zach about what is good so ye winna ruin anything."

Lochinvar grinned as he pulled the cookie off the lobster roll. Then he took another bite and then a sip of Coke with some ice, and asked, "What is this drink called?"

Tracy said, "A Coke? You don't know what Coke is?"

"Tis verra good." He swished his glass around. "I daena understand how tis kept cold. How is ice inside it?"

I glanced around at all the drawn faces. Isla said, "I *know* Uncle Lochie, they didn't have ice at Kilchurn. I missed it very much."

Finch said, "Where are ye from in Scotland that ye've never had a Coke afore?"

Arlo said, "Or ice."

I forced a laugh. "Lochinvar and Isla are just pretending—"

The sky filled with deep black clouds, the kind that meant one of our storms. The wind whipped around the yard, everyone grabbed their plates and cups as lightning struck the water. Beaty screamed. Zach yelled, "Everyone in the house, in the house!"

We were all herded into the house, just in time, as rain and wind picked up and made it feel like there was a hurricane outside. The men behind us were running up the steps, closing the door, except Fraoch, who raced off in the rain after ushering us inside. Lochinvar was watching out the window up at the sky.

I saw Zach and Emma glance at the tracker up on the kitchen counter.

Joe Munro said, "That was an unexpected storm. Did you see a storm on the weather today, Lydia?"

"It sounded like it would be clear all week, but instead there have been daily storms around here."

There was a howling wind, lightning crackling, and a thunderous boom. Arlo climbed onto Finch's lap.

Joe asked, "With this much rain, any danger of the road being impassable?"

Magnus said, "It should be fine, looks like a great deal of rain, but I believe it will end quickly."

Already it did seem like the storm was dissipating.

Joe said, "Man, that was a fluke summer storm, huh?"

The front door opened and Fraoch stuck his very wet head in. "Wanted ye tae ken that we hae company, James and Quentin were walkin' over and got stuck in the downpour."

I looked around at all our relieved faces. Sophie and Beaty rushed out to welcome their husbands.

Emma followed them with a stack of towels.

A moment later James wandered in, drying his hair, soaked through. "Finch Mac is here—?" He stopped dead in his tracks. "I didn't believe Fraoch, at *all*, figured he had the name wrong."

Quentin walked in behind him. "Hey, Finch Mac, big fan."

Finch said, "Thank ye." Then he stood, and joked, "How

many tickets and backstage passes will ye be needing for the next show Magnus?"

Magnus joked, "Looks like about forty-five."

"Ye can give me a headcount, but for now we ought tae be goin'."

Magnus said, "I will walk ye out."

We helped them gather their things to go to their car. The kids ran around looking for lightning bugs and Karrie promised Arlo that they would come back to visit sometime soon. Magnus and Finch were doing that awkward man hug thing, then Fraoch and Finch had a far-apart shoulder clap, and a fist bump, because Fraoch was still wet from the rain. Then Lochinvar fist-bumped Finch, holding onto Finch's fist and shaking it awkwardly.

Then they were gone.

The yard was littered with plates and cups and tree-limbs and the clean party spot of an hour before was now completely trashed. I said, "That was an eventful party."

Magnus said, "Aye, I just explained time travel tae someone who dinna ken it was true."

"How'd he take it?"

"As well as could be expected, he dinna believe me, but... he dinna not believe me. Once he thinks on some of the recent happenings he will realize tis true."

"Why'd you decide to tell him?"

"If he's got threats comin' tae him, he ought tae ken the truth of what he is dealing with."

CHAPTER 71 - KARRIE

*I*n the Escalade on the ride home I said, "That was fun."

"Aye it was."

"I liked your brothers, they were funny. Their clothes were hilarious, all those matching sweats."

He nodded. "They said it was because of being on vacation, they made me feel overdressed."

Joe said, "I could have worn my sweats but none of you would let me."

Tessa said, "That's because Magnus is a *duke*. You don't wear sweats to dinner with a duke."

He said, "I know, I know, I've watched Bridgerton. Historically inaccurate by the way."

We all groaned.

I said, "It's kind of exciting that your brother is a duke."

"Aye, and he's one of those dukes who has a safe and guards and will 'keep things protected for me'. A real duke-with-a-*castle* kind of duke."

"You feel a lot better don't you?"

"Aye, I was verra nervous, I'm glad he kent what was happenin' and what tae do about it."

Tessa said, "They have to be rich, right? Why are they vacationing in that tiny little house? You have a whole bunch of eccentric brothers."

Finch said, "Rich eccentric brothers. The good news is they winna want anythin' from me but tickets and backstage passes."

"I don't want to sound pretentious or shallow, but I really want a personal chef like your brother Magnus."

Finch grinned. "Done, I was thinkin' the same thing."

CHAPTER 72 - KAITLYN

*W*e ate ice cream, the kids chased fireflies, and we gathered in chairs all around the yard with citronella torches lit to keep the mosquitos at bay, and then Tracy had gone home, and Zach collapsed into a chair and said, "Kitchen is closed! I'm not getting anything for anyone."

Quentin said, "Ugh, what a traumatic journey that was."

Zach chuckled and stood, "...unless it's James and Quentin. Can I get anything for you two? But no talking until I'm back."

He brought them drinks and collapsed back in a chair. "Go."

Magnus sat beside me on a bench, leaned forward, resting his arms on his knees. "All right, tell us the damage."

James said, "Not much damage at all."

Quentin groaned and said, "If you don't count the fact that we've jumped over and over and over again."

James said, "Except for that."

Quentin said, "We jumped to 1557, then 1552, then back to 1450, and then 1400, 1350 and then 1290, the date you were crowned. We were never seen. We didn't interact with anyone. We don't know anything about the history, who was king, or whatnot, we just know that we can go to all those dates. The timeline is safe. No need to use the Trailblazer, the path exists."

Magnus said, "Och aye, tis great news. The bad news is by having the route cleared through so many centuries, we hae more centuries tae be responsible for. We used tae hae less timeline tae guard. There are many more years."

Chef Zach said, "Yep, I was rooting for it to get zipped up a bit, so we could just deal with the eighteenth century, a bit of the seventeenth and not much of the sixteenth, but we got a whole hunk of the middle ages to deal with too."

Lochinvar said, "We ought tae go back there, take the kingdoms and make them all bow tae our dominion as Campbell men."

It was perfect how we all paused and then unanimously burst into laughter.

I said, "Lochinvar, I forgot you were new. We've already *done* that. We've been trying to *fix* that."

Magnus said, "I was battling Domnall and Ormr and became a king in the year 1290 when we found the timeline had gone... What was the word ye used, Kaitlyn?"

"Kerflooey."

"Aye, the timeline was kerflooey."

The kids ran up and Isla climbed on my lap, "Mama, lightning bug!" She opened her hands and one crawled around on her palm. She giggled, "Tickly!"

Lochinvar shrugged. "Now it inna kerflooey."

Magnus said, "Exactly, I am a king in the future, I prefer tae live in this time and tae visit family in the past, but I daena want tae control the past. It makes history unstable and is too much power tae wield. That much power is dangerous in one hand, even m'own."

Lochinvar said, "But if ye daena, who will?"

Magnus said, "Listen tae me, the past has been set, and we are victorious in the future. Tis all that is important. From the future we hae a long view of all that happened in the past, and in that view we are safe. If I begin tae change the past, tae alter it in my favor then..."

Chef Zach said, "You can't interfere with your own past, no looping, it's the number one rule of time jumping."

Lochinvar said, "Is this true?"

Chef Zach said, "Yep, God says it. You can't play God, you have to let the world do as it will do."

Fraoch said, "And ye canna change the big things, Og Lochie. We thought the word 'canna' meant 'even if ye wanted tae' but then we learned ye *could* change big things, by aggression or accident, but that ye ought nae tae, because as we learned with James and Sophie, tae try tae change things is tae put all else out of whack."

Lochinvar giggled. "Tae put the kerflooey out of whack?"

"Aye, God said it. Ye canna argue with God." Then Fraoch added, "And what was that, Og Lochie, are ye gigglin'?"

Lochinvar said, "Kerflooey is foonny." He giggled and we all laughed.

Emma asked, "But didn't Sophie get rescued, didn't we change history?"

Zach sighed. "Love of my life, poor sweet Em," he joked, "Sophie is from the future, so rescuing her wasn't really looping, she was already out of time. It didn't change anything to save her."

Magnus said, "And whereas Master Cook wasna able, somehow m'mother was able tae do it. My thinkin' is that the universe was too frightened of her tae argue."

We all said, "Hear hear!" And raised our glasses.

Magnus said, "Lochinvar, does it make sense tae ye? Ye ken I hae a vast kingdom and a great deal of power. Ye understand why I daena want tae push it beyond that time? The greatest emperors in history hae lost everythin' by spreadin' their borders too far."

"I daena believe it."

Magnus said, "I will show ye the histories, ye will see. I daena want tae fight forever, I want tae rest and eat and sleep and enjoy m'life as well, and we already hae all we need. Ye will see, we will hae ye set up on some land and ye will see how it goes, there are plenty of battles tae keep ye busy and ye will be wishing for peace as I am."

Lochinvar said, "I daena ken, I like a good fight."

"I ken, I said the same when I was yer age, how about ye, Fraoch?"

"Aye, but now I prefer tae fish."

Lochinvar jokingly sighed. "Och, auld man, all ye think about is fishing. Tis because ye canna fight?"

We all went quiet.

Fraoch raised his brow. "Ye askin' tae fight me, Og Lochie?"

"Nae, Fraoch, twas just in jest."

Fraoch laughed. "Ye ken, tis the first sensible thing ye said since ye got here. Ye ought tae remember, the men in this circle are yer betters, we are aulder and wiser and every one of us has risked his life for the other. Except Chef Zach."

Zach said, "Hey!"

Fraoch laughed.

Magnus said, "Fraoch is only kidding, Chef Zach, he kens ye are the one keepin' us *all* alive."

Zach said, "Truth, and don't you forget it." Then he looked at Magnus and said, "So seriously, were my ears deceiving me? When the hell did you become a duke?"

Magnus chuckled. "I hae always been a duke."

Quentin said, "Oh no you don't, Boss. Is this like the safe house in NY that you have 'always' had, that I only just recently heard of? When the heck did you become a duke?"

"Lady Mairead has bestowed upon me a title, for cover, twas backdated tae the year 1600, and bears Queen Elizabeth's seal. I believe m'mother went tae her directly for the title. They are great friends."

Emma said, "And this is the first Queen Elizabeth? Holy smokes, there is so much there to ask Lady Mairead about, I want to know all of it."

I said, "Me too, I have so many questions. But, for the present day — are we safe?"

Quentin said, "I declare us safe, we have some unanswered questions, like who pulled you through time, we will figure that out, but for now, we are safe. And since Beaty has asked me, once I made it home from this latest adventure, if I would please, pretty please, take some time off to vacation. I think that's what I'm going to do, enjoy Maine for a minute." He stared out at the dark lake. "Except what does one do on vacation in Maine?"

We all laughed, but agreed that we didn't really know.

Hayley said, "I think what we're supposed to do is stare out at the lake, but frankly that seems like it's going to get old quick. I need a spinning wheel or a—"

Quentin said, "What you need is an AA meeting."

"Yeah, will you come with?"

"Yep, we can go to one tomorrow, there's bound to be one in Orono in the college town."

Fraoch said, "When ye are returned ye can come fishin' with me, Hayley, we can take Archie and Ben out with us."

Archie and Ben said, "Yeah!"

Isla said, "Me too!"

Hayley said, "It's a deal, these little stinkers get their own canoe? Or do we have to paddle them around like a couple of chumps?"

Fraoch said, "We split up in two canoes, but they hae tae do all the paddlin'. Ye canna expect us tae do it, I hae already been called auld taenight. I want the due respect of m'station as the elder of the family."

Magnus said, "Ye're the patriarch?"

"Aye, and everyone kens it. Ye are my wee brother. Ye are so wee we daena talk about it much so we daena hurt yer feelings."

We all laughed.

I said, "James, what are you and Sophie going to do tomorrow?"

He said, "I think I'm going to sleep through most of it, she and I will wear pajamas all day, or these sweats, same difference. Can't believe you all entertained Finch Mac in coordinated sweats. Then we're going to eat something, then a nap, really, that's it all day. Right Sophie?"

She said, "Aye. Then we are going to go buy a telescope."

He said, "I'm going to introduce you to shopping on the computer in pajamas with next day delivery."

I asked, "Beaty what is your plan tomorrow? Now I'm trying to decide who to hang out with."

Isla said, "You can come with me mommy, fishing."

"Perfect."

Beaty said, "I need tae give Mookie a bath and I was thinkin' about goin' up tae the field tae cut some flowers. I will be verra busy, but nae too busy tae go swimmin'. I do love swimmin'."

Quentin said, "You know what we need? We need a big floating raft out there in the sunny part of the lake, maybe tomorrow I should go—"

Fraoch said, "I thought ye were relaxin', Quentin? Already ye are taking Hayley tae a meeting and buyin' us a floaty boat? I daena think ye ken how tae relax."

"What about Zach and Emma?"

"I've got so much shit to accomplish, now I have an employee who doesn't know how to cook."

Emma giggled. "She knows the perfect amount of 'how to cook', she was a huge help today."

He sighed. "I hate it that you're right. What're you going to do, Em?"

"Me? I'm going to keep Zoe from the lake, like every day." She sighed.

"Lochinvar, what are you going to do tomorrow?"

"I daena ken, dost I need tae go tae the stables or the fields?"

"Nae, there are nae stables, or fields."

Emma said, "There are grocery stores, but I'm not sure that's within your wheelhouse. Can you imagine showing up here from the past and going first thing to a grocery store?"

Magnus's eyes twinkled at me. "Aye, tis crazy tae think it."

Fraoch said, "If I had m'knitting needles I could teach him tae knit."

Quentin's eyes went wide.

Magnus said, "There is more of the family land across the road, and an auld family cemetery. I hae been meanin' tae go up there and clear the overgrowth. It haena been done in a long time, and there is a barn up there we ought tae see tae."

I said, "Do you think it needs to come down?"

"I daena ken, tis just something tae go up and see tae. We daena hae tae do the work, as we are on vacation, but we ought tae think about the work we arna doin'."

I laughed.

He said, "I went up there once with yer grandfather, twill be good tae see it again. I like tae ken about the family history."

Emma said, "Speaking of family history, crazy that Joe was studying Mag Mòr and that history is not there any more. Your brother's father-in-law almost wrote a book about you! But now that's been overwritten, completely, as if it never happened."

Hayley brushed her hands together. "One more loose end, done. We're actually getting kinda good at this mind-warping time travel."

Isla was almost asleep in my lap, Zoe was fast asleep on Emma's. Ben and Archie were leaning on their dad's arms, tired from the day.

Magnus clapped a hand on his thigh. "I am verra bothered by one important loose end that still remains. I canna stop thinking about it. Now that I ken the timeline is stable, I think tis a sign, I ought tae go find Haggis."

We all looked at him blankly.

He said, "Ye ken, *Haggis,* m'dog."

I opened and closed my mouth. "But what about... you just got home, we..."

He put his face into a comical frown and made Archie giggle. "But Haggis is the greatest dog in the history of dogs. He has been lost in the thirteenth century, without a friend, and—" His eyes widened. "What if he befriends someone else, like that scoundrel William Wallace?" He growled, "We hae tae rescue him fast, I promised him that he would get tae come live on the beach in Florida with Archie and Ben and Isla and Zoe. I mean tae live up tae my promise."

Archie clapped. Ben sort of woke up and mumbled, "A dog?"

Archie said, "We're going to go get the dog."

Isla, almost fully asleep on my lap, raised a little hand in the air. I whispered, "Did you hear the word dog?"

With her eyes shut she nodded and then went quiet and just like that was fast asleep again.

Magnus said, "I canna leave him behind."

"But what if...what if he's not there?" I chewed my lip. "I mean, don't get me wrong, I met Haggis, he seemed great, but he is seven centuries away. What if he's not there, couldn't we find another...? Ugh. I don't like arguing against this, to talk sense into you. I sound like an ass."

Magnus shrugged. "Ye daena hae tae sound like an arse. Ye daena hae tae argue. Ye could accept that this is m'way. I am loyal and I mean it when I make a promise."

I chuckled. "Listen to you, you didn't even want a dog."

"Aye, and I dinna want a family of brothers either, and look how many brothers I hae."

"Kinda my point. I know you love Haggis, but he wasn't there when the time bridged. He's probably not around there now — what if we found a dog here, in this time? We could..."

Magnus grasped my hand and stroked the back of it. "Kaitlyn, Haggis found me in the deep forest of Scotland in the year 1290. He was at my side through many battles. We lived in a tent on the side of a battlefield, drenched tae the skin, and had tae huddle taegether for warmth. I canna leave Haggis behind. I must go back for him."

"You promised him?"

"Aye, I promised him, I hae tae live up tae my promises. Or I ought tae learn nae tae make them so earnestly."

I sighed, "Well, I would never want the lesson to be to make fewer promises, less earnestly. It's one of the greatest things about you."

Fraoch said, "I will go with ye, Og Maggy. It daena make sense tae do it but if a madman goes on a folly, who am I tae argue? Ye daena get tae be a madman alone."

Hayley said, "Your brother is going to do something crazy and you would follow him into it?"

"Och aye, I hae tae, he's got a sling on his arm, he needs me! Besides, we might nae find Haggis, but we will hae a Fraognus adventure."

Hayley laughed. "Is that your 'ship' name?"

Magnus said, "Wait, why inna our ship name Magnaoch?"

We all laughed.

Fraoch looked at Magnus, "But ye ken this is crazy right, Og Maggy? There is a large chance that we winna find him. The odds are stacked against ye, ye hae tae ken it."

Magnus nodded and swallowed. "I appreciate that ye would accompany me."

"I need tae ken though, how long are we tae look for him? When James was loopin', Hayley and I had tae leave, it got too dangerous. I left him, which I now regret—"

Quentin said, "Me too."

"But I tell ye, Og Maggy, if ye take it too far, if ye risk too much, or put us in too much danger, I winna stand for it."

Magnus joked, "What would ye do?"

"Kick yer arse back here."

Magnus joked, "Like tae see ye try."

Lochinvar laughed. "Now this is what I want tae see. Can I come tae see the elders fight?"

James said, "You don't have to go anywhere to see it, they argue all the time."

Magnus said, "But hae ye ever seen us come tae blows? Nae, because he is afraid tae do it—"

Fraoch chuckled. "Afraid tae hurt ye."

Quentin gestured toward them. "See?"

Magnus said, "Ye are needed here, Lochinvar, if Fraoch and I go tae the past, we need as many men as possible here. Ye will take orders from Quentin, he is yer boss."

James said, "What am I, burnt toast?"

Quentin said, "I have the word Colonel in front of my name, asshole. When shit goes down, I'm the boss."

Magnus gestured toward them. "See, tis nae only us, they are also often arguin' and this close tae coming tae blows."

Hayley said, "All you men are always arguing about—"

I joked, "All you men? I don't know about that, you argue with me all the time."

The men gestured toward us and we laughed.

Magnus said, "All right, thank ye, Fraoch, ye will come. Kaitlyn will stay here with the bairns, as we were gone long enough, and everyone can continue their vacation plans. Lochinvar, I will set ye up with a task on the morrow afore we go."

Hayley said, "I was promised fishing and wait…" She teased, "I can still go fishing, my nephews can paddle me around the lake!"

I said, "How about, instead of fishing, you and I take the kids on an exploration of the south end. It's shallow there, there's lots to find, I used to go all the time with my grandfather."

Chef Zach joked, "I have half the mouths to feed tomorrow, my day got a lot more relaxing."

Emma said, "If there's room Zoe and I will go with you in the canoe. We'd love an adventure."

CHAPTER 73 - KAITLYN

We deposited the kids in the bunkhouse to sleep and then went out to the lawn to sit in chairs, just me and Magnus, everyone else headed to bed. The night was still and dark and cool. He said, "Och, I hae missed this place, ye ken. It has a feel tae it, verra different from Florida, where it is hot and sticky and the air is thick and heavy. Here tis crisp and light, cool and fresh. I did miss it much." His gaze looked up and down the lake shore. "It reminds me of Scotland, from the castle walls I could see a long way. I loved guard duty because of that long view, but here we are on the side of the bank, down low, nestled in the trees, a low house, with nae stairs, too small for all of us, but I like it verra much. The dock there with the canoes. I do like it verra verra much. I just miss yer grandparents here."

"Me too." My eyes swept the darkness, the lake beyond in the light of the moon. "Remember when we were out on the dock and the bear came?"

He chuckled and took my hand, holding it on the armrests between us.

I turned my head to watch his face as he looked out over the lake. "I love you."

"I love ye as well, twas a long time that I was in the past, I ken ye dinna feel the length of time as chronically as I did, yers was more acute."

"Nice science words."

"Thank ye. I heard Emma use them and I thought they worked for time travel. Ye and I were away from each other for a few days, ye believed I might be dead, yer time and loss was acute, I was gone for months, I kent ye were alive, I just had tae get back tae ye, I had tae work the problem, my time and loss was chronic and ongoing."

"Are you always the one looking, I'm the one who is lost?"

He smiled. "Generally speaking."

"You're always rescuing the lost." I sighed. "Like, case in point, your dog, I'm still conflicted about the dog."

"Aye, and I want ye tae ken, Kaitlyn, I understand yer feelings on this, I ken tis nae sensible tae want tae rescue a dog." He looked down, shaking his head. "I daena ken why I hae tae do this… but I hae tae go get him. I feel it in m'heart, that I must get him."

He drew in a deep breath. "When Archie came tae the past, as a grown man, he remembered Haggis. The love between them was palpable. Archie had grown up with Haggis in his life and they played and frolicked with each other. Twas a sight tae behold. I am doin' this for Archie, the bairns are supposed tae grow up with Haggis, tis how it goes."

He turned his head to address me directly, "I need yer help in it, mo reul-iuil, ye ken. I need ye tae tell the kids that I am doin' it out of a sense of responsibility, nae because I am putting them second, or because I dinna love them enough, but because I hae tae. He lives in the past, but he is supposed tae be here, I ken it."

I felt a little like tears were going to well up, but I swallowed them down and blinked them back. "That's beautiful, my love, you're doing it for Archie."

"Aye, and Fraoch will go with me… he will be there tae help."

He added, "I just need… I daena want the bairns tae think I'm crazy, or a madman, or…"

"That bothered you earlier?"

"Aye, I ken how it looks, but I need ye tae pretend like I am wise in doing it." He raised his chin and smiled. "Pretend like ye support me in it, because ye are a good little wife."

I groaned, "You are the worst, did you really just call me a 'good little wife'?"

"I am teasing, but what did ye expect? I am a madman, I just called m'wife a good little wife."

"I'm going to have to do something epic to make myself seem like a badass again."

He tilted his head back, "Ye ken ye just got me out of the thirteenth century? We were in a castle, another king's castle, and I was verra wounded. Ye managed tae help me out of it tae the clearing tae jump. I daena think ye are givin' yerself enough credit. Ye are a plenty big and terrible arse." He chuckled. "Also, if ye can convince everyone that I am nae on the errand of a madman ye will be a terrible arse as well, tis goin' tae be a hard sell."

"You don't seem entirely convinced."

"Well, mo ghradh, tis because I am nae doin' it with m'mind; tis m'heart that is leading."

"I suppose it often leads you well."

"Name a time it haena."

"I can't think of a time, and so I'm going to follow your lead with my heart too."

"Thank ye, mo reul-iuil."

"You're going to go get Haggis for Archie?"

"Aye, the boy needs his dog."

"See, my love, when you put it that way it doesn't sound mad at all."

"I ken, I am the sanest person in the world."

I grinned. "And the sexiest, I really really like you."

He said, "How come we hae once again given up our room tae the rest of the family and we are tae sleep in the bunkhouse?"

"We are so considerate we have put our needs to get some booty last." I said, "Tell me a funny story about being in the past for so long."

He thought for a moment. "Och, here's one, we were on the edge of a battlefield and twas rainin' and verra boring as we waited tae fight and ye ken how Fraoch snores?"

"Boy do I."

"Fraoch was snorin' and it got verra high pitched, like a wheeze, so he would breathe in and then make a sound, whhhh-hheeeeeeeeee as he exhaled, and after about four times, Haggis whimpered along, ee ee, and I chuckled. And Haggis looked at me with his head cocked and then whenever Fraoch snored, Haggis would whimper again and I would laugh, and then for about five minutes Fraoch would snore, Haggis would whimper and I laughed so hard, trying to stifle the sound — it was growin' more and more hilarious. It became clear that Haggis, his head cocked tae the side, was tryin' tae make me laugh."

He laughed and I laughed too and the laughing, holding hands, talking with my husband, felt so much better. "Ye ever heard of such a thing? A dog bein' funny on purpose?"

"I have never heard of such a thing, that's hilarious."

"Aye, twas."

I kissed his knuckles and we stared out at the night.

Later we climbed into our separate beds and went to sleep.

The next morning I did my best to be a supportive good little wife. Over breakfast I asked Magnus what he was going to pack.

He said, "Clothes that fit the time, a tent, some supplies and... dog treats."

I said, "Perfect, Haggis will want those when you find him."

He kissed me, a loving wonderful kiss.

Right after breakfast, Magnus walked Lochinvar and me up through the fields to the family cemetery. It was mind blowing. I hadn't seen this place in ten years or more. It was familiar and shocking to see a place that I remembered so vividly, yet had totally forgotten. The barn was big and dark and I remembered being afraid of it, so close to a family cemetery. The whole place seemed haunted.

My grandparents weren't buried here, the last burial had been in the early 1900s, and the spot was so overgrown it was difficult to see that it was a cemetery at all. Magnus explained that he wanted all the weeds and overgrown bushes cut back. Then he swung the door of the barn open and we stepped inside.

I said, with my hands on my hips, "Well, this is a death trap."

"Aye, there is not a support that will keep it standing in a stiff breeze. Everything needs support." He raised his brow. "Support is necessary."

I laughed, "Nice metaphor, for us."

We closed the door and walked back tae the house.

Hayley and I walked Magnus and Fraoch to the field to say goodbye. He had already said goodbye to the kids. I hadn't been there to listen, that was between them and we had long ago decided that the kids didn't need to go to the clearing to see the storm. The storms were too frightening, watching someone disappear was terrifying.

On our walk back to the house Hayley said, "You are holding up surprisingly well, I thought you were upset he was leaving. I'm furious that Fraoch is going for a dog, and I feel like I shouldn't be the person who is the most emotional about it."

I said, kicking a pebble from the path in front of me, "I had a long talk with Magnus about it last night. I'm being supportive."

"You don't actually think they're going to find the dog do you?"

"I doubt it, I mean how could they? He didn't remember the last time he saw the dog. I was in the room and the room was completely different. I think somehow the time bridge left the dog in an alternate universe or some other bizarre scenario, and he's torn up about it and hopefully Fraoch can talk some sense into him and get him to come home."

"It's really dangerous if there's another king there."

"Yeah, I hope they don't get swept up in the idea of winning the kingdom again. No grandiose plans."

"That's what I told Fraoch, nothing big, just look for the dog, come home, don't die."

"Yeah," I said, "'Don't die' I hope they listen. The trouble is, we've been in so much danger and drama for so long that it seems scary to choose to go somewhere by choice, on an errand, you know? What if something happens while we're vacationing? How sucky would that be?"

"Well, they'll be back tomorrow and if not, we'll send our best men."

"Quentin and James and or Lochinvar."

She said, "You want to go check on him?"

"Sure." We turned on the path and wandered up to the family cemetery. He was there, by himself. He waved and mopped his face with a hand towel, leaving a smear of brown. "Och, hello Queen Kaitlyn, Madame Hayley."

"Hey Lochinvar, we were walking by after taking Fraoch and Magnus to the field."

"I saw the storm, twas verra big, I canna get used tae it."

"I know." He was wearing a pair of yellow sweat pants, and one of Magnus's t-shirts. I added, "That shirt is hilarious."

He pulled it out, stretching it really far to look down, and pointed. "I ken, tis a figure. Do ye see? There is a line here and a spherical shape." He cocked his head left and right and added, "I think tis the head, but also there's a stick here, tis a sword, see? And his arm has come off. Tis verra funny." He giggled, because Lochinvar did indeed giggle, which was hilarious.

Hayley said, "I suppose I should have brought you something to drink, some water, a snack. We'll come back in a bit."

I asked, "How long do you think this will take?"

He put his hands on his hips. "I daena ken, three days or more."

Hayley grimaced. "Yeesh. That sucks."

"I daena mind the work, twould be easier if there were more cookies here."

I said, "Alright, I'll send some up. What's your favorite?"

"I like the ones with the wee dark spots."

"Chocolate chip? That's my favorite too."

Hayley and I returned to the house. She said, "He's ginger, unsophisticated, and has got such a silly giggle, but somehow he's still hot."

"I know, he's like a boy trapped in a superhero's body. It's hilarious. But I remember when Fraoch was like that."

"Fraoch was never that silly. He was very serious about keeping himself and me alive. I don't know if this boy could keep anyone alive."

"I've seen him battle in an arena, he saved Magnus's life, he's a pretty high-functioning hero."

"Yet he's still a boy, how old do you think he is?"

"Probably twenty."

"He's lucky we brought him away from the sixteenth century: he was practically middle aged!"

We told Zach that Lochinvar needed cookies and water and then relieved Beaty of kid duty. Hayley, Emma, and I took the kids in the two canoes out into the lake to the south end where we explored in the pools and shallow spots, drifting around the rocks, watching what Isla called the fairy flies, along with the darner flies, and the dragonflies, as they skirted and skated on the water around us.

CHAPTER 74 - MAGNUS

*W*e landed in the evening. I had chosen a place that was farther from the castle, near a village, so we could visit the pub and ask questions about the castle and the current king.

As we trudged down the path Fraoch joked, "Twill be verra funny if ye walk intae a pub and ye are the king of this world."

"If I was the king would I be trudgin' down the path?"

"Ye ken ye might be missin'. They might be lookin' for ye."

"God, I hope nae, tis a dismayin' prospect tae hae tae be king here again. Tis too much tae worry about. I want tae relax in the lake with the bairns, go out in the canoe, sleep with m'wife."

He chuckled, "The bunkhouse got ye down?"

"Aye, the bed is verra short."

"Ye ken, our bed is a pullout, and it has a bar across the back. Tis nae soft nor comfortable."

"Aye, and ye can be heard snorin' throughout the lands."

"It will teach them, they ought tae give me a proper bedroom."

"Och aye, but ye will be up doin' guard duty most of the night anyway, the private room would be a waste on ye."

"True."

"And Colonel Quentin needs the vacation and Master James has just become reacquainted with his wife after a great deal of worry, and Zach and Emma run the house, they ought tae hae a good night's sleep."

"Aye, tis just for us auld men tae sleep uncomfortably."

"How auld are we?"

"I daena ken, I believe I am past thirty."

"Och, so auld. Lochinvar makes me feel my age."

He scowled as we came tae the village and the Red Lion inn at the edge. Fraoch held the door open.

My eyes scanned the interior, difficult, as it was verra dim, with a small fire along one wall, and a few flickering candles. There were long tables and benches placed near the hearth. But through the gloom, at the far end, I saw that William Wallace was sitting with a small group of men.

Fraoch saw my eyes land and whispered, "Who is it?"

"William Wallace, the man who cut m'shoulder." I was wearing a sling, but my shoulder ached. The bandage on it itched. "I killed him, yet here he sits."

William Wallace's brow drew down, as if he was trying tae remember who I was.

Fraoch and I went tae the proprietor and asked for two flagons of ale.

When Fraoch was handed his flagon, he raised it high. "Tae the king!"

William Wallace scowled.

Fraoch boomed tae the room. "Come on men! Fellow Scots, raise yer ales and hae a drink tae the king — what is his name... I hae forgotten as I hae had too much tae drink!"

The proprietor laughed. "Tae King John."

Fraoch nodded and smiled at me.

"Och aye, tae the good King John Balliol, a man of royal aspirations and folly." He raised his glass toward William Wallace.

Wallace raised his own flagon and nodded. "Tae Toom Tabard."

Fraoch laughed. "Empty coat? Aye, tae Toom Tabard!" He added, "A round of ale for the room," and tossed the proprietor one gold coin.

Then he joined me on a bench near the fire, on opposite sides of the hearth from William Wallace. I kept m'face turned away because he kept lookin' as if he was trying tae figure out who I was, but as time would hae it, I had met him three times and all had been recently. If he couldna place me then this was a good thing, as it meant time had been rewritten.

Fraoch agreed, "The good news is, Wallace daena remember ye, which means he has also forgotten Quentin along with the training and all the guns. I think tis safe tae say history is protected from our machinations."

I rubbed the bandage on my shoulder. I had stitches, I was told that I dinna need tae wear a bandage if I could keep the area clean, but Kaitlyn had forced me tae wear the bandage as she considered the entire thirteenth century as unclean as was possible. "Unless I kill him, I could go over right now and cut him clean through, then we could jump away."

Fraoch said, "Aye, ye could, but inna he important tae history?"

"How important could he be?"

Fraoch said, "I daena ken, Hayley told me there is a famous movie about him."

I scoffed. "A movie? About that sniveling, thieving, conniving arse?" I drank. "It canna be a good movie."

Fraoch chuckled. "I hear tell tis verra good, and that the star is verra handsome in it. Hayley said he wears a kilt and he is brave and…"

I scowled. "I daena understand why they would tell the story of that man, centuries later — now I doubly want tae kill him."

Fraoch leaned back and stretched his legs out, near my feet. He raised his brow. "Ye try and I will trip ye tae yer stomach and then everyone will be laughin' at ye, Og Maggy. Ye will be ridiculous."

I laughed. "Let me understand, Fraoch: the man who cut m'shoulder and almost killed me is sitting right over there, and m'brother has said if I stand tae kill him ye would knock me tae the ground, then laugh at me? Och, ye are an awful person."

He shrugged. "Ye ken ye want history tae be unchanged, ye ken it, ye daena want tae be the king. Ye daena want tae fool around. Ye want tae find Haggis and get the hell out of here without—"

My eyes drew tae William Wallace, standin' and approachin'. He said, "I am Wallace, who are ye?"

I said, "I am Magnus, and this is m'brother Fraoch. We are travelin' through and hae stopped for a drink." I placed my hand on the hilt of m'sword and saw his eyes dart tae the movement.

I asked, "Did ye get the ale m'brother purchased for ye?"

"Aye."

"Good. I will return tae m'friendly discussion with m'brother, twas good meetin' ye."

He said, "Daena cause any trouble here, m'men and I are—"

"We arna here tae cause trouble, we are simply passin' through."

Fraoch said, "Speakin' of which, hae ye seen a dog? He is about this high, and has an expression about his face as if he is tryin' tae decide whether tae eat ye or tae just lick ye."

"Nae." His face clouded over. "What color dog?"

"He is brown, if ye see him will ye tell him Fraoch and Og Maggy are lookin' for him? We hae a deal tae settle."

"With a dog?"

"Aye, with a dog."

Fraoch held his stare.

Finally William Wallace said, "If I see him." He stalked back tae his seat.

I chuckled. "That was tense."

"Aye, and now he is mystified about the dog. He went from

fightn' tae confusion verra quickly." He drained his ale and wiped his mouth with his arm. He looked down at the wet space on his linen sleeve and brushed it with his hand and made a dark mark there. "Och nae, daena tell Hayley, I am a mess a'ready." He continued, "What do we ken? We ken the king is nae Mag Mòr, ye are in the clear. Ye daena hae tae be king of this long ago barbaric land anymore, nae one kens ye, ye can come and go without hassle. This is all good."

I shrugged. "Except we haena found Haggis yet."

He went for more ale and returned. "We daena even ken where tae look."

I said, "Aye, this could take a long time."

CHAPTER 75 - MAGNUS

$\mathcal{W}$e drank a good deal, because the pain of jumping was still on us and we enjoyed it for auld times sake. Then Fraoch looked in the corner, bleary-eyed, and hiccuped. "Looks as if William and his men are about tae leave. We ought tae leave first so they winna lay in wait. I am in nae mood for an altercation."

"Ye are in nae condition for an altercation with four men, we are outnumbered and I only hae one good arm." I stood, accidentally knockin' the bench over and then stumbled tryin' tae raise it again.

I chuckled. "Och, I was tryin' for... tae be stealth-like."

Fraoch said, "Ye were a stealth, ye were like a great... a great... what was it...?" He opened the door and we stepped out intae the medieval night.

"I daena ken, what are ye talkin' on?"

He looked up at the stars. "I daena remember." He added, "Tis good we got Sophie home, inna it?"

"Aye, and we fixed the timeline. We are verra good at what we do. We ought tae get a special award for how good we are." I hiccuped.

He grabbed m'arm and pulled me intae the shadow beside the building. "Wheesht, they are coming out."

I tried tae be verra quiet. They were singing and weavin' down the path headed away from the inn. One said, "Where did they go?"

Another said, "I daena ken, we will find them on the morrow."

Fraoch and I listened tae them leave and then we stepped from the shadow. He said, "Och, twas close. I daena think I could fight them as there were... how many?"

I said, "At least ten I think? Or I was seein' two where there were one."

He said, "Elephant!"

We began walking toward the woods. "What elephant?"

"Tis what ye were like in the pub, ye ken."

"I daena hae any idea what ye are talkin' about."

"Me neither."

We stumbled intae the clearing where our things were hidden under a camouflage tarp with some leafy branches spread on top. There was little ambient light but enough to drag the limbs aside while Fraoch pulled the tarp, stumbling against a tree. "Och nae! Did ye see the tree grab me? It has..." He looked down at his shirt. "It has ripped m'shirt."

I fumbled in a box for my headlamp, turned it on, and we found the tent.

He said, "We ought tae hae paid attention when Quentin told us how tae erect it."

We unzipped the bag and dumped out the tent and sticks intae a big disordered pile. I said, "I daena ken how tae do it, the one I used tae put up dinna look like this." I picked up the instructions, pulled it close tae my eyes and moved it away. Even in the headlamp the words were impossible tae make out.

Fraoch looked up at the sky. "It inna goin' tae rain."

"How far hae I fallen, once a king here, that I will sleep on the ground without a shelter?"

"Ye daena need a shelter over ye, ye need one under ye. Tis the hard ground and the dew that will make us regret our decisions." He lay the tarp out on the ground and then our sleepin' bags, side by side, while I found the flask of whisky I had brought.

"For warmth."

We removed our shoes, took shots of whisky, and climbed in our bags. I propped m'arm under m'head and looked up at the starry night. "Tis a lovely night sky, I daena mind it a bit." A bug landed on my cheek and I smacked it. I laughed. "I forgot my face was under the wee beastie."

Fraoch laughed. "Remind me if ye mind our sleepin' arrangements in the morn." He added, "I'll take first watch."

I woke up a bit later tae the loud snores of Fraoch. I pushed his shoulder, "Och, ye are wakin' me with yer frightful..." I groaned. *He was sleeping without waking me for guard duty.* I pulled my legs up to sit, but there was a heavy weight on them. Twas something alive. I scrambled up out of — a dog barked.

"Haggis?"

My eyes adjusted tae see Haggis, his tail wagging. "Haggis! Cù math! Ye found me!"

He frisked all around, his tail waggin' merrily, jumpin' up and down, trackin' dirt and mud all over m'sleeping bag.

Fraoch sleepily mumbled. "Ye noticed Haggis? He arrived while I was on watch, he offered tae take over guard duty."

I held Haggis behind his ears and looked intae his face. "How are ye doin', cù math? Hae ye been worried?" He squirmed from m'hands and jumped all around some more.

"This is the greatest thing in the world."

Fraoch said, "Was verra easy tae find him, we will hae tae make up some tales so it sounds much more desperate than 'we got drunk in a pub and Haggis found us.'"

We both laughed.

I climbed into my sack and Haggis lay down beside me, his chin on m'arm. I said, "Ye takin' the watch for us, Haggis?"

And I swore he nodded, 'Aye'.

In the morn I woke up tae Haggis looking down on me. I said, "I ken, I am sorry I left ye. I had tae get tae a hospital… Daena look at me like that, I came first thing." I scratched him behind the ears.

Fraoch was up. He had a small fire goin' a'ready. "I'm putting on a pot of coffee, because m'head hurts fiercely and I winna jump until after coffee."

I said, "Sounds good, we accomplished what we needed tae do, now we can relax."

We sat, leaned against a log, Haggis beside us, actin' as if we had never been apart, sippin' from our coffee, talkin' about the weather and the mornin'. I said, "I hae been meanin' tae talk tae ye Fraoch."

"What about?"

"Ye ken ye are m'second, if somethin' happened tae me, I would need ye tae become king of Riaghalbane…"

He joked, "I ken, it daena mean I like the idea."

"The plan would be that ye would pass the throne down tae Archie."

"Aye, we had this discussion afore, we are in agreement on it."

"Well, now there is Lochinvar."

He scowled.

"I ken ye daena like him, but I think ye ought tae give him a—"

"Why? He is just a lad with an overblown opinion of himself, struttin' around — Og Lochie needs an arse kicking."

"Aye, that he does, though tis easy for ye tae say. Ye dinna see him take tae the stadium the other day."

"He is nae so valorous."

I shrugged, "I ken, tis nae the point of it. The point is, I hae brought him intae the family for lack of something better tae do with him, and…."

His brow was furrowed.

I exhaled. "When ye were growin' up, Fraoch, who was the elder of yer clan, the one all the men listened tae?"

"M'da."

"For me twas Uncle Baldie. He only had tae speak and the men listened tae him. He had everyone's respect." I gave Haggis a treat. "Lochinvar is young, he is impetuous, and he has the potential for chaos. He has the ability tae wreak havoc, but that described ye at one time and me as well. We ought tae be the kind of men for him tae look up tae."

"Why are ye mentionin' it now?"

"I want ye tae consider that he is verra useful within the fold, and he is dangerous outside of it. He is a son of Donnan. I daena wan tae kill him. I daena want him tae challenge my throne, Archie's throne. He was born a bastard, orphaned, raised by Ormr, it has been a terrible life. Give him a chance tae find a place in the family, daena fight him at every turn."

"He can hae a place as long as tis nae in front of the window at breakfast, or in front of the whipped cream. He needs tae keep tae his own place as well."

"I ken, twas a difficult situation — ye had tae reach for the whipped cream. I daena ken how ye managed tae eat without mishap."

He chuckled. "I see what ye mean. But he is an arse and deserves tae hae it kicked, but I will try tae help mold his character instead of kickin his arse."

"Good, 'mold his character not kick his arse' are wise words tae live by."

CHAPTER 76 - KAITLYN

*B*eaty, Hayley, Emma, Sophie, and I were frowning around Lochinvar. He was bright red, horribly sunburned on his face and his forearms. His hands and lower legs were covered in vicious looking welts.

He was every shade of pink and red and looked absolutely miserable.

Quentin and James were stifling their laughter.

Emma was Googling. "I think it's Stinging Nettles, a plant." She turned the screen around. "What do you think, did you see a plant that looked like that?"

"Aye, tis likely, twas all green plants everywhere."

"You need a dip in the lake, some scrubbing with soap, then we will put some special concoctions—" She wandered to the kitchen looking for some of her herbs.

Lochinvar grimaced.

"Where does it hurt?"

"It hurts everywhere."

I called to the kitchen, "Emma, do you have aloe too?"

To Hayley I said, "How did we let the Scottish man, fresh off the boat, out in the sun all day?"

She poked my shoulder, also very pink, as we had been canoeing all day.

Zach stuck his head out of the kitchen. "Lochinvar, do you want a cookie?"

He nodded, frowning. "I need all the cookies."

I rolled my eyes. "Man, it runs in the family."

Zach said, "Tracy, can you bake chocolate chip cookies while I finish dinner?"

"Yes, sir."

From the kitchen came loud music and clanking of baking trays as they set to work. Lochinvar went out to jump in the water. The kids stood on the dock and watched. Archie said, "Uncle Lochie, you are very pink."

"Aye, I hae battled the heat of the day and the bushes of the forest and Lochinvar the Fearsome has won."

"Is that what pink means, you won?"

Lochinvar laughed. "Of course I won. Ye ought tae see the bush. He is a broken pile of sticks, vanquished in the grass, the clear loser."

Dinner was delicious, and we played a board game after. Then we all went to bed earlier than usual. We were putting on a strong face for the kids and it was exhausting, so I lay on the bunk in the bunk room, thinking about the empty bunk beside me and how it was supposed to have Magnus in it.

Tomorrow he would be home.

If he wasn't home we would go on a rescue mission.

I would do my best not to think of that until it came to it.

The next morning we had breakfast, and then outfitted Lochinvar in a hat, and bright orange sweatpants, and a buttload of sunscreen before he left for the cemetery. I told him he didn't have to go back to it, but he wouldn't listen. He said, "Magnus told me tae," and left for the morning.

Quentin sat in the Adirondack chair looking like the kind of person who needed something to do. He looked so freaking bored, but when asked, said he was fine.

We got busy doing much of nothing but waiting,

I looked out the window at Quentin, standing in the driveway looking up at the sky.

Then a little while later he was in the back kicking rocks and looking at the foundation of the house.

Then I saw him pick up a fallen limb, dragging it away from the property.

Then I saw him looking up at the sky again.

Archie sidled up and looked up at the sky for a moment beside him then came into the house.

Emma asked, "What do you think Quentin's doing?"

I laughed. "It's his first ever attempt at doing nothing, it's a sight to behold."

Beaty saw us through the window, came up, and watched with her hands on her hips. Her hair was still bright blue, she was wearing sweatpants that she had cut off very short. She shook her head then dragged a tub of sudsy water and placed it in front of Quentin. For the next thirty minutes he scrubbed Mookie in the bath water with all the kids watching.

Then he sat holding the brush looking out at the lake.

After lunch, Quentin passed the house with a ladder and a bucket hat on his head. "Whatcha doing? And where'd you get the hat?"

"Like it? It's my vacation hat. Going to go up and get a new perspective."

"Are you sure you're not checking the horizon for enemy troops? You promised Beaty nothing security related."

"Would I do that?" He chuckled. "Nah, I just want to go see what I can see."

"Coolio, I guess that's vacation-y. Oh and don't let Isla follow you up."

He said, "Just between us, this is really, really boring."

I said, "Yeah, I thought it was, you're not really fooling any of us."

CHAPTER 77 - KAITLYN

A few hours later, in the afternoon, a storm grew overhead, a howling, roiling thundercloud. "Everyone in the house!!!"

We had been sitting outside, worried that the day was gone, now we ran from all parts of the yard into the living room. Quentin and James raced up the road to meet them.

I prayed, *Please God, let it be Magnus, let it be Fraoch, let them both be safe, let them...*

Hayley held my hand. We sat on the couch, watching the storm outside as the thunder clouds filled the sky and whipped the trees. Isla sat on my lap and ducked her head against my shoulder. Lightning lit the room.

Sophie asked, "How dost ye get used tae it?"

Beaty, on the ground with her arms around Mookie's neck, said, "We daena get used tae it, tis always terrible."

The rain and wind and lightning and thunder slowly subsided and then a few minutes later the side door opened and a dog raced into the house, bounded right straight for Archie, and jumped onto him licking his face, his tail wagging wildly. Archie said, "Are you Haggis? Oh my gosh, are you Haggis?"

The kids were all up, jumping up and down, while Haggis

jumped up and down in the middle of them. My husband entered the house, his smile wide.

"You did it!"

He said, "Och aye, I canna believe it, but it worked."

There was a general disorder and merriment as the kids frolicked with the dog and it was too much for one room so we spilled out onto the grass once Zach said, "If you people don't get this dog out of here I'm gonna..."

We didn't wait to hear what he said.

I held on tight to Magnus. He held Isla up but she squirmed to look down on Haggis who was playing hard, wrestling with the boys. We found a ball and he chased that ball like it was the first ball he had ever seen and all of us were blown away by the dog chasing a ball like it was the greatest thing in the world.

Beaty said, her hands clutched together, "I think my heart might explode with love. He is the most beautiful dog in the world."

Emma said, "He for sure needs a bath, first thing."

Magnus said, "I think that ye love him makes all the terrible things we went through worth it, right Fraoch?"

Fraoch laughed. "Aye, we had such a time of darkness. My head is still pained from it."

Magnus asked, "Where's Lochinvar?"

"He's working on the cemetery still, right?" I looked at Quentin.

He looked at his watch. "He ought to be finished by now, he definitely saw the storm."

I said, "Wait until you see him, Magnus, he's sunburnt and he was covered in Stinging Nettle welts, they were gone by this morning, but—"

Quentin said, "I saw him at lunch, but... now I think of it, it's been three and a half hours. Why isn't he here? James, want to go with?"

He and James raced up the hill and were gone for about fifteen minutes while we watched the dog play with the kids. Then we saw them return without Lochinvar but with the box of his tools.

I called out, "He's not there?"

They shook their heads.

My heart sank. *Could he have been taken? Could something have happened?*

Magnus said, "Are all the vessels accounted for?" He called into the house, "Chef Zach! Can ye check the tracker, are all the vessels accounted for?"

Zach came from the house. "Yeah, what's going on? We have all the same vessels as before Magnus left."

Tracy stuck her head out of the door. "Are you asking about Lochinvar?"

We all said, "Yes."

"I took him a drink a little while ago—"

"He was there?"

"Yeah, he probably walked to the pub."

Zach said, "What exactly did he say?"

"He heard some music. We walked up the hill a bit and figured out that there was a bar down the road, the Crazy Loon. He said, 'Like a tavern?' And I told him it was. I figured if he went he would have called to tell you."

Quentin laughed. "Lochinvar might have walked to a bar?"

Magnus groaned.

She asked, "He didn't call you and tell you? That's weird."

I said, "He doesn't have a phone."

Her eyes blinked.

James said, "He looks hilarious too, wearing colorful sweats, what's he doing going to a bar sunburnt to a crisp? He looks like a bouquet of flowers."

Magnus said, "Does he have any money?"

Quentin said, "Nope, none."

I glanced at Tracy and covered, "I doubt he had his wallet with him, doubt he had any ID. This is just great."

Quentin said, "See Hayley, how we worry?"

"Yeah, I get it, this is not cool."

"Where's the bar?"

Tracy looked at her phone. "It's here." She held the phone out for Magnus, but Quentin took it and looked at the map.

"All right who wants to go on a rescue mission to a bar for Lochinvar?"

Magnus and Fraoch chuckled.

Fraoch said, "Och, m'head hurts from the last rescue mission tae a bar, but I ought tae go ahead and start drinkin' again."

Magnus, Fraoch, Hayley, and I got in the Jeep. "We barely fit, we literally need a bigger vehicle, you guys are huge."

Tracy drove her car, with Quentin and James and Zach. Sophie stayed with Beaty and Emma, and the kids while we went on our errand.

It was only a five minute drive and then we pulled up to a little dive bar. The door was open. Music drifted out, which was enticing, but it cracked me up that he had walked to the pub based on the music alone.

We climbed from our cars and the large group of us stood in the door of the bar. It was so dark it took a moment for my eyes to adjust, but there was Lochinvar at the bar.

He slurred, "Och, ye hae come, m'family!"

The bartender said, "This the king?"

He said, "Och aye, the king and a brother and another brother and the..." He waved his hand. "Tis all of them, all of them brothers, told ye they would come for me."

Magnus clapped his hand on Lochinvar's shoulder. "We were wondering where ye were."

"Ye returned from the thirteenth century a'ready? Ye got the dog?"

The bartender said, "He has been telling us stories for almost an hour, we were about to go through his phone to call him an Uber."

Hayley said, "Well, good luck with that."

James bought us a round. "And put Lochinvar's tab on my bill."

The bartender added, "He was drunk when he got here."

Lochinvar pulled a flask from the pocket of his sweatpants and waved it around. "I hae this, tis almost empty though." He unscrewed the lid and turned it upside down. He frowned comically.

The bartender said, "I told you, dude, you can't drink that in here." To us he said, "He's been hiding it, but it's in plain sight."

James said, "Okay, handsome tip since our friend has been an ass."

Lochinvar giggled. "He daena hae any cookies, how come he daena hae any cookies?"

Fraoch laughed. "Og Lochie, ye are pink as a flower and carrying on about cookies, ye are embarrassing yerself."

We took the big table down the middle of the bar. The other customers stared, but they all looked drunk too. If they had heard stories of kings and time travel they probably were too drunk to remember them.

The bartender delivered our drinks to the table. "Ginger here was adamant that you're a king, *insisted* that you were." His eyes narrowed.

"Och, he says a lot of things, none of them are true."

Lochinvar giggled looking down at his beer. "Ye ken tis... tis true, ye are a king, I hae watched them bow tae ye."

Magnus shrugged. "Okay, I am a king."

Lochinvar said, "I kent it! I told ye twas true." Then he slurred. "Ye sure ye daena hae a cookie?"

"I am sure." The bartender walked back to the bar.

We raised our glasses and Magnus made a toast. "Tae Lochinvar the Fearsome, for frightening us by disappearing, but nae truly disappearing, and just going tae the pub, and for that we are grateful, as we daena like disappearances, we ought tae be clear on that."

Lochinvar said, "Nae disappearances, just time travel."

Magnus said, "Ye ought tae wheesht, you're going tae convince everyone that ye are out of yer head, especially Tracy, she is right there."

He looked blearily around. "Och, she is, she is so beautiful, did ye ken?"

Tracy blushed a deep red.

Magnus met my eyes and shook his head. "Well, that toast was ruined."

Lochinvar raised his beer. "Tae King Magnus! King of the whole wide world."

Tracy said, "Boy, you are drunk."

He giggled. "I am, I am so drunk, glè dhroch." He looked at his arms. "And muc pinc, a pink pig and... suns..." Hiccup. "Heat." He giggled again. "Do *you* have a cookie?"

We all burst out laughing. Tracy said, "Hold that thought." She left the bar and returned a few minutes later. "The store next door carries Whoopie Pies, you're welcome." She placed a cake sandwich in front of Lochinvar. He peeled off the plastic, got his fingers all sticky with the creme middle, and licked them each off. "Och, tis delicious."

Fraoch said, "Now I want one as well."

Lochinvar pulled it in half and lay across the table holding out a portion. "A cookie for Frookie, we daena hae a friendship yet... I will share m'cookie with him because we are brothers — we ought tae eat the..." His voice trailed off as if he had forgotten what he was talking about.

Fraoch took the half and bit into it. "Tis delicious, Og Lochie, and ye are right, we do hae a friendship now, twas simple."

Lochinvar said, "Good, because else I might hae tae run ye through with m'sword."

We all laughed, including Fraoch. "Ye ken, I remember

sayin' something like that tae m'uncle John, twas right afore he kicked m'arse."

Lochinvar giggled again. "Do ye think Chef Zachary can make these cookies for us?"

Tracy said, "I can bake them, I do it all the time."

He leaned on the table. "Och, ye are the most beautiful lass in the world."

Hayley said, "Tracy, please don't get too pissed off at him. We'll get him to cut the hitting on you."

She laughed. "Don't worry about it, the silly boy with his pink skin and his funny accent, and his rantings about kings and cookies, I think I can handle his attempts at charm."

We laughed.

We finished our drinks and Fraoch and James put their shoulders under Lochinvar's arms and carried him giggling out to our Jeep.

Quentin ran back inside to tip the bartender extra for the trouble.

CHAPTER 78 - KAITLYN

*O*hen we pulled the cars into the driveway and parked them, we climbed out and stood in the moonlight while James and Fraoch deposited Lochinvar on a chair in front of the fire pit. Magnus got a blaze going and Zach brought out hotdogs, on sticks, for roasting over the fire. Before long the kids were fully sticky with ketchup and greasy potato chips.

Zach said, "Have you ever cooked a meat stick over a fire before, Lochinvar?"

Lochinvar giggled, jiggling his hotdog. "Meat stick!" Then he said, "Master Archie, give me some of the sauce."

"The ketchup?"

"Aye, tè ruadh."

He shoved the hotdog onto the bun too forcefully, dumping it in his lap. He peeled it off. "Och nae! Got m'meat stick on my lap." He giggled. Archie and Ben laughed like there was something naughty going on.

Chef Zach almost doubled over laughing. "Dude, you are so drunk!"

Lochinvar finally got the hotdog balanced on the bun and held it out for Archie to squeeze ketchup on it.

He sighed. "Ye can tell twill be delicious, because it inna like anythin' I hae ever eaten afore, ye ken?"

He took a big bite and chewing said, "Zachary, Tracy said she would bake me a Whoopie Pie. Is she nae a bonny lass?"

Chef Zach said, "Uh oh."

James was roasting a hotdog over the fire. "Man, he is a handful. We'll be carrying him to bed before the night is out."

Quentin said, "I carried your ass to bed many times before."

"We both carried Michael's ass to bed more times than I can count."

Quentin said, "I had forgotten what it's like to be twenty with not a care in the world."

Magnus said, "Did ye ever hae 'nae a care in the world'? I thought ye were at war!"

"Yeah, right, but on leave I could sneak in a lot of rowdy mayhem."

Fraoch said, "I liked a little rowdy mayhem m'self."

James said, "Fraoch, you're cool with Lochinvar now?"

"Nae really, but this night was the most interestin' thing he's done so far."

Magnus joked, "That and helpin' me survive the arena."

Fraoch waved a hand at Magnus. "Och, I dinna see it. It canna be true."

Haggis stood beside Magnus with his eyes locked on the meat. Magnus chuckled. "See it bairns? He is just now arrived and already he kens, there is meat, and he daena hae to hunt for it."

He tossed half a hotdog to Haggis who ate it in one bite and resumed the begging position.

After we ate, Tracy left to go home, and we continued on around the fire pit, a lovely conversation, jokes and fun, and Fraoch sang us an old Scottish song, and Magnus and Lochinvar joined in. Then looking out at the lake, Magnus said, "Tis a beautiful night. Tomorrow I am goin' swimming, then I am goin' canoein', and then I am going tae—"

Lochinvar said, "I am going tae go tae the bar."

We all said, "No."

I said, "Lochinvar, you can't go back to the bar—"

"But why Queen Kaitlyn? Twas an amusement!"

Quentin said, "He's not wrong."

Magnus said, "Aye."

Lochinvar said, "We had a pilgrimage tae the pub for some spirits, tae bring us good spirits, and…" He began to sing. "Twas the spirits of the fae — who-o-o-o led me on that day… tae the braw pub by the light of the mo-o-on." He grinned. "Do ye like the song? I just made it up." He hiccuped and the boys all laughed. He pulled his face down in a frown. "I like ye all so verra much, ye canna understand. In the castle Dunscaith, twas verra brutal and ye daena ken what it is like."

Magnus said, "I think we do, some of us, we lived a tough life."

"Nae, mine was verra hard. Twas the life of an animal until they wanted a man tae fight while they trained. Hae ye seen m'scars?"

He raised his shirt and pointed, "This one, and this one and… so many." His stomach and sides were covered in scars, some long and ugly, one all the way around to his back.

Magnus said, "My back is much the same, Lochinvar, I was whipped."

Lochinvar said, "They liked tae beat me, verra regularly, and stick a blade in me fer practice."

Lochinvar said to Archie. "Ye daena worry about it, Archie, yer da is a good man — he winna beat ye. He kens what tis like. A man who is beaten and wears the scars on his back will ken nae tae beat his sons. Yer da wouldna."

Magnus nodded at Archie with a smile. "He kens I wouldna."

"Good… did I show ye this one?" He showed us a scar on his upper thigh.

Emma said, "I'm surprised that one didn't kill you."

"I had tae go tae the hospital for that one."

"What hospital?"

Magnus asked, "Hae ye always been in the time of the 1580s?"

"Aye, except for the one…" His eyes narrowed as he scrunched up his face comically. "I canna remember it, nae really, I… the hospital was verra white and I was… I canna remember it, nae fully."

Fraoch said, "Great, there's more tae the boy than we kent afore."

Magnus shrugged. "We kent he was the son of a time traveler, tis nae that far-fetched that he has traveled tae the future when he was injured. The question is, who brought him there? Donnan?"

Magnus asked Lochinvar, "Did you ever meet Donnan?"

"Nae, I mean…" He hiccuped. "I think I did but I was verra young."

Fraoch said, "There is a lot goin' on here with Og Lochie that we dinna ken."

Magnus said, "Aye, drunk Lochinvar has confessed a great deal, ask him anything, perhaps we can learn more."

"What do ye want tae ken? I will tell ye anything. Ye're m'family. Og Lochie is verra lucky." His face brightened. "Tis better than 'fearsome' ye can call me lucky now."

Fraoch asked, "Okay, Og Lochie the Lucky, besides Domnall and Ormr, who else did ye ken? Did ye ken Agnie MacLeod? She was m'mum."

"Aye, I kent her, she would visit Domnall and Ormr and was verra mean tae the rest of us in the castle. Auld Arthuretta, who worked in the kitchen, said that someday Donnan would come tae get me, but he never did."

"Donnan is long dead."

He giggled. "That explains why he dinna come tae get me."

I said, "Who was your mother, Lochinvar? How did you end up at Dunscaith?"

He said, "I remember livin' somewhere else and I was taken." He smacked his palm on the arm of his chair. "*Then* I lived with Ormr."

My eyes wide I said, "Lochinvar, that is awful." I said, "Had you ever met or seen Lady Mairead before?"

"Nae."

"Well, that's one good thing. I hope she wasn't involved in your abduction."

Hayley said, "What are the odds that Lady Mairead moved Lochinvar when he was young, to get rid of him?"

Magnus said, "I daena think so, m'mother is a great many things, but I daena think she would remove a son from his mother, even if he was my direct competitor."

I nodded, "I think you're right, she has a pretty horrid nature, but I think that she wouldn't cross that line. She would banish the mother along with the son."

Magnus said, "Aye, she has a weakness there, it has been the one thing that has kept her from losin' her morality all taegether."

Lochinvar said, "I canna remember... whoever twas left me in a terrible state."

He began to sing a sea shanty crossed with a funeral dirge, "Oh ho! The land is nae for me, I hae been drowned since I was wee... I pull up m'ship beside the dock, and I said tae the lassies want tae see m'—?"

Fraoch interrupted, "Ye ready for bed, Og Lochie? Ye hae the look of a man who needs tae lie down." He and James stood, lifted Lochinvar, and dragged him singing and giggling to his daybed on the porch.

Hayley said, "Fraoch and I are going to go down the street to that hotel we passed. I called them when we were in the bar. We want a proper bed. Mags and Katie, y'all can have the sofa bed."

I said, "Perfect."

CHAPTER 79 - KAITLYN

*A*nd then the kids were taken to their beds, and one by one the couples all left. Hayley drove the Jeep to the hotel. Soon it was just me and Magnus outside again, watching as Quentin took a last look around the perimeter of the space to check we were safe.

As he passed us he said, "I was relying on the young'un to do the night guard, but I don't think he's going to be sober enough."

Magnus said, "I will take a turn."

"Nah, that's alright, get some sleep. I'm going to take a walk around."

I checked on the kids, fast asleep, then Magnus and I went into the house to sleep on the sofa bed.

"I am lookin' forward tae a good night's rest on a proper—" The frame creaked as he climbed in. He groaned. "Och, tis springy, and there is a bar here where it inna supposed tae be."

I climbed in and curled up beside him and pulled the crisp sheets and thick blanket over us, not like a cloud, but like a thick heavy spread.

I giggled. "It's so uncomfortable. It was so promising, but instead it's totally disappointing, the bunkhouse might be better."

"But there ye canna hitch yer leg up here on my waist."

"True." I slid my arms around his neck, "And now you mention it, now I've squirmed closer, and gotten a little heat from you and a little skin to skin, I can't even imagine the bunkhouse. That place is awful, I want you right here on this uncomfortable bed."

I kissed him and whispered, "But this might need to be the slowest, quietest, sex we've ever had, because this room is right in the center of the house." I squirmed closer and the bed went squeak, squeak.

Magnus chuckled. "Tis verra noisy, we hae probably awoken the house a'ready. If we vacation here much longer we will need tae ask James tae build a bedroom for us." His breath against my ear he whispered, "I am kiddin'… if we vacation here much longer I will grab a hammer m'self and build m'own bedroom for us."

The room was quiet, very dark and still, even the lapping of the lake against the dock was faint and quiet. His hand rubbed up my thigh and drew my hips closer. I wrapped around him tighter. He said, "Daena breathe, I'm takin' yer…" He pulled the waistband of my panties slowly down my legs, and then used a foot to draw them away from my ankles. I was helpful, but very still through it.

Now that my panties were off, he clung to me. "Och, we did it."

I said, "Now do yours."

"I canna, my shoulder."

"Right, sorry." I held tight around his head, and using my toes, I shoved his pants off, at the very end it required a kick that made a loud squeaking noise but then it was over. We stilled and listened.

He said, "What we need is a bagpiper tae play outside tae cover the sound."

I joked, "What we need is to rouse the family and claim an actual bedroom, this is ridiculous. We are too nice."

He chuckled. "I daena think anyone has ever called me too nice. I killed a man less than a week ago."

His hand rubbed all around my skin, a delicious friction, then dove and played between my legs. "Are we supposed to speak of battles while in bed?"

"Nae, we arna, we are supposed tae say how much we love each other."

"I love you."

His mouth against my ear, the warm breath of him, "I love ye as well, mo reul-iuil."

I tilted my head back and his mouth settled on my throat, kissing— "Say it again."

He whispered, "I love ye, mo reul-iuil."

I pulled him over on me and he drove up into me, holding my hand, his mouth against my cheek — ohmygod, my breaths panting, his hips working. We were quiet, bound, energy and friction, heat, pent up moans. We made love with the smallest of movements and without a word and it was explosive, if I could use that word for an act that went unnoticed by the rest of everyone — we imploded perhaps. His wet lips beside mine, low moans, heat. His excitement shown by the catch of his breath and his eyelashes fluttering against my temple, the way his grip on my hand tightened and we went deliciously slow, that long and lingering he had promised me, writhing against each other, a slow rhythm that built into a climax that was marked with intakes of breath — a gasp and a collapse on me.

He moaned.

We hugged tight and caressed.

"I think we were quiet, but I kind of wonder if I was really really loud for a moment there?"

"Ye were quiet as a mouse, but there inna anyone in the

house awake who dinna ken what we were doing. This bed needs some oil in its springs."

I laughed.

He kissed the side of my jaw. "We hae tae do that more often."

I said, "Vacation, check. Sex, check, more often, check. Build a new bedroom. How long are we staying, do you think?"

He chuckled. "I think for a verra long time, tae really relax and recover from the excitement. But if Lochinvar is determined tae charm Tracy, we might hae tae leave earlier than we would like. I daena think he kens what the dangers are of a modern woman."

"The dangers? How is there a danger in a modern woman?" I had my head on his arm.

"Ye ken, ye are goin' tae argue with us on *everything*."

"That's a danger? It's more likely a help to you. Think of the *insane* ideas you would have if you didn't *occasionally* have someone push back against them."

"Aye, but ye are forgetting, Kaitlyn, that ye are perfect, and yer arguments are always just right. How could Lochinvar ever get so lucky as I hae?"

I playfully smacked him on the shoulder. "Stop teasing, you're going to ruin our after-sex glow."

"I ken and I was only teasin', mo reul-iuil, ye are perfect for me. I daena ken if other men would find it as easy tae find a woman who is perfect for them. I think Lochinvar is desperate and Tracy is the first woman he's seen without a mate, therefore he thinks he can claim her —we might need tae move."

I giggled. "Is it that dire? That a young man likes a young woman? Is it a reason to move?"

"'Tis verra dire, things like this hae caused the fall of empires."

We both laughed. I said, "Well she's just a nice girl from Maine."

"Even worse, I daena ken how we would explain the time traveling tae her. We need tae keep her away from the mysteries."

"Are you tired? You've had such a long day."

His voice was low and rumbly. "I am, I rescued the dog just this morn. Who, I notice, is sleepin' in the bunkhouse with the wee'uns and nae in here with his proper master, I think he is choosin' Archie over me."

I kissed his chest. "Can you blame him? The kids were feeding him all night."

He said, "Did ye notice how he remembered them?"

"I did, he's been in the time loop. I'm really glad he came out the other side with us. I want to say, just for the record, you were right and I was wrong. I'm glad you brought Haggis home."

He kissed my forehead, "I would make a big deal of winnin', but I think I am fallin' asleep."

"G'night m'love."

CHAPTER 80 - KAITLYN

$\mathcal{T}$he next morning, when I woke up, Magnus was sitting on the side of the bed, putting on his shoes. It was just after dawn but I could already hear Zach moving about in the kitchen.

"I love the sounds of our morning, and it's pretty great when it's close by like this. I mean, don't get me wrong, I like a big house, a fortified castle, but it's nice that we're all a few feet away from each other. That's fun too."

He leaned on his good shoulder and kissed me. "I am going tae rouse Haggis and the bairns and go out tae the dock tae see the morn, ye want tae come?"

"I'll be there in a minute. Let me grab a cup of coffee."

A few minutes later I stood on the porch looking out at the lake, my husband standing on the dock with the kids, all four of them gathered around, chattering as they did first thing. Haggis frolicked and frisked around them all. I took a sip of my coffee and enjoyed the warmth, the light of the sunrise on the lapping ripples of the lake, the birds chirping with the changing light, the chill from the darkened woods as the light lifted it away, replacing it with the best that Maine had to offer in summer.

My husband looked up at me, and a smile spread across his face.

This was going to be a great vacation.

After breakfast, Quentin called, "Kaitlyn! Boss!"

Magnus and I went out the back door. "Where are you?"

"In the back shed!"

Magnus and I followed his voice around the house. The back shed was dark and full of furniture and boxes, and I couldn't see what he was doing. "Whatcha doing, Quentin?"

His head popped up from behind an old sideboard. He was wearing the bucket hat, a particularly funny bucket hat made of denim, frayed on the edges and raggedy, completely out of character for him. He had a scruffy beard now, too. "Check this out." He lifted a cardboard box up and placed it on the sideboard. The box had the letters, M.C. written on the side in marker.

Magnus's eyes went wide.

I said, "Ooohhhhh! Magnus! Is this your stuff?"

"Aye, exactly where I left it, but also… I dinna remember it until right now."

Quentin brought the box out to the picnic table. Kids arrived from nowhere to see. Quentin pulled the flaps away and we peered inside.

There was a very old book, Magnus lifted it and blew off dust. The front had the title stamped: The Prodromus Astronomiae. I said, "That looks familiar."

"I hae written in the back of it, how tae use the vessels." Magnus showed us the place.

I said, "I know I've never seen it before but it looks very familiar, that's weird."

There was a photograph of Magnus in a canoe, not far off the shore of the lake. He said, "I remember this moment. I came tae the dock and Barb had made me a sandwich. I had it there in a basket as I paddled away. She took a photo of me."

"You look really happy there. It's so cool that your happy place is also mine."

"'Tis nice tae share a history."

There was another photo, with white edges, very vintage and faded. I was about ten years old in one of the Adirondack chairs with a big grin. He said, looking down on the photo fondly, "I stole this from Barb because I liked it, ye hae the same smile and eyes, yet ye are so wee and silly there."

Isla reached for it. I said, "This is a photo of me when I was a kid."

She narrowed her eyes and dropped it to the side. "What else inside the box?"

Quentin lifted out a bundle wrapped in tartan cloth. He gingerly unwrapped it and there was a vessel.

"Och, we canna escape them, they are everywhere."

I said, "Remember when we thought we could record them all and protect them all in one place?"

Quentin said, "Ah, the folly of youthful time travelers."

Magnus said, "Each vessel exists in every time, so we are finding them over and over, but also, ye ken, there are more we dinna ken about. I thought we did, but we ken less than before."

Quentin said, "Like all your brothers."

I teased. "I wonder if you have more brothers, or more vessels?"

Archie said, "You have so many new brothers. Are they all my uncles?"

Magnus said, "Aye, all of them, and Uncle Lochinvar is older than yer father, I want ye tae ken."

Ben said, "He looks a *lot* younger."

Magnus chuckled. "He is still old, I ken it is confusing. Just like I'm technically older than Fraoch, but if ye lined us up it would go, Fraoch, then me, then m'new brother, the song bird,

Finch Mac, then Lochinvar. And there is yer Uncle Sean in Scotland."

He and Ben looked at each other with their eyes wide. "Wait, Finch Mac is my uncle? That is so freaking cool!"

"Aye, I thought ye heard!"

Archie said, "You don't tell us anything."

Ben, looking so much like his dad, said, "Yeah, you try to," he made finger quotes, "protect us."

Next Quentin pulled from the box a sgian-dubh.

"Tis one of my favorites!" Magnus turned it over in his hand. "See the Campbell crest? Twas from Baldie, I dinna ken where it had gone."

Then there was a small silver box, with beautiful decorations all around it. Magnus said, "Guess what is inside?"

Ben and Archie said, "Gold and jewels."

Magnus said, "Even better." He lifted the lid and inside were five shark teeth.

Everyone oohed and aahed.

He said, "I kept them with me tae guide me, but the last time I jumped tae get back tae yer mother I dinna hae them with me. I suppose they were packed up and put away for my return."

Then he pulled out a few pens.

"You were already collecting them?"

"I wrote ye many letters with them."

"Can I keep them?" I clutched them to my chest.

He nodded and dug through the box and pulled out an embroidery hoop with a rudimentary thistle embroidered in the middle.

My eyes wide, "Did you do this?"

He said, "Aye, Barb was attemptin' tae teach me."

"I love it so much, can I keep it, too?"

"Of course."

Then he said, "Look at this, Archie and Ben, tis a fungus from a tree. They call it an artist's conk. Archie, yer great-grandfather, Jack, showed me how tae pull it from the tree and here I hae carved m'name intae it."

It had the words, Magnus Campbell, Nov 21, 1993 carved into it.

I pulled that into my arms too so that I had an armful. "I know I'm being pretty selfish, but I really really really want all of this. Can I have it all? I'm sorry children, I know it's cool, but I want it."

Magnus laughed. "I think when I collected it all I had ye in mind. I ken I stitched the thistle for ye."

Tears welled up — there was something so wonderful about this time capsule.

The kids ran off to play. "I don't know why I got so emotional about all of this, I think it was that we were so new to each other, and I loved you so much and you loved me and you were at my grandparents house, that's where you came when you were in trouble. It's like we were so completely entwined, already, from day one and… I just love this so much."

"Aye, me too." He ran his hand through his hair, then put his arm around me and we kissed.

Quentin said, "Cool, you guys take all of this, I'm going back in to see what else I can find."

We sat on the picnic bench, our view, the lake.

Fraoch and Hayley were in a canoe offshore, fishing. Lochinvar was sitting on the end of the dock with the kids around him. Zoe wearing her floaty arm bands, the boys, and Isla, all looked like they were listening to him tell a long interesting story.

I leaned against Magnus's shoulder. "It's going to be alright, you know?"

"It feels like it, I feel verra at peace."

"That's a first, huh?"

"It does feel like it."

CHAPTER 81 - KAITLYN

$\mathcal{I}$ stood on the dock holding a blanket as a canoe holding Magnus, Archie, Ben, and Isla slid up beside the dock. Magnus's eyes gleamed. "Och ye read m'mind."

I said, "My turn!"

The kids scrambled out. I kissed Isla on the cheek as she raced past. "I'm going canoeing with your da!"

"Have fun Mommy, make him show you castle rock!"

I climbed into the rocking canoe and picked up the paddle.

We paddled away from the dock to the middle of the lake. I said, "You've only got one good arm, you want me to paddle in the back?"

"Nae, I am twice yer size, I ought tae be in the back even if I am nae much help. Besides, as ye ken, I do like the view from back here."

I laughed. And paddled, enjoying the smooth glide of the canoe through the water, the sound of the small splashes and drips and the 'thunk' of the paddle against the side of the canoe. These were the sounds of my happy place, my childhood, my grandfather Jack would have been in the back, helping to steer as I paddled us through the shallows. The wide blue sky, the trees lining the shore, the darner flies flitting around on the surface of the lake.

He said, "Also, I need ye in my sight line, did ye ken ye disappeared while we were on a procession from Scone tae Stirling?"

"Really?"

"Aye, ye were ridin' behind me and I was talkin'. I turned tae the front of the line, then thought of somethin' else tae say tae ye, and turned back — ye were nae there."

I looked back at him. "Like I *disappeared*? Weird, I left from Scone *before* your procession."

"Ye never saw Blackford, the town where ye disappeared?"

"No, I never saw it. That must have been frightening for you."

"Aye, twas. Cailean heard me speaking tae m'self and I had tae cover my confusion. Twas unsettling tae feel like I was losing my mind, nae sure what was real and what was unreal."

I dipped my paddle in the water and stroked it back, whoosh. "This is as real as it gets."

"Aye."

He said, "See the rocks over there?" He pointed south near the shallow pools. "I saw a place there."

I paddled that direction and he continued, "I think I want tae see m'brother Sean and Lizbeth, I stopped in when I was tryin' tae get tae ye, but it wasna a long enough visit. I am feeling the loss of their company."

"Me too, we'll go, soon." I butted the front of the canoe up against the shore and climbed out, leaping to dry land. Magnus stepped out into the water and waded to shore dragging the canoe behind him. I laughed.

"I daena mind wet feet, ye hae tae get yer feet wet in lake water or the fae think ye are a coward and they tease ye."

I strode into the lake up to my knees then strode out. "Better?"

"Aye, better, tis naething worse than a teasin' fae."

"Says the man who has been chased through time by asshats."

He chuckled and pulled the blanket from the canoe. He bounded up a giant boulder to the top. "There is plenty of sun here and though we hae a view of the lake, we winna be seen."

I unfolded the blanket and spread it across the boulder. Magnus and I sat down. I leaned back on my arms, enjoying the warm sun on my face. "God this is a wonderful place."

"Aye, tis."

And he kissed me, the fresh breeze in my hair, sun on my skin, his warm lips pressed against mine. He nibbled my lip and his tongue played against my tongue, sweet and oh so sexy, as his hand caressed up under my shirt fondling and playing with my breasts. We were out in the wide world exposed but intimately focused, his breath, his skin, the glistening moisture on his cheek, the fluttering of his lashes, his mouth on my breast, as we were so close and caressing, kissing along each other's skin. Long. Rubbing the length of him, being caressed, kisses on my throat, stroking. Lingering.

Finally after oh so long and lingering, I rolled him to his back and climbed on him and rode him, breaths against his cheek, as I found a rhythm, meandering for a while, pushing and pulling against him, teasing, making him beg for it, more and faster, and — *yes, you like?*

Aye, mo reul-iuil.

Then when I could sense he was about to finish with me or without me, I arched back, sat deep, and rode him hard, a roar rolling though me, rocking his fucking world. Then I collapsed on him, o*h god.*

I ken.

And then I just held on, the warm sun on my ass. His kisses on my cheek. The exertion lulling us into a comfortable resting silence. His breath, *I love you,* in my ear.

•   •   •

Then we kissed and rose and sat for a time, looking out over the lake. "That was necessary."

"Twas."

I pointed. "See there, that tree? My grandfather and I planted it when I was four. And there, see that area? That's where I used to paddle and just sit in the canoe and let it spin and think, the rocks create a little eddy."

He pressed his lips to my shoulder. "Kaitlyn, I daena tell ye often enough, it has been a wonderful life with ye. Ye hae made it all so much better."

"Thank you my love, I feel the same way." I kissed his temple and we held an embrace for a long time.

Then he said, "Ye ready tae go back tae the family?"

Yes.

We folded up the blanket, climbed down to the canoe and I took the long route paddling him back home.

CHAPTER 82 - KAITLYN

The next night Magnus said, "Master Cook, how much trouble would it be for ye tae add an extra bedroom tae the house?"

Hayley said, "Two extra bedrooms!"

James laughed. "Y'all want me to build this out into a big family compound? Okay, will do, but first I gotta get permits."

"Permits for what?" asked Magnus

"Remember how we had to ask to put the stables in at the house?"

"They wouldna let me."

"Yep, they might not let you."

"Why nae, what sense does it make?"

"They have to look at easements, property lines, how many toilets on the septic tank, the seasonality, and the codes."

Magnus said, "Och, well we will hae tae find the man who we pay tae make it happen." We all laughed.

Tracy chuckled, shaking her head, "So this is pretty great, right?"

Everyone nodded.

"But you've *never* been here during a Maine winter?"

Everyone shook their heads.

She looked incredulous. "Now how are a bunch of *Floridians* going to decide to live full time in Maine? *Also*, the road out here is impassable much of the year — you cool with that?"

We all kind of looked at each other.

She said, "Zach here goes to the grocery store every single day."

He looked sheepish. "I do do that, but it's just because I want everything to be special."

"I think all of you need to decide if you want to put up with the worst weather ever and then you can decide to add on. *Or*, if you decide to add on anyway, pay someone to do it for you, so that James here isn't stuck in Maine figuring out how to lug lumber through the snow on top of your old Jeep."

James raised his beer, "Good point, Tracy, and now you mentioned it, wasn't it getting cold today?" He shivered.

She laughed.

Zach said, "Tracy are you telling us that you don't want to work for me anymore?"

"Nah, not at all." She pretended to wipe her eyes. "This has been the best job I ever had, but *seriously*, I can't let you decide to live here during the one good two week stretch this year. What kind of Maine native would I be to let a bunch of southerners think that Maine is all canoes and fishing?"

Magnus said, "Some of us are from Scotland."

She waved her hands. "Scotland? I'm not even sure that place exists, when *you're* talking about it you're always saying castles and fireplaces and horses and—"

Sophie said, "We had a verra long winter last year, we had tae all huddle in one room for warmth."

She said, "See! I think half the time you're kidding me and I don't believe you know anything about winter weather at all."

Magnus shrugged, "So ye think we ought tae move back tae Florida?"

Chef Zach said, "Won't you miss us?"

She said, "I'll come visit, promise." I saw Magnus follow Lochinvar's eyes as he gazed at Tracy's face.

Magnus looked at me, briefly, his brow raised, wordlessly: "Did ye see?"

I nodded. *Aye.*

Magnus said, "First, we ought tae vote on our vacation." He scratched Haggis's head between the ears. "It haena been long, but does everyone feel relaxed from it? Let's go around the table. Tracy, ye daena get a vote." He chuckled, "Ye already told us ye think we ought tae go home. Lochinvar, ye haena been tae Florida, so ye daena ken what ye are votin' on, but how about this, are ye done with the graveyard?"

"Aye, I vanquished the weeds." He grinned and drank from a beer.

Magnus said, "Okay, James?"

"I'm ready to go back to Florida, I would like to show Sophie around. I've got some confused memories, it's time to make new ones."

"Sophie?"

"I hae a vote?"

Hayley said, "Of course you have a vote!"

Sophie raised her chin. "I do verra much like the loons in the evenin' when they are callin' and—"

James said, "But if we stay I have to build an extra room."

Sophie laughed. "Och, I forgot all the points, ye ken, James daena want tae build a room in the snow. We hae had enough snow for a lifetime. Did I vote right, Master Cook?"

He laughed. "Perfectly."

Tracy's eyes widened at their exchange. "You guys are so old-school sometimes."

Magnus moved the conversation on. "How about ye, Madame Beaty?"

"As ye ken, I am pleased tae be anywhere as long as Quennie is there, and ye also ken that I asked Quennie tae relax and take some time tae nae be working as hard as he does, well, I want tae go on the record and say, twas difficult tae watch. He daena want tae relax. He likes tae work, so I hae decided that he is done with his vacation—"

Quentin jokingly collapsed on the table. "Thank God I don't have to vacation anymore."

She continued, "I winna ask him tae go against his nature, and, I think we ought tae return tae Florida. The bairns and I hae been here for a couple of weeks now, I miss our beach."

Quentin said, "I'm going to let Beaty's vote count for both of us, I am happy to go wherever I'm needed."

Magnus said, "This is somethin' tae consider, many of ye hae been here for quite a while, I feel like I just returned. But I would like m'own bed. I do miss it. Madame Emma?"

Emma said, "I wouldn't mind returning to Florida, if it's safe. We've had some lovely days here, but we can always come back. After James hires the contractor to sort out all the new bedrooms." She grinned.

James groaned. "I don't know which would be worse, doing the work or hiring someone to do the work."

Zach joked, "When you hire the contractor, we need a kitchen redo too. If it's going to be our vacation home, it ought to be good." Then he added. "I'd like to hit the road, man, the granite countertops of home are calling me."

Magnus said to the kids, "Got a vote?"

The kids all jumped up and down yelling, "Yay!" but we weren't really sure what that meant. Emma asked for clarification, "Go to Florida?"

They yelled yay again. Haggis barked merrily.

Magnus said, "I suppose we are de—"

Fraoch said, "What of me and Hayley?"

Magnus said, "I already counted yer vote, twas aye, take me tae Florida tae go fishin'."

Hayley said, "Yes, exactly, and I'm over the hotel, let's head home."

I said, "It will take a moment, I think we're going to need to rent a van for the drive down—"

Magnus said, "Why a van?"

"Do you want to take Haggis on an airplane?"

Magnus's eyes went wide. "Och, they would put Haggis in a seat with the belt on his lap? Nae, I daena think he would like flying at all." He scratched Haggis behind the ears again.

CHAPTER 83 - KAITLYN

The last night of our vacation was bittersweet. Hayley said, "I am going to miss this place, can we change our votes?"

Quentin said, "I've rented a fifteen-person passenger van and James and I have been strapping stuff to the roof, no, we are leaving, headed south, but we can come back."

Magnus said, "We can always come back."

The sun was almost completely set, it was late, we had eaten and had homemade Whoopie Pies from Tracy. I led the kids down to the dock explaining, "We skip stones to say goodbye."

We collected a tiny pile of pebbles and I taught them to skip stones. Archie and Ben got the hang of it really quick. Isla tossed hers. Zoe's dropped, 'plunk', and she giggled and plunked pebbles into the lake, merrily. Isla complained, "Zoe isn't doing it right."

"Zoe is doing it right. Archie's rock is saying, 'A fond farewell to you, lake.' Ben's rock is saying, 'See you soon, I hope.' Your rock is a long toss, as if you're saying, 'Goodbye I will miss you,' and Zoe's pebble is saying, 'Bye-bye.' It's all valid."

Zoe plunked in a pebble and said, "Bye-bye."

Isla said, "That's good, Zoe, it all valid."

Someone turned on some music from the house. "I love this song." I turned and drew in a breath at the sight of my family, there in chairs all over the lawn. Like decades ago when it had been my grandparents and their brothers and sisters and....

"God, I love you all so much,"

Hayley said, "What brought this on?"

"You're all sparkling in the firelight, the darkness around you, it's magical, thank you for coming—"

James said, "I think most of us were totally chased here."

Quentin chuckled, "Again, your fault, James"

I said, "But still, whether we were chased, or escaping, or gathering, or vacationing, it's been lovely seeing you all here at my grandparents' house. This is kinda making me weepy." I waved my hand trying to keep the tears from coming.

Magnus stood. "Dost ye ken what we need? We need a dance tae say goodnight tae the shore." He crossed to the middle of the lawn, the gentle grassy slope to the lake and held out a hand. I met him there and he put an arm around me and we danced in the night to my favorite song. A moment later Zach and Emma came to dance near us, then Beaty and Quentin, Sophie and James, and Hayley and Fraoch. It was a lovely moment all of us slow-dancing in the night.

I said, "This is perfect."

We rocked back and forth, held close in his arms, the scent of smoke and lake, the dirt of the ground, and the fresh cool grass, the pine around us. "I ken, I once saw Barb and Jack do this, twas a lovely sight. I am verra glad tae hae ye in my arms and I am sure they are smiling down on us."

The music lilted through the air. I met Hayley's eyes as she passed by in Fraoch's arms, genuinely happy. Beaty beaming up into Quentin's eyes, Emma and Zach, holding each other with Zoe in their arms too. Sophie and James rocking back and forth, so in love, our newlyweds. Then Magnus spun me around and we met eyes, kissed, and hugged, then I heard him say, "Och," and I turned to see Lochinvar leading Tracy by the hand to a patch of grass where they danced together too.

"Uh oh," I said.

"Aye," he agreed.

But I supposed summer was made for love, and vacations were meant for meeting people, and we were leaving in the morning, so whatever was going on with that would all probably figure itself out.

~

The next morning was spent with last minute packing, loading, and soon enough we were all in the passenger van. Tracy was there to say goodbye, to clean up when we were gone, and we were sending her a stipend for house sitting for us while we were gone.

I received a call as we were busying to go, from Karrie, my half-sister-in-law. "Hi, I wanted you to know, after our talk, I took an interest in your public relations, so I set up some alerts... I know it's weird, but I know you and Magnus want your privacy — I get that, believe me, Finch and I are so protective of our privacy, but anyway, you're a little viral on Instagram."

"What... what do you mean?"

"Some local bar has photos of you, calling you King Magnus and Queen Kaitlyn and Prince Lochinvar. It's all a little silly but I wanted you to know, it's got a lot of views and comments and a few of the comments mentioned your past YouTube channel..."

"I guess it will always follow me. Thank you so much for paying attention to it for us."

"No worries, it's what I do. Will you be around there much longer?"

"We're leaving this morning actually, headed to Florida."

She said, "It was a pleasure meeting you, hope to get the brothers together again someday."

"Me too."

Piling into the van was not easy. We put kids along the back row, then Emma, me, then Zach, Sophie, James, Hayley, Fraoch, and Lochinvar with Magnus riding in the front. Quentin was driving. Everyone else offered but he said, "No, I'll drive, it's only seven hours to New York City, and now that I see you all packed in there I am happy with the front seat." Beaty rode between Quentin and Magnus, and Mookie sat between the first and second rows. Haggis went to the all-the-way back and sat awkwardly on Archie's lap, looking very happy to be in a van for his first time, and occasionally licking a kid's face.

Quentin got in the van and started the engine. He pulled us down the driveway. We rolled down the windows and everyone waved goodbye to Tracy. Lochinvar twisted all the way around in his seat to watch her as long as he could.

Then Quentin pulled us out onto the main road. "Next stop, New York City!"

He joked, "Finally, Boss is going to prove that he has the safe house he's promised me he has 'always had'."

Magnus chuckled. "I hae always had it, I just canna remember when I got it."

We all laughed.

CHAPTER 84 - LADY MAIREAD

*A*bby Rockefeller was having a soiree at the museum for the opening of her new show. It was 1929 and all the most important people would be there. I had been living at my favorite house, Elmwood, one of the stately manors along the park, but I was so busy helping Abby plan the party that I was rarely home, instead staying in Abby's guest room.

But today was the day and I was home. I had a bath drawn, then I dried off and my hair was brushed and styled intae elegant waves. My makeup was applied, my gown pulled on. I wore stockings and the final touch was my jewelry, a necklace given tae me for the occasion by my new lover, Cornelius Vanderbilt Whitney.

His mother, Gertrude, had introduced us. She was an accomplished sculptor who studied in Paris under Auguste Rodin, and we were great friends. Cornelius would accompany me tae the party, which was a lovely thing, as he was gorgeous and looked verra good on m'arm.

I was so looking forward tae the party that I was ready early, with my sable wrap folded on the stair rail, my purse waiting for me over my butler's arm. I had tae wait impatiently at the window for the car as I couldna think of much else tae do. Twas hard tae keep the dress straight and pressed and m'makeup perfect while in motion, so I stood, and thought.

I hadn't had much time tae think on all that had happened. The excitement of the time twists — how m'son in his irresponsibility had allowed one of his group tae loop and put us all in peril. I sighed. He had fixed it in the end, but the Bridge was a verra powerful mechanism.

I regretted allowing Lochinvar and Magnus tae take it with them. It weighed on my mind.

But, Lochinvar had helped Magnus kill Domnall and Ormr.

I spoke the words out loud: "Ye are welcome for finding him." Because I *had* found him.

I had found Lochinvar years before, when his mother begged me tae locate him — I had. He had been held captive at Dunscaith, where that bitch Agnie MacLeod had left him.

She was a terrible person.

She was also Fraoch's mother.

And Fraoch had been a help tae me. Lochinvar had been a help as well.

I wondered if I might get Lochinvar tae kill Agnie, twould be the last thing I needed done.

Then we would be mostly alone on the timeline. Not all alone, but alone enough tae be the most powerful.

I pulled my book from my purse and turned tae the page where I had listed the challengers tae Magnus's throne. Domnall and Ormr had their names scratched through. Then there were Samuel and Roderick, their names scratched through as well. A few other men, the three challengers that we haena met afore, Scot Hepburn, Aodh Menzies, and Ian the Troublesome. I had visited them, though, tae see their merit. They were nae a true threat, I felt sure, but there were more men, I kent, I just hadna located them yet. There was a woman in the year 1890 who received payments from Donnan. She concerned me. I had looked at past accounts but found that Samuel and Roderick hadna kept records of their mistresses and their sons. Twas a terrible mess. The world would be a much better place if the men would simply keep their pants on.

I dinna want tae harm Agnie Macleod, I had nae reason tae wish harm upon her, I had won everything I had ever wanted, and had the strength of m'son tae guard me, a long line of children and grandchildren after us.

And a kingdom.

What did she have?

Two dead sons.

Och, she was going tae be trouble.

A car slid up tae the curb out front. I raised my chin, and waited for my butler tae answer the call. Then I met Cornelius in the entryway.

"Mairead! You are ravishing!"

I smoothed my hair, "Thank ye, Cornelius, ye are verra fine yerself. Would ye like a drink afore we go?"

"No, Mairead, I would like to show you off, we ought to be there to do it."

He put his hand on the small of my back and led me to the car, opening the door for me, and then climbing in the driver's seat. Twas all verra elegant, but then he drove like a madman tae the party, the vehicle bouncing and careening terribly. I wished desperately for a properly chauffeured limo, but he assured me he loved the freedom of his own automobile.

We pulled up in front of the museum. I had been quite shaken, and having been stuck in traffic, with a thick cloud of smoke settled around the car, covered in a bit of grime.

I pulled a compact from my purse, powdered my nose, reapplied lipstick, smoothed down my hair, and straightened the rhinestone comb. I made sure the diamond necklace was centered.

He asked, "Have you had a good week, Mairead? You have been too busy to see your poor Cornie."

"Ye ken, I was occupied with Abby and Flora, busy organizing the details of this party."

He scowled as he looked out of the window. "You say it with such assurance, but I am certain you have been with your lovers."

I huffed. "I hae been planning a party. Ye daena hae tae be jealous, I am nae seeing anyone—"

"What of your General?"

I pursed my lips. "I shouldna hae told ye of him."

"You did it to keep me at the beckoning of your whims."

I took his hand. "Dear Cornie, ye must stop the jealousy. Tis unbecoming. We are here in New York, and ye are my only... my one and only."

He kissed my gloved hand.

"You have not taken a lover here in Manhattan? I wonder sometimes if I am passing him on the street. I do not believe I could bear it."

"I am growing bored of the questions, Cornie, I haena taken another lover, not in this whole glorious decade."

"Good, and I will keep you to myself the following decade as well. I will persuade you to live here always, Mairead. There is nowhere in the world as grand and luxurious, no finer city than New York."

I said, "True, though Paris is verra fine."

He laughed. "Paris? With the artists? No, not Paris, it has one Eiffel tower, it cannot even compete with New York." He passed our keys to the valet and came around tae open the door for me. On the sidewalk I straightened my gown.

He gave me his arm as we climbed the steps to the museum, walked through the main doors, and followed the sound of the music through tae the party tents in the sculpture gardens. There were large tables set up with a buffet and smaller tables for dinner seating, and a dance floor in front of the band. The doors were open tae the galleries, so that we could view the new exhibits and the grand collection.

The lights twinkled. Fragrant perfume floated on the night air mingling with the scents from the flowerbeds. The men were all more handsome than usual in their tuxedos, the women glorious in their gowns.

"We ought tae hae a drink." Cornelius raised his hand as a waiter walked by carrying a tray of drinks.

Passing me a glass, he asked, "Do you see Abby and John?"

"Nae, not yet."

"I see Mortimer against the far wall, dear me he is dreadful, if he comes over you must rescue me..." The gardens were crowded, and many more were still arriving.

My eyes swept the crowd and landed on — *och.*

Twas Agnie MacLeod. She was in conversation with Marjorie Gleason and yet, she raised her eyes and met mine. Her brow raised, a bit of a malicious smile tugged at the edge of her lips, and her gaze was so direct it sent a chill over my heart.

My hands shook. She was here. *What did this mean?*

We had been locked in conflict for so long, I had believed that we had come tae an agreement — the world had been split and we never crossed paths, yet here she was, at my party? I found it infuriating.

The last thing that needed tae happen was a scene, but she was headed toward me across the party.

My son had killed her sons, I guessed she was not there for pleasant reasons.

CHAPTER 85 - KAITLYN

*W*e all but fell from the van all over the sidewalk and everyone gaped around at the skyline, the park across the street, the crowds of people bustling by, the traffic. Beaty stood on the sidewalk with Haggis and Mookie on leashes, staring up at the sky saying, "What in the world, Quennie, dost ye see it?"

"I do see it, I just drove into the middle of it with a van carrying my wife, a pig, a dog, four kids, a bunch of other people, and a king, like a goddamn insane person."

Magnus said, "More importantly though, Colonel Quentin, here is a house, and tis mine."

Quentin said, "How about I believe it when they let you in the front door."

Magnus said, "I will go up tae speak tae the butler for a moment, I will return in a moment."

"And who is the butler?"

"What year is it?" Magnus jogged up the steps.

We were quite the spectacle, all of us in our sweatsuits and t-shirts, desperately needing a shopping trip, surrounded by kids and animals, staring up at the mansion as Magnus disappeared into it. Emma said, "He probably could have called."

I said, "Yep, it's not his way to even think about it."

Hayley said, "Instead he just drops in unannounced."

A few moments later Magnus waved us all up.

"How the hell did he prove he lives here? They know him?" I muttered, going up the stairs. "I haven't even been here before."

As we passed, the butler did his best to pretend like none of us were bringing a pig into the house. I whispered to Magnus, "When have you been here?"

He said, "I haena ever seen it afore, but Helms, the butler, is from m'kingdom. Daena tell Quentin, I am havin' fun with him."

We were invited to sit, but instead we sprawled all over the sitting room, which was opulent, full of antiques and the walls covered in art. It looked like a Victorian palace and because I knew Lady Mairead had decorated it, I knew it was all authentic and priceless.

The kids raced around like little uncivilized monsters, but it was hard to blame them as they had been cooped up in the van for hours. Besides, Magnus said it was okay and it was his house.

He collapsed on the couch beside me. "What dost ye think, mo reul-iuil. Lady Mairead likes a grand house."

"That she does. It's epic. Not sure we should be in here with a pig and a medieval dog."

Haggis jumped up beside us on the couch and dropped down on the cushion.

Magnus laughed, "Och aye, m'mother would *love* a medieval dog on her settee."

He added, "That reminds me, we ought tae check the safe, tae see if she has left us a message." He went up the stairs, returning a bit later, looking distracted.

"Was there something?"

"Nae, we ought tae... we ought tae feed the bairns. Does everyone want some food?" He called the butler in. "Helms, how does a family of..." He pretended tae count heads, and finished, "this many people eat dinner here in New York City?"

"Well, sire, I could ask your mother's chef to come in, though it was her day off and..."

"Nae, that inna necessary." The kids ran through yelling with the dog and the pig close at their heels. "We probably daena want anyone witnessin' how we are behavin' in this fine grand house. Daena report on me tae m'mother, Helms, she will be wrathful."

"I wouldn't dream of it, sire. You might go to a restaurant?"

Emma groaned. "I cannot imagine taking all these littles out somewhere, they are in the mood for chaos."

Helms said, "You could order in, sire, enough for a hundred and thirty-three people and a menagerie of animals."

Magnus chuckled. "Och aye, let's order in, Kaitlyn, would ye make a list?"

Emma figured out some of the closest restaurants. I took orders: we needed Italian for some, Chinese for others, and Zach ordered a pile of meatballs from a famous restaurant he had seen on a morning show. Also, there had to be a cookie delivery for Lochinvar. Then he stood on the front stoop waiting for the food, his mouth hanging open in amazement.

It took so much wrangling and cost a fortune to get three cars converging on the front step at about the same time. Lochinvar's eyes were wide as we all grabbed boxes and bags from drivers. "What are we doin'?"

I joked, "Making dinner!"

We placed the food out on the countertops in the giant gourmet kitchen. Zach said, "Do you see all this counter space? Now this is great kitchen. If we knocked out the living room and two of the bedrooms at the lake house, we might have a proper-sized kitchen there."

Magnus joked, "Ye want even fewer bedrooms in the lake house than we had? I think next time ye get the bunkhouse."

We filled plates and sat the adults down the long table in the opulent dining room. The walls were painted a pale blue, there were ornately carved shelves, a giant fireplace and an exquisite chandelier. There were four Picasso paintings on the wall.

Magnus, digging his serving spoon into a container of orange chicken, said, "Are all the houses in Manhattan this big and fancy?"

James and Quentin laughed. James said, "Hell no, this is a freaking palace."

Emma said, "It's like she is competing with her brother, 'Fine, you have a nice eighteenth century castle, I will have a bigger, better castle in the middle of Manhattan in the twenty-first century.'"

Magnus said, "Also in the nineteenth and twentieth centuries, I think she had this manor house built for her. I suppose compared tae m'uncle keeping Balloch for four decades, keeping a mansion in New York for three centuries is exceptional."

We finished our meals and then went out for a night stroll around the block with the whole family, showing them the skyline of the city. It was a cool night, and everyone, even those of us who had lived in the modern world were blown away by the lights and sounds and crowds of New York, but for our friends and family who were visiting from the past, it was absolutely shocking.

Lochinvar gaped at the sky and spun in circles trying to see the tops of buildings. Beaty kept pointing and gasping and Sophie took small peeks and hid her face in James's shoulder. Central Park was right beside us, people bustling everywhere, bumping and jostling us on the sidewalk. The traffic, the noise, the smells, bags of trash along the sidewalks. A horse-drawn carriage went by and the Scottish men stood dumbfounded. Fraoch asked, "Why...?"

James said, "Those belong to people who weren't able to pass their driver's tests."

Fraoch said, "Och aye, that makes sense."

Magnus, carrying Isla, felt it was his duty to listen to every song being played by every musician, dancing and nodding along, and cheering when it was done. Zach followed behind him, giving Archie and Ben money to toss in the hats.

Fraoch criticized the city, full of judgments on it. "Ye ken, ye ought nae hae these many buildings, this tight," and, "Why would ye put a shop that close tae the street?" And startled by the metal plates on the sidewalk, "Why dost they hae these doors here, we might fall in!" He shook his head. "Tis nae sensible tae hae this many people in one place..."

On our way home, Isla was growing sleepy, her wee head heavy on Magnus's shoulder. He held my hand. I said, "What're you thinking about?"

"A few things, but one of them is I am pleased I can show m'family a night like this, twas a braw meal in a good house, and a proper large family all out for a stroll. Tis a bit like being at Kilchurn but even better."

Lochinvar was carrying the big bag of cookies and he came up right then with one for Isla. "Cookie?"

"Thank you, Uncle Lochie."

"Ye're welcome, Niece-wee-Islee." She giggled.

We meandered back to the house and everyone was wound down enough to go to their guest rooms to sleep, except Magnus. He said to me and Hayley and Fraoch, "Would ye remain downstairs for a moment? I need tae speak tae ye."

Hayley and Fraoch and I all sat on the couch with Magnus in a chair across from us.

She said, "Uh oh."

He pulled a letter from his pocket. There was a red seal on it that was already broken. "I read it earlier, but I dinna want tae spoil the evening."

Fraoch said, "What is it?"

Hayley said, "It looks like a letter from Lady Mairead."

Magnus nodded, opened the letter and read aloud:

Dearest M,

I am in trouble, Agnie MacLeod is here, and I need ye tae come.

Lady Mairead

He said, "This was with it." He held out an invitation to a party that was held on November 7, 1929. "I included ye, Fraoch, as it involves yer mum."

Fraoch exhaled. "Aye, that it does. I think tis time, we hae tae deal with her."

Magnus said, "Aye, I think we do."

≈

The end.

THANK YOU

*T*here will be more chapters in Magnus and Kaitlyn's story.

If you need help getting through the pauses before the next books, there is a FB group here: Kaitlyn and the Highlander

I would love it if you would join my Substack, here: Diana Knightley's Stories

Thank you for taking the time to read this book. The world is full of entertainment and I appreciate that you chose to spend some time with Magnus and Kaitlyn. I fell in love with Magnus when I was writing him, and I hope you fell in love a little bit, too.

As you all know, reviews are the best social proof a book can have, and I would greatly appreciate your review on this book.

Some photos of my grandparents' house in Maine:

THE KAITLYN AND THE
HIGHLANDER SERIES

BOOKS IN THE CAMPBELL SONS SERIES...

Why would I, a successful woman, bring a date to a funeral like a psychopath?

Because Finch Mac, the deliciously hot, Scottish, bearded, tattooed, incredibly famous rock star, who was once the love of my life... will be there.

And it's to signal — that I have totally moved on.

But... at some point in the last six years I went from righteous fury to... something that might involve second chances and happy endings.

Because while Finch Mac is dealing with his son, a world tour, and a custody battle,

I've been learning about forgiveness and the kind of love that rises above the past.

We were so lost until we found each other.

I left my husband because he's a great big cheater, but decided to go *alone* on our big, long hike in the-middle-of-nowhere anyway. Destroyed. Wrecked. I wandered into a pub and found... Liam Campbell, hot, Scottish, a former-rugby star, now turned owner of a small-town pub and hotel.

And he found me.

My dear old dad left me this failing pub, this run down motel and now m'days are spent worrying on money and how tae no'die of boredom in this wee town.

And then Blakely walked intae the pub, needing help.

The moment I lay eyes on her I knew she would be the love of m'life.

And that's where our story begins...

THE SCOTTISH DUKE, THE RULES OF TIME TRAVEL, AND ME

Book 1

Book 2

SOME THOUGHTS AND RESEARCH...

A prototype of the vessel:

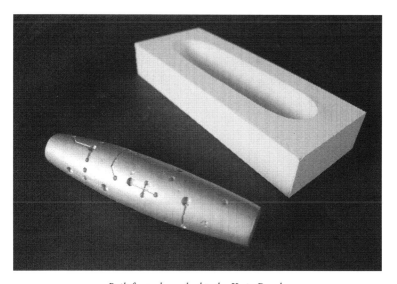

Built for me by my husband... Kevin Dowdee

Characters:
Kaitlyn Maude Sheffield - born December 5, 1993

Magnus Archibald Caelhin Campbell - born August 11, 1681

Baby Archibald (Archie) Caelhin Campbell - born August 12, 2382

Isla Peace Barbara Campbell - born October 4, 2020

Lady Mairead (Campbell) Delapointe - Magnus's mother, born 1660

Hayley Sherman - Kaitlyn's best friend, now married to Fraoch MacDonald

Fraoch MacDonald - Married to Hayley. Born in 1714, meets Magnus in 1740, and pretends to be a MacLeod after his mother, Agnie MacLeod. His father is also Donnan, which makes him Magnus's brother.

Quentin Peters - Magnus's security guard/colonel in his future army

Beaty Peters - Quentin's wife, born in the late 1680s

Zach Greene - The chef, married to Emma

Emma Garcia - Household manager, married to Zach

Ben Greene - born May 15, 2018

Zoe Greene - born September 7, 2021

James Cook - former boyfriend of Kaitlyn. Now friend and frequent traveler. He's a contractor, so it's handy to have him around.

Sophie - wife of James Cook. She is the great-great-granddaughter of Lady Mairead, her mother is Rebecca.

Lochinvar - A son of Donnan.

Finch Mac - Rockstar. Dad to Arlo.

His story is here: Karrie and the Rock Star

Karrie Munro - Married to the rock star

Joe, Lydia, Tessa Munro - also from Karrie and the Rock Star

Sean Campbell - Magnus's half-brother

Lizbeth Campbell - Magnus's half-sister

Sean and Lizbeth are the children of Lady Mairead and her first husband.

Grandma Barb - Kaitlyn's grandmother

Grandpa Jack - Kaitlyn's grandfather

General Hammond Donahoe - Magnus calls him Hammie, (he's a cousin) in a relationship with Lady Mairead.

Rebecca - Lady Mairead's great-granddaughter

Agnie's sons - Ormr, Domnall, and Fraoch. Ormr and Domnall are now dead.

The kingdom of Riaghalbane, comes from the name *Riaghladh Albainn*, and like the name Breadalbane (from *Bràghad Albainn*) that was shortened as time went on. I decided it would now be **Riaghalbane.**

The line of kings in Riaghalbane

Normond I - the first king

Donnan I -

Donnan II - Magnus's father. murdered by Kaitlyn Campbell in the year 2381

Magnus I - crowned August 11, 2382 the day before the birth of his son, Archibald Campbell, next in line for the throne.

Some **Scottish and Gaelic words** that appear within the book series:

Dreich - dull and miserable weather

Mo reul-iuil - my North Star (nickname)

Osna - a sigh

Dinna ken - didn't know

Tae - to

Winna - won't or will not

Daena - don't

Tis - it is or there is. This is most often a contraction 'tis, but it looked messy and hard to read on the page so I removed the apostrophe. For Magnus it's not a contraction, it's a word.

Och nae - Oh no.

Ken, kent, kens - know, knew, knows

mucag - is Gaelic for piglet

m'bhean - my wife

m'bhean ghlan - means clean wife, Fraoch's nickname for Hayley.

Cù-sith - a mythological hound found in Scottish folklore.

cù - dog

cù math - good dog

in ùine air fhuasgladh - time unraveled

steach far a bheil bruachan na h-aibhne air leth - the place where the banks of the river are distinct

Fhuasgladh - Unraveled

an abhainn dhubh - means the black river

Whoopie Pies are the official state treat of Maine! And writing about them made me hungry... my mother used to make them for me. Below are her recipe cards.

Whoopie Pies   Aunt Emma

½ cu. shortening } Cream.
1 cu. sugar

    Add 2 egg yolks. Beat 'til
light colored.

5 tbsp cocoa ⎤ ⅓ cup
2 cu. flour   ⎥
1 tsp b. powder ⎬ Sift together
1 tsp soda   ⎥
1 tsp salt   ⎦

    Add alternately with

Whoopie Pie Filling

2 cu. margarine
2 cu. conf. sugar
2 egg whites
½ tsp salt
1 tsp vanilla

    Beat egg whites 'til stiff.
Fold in some conf. sugar.
Cream shortening, add rest
of sugar & more if needed.

Add salt & vanilla
in beaten whites.

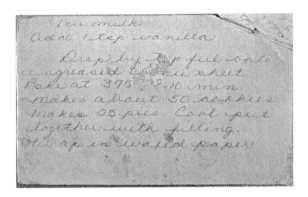

Locations:

Fernandina Beach on Amelia Island, Florida, present day. Their beach house is on the south end of the island.

The lake house in **Maine**. Specifically Holbrook Pond.

Magnus's homes in Scotland - **Balloch**. Built in 1552. In the early 1800s it was rebuilt as **Taymouth Castle**. (Maybe because of the breach in the walls caused by our siege from the future?) Situated on the south bank of the River Tay, in the heart of the Grampian Mountains. In 2382 it is a ruin.

Kilchurn Castle - Magnus's childhood home, favorite castle of his uncle, Baldie. On an island at the northeastern end of Loch Awe. In the region Argyll.

The kingdom of Magnus the First, **Riaghalbane**, is in Scotland.

His castle, called, **Caisteal Morag,** is very near Balloch Castle situated on the south bank of the River Tay about a mile from Loch Tay.

Dunscaith Castle is a ruined castle on the coast of the Isle of Skye. Originally belonging to a branch of Clan MacDonald, it has also been claimed by Clan MacLeod.

Legend has it the castle is featured in Irish mythology as the place where Scáthach the Shadow, a legendary Scottish warrior woman and martial arts teacher, trained heroes. Scáthach's brother was named Domnall. (Note: Ormr means dragon.)

Stirling Castle, one of the largest and most important castles in Scotland, both historically and architecturally. The castle sits atop Castle Hill, an intrusive crag, surrounded on three sides by steep cliffs, giving it a strong defensive position.

The first record of Stirling Castle dates from around 1110, when King Alexander I dedicated a chapel there. It appears to have been an established royal centre by this time, as Alexander died here in 1124, and Alexander III laying out the New Park, for deer hunting, in the 1260s.

Stirling remained a centre of royal administration until the death of Alexander III in 1286. His passing triggered a succession crisis, with Edward I of England invited to arbitrate between competing claimants.

∽

True things that happened:

Cailean Mór Caimbeul is one of the earliest attested members of Clan Campbell and an important ancestor figure of the later medieval Earls of Argyll.

November 7, 1929 Abby Aldrich Rockefeller did indeed have a big party for the opening of the Museum of Modern Art.

And **Cornelius Vanderbilt Whitney** was a real person: businessman, film producer, philanthropist, polo player, writer, and breeder of Thoroughbred racehorses

Thomas Wagstaffe was a noted maker of fine clocks and pocket watches, including one in gold that was listed in Benjamin Franklin's inventory at time of his death.

John Balliol was King of Scots from 1292 to 1296. After the death of Margaret, Maid of Norway, Scotland entered an interregnum during which several competitors for the Crown of Scotland put forward claims. Balliol was chosen from among them as the new King of Scotland by a group of selected noblemen headed by King Edward I of England.

Sir William Wallace was a Scottish knight who became one of the main leaders during the First War of Scottish Independence.

ACKNOWLEDGMENTS

Thank you so much Cynthia Tyler, for your bountiful notes, for reading through twice as you do, your edits, thoughts, historical advisements, and the proofing. From language, to grammar, to landscapes and interiors, I'm filled with gratitude that you're so good at this, thank you.

~

Thank you so much David Sutton for your abundant notes and for reading even though the manuscript was such a mess. You are so great at keeping the characters consistent with their archetypes, and keeping me on my toes. And for finding that last minute time burp. Phew, so glad you helped!

~

Thank you to Kristen Schoenmann De Haan for your notes and for still being here after so many books, thank you thank you thank you!

~

Thank you to Jessica Fox for the notes. You found things that I missed after five read-throughs! My favorite was how Kaitlyn was in jeans and then somehow in a skirt, so relieved you noticed. I appreciate your attention to detail so much!

~

Thank you to *Jackie Malecki* and *Angelique Mahfood* (the admins) for letting me watch your 'chapter dashes' (reading at the same time) and for helping me keep timelines, family trees, and details straight!

~

And a very big thank you to Keira Stevens for narrating and bringing Kaitlyn and Magnus to life. I'm so proud that you're a part of the team.

~

And thank you to Shane East for voicing Magnus. He sounds exactly how I dreamed he would.

~

Thank you to Gill Gayle and Emily Stouffer for believing in this story and working so tirelessly to bring Kaitlyn and Magnus to a broader audience. Your championing of Kaitlyn means so much to me.

~

And more thanks to Jackie and Angelique for being admins of the big and growing FB group. 7.2K members! Your energy and positivity and humor and spirit, your calm demeanor when we need it, all the things you do and say and bring to the conversation fill me with gratitude.

You've blown me away with so many things. So many awesome things. Your enthusiasm is freaking amazing. Thank you.

～

I have a new venture, Patreon, and thank you to those of you that followed me there whether it's fan level or 'I love Liam and Blakely' tier, or both. Thank you for being a part of the magic, Tasha Sandhu, Jackie, Angelique, Paula Seeley Fairbairn, Diane Porter, and Sandy Hambrick for being the very first.

～

Which brings me to a huge thank you to every single member of the FB group, Kaitlyn and the Highlander. If I could thank you individually I would, I do try. Thank you for every day, in every way, sharing your thoughts, joys, and loves with me. It's so amazing, thank you. You inspire me to try harder.

And for going beyond the ordinary and posting, commenting, contributing, and adding to discussions, thank you to Mariposa Flatts, Anna Shallenberger, Dawn Underferth, Linda Epstein, Debra Walter, Sarah Bergeron McDuffie, Tina Rox, Fleur Garmonsway, Kathleen Fullerton, Lori Balise, Ginger Duke, Christine Todd Champeaux, Liz MacGregor, Linda Rose Lynch, Cynthia Tyler, Lauren Scarlett-Johnson, Makaylla Alexander, Lillian Llewellyn, JD Figueroa Diaz, Michelle Wimberly Dorman, Bev Burns, Marcia Coonie Christensen, Harley Moore, Christine Cornelison, Karen Scott, Carol Wossidlo Leslie, Jenny Bee, Mitzy Roberts, Debi Mitchell-Kirchhof, Crislee Anderson Moreno, Melissa Myers, Lauren Mccorquodale, Kelli Hawkins Dart, Debi Mahle O'Keefe, Katie Carman, Marge Robbers Ebinger, Irene Walker, Michelle Lynn Cochran, Teresa Gibbs Stout, Debbie Carroll Houston, Flori Gulik, Tori Smith, Toni Escudier Plonowski, Yasmin Alsahlani Yasir Mekki, Sam Broxterman, Jeanne Collins, Patricia Anne Keith-Thornton, Christine Ann, Kathleen Anderson, Melissa Russell Hallman, Paula Seeley Fairbairn, Brenda Raley, Betsy

Elizabeth, Enza Ciaccia, David Sutton, Julie Dath, Marie Smith, Katheryn Brown, Jacqueline Modell, Jackie Briggs, Azalee Salis, Joann Splonskowski, Linda Carleton Stoops, Amanda Ralph Thomas, Dianna Schmidt, Sonia Nuñez Estenoz, Irene Pinho, Anna Spain, Helen Ramsey, Mary Perkins Wells, Kim Curtner-larson, Lupe Skye, Alysa Isenhower Hill, Susan Sparks Klinect, Maureen Mukhlis, Dorothy Chafin Hobbs, Jenny Parlier Fowler, Dee Mecklin, Maria Sidoli, Theresa Partridge Fuller, Lesli Muir Lytle, Vicky Faherty, Joy Alpuche Antell, Debora C Snyder, Cathy Babcock, Jennifer Dunaway Cormier, Beth Schwartz, Bonnie Leslie Irving, Melissa Harper Rasmussen, Kathy Ann Harper, Jennifer Goerke, Cindy Straniero, Madeline Benjamin Gonzalez, Amy Brautigam, and Jeanne Ford.

When I am writing and I get to a spot that needs research, or there is a detail I can't remember, I go to Facebook, ask, and my loyal readers step up to help. You find answers to my questions, fill in my memory lapses, and come up with so many new and clever ideas... I am forever ever ever grateful.

And when I ask 'research questions' you give such great answers...

I asked:
Lady Mairead has something in her bag that she likes to eat and she never goes anywhere without it. It's her treat. What is her favorite thing, brand, recipe, style?

I went with Carol Wossidlo Leslie for Reese's Peanut Butter Cups (popular in the 1920s) I can imagine Lady Mairead has them tucked away and Lochinvar loves them.

Speaking of Lochinvar, I also asked:

I need a name.

A Scottish male name. (Shhhh, it's for a secret person.)

I have been using Domangart. But there are a couple of 'Do' names already, might be confusing... So here's a poll!

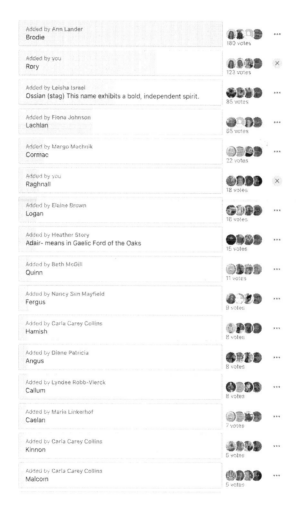

Added by Ann Lander **Brodie**	180 votes
Added by you **Rory**	123 votes
Added by Leisha Israel **Ossian (stag)** This name exhibits a bold, independent spirit.	85 votes
Added by Fiona Johnson **Lachlan**	65 votes
Added by Margo Machnik **Cormac**	22 votes
Added by you **Raghnall**	18 votes
Added by Elaine Brown **Logan**	16 votes
Added by Heather Story **Adair-** means in Gaelic Ford of the Oaks	15 votes
Added by Beth McGill **Quinn**	11 votes
Added by Nancy Sim Mayfield **Fergus**	9 votes
Added by Carla Carey Collins **Hamish**	8 votes
Added by Diane Patricia **Angus**	8 votes
Added by Lyndee Robb-Vierck **Callum**	8 votes
Added by Maria Linkerhof **Caelan**	7 votes
Added by Carla Carey Collins **Kinnon**	5 votes
Added by Carla Carey Collins **Malcom**	5 votes

I tried so many of these names before deciding on Lochinvar, which I absolutely LOVE.

Thank you, Candis Lively for the idea and Jenniffer Vasiento for the vote.

I asked a couple of other questions, but they didn't end up in the book this time, sometimes the story veers off in other directions.

If I have somehow forgotten to add your name, or didn't remember your contribution, please forgive me. I am living in the world of Magnus and Kaitlyn and it is hard some days to come up for air.

I mean to always say truthfully, thank you. Thank you.

Thank you to *Kevin Dowdee* for being there for me in the real world as I submerge into this world to write these stories of Magnus and Kaitlyn. I appreciate you so much.

Thank you to my kids, *Ean, Gwynnie, Fiona,* and *Isobel,* for listening to me go on and on about these characters, advising me whenever you can, and accepting them as real parts of our lives. I love you.

ABOUT ME, DIANA KNIGHTLEY

I write about heroes and tragedies and magical whisperings and always forever happily ever afters.

I love that scene where the two are desperate to be together but can't be because of war or apocalyptic-stuff or (scientifically sound!) time-jumping and he is begging the universe with a plead in his heart and she is distraught (yet still strong) and somehow — through kisses and steam and hope and heaps and piles of true love, they manage to come out on the other side.

My couples so far include Beckett and Luna, who battle their fear to search for each other during an apocalypse of rising waters.

Liam and Blakely, who find each other at the edge of a trail leading to big life changes.

Karrie and Finch Mac, who find forgiveness and a second chance at true love.

Hayley and Fraoch, Quentin and Beaty, Zach and Emma, and James and Sophie who have all taken their relationships from side story in Kaitlyn and the Highlander to love story in their own rights.

And Magnus and Kaitlyn, who find themselves traveling through time to build a marriage and a family together.

I write under two pen names, this one here, Diana Knightley, and another one, H. D. Knightley, where I write books for Young Adults. (They are still romantic and fun and sometimes steamy though because love is grand at any age.)

DianaKnightley.com
Diana@dianaknightley.com
Substack: Diana Knightley's Stories

A POST-APOCALYPTIC LOVE STORY
BY DIANA KNIGHTLEY

Can he see to the depths of her mystery before it's too late?

The oceans cover everything, the apocalypse is behind them. Before them is just water, leveling. And in the middle — they find each other.

On a desolate, military-run Outpost, Beckett is waiting.

Then Luna bumps her paddleboard up to the glass windows and disrupts his everything.

And soon Beckett has something and someone to live for. Finally. But their survival depends on discovering what she's hiding, what she won't tell him.

Because some things are too painful to speak out loud.

With the clock ticking, the water rising, and the storms growing, hang on while Beckett and Luna desperately try to rescue each other in Leveling, the epic, steamy, and suspenseful first book of the trilogy, Luna's Story:

ALSO BY H. D. KNIGHTLEY (MY YA PEN NAME)

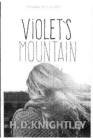

Bright (Book One of The Estelle Series)

Beyond (Book Two of The Estelle Series)

Belief (Book Three of The Estelle Series)

Fly; The Light Princess Retold

Violet's Mountain

Sid and Teddy

Printed in Great Britain
by Amazon

17134123R00221